FACING HER FEAR

"Oh!" Stevie said. "By the way, Callie, I almost forgot to tell you. George has been looking for you for a couple of days now."

Callie froze, her fingers gripping the bridle. "What?"

"George," Stevie repeated. "I guess he wanted to, like, thank you or whatever. Because of what happened the other day with the paramedics and all."

That was all Callie could take. Without another word, she pulled the bridle down and practically ran out of the room, ignoring Stevie's surprised-sounding calls. *I knew it,* she thought desperately as she made a beeline for Scooby's stall, careening through the entryway and barely avoiding collisions with several other riders. *I knew this wasn't going to be easy.*

Don't miss any of the excitement
at PINE HOLLOW,
where friends come first:

#1 *The Long Ride*
#2 *The Trail Home*
#3 *Reining In*
#4 *Changing Leads*
#5 *Conformation Faults*
#6 *Shying at Trouble*
#7 *Penalty Points*
#8 *Course of Action*
#9 *Riding to Win*
#10 *Ground Training*
#11 *Cross-Ties*
#12 *Back in the Saddle*
#13 *High Stakes*
#14 *Headstrong*
#15 *Setting the Pace*

And coming in February 2001:

#16 *Track Record*

PINE HOLLOW®

SETTING THE PACE

BY BONNIE BRYANT

BANTAM BOOKS
NEW YORK • TORONTO • LONDON • SYDNEY • AUCKLAND

Special thanks to Sir "B" Farms and Laura Roper

RL 5.0, AGES 012 AND UP

SETTING THE PACE
A Bantam Book/December 2000

ISBN: 0-553-49305-1

Visit us on the Web! www.randomhouse.com/teens
Educators and librarians, for a variety of teaching tools, visit us at
www.randomhouse.com/teachers

Published simultaneously in the United States and Canada

Bantam Books is an imprint of Random House Children's Books. BANTAM
BOOKS and the rooster colophon are registered trademarks of Random
House, Inc. Bantam Books, 1540 Broadway, New York, New York 10036.

PRINTED IN THE UNITED STATES OF AMERICA
OPM   10 9 8 7 6 5 4 3 2 1

*My special thanks to Catherine Hapka
for her help
in the writing of this book.*

ONE

"Did you decide on your music yet?" Stevie Lake asked Denise McCaskill as she stepped into the stall where an Appaloosa gelding named Chip was sniffing at his empty grain bucket. The horse cocked his head at her hopefully. "Sorry, boy." She gave him a pat. "Not dinnertime yet."

She continued to stroke the horse as Denise entered the stall. At twenty-four, Denise was only eight years older than Stevie, but she had a lifetime of experience riding and caring for horses. That was why Max Regnery, the owner of Pine Hollow Stables, had made her his full-time barn manager.

"Well?" Stevie asked expectantly when Denise didn't answer.

"You mean for the reception?" Denise sighed and checked the dosage of the dewormer she was holding. "No. I guess that's one more detail to think about."

"Oh, but you've got to think about that!" Stevie

exclaimed. She wrestled Chip's head down so that Denise could shoot the dewormer into his mouth. The gelding pinned his ears back, shook his head, and rolled his eyes distastefully. Stevie gave the gelding's shoulder a comforting pat and glanced at Denise. "The music is important. You don't want to be scrambling at the last minute. Or dancing to one of Maxi's or Jeannie's CDs." She grinned at the thought of what kind of music Max's five- and three-year-old daughters liked as she followed Denise down the aisle to the next stall. There, a tall chestnut mare named Calypso was eyeing them suspiciously from the farthest corner. "But don't worry. I'm sure Deborah can give you some ideas."

"I'm sure she can. I just hate to lay one more thing on her when she and Max are already being so generous."

Denise sounded frazzled, and Stevie shot her a sympathetic glance. Max and his wife, Deborah, had offered to throw a New Year's Eve wedding for Denise and her fiancé, Red O'Malley, who was the head stable hand at Pine Hollow. The couple had been together for years, but recently, when Denise discovered she was pregnant, she and Red had decided it was time to get married. Now the wedding was less than a week away, and although Denise seemed more than a little nervous about the big event, Stevie could hardly wait.

2

Stevie entered Calypso's stall and stroked the mare soothingly as Denise prepared the next dose of dewormer. "Don't worry, all the fast planning will be worth it," she assured the bride-to-be. "Phil and I are totally looking forward to it." She smiled, imagining how romantic it would be to dance the old year away and greet the new one with her long-time boyfriend, Phil Marsten. For once they would have New Year's Eve plans worth mentioning. "It'll be a real change of pace for us from last year," she added. "Of course, nothing can compare to listening to my brothers have an hourlong argument about whether Batman could beat Superman in an arm wrestling contest, but we'll just have to make do with a nice, romantic wedding instead."

"I'd vote for Superman myself." Denise smiled, then glanced at the roof as a sudden gust of wind howled around the building. Stevie followed her gaze with a shiver, even though it was warm and cozy inside the stable. Until just a day earlier the weather had been unseasonably mild. But suddenly, on Christmas Day, winter had arrived full force, making the northern Virginia town of Willow Creek feel more like the North Pole. The temperature had dropped about fifteen degrees, and a cold wind had been moaning around the eaves and jostling the bare branches of the trees for the past thirty-six hours.

The conversation paused as Stevie and Denise focused on getting a full dose of dewormer into Calypso, who was always difficult to treat. They had just finished and were heading for the next stall, which belonged to a longtime Pine Hollow school horse named Diablo, when Stevie heard someone in boots approaching from the far end of the aisle. Glancing over her shoulder, she saw George Wheeler hurrying toward them.

The pudgy, pale, somewhat socially awkward sixteen-year-old was a familiar sight around the stable. George boarded his Trakehner mare, Joyride, there. Like Stevie, he was a junior at Fenton Hall, Willow Creek's oldest and most respected private school. But although their paths crossed several times during the average day, Stevie couldn't say she knew George well. He had a way of disappearing into the corners of life that made him hard to notice at all, let alone know. Shooting him a polite smile, she prepared to follow Denise into Diablo's stall.

George cleared his throat. "Stevie?" he said in his soft, uncertain voice.

Stevie stopped and glanced at him again. "Yes?" she said, expecting him to mention something about his mare's deworming schedule.

"I was just wondering," George said hesitantly. "Um, have you seen Callie lately?"

Stevie blinked in surprise. It had been painfully

apparent for some time that George had a monster crush on Stevie's friend Callie Forester. At first Stevie had found the whole thing cute, especially when it had seemed that Callie was making an effort to befriend George. But lately George's attention had become so relentless that it was making Callie uncomfortable, and the last Stevie had heard, her friend had told George in no uncertain terms that she wanted him to leave her alone. "As a matter of fact, I haven't seen Callie in, like, three days," she said. "I guess she's been busy at home. You know, what with Christmas and all."

"Oh," George said, looking disappointed. "Right."

Suddenly Stevie realized why George must be looking for Callie now. Three days earlier there had been some sort of accident out on the trails. George had been hurt, and Callie had been the one to call the paramedics. Stevie still wasn't quite sure of all the details. She figured Callie would fill her in when she saw her next, but as near as she could figure it, George had been kicked by his horse while he was picking a stone out of her foot, and Callie had happened by in time to see him hit his head on a tree.

Feeling a little more sympathetic toward George—after all, even with everything they'd been through, surely Callie would allow him to thank her for helping him out of a crisis like that—Stevie smiled at him. "Don't worry," she said kindly. "I'm sure she'll be along sometime today. After all, she's got a new horse to take care of, remember?"

Noticing that Denise was waiting for her inside Diablo's stall, Stevie shot George one last smile and hurried inside to help, thinking about Callie's new horse. Callie had been a junior endurance champion in her old hometown on the West Coast. About six months earlier, her family had moved to be closer to her congressman father's office in nearby Washington, D.C. Callie had been injured in a car accident soon after the move, but she was finally back in training. Less than a week earlier her parents had bought her a horse to train with, a spunky Appaloosa named Scooby that had all the makings of a fantastic endurance partner.

As Stevie and Denise emerged from Diablo's stall a few minutes later, Stevie noticed that George had disappeared. At the same moment she heard a familiar voice calling her name. Turning to glance down the aisle, she saw one of her best friends, Lisa Atwood, hurrying toward her.

"Hey!" Stevie called brightly. "What's up? Merry day after Christmas!"

Lisa grimaced slightly in return. "Thanks. Same to you."

Stevie peered at her closely. "What's the matter?"

Lisa shrugged and sighed. "Oh, just the usual,"

she said with a touch of bitterness in her voice. "I just finished having another lovely discussion with Mom about moving."

Stevie winced. By *discussion,* she knew that Lisa actually meant *argument.* There had been a lot of "discussions" going on in the Atwood household ever since Mrs. Atwood had decided, out of the blue, that she wanted to move to New Jersey, where her sister, Marianne, lived with her family. Stevie knew Mr. and Mrs. Atwood's divorce had been hard on Lisa, but it had been even harder on Mrs. Atwood. Lisa's mother had never really recovered from the blow of having her husband of twenty-seven years walk out on her, and she wasn't afraid to share her pain with those around her, particularly Lisa.

Denise greeted Lisa and then glanced at her watch. "Since we're done here, I suppose I'd better go see if Maureen needs any help with the schedule," she told Stevie.

Stevie wrinkled her nose slightly at the mention of Maureen Chance, Pine Hollow's newest full-time stable hand. She wasn't sure why that reaction came so automatically. Stevie tended to like most people until they gave her a reason to feel otherwise. And Maureen certainly hadn't done anything to her in the three and a half days she'd been working at Pine Hollow. *Well, not unless you count sneaking a cigarette in the bathroom,* Stevie added to herself, remembering how she'd caught the woman smoking despite Max's strict rule against it. At the time she'd planned to say something to Max, but after thinking it over, she'd decided that was too much like squealing. Instead, she had determined to keep a close eye on Maureen whenever she could. If it happened again, she would have to say something. Stevie wasn't a tattletale, but she knew better than to take any chances when it came to fire safety around the stable.

"Do you need us to do anything else?" Stevie asked Denise. It was a long-standing Pine Hollow tradition that all riders helped out with stable chores. That allowed Max to keep his staff small and his prices low.

Denise scratched her ear and shrugged. "If you wouldn't mind, Patch and Congo need to be brought in from the south pasture," she said. "Red is using them in a lesson this evening, so don't worry about grooming. The students can do it."

"Sure, no problem." Stevie waved as Denise hurried off, then turned her full attention back to Lisa. "So let's hear it," she said bluntly. "Did she change her mind yet?"

Lisa sighed. "No. In fact, she seems more excited than ever about the whole idea. It's like she thinks New Jersey is some kind of promised land where all her dreams will come true, and I'm the evil grinch who wants to steal her happiness."

"Really?"

"Just about." Lisa rolled her eyes. "Anyway, she really does seem psyched. She talks to Aunt Marianne like every hour on the hour, practically." She grinned weakly. "Hey, maybe if I'm lucky, she'll eat up so much money on long-distance bills that there won't be enough left to pay for a moving van."

Stevie smiled automatically, though she didn't think anything that Lisa was saying was very funny. *She sounds as if she's starting to accept this,* she realized uneasily. *It sounds like she doesn't think there's even a chance of changing her mom's mind anymore.*

The thought was very disturbing. If Lisa wasn't going to fight to stay in Willow Creek, what was stopping her mother from packing them up and leaving right after New Year's as she planned?

For the first time the full weight of that possibility started to sink in. When Stevie had first heard about Mrs. Atwood's plans, she had scoffed—no way would any mother force her daughter to move right in the middle of her senior year. Mrs. Atwood might be a little nuts, but she wasn't totally crazy. At least Stevie hadn't thought so before this had happened. Now she wasn't so sure.

Lisa can't move, she thought, suddenly overwhelmed at the thought of losing one of her best friends. She and Lisa and their other best friend, Carole Hanson, had been virtually inseparable for years, ever since they'd met at riding lessons back in junior high. *She just can't. Impossible. No way.*

After all those years, though, she knew Lisa well enough to know that blurting out what she was thinking would only upset her friend more. Lisa was a planner, a rational, thoughtful person who liked to go about things the logical way. Stevie was more of a seat-of-her-pants kind of person, which could make her a little frustrated with Lisa's cautious ways. In this case, however, she did her best to control her impulse, which was to start shouting about the unfairness of it all.

"Um, so did your mom say anything else?" Stevie asked cautiously. "You know, about actual plans or anything?"

"Not really." Lisa shrugged. "By the way, shouldn't we be heading out to get Patch and Congo?"

"Oh, yeah." Stevie had almost forgotten their promise to Denise. She turned and walked toward the main entrance with Lisa at her side. "Come on, let's grab some lead lines and get started. You know how Patch can be."

As the two of them emerged into the biting wind and dull gray sunlight of the late-December afternoon, they were just in time to see a familiar rust-and-red car wheeze and sputter its way to a stop in the gravel parking area nearby. "Hey, there's Carole," Lisa said.

Stevie waved; then she and Lisa waited as Carole pocketed her keys and hurried toward them. "Hey," she called when she was close enough. "What are you two up to? You're not leaving, are you?"

Lisa shook her head. "I just got here."

"We're going out to catch Congo and Patch," Stevie explained. "Want to help?" Normally she wouldn't even need to ask, but those days Carole's time at the stable was limited. She had cheated on a test a couple of months earlier, and as part of her punishment she was only allowed to come to Pine Hollow four times a week for two hours a day. Stevie knew that her friend was counting the days until New Year's, when her grounding would finally be over.

Carole glanced at her watch, then nodded. "Let's go."

The three friends fell into step as they hurried toward the pasture. "So how was your Christmas?" Stevie asked. Another condition of Carole's punishment was that she couldn't talk on the phone, so Stevie hadn't spoken to her since seeing her on Christmas Eve at Pine Hollow. "Did Santa bring lots of goodies?"

"A few," Carole replied with a grin. "Including a new pair of breeches and some training videos that I've been wanting."

Noticing that Lisa was hardly paying attention to their conversation, Stevie elbowed her. "Hey," she said. "Earth to Lisa." She glanced at Carole. "You'll have to forgive her. She's still recovering from another 'discussion' about her mother's crazy plan to move them away to the ends of the earth."

"I can't believe your mom is still on that," Carole said, chewing her lip anxiously as she cocked her head and gazed at Lisa.

Lisa kicked at a half-frozen clod of dirt. "Believe it," she said grimly. "She's totally serious about this."

Stevie blew out a loud sigh. "This is insane," she said. "We've got to do something to change her mind."

"Like what?" Lisa said with a hint of sarcasm. "Convince Aunt Marianne to move down here instead?"

Stevie shrugged. "It just seems like there's got to be something we could do," she said. "Like back when we were kids. Remember? We never would have stood for this sort of thing then. We would definitely be planning and scheming by now, not just sitting back and waiting for the worst to happen."

Carole grinned. "You're right," she agreed. "Knowing us—or rather, you"—she stared pointedly at Stevie—"we would probably be trying to convince Lisa's mom that New Jersey is about to be swept away by a tidal wave or struck by an earthquake or something."

Stevie snorted. "Yeah, like she'd really believe that," she said. "Personally, I was thinking more along the lines of paying off one of my brothers—probably Michael, he's always desperate for money—to disguise himself as Lisa and move to New Jersey in her place."

Carole giggled. "Good plan," she said. "But I'm not sure Michael would be all that thrilled about wearing a long blond wig."

"No problem." Stevie shrugged again. "We'd just have to explain to Lisa's mom that short hair is all the rage in New Jersey, so she cut it in honor of the move." She smiled, imagining her thirteen-year-old brother dressed up in one of Lisa's classic khakis-and-polo outfits instead of his usual sloppy jeans and heavy metal T-shirts. She was actually starting to feel a little inspired by the conversation. Maybe the plans they were joking about were on the wacky side, but that didn't mean there was absolutely nothing they could do to help Lisa out of her jam. All they had to do was think seriously about it, figure out the best way to proceed . . .

"Whatever," Lisa said, her voice rather heavy. "Um, could we maybe talk about something else for a while?"

Stevie glanced at her friend and noted her sad expression. "Sure," she said instantly. The last thing she wanted to do was bring Lisa down more.

Of course, that doesn't mean I'm not going to stop thinking about it, she thought, shooting Carole a quick look. Maybe the two of them could brainstorm about this later.

"I know what we should talk about," Carole said as they reached the pasture gate. She swung it open and held it for her friends to pass through ahead of her. "The wedding. What are you guys going to get them?"

"Get them?" Stevie said blankly. Then she gulped. "Oh. You mean, like as a present? I sort of forgot about that." Doing some quick mental arithmetic, she grimaced. She'd spent most of her holiday money, as well as the three-week advance on her allowance she'd wheedled out of her parents, on a gift for Phil.

Carole was watching her with an amused smile. "Don't worry," she told Stevie. "My relatives sent cash this year. I can loan you some money if you need it."

"Thanks." Stevie shot her a grateful smile. "Okay, so what are you getting them?"

14

Lisa shrugged. "Deborah said they're registered at Dylan's," she said. "I guess we could go over to the mall together and pick out some stuff from the registry."

Stevie wrinkled her nose. "You mean like gravy boats and crystal vases?" she said, glancing ahead as they approached a small knot of horses grazing on the stubbly winter grass. "Ugh. But that's so boring."

"I know," Carole agreed. "I can't imagine why they didn't just register at The Saddlery instead."

Stevie laughed. "I guess there's no question where you and Cam are going to register when you get engaged, huh?" She grinned as her friend blushed deeply. Carole had always been more interested in horses than in guys, but all that had changed recently when Cam Nelson, an old friend who had moved to California years earlier, had suddenly returned and swept Carole off her feet. It was obvious to anyone who saw them together that Carole was blissfully happy, but she was still a little shy about discussing her new boyfriend, as if fearing that talking about it would jinx the whole thing.

"Anyway," Carole said quickly, "I guess we could just get Red and Denise a Saddlery gift certificate or something."

Lisa looked uncertain. "I guess," she said slowly. "But they probably need that stuff they registered for a lot more than another pair of breeches or whatever."

Stevie rolled her eyes. "Right," she said. "They really need a gravy boat."

"I'm sure they've registered for stuff other than gravy boats, Stevie," Lisa said as they reached the edge of the small herd and stopped. "They probably need, like, silverware and wineglasses and stuff."

Stevie wasn't convinced. As the three of them spread out and got to work, calmly and quietly approaching the two horses they wanted, she kept thinking about their conversation. She had visited Red and Denise's small apartment, and as far as she could tell, they had all the necessities already. What good would another soup spoon or two do them? How could that possibly be as special as something their friends picked out themselves?

Fortunately, both Patch and Congo seemed more than willing to head inside, and soon the two horses were obediently trailing along behind the girls. As they turned and moved back toward the gate, Stevie cleared her throat. "I don't know," she said. "I just can't believe that Red and Denise really want all that boring stuff. I'd rather give them something they'll appreciate." Suddenly an idea occurred to her. A brilliant idea. "I know! What they really need is . . . a honeymoon!"

Lisa's eyes widened. "You know, that's not a bad

idea," she said. "I mean, the only reason they're even having a decent ceremony and reception is because Max and Deborah are giving them the whole shebang as their wedding gift. Why not follow their example?"

"You mean pay to send them on a honeymoon?" Carole said uncertainly. "That sounds kind of expensive."

"It doesn't have to be." Stevie shrugged, her mind working a mile a minute. "You know how Red and Denise are—they wouldn't care about lying around on some Caribbean island or anything anyway. All they need is a little getaway. You know, a chance to recover from their whirlwind engagement and all. Maybe we could book them a nice room at a hotel in D.C. for a couple of nights."

"Stevie, you've done it again," Carole said with a grin. "I think it's a great idea! I'm in for sure." She paused and added shyly, "Cam, too."

Lisa nodded. "Agreed. We can all chip in. I'm sure Scott and Callie will want to be in on this. If we get enough people, we can probably buy them a couple of nice meals, too, and maybe some show tickets or something."

"Great!" Stevie rubbed her hands together, rolling Patch's cotton lead line between them. "I'll call some hotels tonight to check on prices and stuff. We probably won't be able to get them in on their actual wedding night, since it's New Year's Eve, but by the next day—"

"Hey, check it out," Carole said abruptly, gazing into the distance over Stevie's shoulder. "That's weird."

"What's weird?" Stevie turned to see what Carole was looking at. Almost immediately, she spotted a dramatically marked Appaloosa grazing peacefully in the next pasture. She frowned. "Hey, that's Scooby," she said. "What's he doing out here?"

Carole shrugged. "That's what I'm wondering, too," she said, giving a gentle tug on Congo's lead line to get him moving. "It seems weird that he would need turning out if Callie has him in training. Why would she waste a whole school-free day when she's so eager to get back into shape?"

"He didn't get hurt the other day, did he?" Stevie asked, keeping stride beside Carole, with Patch trailing obediently at her shoulder. "You know, out in the woods with George and all that?"

Carole shook her head slowly. "I don't think so," she said. "As far as I know, he was fine the next day."

"It's probably no big deal." Lisa didn't seem terribly interested in the whole issue as she glanced at the leopard-spot gelding. "Callie's probably just taking a few days off to do the holiday thing with her family."

"Maybe." Stevie turned her head and stared at

Scooby for a moment as she walked. "I guess that's probably it. I just hope Maureen the new wonder stable hand didn't screw up and turn him out by accident."

"Yeah," Carole agreed. "That would be a real shame."

Stevie shot her a quick, curious glance over Patch's withers. She knew that it couldn't be easy for Carole to watch a newcomer take over the job that used to be hers, especially when there were only a few days left until her grounding was officially over. "So has the colonel said anything about letting you work at the stable again?" she asked.

Carole bit her lip. "Not exactly," she said. "I mean, I haven't really mentioned it. Besides, I've been so busy trying to figure out what to get Cam for Christmas, I've hardly had time to think about anything else."

Stevie nodded and gave Lisa an amused glance. The two of them had been saying for years now that it was high time some nice guy came along and swept Carole off her feet. At last it seemed to have happened.

They discussed Carole's grounding for the rest of the walk back to the stable building. As they entered the wide entryway with the two horses in tow, Ben Marlow emerged from the stable aisle, pushing an empty wheelbarrow. Ben had been a stable hand at Pine Hollow since graduating from high school a year and a half earlier. Stevie had to admit that he had a truly amazing touch with horses—they responded to him almost as if he were one of their own, not human at all. That was just as well, in Stevie's opinion, since Ben seemed to be much less skilled in communicating with his own species. Or maybe he was just much less interested in the human race. In any case, he had never tried very hard to make friends.

Still, Stevie knew that while Ben might not have a lot to say, not much happened around Pine Hollow that he didn't know about. "Yo, Ben," she said. "What's the deal with Scooby? We just saw him turned out."

As always, Ben seemed a little surprised that someone was speaking to him. "Callie called," he replied gruffly. "Her orders."

"You mean she's not coming to ride today?" Stevie asked, more than a little surprised. One of the first things she'd noticed about Callie was her intensity. Now that Callie finally had her own horse, Stevie had expected her to spend more time than ever at the stable, not less.

Ben merely shrugged in response. Without another word, he turned and moved off, pushing his wheelbarrow toward the other aisle.

"That's weird," Stevie said, turning back to face

her friends as Ben disappeared around the corner. Even in the midst of her surprise about Callie's odd decision, she noticed that Carole was staring off in the direction Ben had gone. Stevie grimaced slightly. She knew that her friend had had some feelings for Ben before Cam had come back into the picture. Stevie had been glad at her friend's change of heart—Carole wasn't exactly the most confident person when it came to guys, and Stevie had been sure that no good could come of her trying to make a go of it with a difficult, uncommunicative, fiercely private guy like Ben.

But was Ben really out of the picture? The way Carole was staring after him, Stevie was no longer certain. She opened her mouth, tempted to ask Carole about it.

Instead, she cleared her throat. "So, Carole," she said casually, "what were you just saying about Cam's Christmas present? Does this mean you haven't made any progress on your shopping? He gets back from his relatives' house on New Year's Eve, right?"

Carole blinked. "Oh!" she said, finally turning to face her friends. "No, I still haven't found the perfect gift. I just don't know what to do. Whatever I give him really has to be special."

Stevie nodded and smiled, relieved to see the way Carole's face had lit up at the mention of Cam's name. As Lisa listed a few shopping suggestions, Stevie glanced one more time down the aisle after Ben.

Whew, she thought. *Must've just been a momentary lapse. Just as well, too. Carole has a good thing going with a good guy now. She doesn't need Ben Marlow messing with her head.*

TWO

Callie rested her chin on her hand and stared at the tall bookcase on the far side of her bedroom. The bottom three shelves held books, but the top three were crowded with the trophies and plaques that she had won in her many years of riding. Above the bookcase was a large bulletin board that was almost completely covered by row after row of show ribbons.

Callie's gaze slipped from the first small cup she'd ever won—at an equitation schooling show at her first training barn—to a plaque proclaiming her triumph at a major endurance competition the previous spring. *I remember how tough that one was to win*, she thought, running her eyes over the familiar inscription. *It was raining so hard that day, I was afraid the whole mountain was going to slide down on top of us. Three other riders dropped out before the five-mile mark.*

She looked next at a particular yellow ribbon

fluttering near the bottom of the bulletin board. Earning that one had required a different kind of courage, the kind she'd needed to overcome her jitters the first time she'd ever jumped in a show. She had been just eight years old and riding a school horse, a recalcitrant pony appropriately named Mule. For two solid weeks prior to the show, Mule had misbehaved every time she rode him into the ring, refusing more jumps than he took. Callie's instructor had offered to let her switch mounts, but Callie had been almost as stubborn as the pony. When she and Mule had entered the ring for their round, the four low cross rails had seemed as daunting as those in a Grand Prix course.

But I did it, she thought with a small smile. *I kicked that pony like I meant it, and we went out there and jumped without stopping for the first time ever.*

She sighed, wondering when that kind of courage had deserted her. Had it been the moment out there in the woods the other day, when she had suspected that George had sabotaged her horse? Or had it happened even earlier—when she'd first heard him shout her name and realized he had tracked her down like a foxhound trailing his game?

She shook her head, trying to shake all thoughts of George Wheeler out of her mind. Glancing at the bulletin board again, she focused instead on another ribbon. This one was blue, but she remembered that she had almost lost her shot at getting a ribbon that day at all. She had lost a stirrup during an equitation class, but luckily it had been on the side facing away from the judge. Without allowing even a hint of consternation to cross her face, Callie had calmly continued her ride, managing to regain the stirrup without the judge ever noticing. By the time the judge called for a reverse, both of Callie's feet were firmly in the stirrups again, and she had wound up winning the class.

Okay, so maybe that wasn't exactly what most people would call a terrifying experience, she thought with a hint of a smile. *Still, my instructor said it took guts to carry on like that without letting the judge see I was upset.*

She sighed and leaned back on her bed, closing her eyes to rest them. She had hardly slept the night before. In fact, she hadn't slept more than an hour at a stretch since the encounter in the woods the other day. She had been haunted by nightmares that she barely remembered upon waking, though she was pretty sure that a certain pale, pudgy, and oddly menacing guy had figured prominently in most of them. She had spent most of Christmas Day feeling cranky and exhausted, not to mention guilty for constantly snapping at her family.

But that wasn't even the worst part. The worst

part was, she was afraid to return to Pine Hollow. Afraid to face George again.

But that's stupid, she told herself, clenching her hands into fists. *What do you think he's going to do?*

Before the thought was fully formed, she knew it sort of missed the point. It was true that George had suddenly, in one relatively brief encounter, become a much more complicated and mysterious person, and that she would never look at him the same way again. But she really wasn't worried about what he might do when she saw him again—not rationally, anyway. The stable was almost always full of people when she was there, so the thought of what other bizarre tricks he might pull wasn't nearly as frightening as wondering what *she* might do when she saw him.

What if I freak out, get hysterical? Callie could feel her cheeks turning pink at the idea. *What if I make a total fool of myself? Then not only will George know that he scared me, but everyone else will know it, too. And I really couldn't stand that.*

She sighed again, feeling hot tears well up. She stared at her trophies, trying to figure out exactly what had gone wrong inside her head the other day. How had this happened? How had the girl who'd fought so hard for all those ribbons—the girl who wasn't afraid of anything—turned into this quivering, whimpering coward?

This is ridiculous, she thought, tracing the pattern on her bedspread with one finger. *I mean, what really happened, anyway? George stumbled upon my route map in the stable office and decided to follow me around like the lovesick, pathetic puppy dog I already knew he was. He wanted to play hero and pry that stone out of Scooby's foot, and in the process he accidentally jammed the pick too hard and loosened the shoe. When that happened, he was so clueless that he convinced himself the shoe was loose before he got to it. By then he was so worked up with his own helpfulness that he got clumsy and accidentally knocked my cell phone into the stream so that I couldn't call for some real help. And to top it off, he managed to put himself right in the way of Scooby's hoof and ended up knocking himself out on a tree. No big deal.*

She focused on the idea that that was all that had really happened. It had all been just a series of unfortunate coincidences. Accidents. A run of bad luck.

But she couldn't quite manage to make herself believe it.

"Callie?" Scott knocked gently on her half-open door and stuck his head into the room. "There you are. What are you up to?"

Callie took a few quick breaths, regaining control of herself and willing the threatening tears away.

27

"Nothing," she said quickly. "Um, just hanging out."

"Cool. Um, I was just wondering if you wanted me to drop you at the stable or anything." Scott blinked at her, his blue eyes wide and guileless.

Despite her present mood, Callie almost smiled. Her brother could fool most people with his gee-shucks innocent act, but not her. It was as clear as water that he was just looking for an excuse to go over to Pine Hollow. And Callie knew why. He was hoping Lisa would be there.

And I'm hoping George won't be there.

Callie's smile faded as she thought about Scott's offer. It would be so nice to go over and see Scooby. . . . She was tempted to spill her guts to her brother right then and there. Maybe talking to Scott about what had happened would help her put it all in perspective, give her a handle on how to deal with it.

No way, she thought firmly, getting control of herself once again. *That would be giving the whole stupid situation too much importance. All I need to do is get over this ridiculous, pointless, totally idiotic fear and forget it ever happened.*

Of course, that didn't mean she was ready to go back to Pine Hollow. Not yet.

"Um, no thanks," she told him. "I think I'll just hang out around here today."

"Are you sure?" Scott looked surprised. More than a little disappointed, too. Callie guessed this was his best chance to hang out with Lisa, especially since he'd decided not to ask her out again until *she'd* decided whether or not to get back together with her ex-boyfriend, Alex Lake.

But as much as she would otherwise like to help him out, she just couldn't do it. Not today. She shrugged. "I'm sure," she mumbled. "Totally."

As Lisa let herself into the front hall of her house, she heard her mother's voice in the kitchen. She thought about going straight upstairs to avoid any chance of another unpleasant confrontation, but she was thirsty. Taking a deep breath and vowing to stay calm, she headed into the kitchen. Her mother was leaning against the counter with a glass of white wine next to her right hand and the phone tucked into the crook of her left shoulder.

". . . and it would be nice to have that traditional Christmassy look instead of just—Oh! Here's Lisa now." Mrs. Atwood lowered the phone and smiled at her. "Hello, sweetie. How was the stable today?"

Lisa shrugged. "Fine."

"That's good." Her mother hardly seemed to have heard her. She took a sip of wine. "Guess what? I have your aunt Marianne on the phone, and she says they had a white Christmas! That cold snap that just made everything windy and miserable here brought them three inches of bright, beautiful snow."

"That's nice." Lisa gritted her teeth, willing herself to stay cool as she reached into the refrigerator for a soda. But she couldn't keep the sarcasm out of her voice as she added, "Maybe you should go up there and build a snowman or something."

Her mother frowned and gave her a look she'd perfected over the years, one that told Lisa she was being so childish that she might as well go out in a diaper. Then she raised the phone again. "Marianne? Lisa says hello."

Lisa rolled her eyes and headed for the door. Leave it to her mother to get all excited about snow. *I remember last winter when we got two inches, she was practically hysterical about all the salt mush that splashed up on her car while she was driving,* she thought with a grimace. *But I guess this is different. This is wonderful, magical* New Jersey *snow, so of course it's all good.*

As she walked into her room, Lisa swept her eyes over the comfortable, familiar space. It had hardly changed at all since she had helped her mother decorate it years ago. She lingered lovingly over every inch of the muted, rose-toned floral fabric and wallpaper and clean white wicker. Her childhood dolls and stuffed animals were carefully lined up atop her tall dresser, and a pair of bookshelves held a collection of her favorite novels and schoolbooks, as well as a set of Pony Club manuals and other horse books, many of them gifts from Carole.

Lisa tried to picture it all shoved into some dark, depressing little room somewhere in New Jersey, her favorite rag rug spread over ugly parquet or beige carpeting instead of wide wooden floorboards.

"Ugh," she said aloud.

With a sigh, she walked over to her desk chair and flopped into it, feeling depressed. For a little while at the stable that day, she had actually started to feel a twinge of hope that things might work out somehow or other. Stevie had a way of bringing that out in people. But after a few minutes, even Stevie's boundless optimism had started to rub her the wrong way.

We aren't kids anymore, she reminded herself, leaning her chin on her hand and staring fixedly at the wall. *Back then, we thought we could find a way to fix any problem that came along. But the truth is, there are some things you just can't change, no matter how much you want to.*

At that, her mind wandered to Alex. The deadline for their temporary breakup, New Year's, was rapidly approaching, and she still wasn't sure what she wanted to do. It still felt strange even to have to think about it—he was the first guy she'd ever really loved, and she still couldn't quite believe it had come to this. She couldn't believe she was actually considering whether or not she still wanted him in her life. Of course, if she was going to be moving to New Jersey in a week or two, the whole question could be moot.

Noticing her diary lying on the edge of the desk, Lisa grabbed it and flipped it open. Picking up a pen, she began to write.

Dear Diary,
   Another depressing day. Why can't I have my old life back?

She stopped and chewed on the end of her pen. She had already filled several pages with similar whining and complaining, and what good was it doing her? She'd be better off trying to be logical and mature, maybe figure out how to deal with things. She decided to make a list of pros and cons to give herself some perspective on her life. She started with the cons, since that seemed easier just at the moment.

My life right now—Cons:
   I might have to move to New Jersey with Mom.
   I still don't know what to do about Alex.

I still don't know how to feel about Scott.
Mom and Dad are still on my case about college.
Everything sucks.
My life right now—Pros:
  Only a few months until I'm eighteen and can
    do whatever I want, legally.
  I'm not starving or paralyzed or homeless or
    terminally ill.
  Stevie and Carole will always be my best
    friends, no matter what.

The last entry made her feel better, but only for a moment. Then she felt even worse. How could she move so far away from them? It just wasn't fair. And no amount of pros or cons would change that.

Tossing aside the diary, she walked over to her bed and flopped down on her stomach. She was tired. She'd tossed and turned for most of the night before, thinking about moving. With a yawn, she rolled over and grabbed her pillow, deciding she could use a nap. . . .

Lisa awoke with a start. For a second she didn't know where she was. Then she remembered. She'd been having some sort of weird dream. She and Carole and Stevie had all been kids again, back in the days when they were The Saddle Club, and they'd come up with a plan to stop Lisa's mother from moving to New Jersey. For a second, Lisa felt tremendously happy.

Then a knock came on her door and her mother stuck her head in. "Lisa?" she said, sounding vaguely annoyed. "Didn't you hear me calling you?"

Suddenly Lisa snapped back to the here and now, and her whole life came crashing down around her once again. Her problem wasn't solved—not even close. The Saddle Club hadn't ridden to the rescue, her mother hadn't changed her mind, and Lisa didn't get to stay in Willow Creek where she belonged. No, things were just as bad as ever, and no dream could change that.

"Uh, sorry, Mom," she mumbled, shaking her head to try to clear it. "What is it?"

Mrs. Atwood started chattering about Aunt Marianne and New Jersey as Lisa blinked away the last few remnants of her dream. It was almost painful to recall how pitifully excited she'd been at the thought that she was saved. How could she have believed it could ever be that simple, even in a dream?

She was so distracted that it took a moment or two to focus on what her mother was saying. ". . . and so I just called in and took a few days off."

Mrs. Atwood grimaced. "My boss gave me grief about that, of course, but who cares? It's not like I'll need that job much longer anyway."

"Wh-What are you talking about?" Lisa asked, trying to keep up. "Why did you take time off?"

Mrs. Atwood sighed loudly. "Weren't you listening?" she practically shouted. "I just told you. I'm going to drive up to Marianne's for a few days. I want to take a look around the area, maybe talk to some real estate agents. You can come along if you like," she added, her expression suddenly hopeful. "After all, you don't have school this week. It could be the perfect opportunity for you to come up and help pick out where we should live."

Lisa frowned, finally focusing completely on what her mother was saying. "No thanks," she snapped. "Unlike you, I don't have any interest in visiting New Jersey at all."

"Well!" Mrs. Atwood looked slightly taken aback for a second. Then she returned Lisa's frown. "With that attitude, you're not going to have an easy time adjusting to your new home," she said frostily.

"Whatever," Lisa muttered, knowing that she sounded like a sulky brat but not caring. Her mother deserved it. After all this time, did she really think she was ever going to convince Lisa that this moving idea was a *good* thing? Was she that clueless?

Throwing her hands up and sighing loudly and dramatically, Mrs. Atwood stormed out of the room, leaving Lisa alone with her thoughts. Dream or no dream, it was time to face reality. And the reality was, her mother was serious about this. She wasn't changing her mind. They were really going to move.

THREE

"Hanson," Carole told the bored-looking college-aged girl behind the counter. "There should be two rolls."

The girl snapped her gum, then turned and lazily surveyed a rack behind her that was stuffed full of stiff white envelopes. "Henderson?" she asked.

"Hanson," Carole repeated patiently. "I dropped them off three days ago."

The girl grabbed two of the envelopes. "Carl Hanson?"

"That's it," Carole said, hiding a smile. "Thanks. How much?"

She quickly paid the girl, then took the film and hurried outside. Ripping open the first envelope, she pulled out a fat stack of photos. She flipped through them quickly, then went back to the beginning and examined them more slowly. Most of the photos had been taken at Pine Hollow, and many of them featured her and Cam. She gazed at those happily, running her eyes over his handsome physique and wondering just how she'd become the luckiest girl on the planet.

I can't believe this hot guy is really my boyfriend, she thought in amazement as she pulled up a photo of Cam grooming Starlight. *I can't believe he's real, and he loves me, and we're going steady.*

It really did seem hard to believe, especially now, after Cam had been out of town visiting relatives for several days. It felt like forever since he'd left. Still, the special shiver she felt down her spine when she remembered kissing him good-bye on Christmas Eve reminded Carole that this was for real.

She pulled up the next photo. This one didn't feature Cam at all. It was a picture Carole had taken more than a month earlier, way back at the beginning of the roll. The photo showed Firefly, a flashy young mare that Max had recently added to the stable, trotting around the schooling ring with Ben Marlow in the saddle.

Carole gulped as she automatically noted Ben's flawless position and firm control of the flighty young horse. It had been so long since she'd seen him ride that she'd almost forgotten how good he was. In fact, it had been a long time since she'd seen much of Ben at all.

It's just because I haven't been working at Pine Hollow since I got grounded, she reminded herself, quickly moving past that picture and several others taken at the same training session.

Soon she came to another picture of Cam. She lingered over it for a moment, smiling at the funny expression on his face as he mugged for the camera.

"I really am awfully lucky," she murmured aloud.

Realizing that her cheeks were starting to go numb from the cold, she stuffed the pictures back into their envelope and hurried toward her car, shivering. Her father would be expecting her home soon, and she still had one more errand to run.

When she reached her car, she tossed the photo envelopes on top of her father's dry cleaning, which was taking up most of the backseat. Then she climbed into the driver's seat and started the engine, which muttered in protest at the cold. Turning down a narrow side street, she found a parking space near the entrance of Willow Creek Feed and Grain, a modest farm supply store tucked between an accountant's office and the local VFW hall. It didn't have nearly the selection of The Saddlery, the fancier tack shop at the mall, but it did carry some basic necessities, including the mineral block that she needed to pick up for Starlight.

When she hurried into the store a moment later, she was surprised to spot a familiar face. Usually the only people she encountered at the feed store were crusty old farmers or 4-H'ers buying chicken or sheep pellets.

"Callie?" she said. "Is that you? What are you doing here?"

Callie spun around, looking startled. Dropping the nylon halter she was holding back onto the shelf, she ran a hand over her long blond hair and smiled, though it looked slightly forced. "Oh, hi, Carole," she said. "Um, I was just browsing."

Carole cast an uncertain glance around the cramped, poorly lit store. It wasn't really the kind of place that was set up for browsing. The shelves were sparsely stocked with prosaic items such as fencing supplies and poultry waterers, and aside from half a shelf of equine items—feed supplements, deworming paste, a few halters, and bell boots—there really wasn't much to look at.

Carole shrugged, deciding her friend's shopping habits were her own business. Besides, there were more interesting things to talk about. "Are you going over to Pine Hollow after this?" she asked eagerly. "Or were you already there?"

Callie didn't answer for a moment, instead gazing at a stack of fly strips as if they were the most interesting things she'd ever seen. Finally, she lifted one shoulder slightly in a sort of half shrug. "I don't think I'll make it over there today."

"What?" Carole wondered if she'd misunderstood somehow. "But you haven't been there in days, have you? I mean, Scooby—"

"Scooby will live," Callie said with a slight frown. "I'm just really busy right now, okay? Don't worry, though, I called and asked them to turn him out this afternoon when it warms up a little." She turned away again, clearly wanting to drop the subject.

Carole wasn't normally a pushy person, but she couldn't just let it drop—not when there seemed to be a serious problem brewing between Callie and her new horse. Was Scooby not the mount she'd expected? Were they having some kind of personality clash, or maybe a training problem?

"Listen, Callie," she said sincerely. "I know it's hard sometimes—you know, getting used to a new horse. You've been riding Barq a lot lately, and I'm sure Scooby is really different in a lot of ways. But maybe all you need is—"

"All I need is to stop talking about this," Callie interrupted, her voice as sharp as a blade. "Now, if you'll excuse me . . ." She spun on her heel and left. Carole gaped after her, reeling from the icy retort. She knew that Callie had a temper, but this was the first time it had been leveled at her.

What did I say? she wondered, feeling wounded and a little shaky. *I was just trying to help.*

Still, she tried not to take it personally. If Callie

was having trouble with Scooby, she needed her friends to stick by her. And now that she knew there might be a problem, Carole planned to do just that.

"It's the next driveway, there on the right," Stevie said, pointing. "You can just drop me at the curb. It's hard to turn around when Alex parks right in the middle of the driveway like that." She rolled her eyes and grinned.

"Okay," George said, steering to the curb and shifting into park. "Here you go."

"Thanks a ton, George. Really." Stevie unhooked her seat belt and turned to grab her duffel bag from the backseat. "I owe you one. I really wasn't looking forward to walking home in this arctic blast."

"No problem," George said with his usual timid smile.

Stevie shivered as she opened the car door. She hadn't been kidding about the arctic blast. The temperature had dropped several more degrees since she'd arrived at the stable that morning, and a brisk wind was blowing in from the northwest, making things even chillier. Hugging her duffel to her chest for warmth, she gave George one last quick wave and hurried toward the front door.

That was nice of him to offer me a ride, she thought idly. *Especially since he lives in the opposite direction.*

Still, that kind of lucky break was only what she would have expected after the great day she'd had. Except for the fact that neither Carole nor Callie had showed up at Pine Hollow all day, things had been practically perfect. Belle had kept herself pristinely clean in her stall for a change, so all Stevie had had to do was pick out her feet and run a body brush over her before tacking up. The spirited bay mare had performed like a dream, turning in picture-perfect canter departs and flying changes as if she'd been born doing them.

After her ride, Stevie had spent a pleasant hour in the tack room with Lisa and Denise, chatting about the upcoming wedding as they cleaned tack together. It had taken all the self-discipline she possessed to keep from blurting out any hint of the fantastic wedding present she had planned. Finally Denise had been called away to the phone, and Stevie was able share it all with Lisa. She told her how she'd arranged for a fancy suite at a nice hotel downtown, with a champagne breakfast and a nice dinner in the hotel restaurant. Lisa had quickly volunteered to call around and reserve tickets to a show. It wasn't what Stevie would consider a super-deluxe honeymoon, but she was sure Red and Denise would love it. And after talking it all over with Lisa, Stevie's mood was better than ever.

And the best part is, I have another five whole days

until school starts again! she thought gleefully as she all but skipped up the front walk. She slowed her pace when her boot slipped on an icy patch, but even the frigid weather couldn't dim her sunny mood.

Then she entered her house. As soon as she let herself into the front hall, she wrinkled her nose. "What's that smell?" she muttered as a sickly sweet, flowery odor tickled her nose. Tossing her coat and bag in the general direction of the closet, she hurried down the hall toward the kitchen.

As soon as she rounded the corner, her mood plummeted. All three of her brothers were sitting at the kitchen table. And right in the middle, laughing and tossing her blond hair around, was Nicole Adams. Nicole was a classmate of Stevie's at Fenton Hall, but the two of them had never been close. In fact, Stevie had barely had reason to speak to her before her twin brother had suddenly decided to ask her out. Nicole hung with a crowd of snobs who never debated anything deeper than whether the latest shade of lipstick looked good on redheads or which player on the basketball team had the cutest butt.

"What are you doing here?" Stevie blurted out before she could stop herself.

Alex glared at her, but Nicole smiled sweetly. "Hi, Stevie," she said. "How's it going?"

Michael and Chad mumbled something that may have been a greeting, though neither of them took his eyes off Nicole. Stevie frowned. "Hi," she said shortly. She glared at Alex.

He glared back. "Did you need something, Stevie?" he said. "We were having a conversation here."

"I'll bet," Stevie muttered.

Alex scowled. "Stevie, could I speak to you for a minute?" he said through clenched teeth. *"Privately?"*

"Whatever." Stevie shrugged and followed him into the hall. She still couldn't quite believe that Nicole was in her house. It was bad enough that Alex had gone out with her a few times—he was male, he'd been suckered in by her blond hair and tight sweaters, it was almost understandable—but to bring her home? What was he thinking?

Alex whirled to face her as soon as they were out of earshot of the group in the kitchen. "Okay, what's the big idea?" he demanded, crossing his arms over his chest.

Stevie blinked. "Huh?" she said. "I was about to ask you the same question. What's she doing here?"

"I invited her to dinner," Alex said rather stiffly. "Mom and Dad said it was okay."

Stevie goggled. "What?" she cried. "She's eating here, with us? Talk about an appetite killer."

Alex scowled. "Very funny, Stevie," he said. "But

you'd better get it out of your system now. Because I don't want you making any more snotty comments in front of Nicole. She's supposed to be a guest here, remember? And you know how Mom and Dad feel about making guests welcome."

Stevie opened her mouth for a sharp retort, then bit it back and shook her head. "What are you thinking, anyway?" she asked, her tone subdued. "Aren't you even the slightest bit worried that all this"—she waved her hand in the general direction of the kitchen—"is going to blow your chances of getting back together with Lisa?"

Alex didn't quite meet her eye. "What difference does it make?" he mumbled. "She's probably moving to New Jersey soon, right? So it's just as well."

Stevie's jaw dropped. Was she the only one who was still convinced that Lisa's move wasn't going to happen? "Fine!" she snapped. "If you're ready to give up on Lisa, go ahead. But I'm not." Whirling away, she stomped off toward her room, dreading dinner.

FOUR

Lisa speared a bright orange ravioli with her fork and bit into it, grimacing as she realized it wasn't heated all the way through. Dropping her fork onto the cardboard tray, she stood up with a sigh and headed for the kitchen to nuke it a little longer. "Stupid microwave directions," she muttered, dumping the fork onto the counter. "If they aren't telling you to burn it to a crisp, they're leaving it half frozen."

She shoved the tray into the microwave and turned it on, punching the buttons a little harder than necessary. Aside from the whirring of the microwave's motor and the distant chatter of the TV, the house was very quiet. Lisa's mother had left earlier that day on her New Jersey house-hunting odyssey, and Lisa's mood had been going downhill ever since. She couldn't seem to stop imagining how her mother's trip might go. With the way things were going lately, she would probably find some perfect, amazing house right away. Maybe she would even put an offer on it before returning home on Monday. Then it would be a done deal, and there would really be nothing more for Lisa to do.

Not that there's a whole lot I can do as it is, she thought sourly, leaning on the counter as she waited for her food to cook. She couldn't seem to think of one thing she could do to change her mother's mind.

The microwave beeped at almost the same moment the phone rang. Lisa quickly pulled the tray out of the oven and then grabbed the phone. "Hello?" she said, realizing too late that she should have let the machine get it. It was most likely her mother calling to check in, and Lisa had no interest in talking to her at the moment.

"Hey, it's Carole. What's going on?"

Lisa smiled in relief. "Hi," she said, licking tomato sauce off her finger. "I was just having dinner."

"Oops! Sorry. Do you need to go?"

"No, that's okay." Lisa tucked the phone between her ear and her shoulder and grabbed the microwave tray and her fork. "I can talk, as long as you don't mind if I chew in your ear."

"Deal," Carole agreed. "Because the phone is busy at Stevie's house, and I just have to tell someone what happened today. Luckily Dad is already easing off on the phone ban."

"That's good," Lisa said, feeling a little sad. Soon Carole's grounding would be over. But how long would Lisa have to enjoy hanging out with her friend before her mother yanked her off to snowy New Jersey? "Um, so what happened?" she asked, trying to take her mind off that.

"It's Callie," Carole said. "I ran into her today in town, and I'm kind of worried."

Lisa ate her dinner and listened as Carole described the way Callie had acted that day at the feed store. "Weird," she said when her friend had finished. "What do you think that was all about?"

Carole sighed. "I don't know, but she really seemed upset. Almost angry. And I don't think it had anything to do with me. You know how intense she can be. What if she's decided already that Scooby isn't the right horse for her?"

"Do you really think that's it?" Lisa said, remembering how excited Callie had been about her new horse. "I mean, maybe she was just in a bad mood or something. Some people get cranky around the holidays anyway."

"I guess." Carole didn't sound convinced. "I'll have to see how she acts tomorrow at the stable, if she shows up." She sighed. "Anyway, what's new with you?"

Lisa didn't really feel like getting into her own problems just then. "Not much," she said quickly. "Hey, did you figure out a gift for Cam yet?"

"Not yet," Carole said sheepishly. "Actually, just this afternoon I started going through some old photo albums for inspiration." She laughed self-consciously. "You know, looking for hints of what kind of stuff he might like."

"Any luck?"

"Nope." Carole sighed loudly into the phone. "I don't know what I'm going to do. On the one hand, I can't wait to see him again, and four days seems like forever. But on the other hand, four measly days doesn't seem like nearly enough time to figure out this present thing."

Lisa made understanding noises, though she couldn't really work up much sympathy for Carole's plight. *I know she's new to this relationship stuff,* she thought. *But really, what's the big drama about this gift? Cam loves her—he'd be perfectly happy if she just went out and bought him a nice sweater or a new wallet or something. Or even if she just cooked him dinner.*

Besides that, she couldn't help feeling a little resentful. Here she was, possibly only days or weeks away from leaving Willow Creek for good, and all Carole could seem to talk about was some stupid Christmas gift for her boyfriend.

Lisa immediately realized she wasn't being fair. How could her friends know how she was feeling if she didn't tell them? She opened her mouth to tell Carole about her mother's trip to New Jersey, which she hadn't mentioned yet. But at the last second, she decided against it. What good would it do to re-hash her problems? It would only make Carole feel just as bad as Lisa was feeling, and Lisa didn't want to do that to her.

Besides, she thought sadly as she and Carole said good-bye and hung up, *what more is there to say?*

Callie poked at a glazed carrot with her fork, her stomach churning at the mere thought of trying to eat it. She hadn't had much appetite for food lately. Just about the only thing she could stomach was microwave popcorn, which she'd been sneaking at night after the rest of the family had gone to bed.

"Callie?" her mother said, glancing at her. "Are you okay, honey? Do you want some potatoes?"

"No," Callie said. Noticing her mother's raised eyebrow, she quickly added, "Um, thanks. But I'm really not that hungry today."

She forced herself to smile blandly until her mother's attention returned to whatever it was that Callie's father had been talking about for the past fifteen minutes. Then she sighed and returned her gaze to her plate, feeling tired and very much alone, even sitting there with her parents and her brother. Her lack of sleep was making her moody, and she was afraid her family was starting to notice. Scott had been shooting her curious looks at odd times, and she could tell her mother was starting to worry about her, too.

Still, she couldn't seem to help herself. The nightmares were coming every night. Even in her waking hours, odd thoughts kept intruding at random times. The image of George holding a hoof pick would pop into her head while she was loading the dishwasher. Or she would suddenly think about the way Scooby had rolled his eyes at George while she was brushing her teeth or dumping her clothes in the laundry hamper.

When am I going to get over this? she wondered wearily, feeling frustrated and helpless. *When is my life going to go back to normal?*

Stevie gritted her teeth as Nicole cleared her throat and politely asked for a second helping of shrimp. It already felt as if dinnertime had gone on for days, though when Stevie sneaked a peek at her watch, she realized with a sinking heart that they'd only been at the table for about fifteen minutes.

"Here you go, Nicole," Stevie's mother said with a smile, passing the bowl of shrimp.

"Thanks!" Nicole accepted the dish and helped

herself to a generous serving. "This whole dinner is really great, Mr. and Mrs. Lake. Thanks again for having me."

"Don't be silly!" Mr. Lake replied in his most jovial tone. "It's our pleasure. Any friend of Alex's is always welcome here."

Stevie rolled her eyes. She couldn't believe the way her whole family was making such a big, fat fuss over Nicole. They were acting as if they'd never had a guest for dinner before—or at least not one they liked so much. It was making Stevie want to gag.

It's not as if Nicole doesn't get enough undeserved attention at school, she thought sourly. *Male attention, that is.*

"More water, Nicole?" Stevie's older brother, Chad, said, reaching for the pitcher at his elbow. "That shrimp is pretty spicy."

Nicole giggled, even though Chad hadn't actually said anything funny. "Thanks, Chad," she cooed, holding out her glass. "That would be great."

With difficulty, Stevie held back a snort. Chad had been a love machine wannabe since he'd first discovered girls at age thirteen or fourteen. Now that he was a college sophomore, he still tended to act like a goofy adolescent when an attractive girl was in the room. And he wasn't making any secret of the fact that he thought Nicole was attractive.

Not that Chad's behavior is any huge surprise, Stevie told herself, scooping up a forkful of rice and shoving it into her mouth. The faster she ate, the sooner this painful meal could be over. *He's always been a major hound dog. Still, I would have expected better from Mom and Dad. They've always loved Lisa—how can they act so happy about having Nicole here in her place?*

Somehow Stevie managed to survive the next twenty minutes without either telling Nicole off or hurling on her own plate. Finally her father pushed his chair back and excused himself to go and watch the news. The rest of the family took that as a cue to scatter. Stevie's mother corralled Michael into helping her clear the table, Alex and Nicole headed for the basement rec room, and Chad wandered aimlessly into the hall.

Stevie followed him. "Well," she said sarcastically when they were out of their mother's earshot. "Congratulations. You actually managed to avoid drooling all over yourself. Well, mostly, anyway."

Chad grinned. "Stuff it, Stevie," he said cheerfully. "Nicole's hot, and you can't deny it. So sue me—I noticed."

Stevie grimaced. "There's more to a woman than how she looks, you know," she snapped. "Like personality and brains and stuff like that."

"Whatever." Chad shrugged. "Anyway, what are you getting on my case for? Alex is the one who's seeing her, not me." He smirked. "Bummer for me, huh?"

"Get a life," Stevie mumbled, though her heart wasn't really in it. Chad was right. Alex was the one she was really annoyed with.

She sighed and turned away as Chad loped up the stairs. Then she wandered back down the hall toward the kitchen. Before she got there she passed the half-open basement door. Hearing strange noises coming from behind it, she glanced over.

She immediately wished she hadn't. Alex and Nicole hadn't even made it down the stairs. They were standing only a few steps down. Nicole's back was pressed against the wall and her hands were wrapped around Alex's waist. He was kissing her passionately, one hand buried in her hair and the other . . .

Stevie shuddered and turned away quickly, hurrying past the door before they noticed her presence. She stopped and leaned against the wall, feeling sick to her stomach.

For the first time she considered the possibility that this wasn't just some passing fling. Maybe Alex really did like spending time with Nicole. Maybe he really was moving on rather than just marking time before he could get back together with Lisa.

But they have *to get back together,* Stevie thought hopelessly, wrapping her arms around her waist. *They have to!*

She couldn't stand the thought that her brother might not be in love with Lisa anymore. How could someone's feelings change so drastically, practically overnight? And what would Lisa say when she found out? How would she feel if she wanted to get back together and Alex didn't?

Then again, maybe I'm totally overreacting because of what I just saw. Stevie stood up a little straighter, feeling a flicker of hope. *I mean, like Chad said, Nicole is hot. Maybe Alex is just getting a little carried away because all his guy friends think he's a big stud now.*

She smiled, liking the idea. Alex had always been a sucker for flattery, and Nicole was awfully good at flirting and making guys feel like big shots. Plus, with Chad and Michael and probably every other male he knew telling him how lucky he was—well, it was no wonder Alex was acting like Nicole was the girl of his dreams.

But he'll get over that the second Lisa decides she wants him back, Stevie assured herself. *I'm sure that's all it will take to wake him up and make him realize who he really cares about. Then it will be Nicole who will have to deal with rejection.*

She almost smiled at the thought. Almost. Then she glanced toward the basement door and shuddered slightly instead.

FIVE 5

Stevie slipped the reins over Belle's head, keeping a grip on them with her left hand as the mare danced in place. "Okay, girl," Stevie said firmly, stepping up on the mounting block near the outdoor schooling ring. "Hold still."

She grabbed some mane and swung into the saddle. Slipping off one glove, she reached down to double-check her girth. Her fingers began to go numb almost immediately, and she quickly pulled the glove back on.

"Whew!" she muttered, wishing the indoor ring were free. Max was giving a private lesson in there at the moment, and another set of students was due as soon as the current rider was finished. "Chilly out here."

Belle blew out a snort, her breath visible in the cold air. Stevie urged her forward, heading for the open gate of the schooling ring.

Soon she was inside, bending her horse as Belle

walked around the ring. The horse settled down to work almost immediately, though she tossed her head at every gust of wind.

Stevie gave her a pat as she turned her to the inside. "This gives the term *warming up* a whole new meaning, doesn't it, Belle baby?" she commented to the horse.

Deciding it was time to trot, Stevie lifted herself into two-point position to give the mare's back a chance to warm up. She signaled for the change in gait, but Belle stumbled. Stevie lost her balance and landed hard in the saddle. "Whoa!" she exclaimed, startled by the impact. She gritted her teeth, keeping her temper and reminding herself that it wasn't the horse's fault. If she'd been properly balanced, she would have been able to hold her position better. Reaching down to give Belle another pat, she blew out a slow breath. "Sorry about that, girl," she murmured.

She gathered her reins and tried again. *I've got to focus,* Stevie thought. *Belle and I haven't gotten as much work done during break as I'd hoped, and we only have a few days left.*

Now that Stevie thought about it, it really had been a busy week or two. And she'd expended an awful lot of energy worrying about her friends' problems, particularly Lisa's possible move and her breakup with Alex. And the really depressing thing was, both problems just seemed to get worse and worse as time went on. So far Stevie hadn't been able to do a thing to help solve them. With a grimace, she forced those sorts of thoughts out of her head and signaled again for the trot.

This time they made it more than halfway around the ring before Stevie's mind started to wander and Belle decided that meant it was time to break down to a walk and suddenly lower her head to rub it on her leg. Stevie jerked forward and almost came unbalanced again.

"Ugh!" she exclaimed, regaining her seat and fishing for the stirrup she'd lost.

She sighed. Enough was enough. She was riding like a rank beginner, and Belle wasn't the kind of horse to let her get away with it. Reluctantly, she decided it would be best for them both if she called it a day right then and there.

"Sorry, girl," she said with a quick pat, turning the mare toward the gate. "I don't think we're up to a schooling session right now. How about a nice long turnout instead?"

The horse flicked her ears back, which Stevie took as an assent. Dismounting, she led her horse into the stable entryway. Just inside, she found Maureen talking with George.

"Hey," Stevie greeted them both. She turned to Maureen. "I decided to turn Belle out instead of riding her today," she explained, feeling slightly sheepish. "Um, which pasture should I put her in?"

Maureen shrugged. "Take your pick," she said. "Max and Red have lessons scheduled all day, so most of the horses are in. The only troublemaker out right now is Geronimo, and he's in the back paddock by himself. So why don't you put her out front with Pinky and Topside?"

"Okay." Stevie glanced at Belle and smiled. The mare had a special fondness for Pinky, a fellow boarder's quarter horse gelding. And Topside got along with just about everyone except Geronimo, Pine Hollow's resident stallion. "Thanks."

Maureen nodded and returned her attention to George, who seemed to be telling her his life story. Stevie clucked to Belle and moved on.

A few minutes later Belle's tack was off and her turnout rug was on. Stevie led the mare back out of the stable and a short distance along the driveway to the large pasture that lay between the stable building and the road.

Opening the gate, she led the horse inside. "Okay, have fun, girl," she said, unclipping the lead line and stepping back. Belle stood stock-still for a moment, her ears pricked in the direction of the pair of horses grazing in the middle of the field. Then, with a snort, she trotted off toward them.

Stevie watched her go, then turned and left the

pasture, carefully latching the gate behind her. She walked slowly up the driveway, wondering what to do. None of her friends had arrived at the stable yet as far as she knew, and she was afraid that if she hung around waiting for them, Max would put her to work, probably doing something really fun like chipping frozen manure chunks off the ground or cleaning out half-frozen water tubs.

As she approached the stable building, she winced, spotting Max himself standing just outside the big double doors and staring thoughtfully at the wall. For a moment she was tempted to slip past as quietly as possible—what if he was thinking of rustling up a volunteer crew to repaint the entire building or something?—but at the last second she felt guilty. There was an awful lot of work that went into keeping Pine Hollow running smoothly, and Max needed all the help he could get.

She cleared her throat. "Hi, Max," she said. "What's up?"

Max blinked and glanced over at her. "Oh, hello, Stevie," he replied. "I was just thinking."

"You weren't thinking about, um, painting, by any chance?" Stevie asked cautiously. "It's probably a little cold for that, right?"

Max looked confused. He shook his head. "Actually, I was trying to visualize the best way to expand this building."

"Really?" Stevie glanced up at the stable wall. "Cool. Are you thinking of giving all the horses twenty-by-twenty-foot stalls? Or were you planning to put in a nice sauna and hot tub for tired, over-worked riders?" She grinned.

Max rolled his eyes. "Very funny," he said gruffly. "In case you haven't noticed, things are getting pretty busy around here. Willow Creek is an up-and-coming suburb, and more people are moving here all the time."

Stevie nodded. She'd seen several signs for brand-new housing developments going up around the area just in the past few weeks.

Max wasn't finished. "Pine Hollow is busier than it's ever been," he said, rubbing his chin thought-fully as his gaze strayed back to the building. "And now that Maureen's on board and Carole will be re-turning soon—I hope—well, it just seems like the right time to think about expanding. I want to start shopping for a few more horses, and maybe add on another row of stalls to house them."

"Wow!" Stevie grinned, thrilled that there could be a whole new group of horses at Pine Hollow be-fore long. "Talk about major news! I had no idea."

"Well, I haven't been talking about it much yet." Max fixed her with a stern look. "In fact, I'd appre-ciate it if you kept quiet about this for the time be-ing. I know there's no way to stop you from filling in your cronies, but I'd rather not have all the younger kids buzzing about it and getting more distracted than they already are."

Stevie giggled. "No problem," she said, pleased that Max had confided in her. Knowing this exciting news before almost anyone else gave her the same feeling she got when she turned in an article for the school newspaper.

You know, that's just about the only good thing about going back to school next week, she thought as she waved good-bye to Max and headed inside. *I hadn't really thought about it, but I really do miss working on my articles for the* Sentinel.

She smiled as she thought about it. Max's wife, who was a reporter for a major Washington daily, had been the one who had first inspired Stevie to give journalism a try. She had also been the first one to warn Stevie that it wasn't going to be all fun and games and glamour, and she'd been right about that. Researching and writing newspaper articles took a lot of hard work, and Stevie had already had to sacrifice a few dates with Phil or outings with her friends to make a deadline. But in the end, when she saw her name on a byline and realized she was the one who'd made the story happen, it was all worth it.

It's kind of like when I was first learning to ride, Stevie thought as she passed through the entryway and into the locker room. *Back then, every lesson or trail ride taught me something new and interesting, whether it went well or not. And now, every article I write makes me feel the same way. Even the boring ones.*

She sat down on the bench in front of the cubbyhole where she'd stowed her sneakers. Pulling off her boots, she tossed them inside. Now that she was thinking about the *Sentinel* again, her mind started buzzing with ideas for articles she could write when the holiday break ended after New Year's. She couldn't wait to get started.

Of course, she added with a smile as she leaned over to yank on her sneakers, *that doesn't mean I actually miss school or anything. Ha!*

As Carole pulled her car into an empty spot in Pine Hollow's gravel parking area, she saw Maureen walking across the lot in the direction of the stable. Maureen saw her, too. She paused and raised a lazy hand in greeting as Carole climbed out of her car.

"Hey," Maureen said. "How's it going, Carole? Cold enough for ya?"

Carole smiled uncertainly. "Um, yeah. I mean, I know. It's really freezing." As usual, she found herself feeling a little tongue-tied around the new stable hand. Maureen just seemed to have that effect on her—her cool, gold-flecked brown eyes always seemed to see a little more than they should. Whenever those eyes fixed on her, Carole could almost feel herself shrinking back under their direct, curious gaze.

The two of them fell into step together, Carole picking up her pace slightly to keep up with the tall, lean woman's easy stride. As they walked, Carole couldn't help noticing an unpleasant smell emanating from Maureen's general direction. Carole wrinkled her nose, feeling her stomach clench as she recognized the odor as cigarette smoke and remembered the time a few days earlier when she'd caught Maureen smoking in a storage shed.

Shooting the stable hand a quick, nervous glance, Carole wondered if Maureen had just been out in the parking lot sneaking a cigarette. *Of course, it's really none of my business if she wants to smoke in her own car, I suppose, even if it's parked here,* Carole reminded herself. *Much less if she chooses to smoke on her way over to Pine Hollow, when she's not even on stable property.*

Carole bit her lip, wondering if she should ask Maureen if she'd been smoking in the parking lot. She wasn't a fan of cigarettes in general—in her opinion, they smelled worse than the stinkiest, most poorly managed manure pile in the world— but that didn't give her the right to tell someone else what to do with their own lungs.

It's different if she keeps smoking around the stable, though, Carole thought. *That's really dangerous, and it's why Max has such a strict no-smoking rule here at Pine Hollow. One stray spark or a butt that's not completely out could start a fire that would put the lives of every horse and person in the place at risk.*

Still, she really had no evidence that Maureen had posed such a risk. And Carole wasn't sure she wanted to make an enemy of the new hand, or face down those cool brown eyes without good cause. Feeling confused and vaguely anxious about the whole situation, Carole excused herself as soon as she and Maureen reached the entrance. Then she turned down a stable aisle in search of her friends.

She didn't have far to go before she found Stevie, who was standing in front of Talisman's stall chatting with Red. Red had the chestnut gelding in cross-ties and was pulling his mane. Denise was standing by as well, along with Deborah, who was holding her sleepy-looking three-year-old daughter, Jeanne.

"Hey!" Stevie called as soon as she spotted Carole. "It's about time you got here. We were just talking about the wedding."

Carole smiled, instantly forgetting all about Maureen Chance and her nicotine habit. "Cool," she said, feeling a flash of excitement at the thought that the wedding was only a few days away. "Need any help with Tally?"

Stevie patted Talisman's neck. "He's being pretty good so far," she reported.

Carole nodded, pleased to hear that. When the talented jumper had come to Pine Hollow two years earlier, his ground manners had left a lot to be desired. It had taken four people to give him a bath and three to catch him and bring him in from the pasture. His remedial training had become something of a stable project, with the entire staff and many of the regular students helping to teach the spirited horse that it was in his best interest to cooperate with people.

As she was thinking back on those days, Denise sighed loudly. "Thanks again for helping out with him, Stevie," she said. "I'm still feeling a little shaky after that last trip to the john."

For the first time, Carole noticed that Denise was leaning heavily against the wall. Her normally tanned face looked pale. "Are you okay?" she asked worriedly.

"I'll live," Denise replied with a grimace. "Although I really think I'll be the only woman in the history of pregnancy to have morning sickness right through month nine." She smiled, though she still looked a little green around the gills. "Whoever came up with the name *morning sickness,* anyway?

It's more like morning, noon, and night sickness if you ask me."

Carole was sympathetic—she guessed that suffering through a nausea-filled pregnancy had to be especially hard on Denise, who was usually so energetic and athletic—though she couldn't help being a little distracted by thoughts of the upcoming wedding. The big day would surely be one of the most romantic days of Denise's life, and Carole was sure it would be an incredibly romantic day for her, too. Cam was due to return from his trip that morning, and he and Carole had arranged to meet before the wedding to exchange Christmas gifts. Then, later, they would attend the wedding together and dance New Year's Eve away at the reception.

Of course, our gift exchange will be kind of a bust if I don't manage to get my act together and actually get something for him soon, Carole thought ruefully.

Before she could follow that line of thought any further, she heard hoofbeats approaching from the end of the aisle. "Oops," Ben Marlow's quiet, unassuming voice commented. "I'll go around."

Carole gulped. Peeking past Talisman, she saw that Ben was leading a horse named Romeo, whose stall was just beyond them.

"No, wait," Red called. "It's okay. It will be good practice for Tally to step aside and be patient."

Red and Stevie bustled about, unhooking one of the cross-ties and moving the tall chestnut gelding to one side so that Ben could pass. Through it all, Carole kept her gaze carefully trained on the horses, not quite daring to meet Ben's eye. She still felt a little strange whenever she encountered him. Even though she was happy with Cam now, she couldn't help remembering the day, more than a month before, when Ben had kissed her and then pretended it had never happened.

"Hey, Ben," Denise said as the stable hand led Romeo into his stall. "We were just talking about the wedding. You're coming, aren't you?"

Carole winced, waiting for Ben to mumble one of his famous noncommittal replies. She only hoped Red's and Denise's feelings wouldn't be hurt when Ben—

"Uh-huh." Ben glanced out of the stall as he unclipped Romeo's lead line. "I'll be there. Wouldn't miss it."

Carole blinked in surprise. *Wow,* she thought. *Talk about a surprise. I wouldn't think a big New Year's Eve party would be Ben's kind of scene at all. I figured he'd come up with some kind of excuse to get out of the whole wedding celebration.*

For some reason, the idea that Ben was going to be there—right smack in the middle of her big, romantic daydream New Year's Eve—made her feel vaguely unsettled. But she did her best to shake off the feeling, reminding herself that Ben wasn't the one she was going to be thinking about. She would be too busy enjoying herself with Cam.

Soon Ben moved on, and Stevie started chattering about something Max had said earlier that day. As near as Carole could follow, it sounded as though the stable owner was thinking of expanding, maybe buying some new horses soon. Carole couldn't help feeling a little left out—in the old days, she would have been the one sharing that kind of news with Stevie, not the other way around—but she didn't spend much time worrying about it. She would be back at work at Pine Hollow soon enough. In the meantime, she had a more immediate worry.

Okay, this is getting truly ridiculous, she told herself. *What in the world am I going to give Cam for Christmas?*

.

SIX

"Callie?" Congressman Forester said, sticking his head into the kitchen. "Phone."

"Really?" Callie looked up from the magazine she was reading and cocked her head in surprise. "I didn't even hear it ring."

"It didn't. I was on the other line." Callie's father tossed her the portable phone.

Callie caught it. "Thanks." She put the phone to her ear. "Hello? This is Callie."

"Hey, it's Maureen." The stable hand's voice sounded even deeper and raspier than usual over the phone. "Max wants to know what you want us to do with Scooby today. Should we turn him out or keep him in?"

Callie winced. This was the moment she'd avoided thinking about all this morning—the moment she had to make a decision. Was she going to ride today, or was she going to allow her fear to take away yet another day of doing what she loved to do?

When she thought about it that way, she knew there was only one response she could give Maureen if she wanted to be able to look herself in the mirror. "Keep him in," she replied, her voice firm. "I'll be over to exercise him in a little while."

"Okay." Maureen sounded rushed. "Later, Callie."

"Bye," Callie said, though the stable hand had already hung up. She shrugged, guessing that Pine Hollow must be hopping that morning. She wasn't sure if that made her more or less nervous about going back.

It doesn't matter either way, she told herself firmly. *I've got to just do it.*

Tossing her magazine and the phone onto the kitchen table, Callie hurried toward the coat closet to dig out her jacket and the bag containing her boots and hard hat. She knew Scott was taking a shower upstairs and she could hear the water running, which meant she had a few minutes to make her escape. She knew he would want to come with her, but she also knew she had to make this visit on her own if she was ever going to put the incident behind her.

Soon she was crossing the last field on the ten-minute walk to Pine Hollow. When she caught a glimpse of the long, low-slung stable building, her heart started to pound a little faster.

Chill, she chided herself. *This is no big deal. It's no big deal.*

The parking lot was full, and a couple of adult riders were practicing over cross rails in the outdoor ring. But Callie didn't see anybody she knew, either outside or in the entryway. In fact, she managed to make it all the way to Scooby's stall without encountering any familiar faces at all aside from a trio of intermediate riders, who paid no attention to her whatsoever, and Ben Marlow, who merely nodded and moved on with the wheelbarrow he was pushing.

Whew! Callie thought as she darted into Scooby's stall. Her horse seemed mildly pleased to see her, ambling over and snuffling at her shoulder. She patted him, a feeling of resentment washing over her as she realized just how long it had been since she'd seen him. *It's ridiculous,* she thought, straightening the spotted gelding's forelock. *I've only had him for like a week, and I've already missed so much time with him. And it's all my own stupid fault for being such a wuss.*

"Want to go for a ride, buddy?" she asked the horse softly.

Pulling a hoof pick out of her bag, she quickly cleaned his feet. Someone had obviously given him a quick brushing sometime that day, so after running her hands over his body and legs to check for any problems, she poked her head out into the aisle. It was time to grab his tack and get out of there.

"Back in a sec, Scooby," she whispered.

She let herself out of the stall and scurried down the deserted aisle. As she crossed the entryway, the adult riders were coming in with their horses. They nodded politely to Callie and she smiled back. Then she ducked her head and scooted into the hallway leading to the tack room. Rounding the corner, she stopped short, realizing too late that the small room was occupied.

Stevie spotted her immediately. "Callie!" she exclaimed, glancing up from adjusting a bridle. "Long time no see, girlfriend!"

"Hi there," Phil added with a smile. "I just checked out your new horse. He's pretty hot stuff."

"Thanks." Callie forced herself to smile in return, though she felt more like screaming. Normally she would have been perfectly happy to hang out and chat with Stevie and Phil for a few minutes. But that day wasn't a normal day. "Um, what are you guys doing? Going for a ride?"

"Yep." Stevie bent over to fish a fleece saddle pad out of the stack near the door. "Probably a short one, though, since the weather still sucks. I hope it's not this cold on Tuesday for the wedding." She shivered dramatically to punctuate the comment.

The wedding. Callie had almost forgotten about that. There was no way she could get out of going, but what would she do if George went, too? What would she say if he tried to talk to her about what had happened?

"Right," she said, doing her best to sound normal. "Well, okay then, I guess I'd better—"

"Oh!" Stevie stood up straight and glanced at her. "Hey, did I ever tell you what happened with A.J.? He decided to try to track down his birth mother, and so he called this woman I saw in a picture in the paper, and . . ."

Callie tried hard to look interested as Stevie chatted on and on about Phil's friend A.J. McDonnell, who had recently discovered he was adopted. She seemed to have an endless supply of information about the topic that she felt she had to share with Callie, with Phil adding comments here and there. Eventually Stevie switched over to talking about some new plan of Max's to buy new horses, and Callie cleared her throat forcefully.

"Um, listen," she interrupted during a brief pause in Stevie's monologue, "I should really get going. I left Scooby tied in his stall, and—"

"Oh! Sorry." Stevie looked sheepish. "Guess I was kind of babbling."

Phil rolled his eyes. "Kind of ?" he said teasingly.

"Okay, then, I'll catch you guys later," Callie said hurriedly, not wanting to get trapped in another lengthy conversation.

Before Stevie or Phil could respond, she strode

across the room and grabbed Scooby's saddle off its designated rack. She slung a saddle pad over it and was reaching for the bridle when Stevie spoke up again.

"Oh!" she said. "By the way, Callie, I almost forgot to tell you. George has been looking for you for a couple of days now."

Callie froze, her fingers gripping the bridle. "What?"

"George," Stevie repeated. "I guess he wanted to, like, thank you or whatever. Because of what happened the other day with the paramedics and all."

That was all Callie could take. Without another word, she pulled the bridle down and practically ran out of the room, ignoring Stevie's surprised-sounding calls. *I knew it,* she thought desperately as she made a beeline for Scooby's stall, careening through the entryway and barely avoiding collisions with several other riders. *I knew this wasn't going to be easy.*

She didn't take a full breath again until she was safely inside Scooby's stall with her back pressed against the wall. The horse gazed at her curiously for a moment before turning to take a drink out of his water bucket.

Callie stood there for several minutes, waiting for the pounding of her heart to slow. She prayed that Stevie wouldn't be worried enough to come looking for her. She wasn't sure she could explain what was going on inside her own head right now even if she wanted to, which she most definitely didn't.

"Okay, Scoob," she said when she had control of herself again. "Let's get going. Enough messing around."

After quickly tacking up her horse and checking the aisle for familiar faces, she headed outside. Soon she was mounted and adjusting her stirrups as she glanced around, wondering what to do next. She couldn't quite bring herself to hit the trails again, though she felt like the world's biggest loser for being afraid.

What am I going to do? she thought sarcastically. *Only enter races that don't go into any woods? That's going to limit me just a tad.*

She grimaced, irritated with herself anew. Still, she decided that she wouldn't push it that day. The important thing was that she was there at Pine Hollow, in the saddle again. She and Scooby could just do some schooling in the far corner of the back pasture. That would be enough for the moment.

"Okay, let's get moving, then," she murmured, sending Scooby into a walk. As they crossed the stable yard, Callie tried to gather her thoughts and form a plan of action. She would warm him up on the way out to the pasture, then get straight to work on some exercises to loosen him up. Then—

She froze in mid-thought as she happened to glance toward the driveway. A white car had just pulled in. A very familiar white car belonging to George's mother, with a very familiar round face just visible behind the wheel.

Callie didn't think. She just reacted. "Yee-hah!" she cried, kicking her heels into Scooby's sides.

The Appaloosa, who had been ambling along willingly, let out a startled snort. With a slight buck, he took off at a gallop, racing across the yard at top speed. Almost too late Callie realized that the pasture fence—five and a half feet tall and very, very solid—was just a few strides ahead. Pulling Scooby around, she nearly knocked her knee on the fence as he careened alongside it, nostrils flared. In a matter of seconds they reached the corner of the fence, crossed a small open area beyond, and entered the woods.

Realizing the danger of crashing through the underbrush at top speed, Callie sat back and pulled back on the reins. For a second Scooby shook his head and seemed inclined to race on, but then his pace slowed to a canter, then a trot. Finally he stopped, his breath coming in loud snorts.

Callie slumped in the saddle, her head pounding.

"What's wrong with me?" she whispered as guilt washed over her, deep and bitter. Taking off like that had been a truly stupid move. Scooby wasn't even properly warmed up yet, and there she was, spurring him on like a racehorse in the homestretch.

What if he'd stumbled? she thought furiously. *What if he'd snapped a cannon bone or thrown me or run right into that fence or tried to jump it and crashed or—*

She stopped herself. The list of possible disasters was just too long. Besides, none of it mattered. The important thing was that it was over now.

Callie slid out of the saddle and spent a few minutes stroking and comforting Scooby, who seemed to have recovered from their sudden flight faster than she had. Then she bent over each of his legs in turn, making sure all was well.

When she was satisfied that he was really all right, she gave him a pat and then remounted. *Now what?* she wondered, feeling a stab of apprehension as she glanced over her shoulder in the direction of the pasture.

The question had barely formed in her mind when she knew the answer. She couldn't go back out there. Her horse, with his dramatic black-and-white leopard-spotted coat, was just too noticeable.

Even tucked away in the far corner, Scooby would be all too visible in the pasture to anyone who so much as glanced in that direction.

Like George, for instance, Callie thought grimly. *What if he saw us out there? What if he decided to ride out and join us?*

She really didn't know how she would react to that. But she didn't want to find out.

"Come on, Scoob," she said wearily. "Let's just take a little hack through the woods here."

She urged him down the trail at a walk. The area they were in was a familiar one, with wide, straight trails and no tricky spots. Usually it was an easy ride, even for beginners. But Callie was so distracted by thinking about what had just happened—What if George had seen them on his way up the driveway? What if he was tacking up his horse right that very minute, preparing to ride out after them?—that she was having a hard time concentrating on her riding. Scooby was clearly picking up on her nerves, since he kept shaking his head and spooking at nothing.

Finally, after the horse nearly unseated her jumping over a twig on the trail as if it were a Grand Prix oxer, Callie gave up. Patting Scooby apologetically, she dismounted and led him off the trail into a small clearing with a few tufts of winter-brittle grass.

Soon Scooby was grazing calmly. Callie felt anything but calm. Sitting down with her back against a tree, she buried her face in her knees. Taking deep breaths, she tried to figure out exactly what was wrong with her. Because until she knew, she had no idea how to fix it.

SEVEN

Pine Hollow's entryway was empty when Lisa stepped into it a little later that day. She felt silly for coming to the stable again—she hadn't been a daily visitor to Pine Hollow, even during school vacations, since sometime around ninth grade. But somehow, now that her whole life could be changing so soon, Pine Hollow was where she wanted to be. It was the place that held most of her fondest memories—the place where she and her best friends had met and bonded over their common love of horses.

Unfortunately, neither of her best friends seemed to be around at the moment. Lisa poked her head into the student locker room, where several younger riders were gossiping as they changed into their boots. Then she walked down the hallway to check the tack room and office. There was no sign of her friends there, either, though Denise was doing paperwork in the office.

"Hey," Lisa greeted the stable manager. "Have you seen Carole or Stevie lately?"

Denise glanced up. "I think Stevie's out on the trails with Phil. And I haven't seen Carole at all."

"Okay, thanks." Lisa sighed and left the office, feeling restless and lonely. There was no telling when Stevie would be back—when she and Phil got out there in the woods together, they could sometimes rival Callie in the length of time they spent on the trail. Still, Lisa didn't want to leave the stable. Where else would she go?

She wandered across the entryway into the stable aisle opposite. On her way in, she had noticed that only a handful of horses were turned out, probably because of the weather. Half a dozen more were probably in use. That meant a good number of heads poked out over the half doors of their stalls as she walked down the aisle.

Lisa paused at the first occupied stall, where a big bay gelding was gazing at her placidly and munching on a mouthful of hay. "Hi there, Topside," she murmured, reaching up to stroke the horse on the cheek. She smiled as Topside nuzzled her, clearly hoping for a carrot or other treat.

Lisa still remembered the days before Stevie had gotten Belle, when she had ridden the handsome Thoroughbred regularly in lessons and on the trail. She also remembered the time even longer ago when Topside had been a champion show jumper, winning national competitions for his previous owner.

Hearing a snort from across the aisle, Lisa turned to see Barq watching her curiously. She stepped over to give the spirited Arabian a pat. "Hi, guy," she crooned. She had a special fondness for Barq, since he had been one of the first horses she had ridden.

After spending a few minutes scratching and patting the friendly gelding, Lisa moved on down the aisle, stopping in turn to visit several other horses.

"You know, I hadn't really thought about it," Lisa whispered to Carole's horse, Starlight, as she scratched his topknot. "But it's not just my human friends I'm going to miss. It's all of you guys, too."

She took a step back from the stall, startled as she realized what she'd just said. *I'm talking as if this move were a done deal,* she thought uneasily. *I think I'm starting to accept it—to assume that it's definitely going to happen, for real.*

That was a disturbing idea. For a moment Lisa tried to convince herself that it didn't have to be that way. She clutched the edge of Starlight's stall door. Stevie was right—they just hadn't tried hard enough. There had to be a way. . . .

But then Lisa sighed and relaxed, leaning against the wall as Starlight nudged at her curiously. What was the use? Her mother was going to do what she wanted to do; she'd made that pretty clear. It would be a lot easier if Lisa just accepted that and started dealing with it.

Glancing across the aisle, she saw that she had almost reached the stall where her favorite horse, a beautiful Thoroughbred mare named Prancer, had spent the last few months of her life. Prancer had died less than two months earlier, and Lisa still missed her every day.

She walked over to the stall, which had been vacated recently when Max moved a few of the horses around. The half door was open, and Lisa stepped through it tentatively. Suddenly she was overwhelmed by an image of Prancer coming forward to meet her, her soft brown eyes eager and joyful. That was all it took to bring the tears to Lisa's eyes.

Sliding to the floor, Lisa buried her face in her hands, crying first for Prancer and then for herself. But soon the tears stopped, leaving her feeling a little better than she had in days.

This doesn't have to be a huge deal, she told herself as she wiped the moisture from her face with one sleeve. *Really, it's all just temporary if you think about it. Yes, it will suck big-time to have to start school somewhere new, especially in the middle of my senior year. But it's just for a few months, and then I'll be off to college anyway. So I'll be back in this area by August at the latest.*

She blinked and sat up straight, suddenly realizing just how true that was. Earlier that fall, she had committed to attending Northern Virginia University, a good local college located an easy forty-minute drive from Willow Creek.

And no matter what Mom and Dad think, I'm not changing my mind about that, Lisa thought fiercely. Her parents hadn't been able to agree on much since their divorce, but they had been unanimous in their anger and dismay after discovering that Lisa had sent back her acceptance to NVU without consulting them. Lisa was still a little surprised at their reaction—it was her life, after all, and she was the one who would have to spend four years living with her decision, not them.

Six to eight months. That was all the time she'd have to spend in New Jersey. Still, six to eight months seemed like forever.

As she took a deep breath, trying to avoid crying again, Lisa wrinkled her nose. What was that smell?

She sniffed again and climbed to her feet. "Is that smoke?" she murmured, suddenly forgetting all about her own problems. The smell of smoke in a stable was a serious thing. A stray spark from an electrical short could set the hayloft ablaze in a matter of moments.

Her heart pounding, Lisa hurried out of the stall and grabbed the nearest fire extinguisher, which was hanging on the wall halfway down the aisle. Then she followed her nose, praying she would remember how to use the extinguisher if she needed to.

Of course, it could be a false alarm, she reminded herself, trying not to panic. *It's pretty windy today, and the smell could just be blowing in from a neighbor's chimney or—*

She stopped short as she turned the corner of the U-shaped stable aisle and glanced toward the back entrance, which led out to the sheltered area between the stable and the path to the Regnerys' farmhouse. Thick gray smoke was clearly visible drifting in through the propped-open doorway.

Frowning slightly, Lisa walked toward the door. Glancing outside, she saw Maureen leaning on the fence of the back paddock and puffing on a cigarette.

Lisa scowled, too angry to react for a second. "What are you doing?" she blurted out at last. "Are you clinical? You can't smoke here!"

Maureen frowned and puffed out a smoky breath. "Why not?" she retorted sharply. "The rule is, no smoking in the stable." She gestured expansively around her. "Am I in the stable?"

Lisa couldn't believe her ears. Did Maureen really think that excuse would fly? True, she was a good dozen yards from the stable building. That was still way too close for comfort, at least as far as Lisa was concerned. But before she could say a word, the sound of voices came from just around the corner of the building. Lisa glanced over her shoulder, recognizing Stevie's distinctive laugh.

"Excuse me, but I have work to do," Maureen muttered, quickly grinding out her cigarette on the gravel path and then kicking away the ashes. She grabbed the handles of a nearby wheelbarrow and pushed past Lisa before she realized what was happening.

"Wait!" Lisa exclaimed, unwilling to let it drop.

But it was too late. Maureen was already disappearing around the corner into the stable, only one last puff of smoke lingering to mark her departure. Lisa waved a hand in front of her face to chase away the foul-smelling cloud, wondering what to do. Once she thought about it, she realized that the stable hand was technically right—she hadn't actually broken any stable rules. Max hated smoking in general, but Lisa knew that he overcame his personal feelings enough to allow some of the adult riders to smoke in certain areas near the stable, including the parking area and the driveway. Did that mean he wouldn't mind Maureen's behavior?

Maybe Stevie will have some idea about what to do.

Lisa hoisted the fire extinguisher and headed inside to hook it back in place on the wall.

Stevie was glad she'd decided to take a nice, relaxing trail ride that day instead of attempting another schooling session. She and Belle had both enjoyed themselves, and it had been great spending time alone with Phil. She always loved getting together with friends, but sometimes it seemed as if she and her boyfriend were left with practically no time together, just the two of them.

"This was nice," she said, patting her mare on the neck as she waited for Phil to lead his mount, a Pine Hollow school horse named Rusty, into his stall.

Phil glanced over his shoulder with a grin. "It didn't suck," he agreed. "Except for the weather, that is."

"I know." Stevie grimaced and flexed her gloved fingers on Belle's reins. "I'll be lucky if I don't end up with frostbite after . . ." Her voice trailed off as she spotted Lisa hurrying toward them.

"Stevie!" Lisa called breathlessly. "I'm glad you're here. I—"

"I'm glad I'm here, too," Stevie said. Lisa's eyes were red and puffy, and a telltale smudge of eyeliner told Stevie as clearly as words that her friend had been crying. Phil had just emerged with Rusty's tack, and Stevie tossed him Belle's reins. Rushing to Lisa's side, Stevie put an arm around her shoulders. "You look terrible! What's wrong?"

"I'm fine," Lisa said. "Never mind that. Did you know Maureen smokes?"

Stevie hardly heard her. "Huh?" she said. "Yeah, I guess. But listen, what's up with you? You look totally bummed." As she said it, the image of Alex and Nicole making out popped into her head. Had Lisa somehow heard that the two of them were an item? Was that why she was so upset?

But Stevie almost immediately realized that probably wasn't it. This had to be about the move. Feeling a little guilty—she'd vowed to come up with a solution but had barely thought about the problem all day—she squeezed Lisa's shoulder tighter.

Lisa sighed. "Um, I guess I was a little upset before. You know, about Mom and . . . you know. But then after that—"

"Hey, Stevie," Phil broke in. "Belle looks a little bored. How about if I take her down to her stall for you?"

Stevie shot her boyfriend a grateful glance. She knew he wasn't making the offer for Belle's sake. The mare was tired from the long trail ride and seemed perfectly content to stand in the aisle. But her stall was in the opposite arm of the stable aisle, which would give Stevie and Lisa some privacy.

"Thanks," she told Phil simply, vowing to show him later how grateful she was.

He headed off down the aisle with the mare in tow. As soon as he was out of earshot, Stevie turned to face Lisa. "Okay, what's your mother up to now?" she asked bluntly.

Lisa blinked. "Mom? Nothing. She's not even here."

"Huh?" Stevie peeled off her gloves and glanced at Lisa in confusion. "Where did she go? Don't tell me she decided to move to New Jersey without you."

"Not exactly." Lisa sighed. "I meant to tell you guys earlier. Um, she drove up to New Jersey to look at houses and stuff."

Stevie gulped. That sounded serious. They could be running out of time, which meant it was way past time to start doing something about it. As Lisa started to say something else about Maureen, Stevie waved her hands in the air. "Wait," she demanded. "Are you serious? She's in New Jersey now?"

"Uh-huh. She's spending the weekend with my aunt. She left on Friday and she's coming back to-morrow morning."

"Yikes," Stevie said succinctly, her mind working fast. Enough was enough. It sounded as though Mrs. Atwood wasn't going to change her mind on her own. That meant Stevie would have to change it for her. But how? This was going to require some thought. "Um, listen, Lisa. Are you okay? Because I really need to go groom Belle, and then I have to rush home—it's my turn to cook."

"Oh. Okay." Lisa shrugged, looking disappointed. "I mean, sure, I'm fine. I should probably get going, too."

"Good. Then I'll catch you later, okay?" Stevie felt bad about ditching Lisa when she was obviously in such a sad mood, but she figured it would all be worth it if she could come up with a plan to keep her in Willow Creek.

As Lisa wandered off toward the entryway, Stevie stuck her head over the stall door to check on Rusty. Then she hurried off to find Phil.

"There you are," Phil said as Stevie arrived at Belle's stall. "Just in time to miss all the work." Grinning to show that he was kidding, he hoisted Belle's saddle and bridle and let himself into the aisle.

"Thanks a million." Stevie stood on tiptoes to give him a grateful kiss on the cheek. Then she fell into step beside him as he headed for the tack room. "But listen, this is important. Lisa just told me her mom went up to New Jersey to look at houses."

Phil let out a low whistle of dismay. "Sounds serious," he commented.

"That's what I said." Stevie chewed her lower lip

thoughtfully. "You know, I was just kidding before about all those wacky plans we were talking about the other day. But now . . ."

"Yeah, right." Phil rolled his eyes. "Like the one you told me about where your brother dresses up as Lisa's clone? Or the one where we hijack the Weather Channel to make it look like New Jersey's been swept out to sea? Get real."

"I'm serious," Stevie protested, glancing around as they crossed the entryway to make sure Lisa wasn't within earshot. "I mean, those particular plans might need some fine-tuning. But we have to try something, right?"

Phil glanced at her soberly. "I guess so. But seriously, don't you think we're getting a little too old for the kinds of crazy schemes you're talking about?"

"Maybe you are, Gramps," Stevie shot back, annoyed that he wasn't being more supportive. "All I know is, I don't want Lisa to go. I couldn't stand it if her mom really made her move. And I'm going to do whatever I can to stop it."

"Relax." Phil smiled appeasingly. "We're on the same side here, remember? I'm just saying, if you're going to put your energy into something, make it something that could actually work. Not something that's just going to piss everybody off and make Lisa more miserable than ever."

Stevie made a face at him. But then she relented. "Okay, then, Mr. Mature," she said as they reached the tack room. "Maybe you have a point. But I'm not going to stop thinking about this." She dumped Belle's saddle on its assigned rack and hung up her bridle.

"Come on," Phil said. "Let's go give Rusty a quick grooming. Then maybe we can get out of here and grab a snack. All that riding made me hungry."

Stevie nodded, though she was distracted by her thoughts. What could she do to help Lisa? What kind of mature, rational plan could actually work?

As they stepped into the entryway, a flash of blond hair caught her eye. Stevie gulped, thinking for a second that it was Lisa. But instead, she recognized Callie reaching for the door.

"Yo, Forester!" Stevie called, remembering how strange and anxious Callie had acted earlier that day.

But Callie didn't seem to hear her. She hurried through the door without a backward glance.

"Weird," Phil remarked, gazing after her.

Stevie nodded slowly, wondering if everyone around her had decided to go crazy for the New Year. *First Lisa starts acting like she's all ready to pack up and move,* she thought. *Callie gets her own horse and then suddenly decides she only wants to ride, like, once a week. And of course, there's Carole and the weird way she still looks at Ben sometimes, even though she already has an amazing boyfriend who's nuts about her.*

She sighed. When she really thought about it, just about everything seemed strange and topsy-turvy. And the worst part was, she had no idea how to fix any of it.

EIGHT

"Just one more day till the big one, huh?" Deborah commented cheerfully as Carole walked into the stable office the next morning.

"Yep," Carole agreed with a secret smile. Deborah was referring to Red and Denise's wedding, of course. But Carole was looking forward to the next day for her own reasons as well. She was still anxious about finding Cam a gift—she planned to hit the mall as soon as she was finished at the stable, and not leave until she'd found something. But more than that, she was increasingly eager to see Cam. She had missed him all week, but now that they would be together again in twenty-four hours, she could hardly stand to wait another second.

"By the way," Deborah said, "if you're looking for my husband, he's not here. He went with Justine Harrington to look at a horse her parents are thinking of buying for her."

"Really? Cool." Carole raised an eyebrow, guessing that the intermediate rider was about to receive an excellent, if slightly belated, Christmas present. "I just wanted to talk to him about Starlight's next shoeing, but it's no big deal. I'll just leave him a note."

"Good luck finding a pen that works," Deborah said with a smile. "I swear, I think the stable cats steal them at night." With a wave, she hurried out of the office.

A minute or two later, as Carole was scribbling her note with the stub of a pencil, the office phone rang. Carole grabbed it. "Pine Hollow Stables," she said automatically. "Can I help you?"

As soon as the words were out of her mouth, she felt a little awkward. She had answered the phone that way hundreds of times when she worked there. But technically she didn't work there now. Soon, but not yet.

"Hello?" a slightly quavery voice said on the other end of the line. "This is Mrs. Rand. Is Mr. Regnery there?"

Carole couldn't help smiling at the caller's formal tone. Everyone from the feed delivery man to the tiniest beginning rider called Max by his first name. But she responded politely. "I'm sorry, he's not here at the moment. Could I help you with something?"

"Well, I don't know." The woman's uncertainty

was clear. "I wanted to speak with him about some horses."

"Were you looking to buy?" Carole asked, sinking down into the desk chair and twirling the phone cord between her fingers. "Because I don't think we have anything available right now."

"No, no," Mrs. Rand replied. "You see, my granddaughter just got married, and her husband is in the service. They're moving to Germany next month. My granddaughter has two horses, and we need to find a new home for them as soon as possible. Mr. Regnery was recommended as someone who might want them to use as school horses."

"I see," Carole said, her mind racing. Should she simply take Mrs. Rand's name and phone number and leave a message for Max to call her back? Or should she try to get more information about these alleged school horses first? After a very brief struggle, her curiosity won out. "Um, why don't you tell me a little more about them?"

"Who is this, anyway?" Mrs. Rand asked suspiciously.

"My name's Carole Hanson," Carole replied politely. "I, uh, work here."

Mrs. Rand seemed satisfied with that. "There are two horses," she said. "The mare, Madison, is a quarter horse. She's twelve years old and has quite a bit of show experience." She quickly described the mare's record, which sounded very good. "The other horse is an older gelding named Jinx. He—" For the first time, Mrs. Rand hesitated. "Well, he's a bit of a rowdy one. Not too good when it comes to grooming and such, or under saddle, either. But he has a heart of gold," she added hastily. "Wouldn't hurt a fly. Not on purpose, anyway."

As Mrs. Rand talked, Carole scribbled down all the information with her pencil stub. "Okay," she said when the woman was finished. "Um, I'll pass this along to Max. I suspect he'll be very interested in taking a look at Madison."

"Oh, he has to take them both," the woman said quickly. "They're a package deal."

"Oh." Carole gulped. She had the funniest feeling that Max wasn't going to be leaping at the chance to bring home a troublesome, untrained older gelding with a "heart of gold." "All right, I'll mention that, too. I'm sure he'll be calling you back soon."

She hung up, wrote out a brief note at the top of the page explaining what it was about, and tucked the message into the day book where Max would be sure to see it as soon as he returned.

Who knows? Carole thought as she headed for the office door. *Maybe old Jinx isn't as bad as that woman made him sound. Maybe all he needs is some consistent training. Ben and I*—She paused, feeling her face flush slightly. *Ben and I could probably help him a lot.*

She was so deep in thought that she almost walked straight into Maureen and Denise, who were entering at that very moment. "Oops!" Carole said. "Sorry. I'm a little distracted—an interesting phone call just came in."

"What?" Denise looked anxious. "It wasn't the caterer changing the menu again, was it?"

"No, no, nothing to do with the wedding at all," Carole assured her. "It was someone looking to sell a couple of horses." She quickly described her conversation with Mrs. Rand.

When she finished, Maureen snorted. "Why'd you bother stringing the old broad along?" she asked. "You should've just told her it was a no go."

"What do you mean?" Carole wasn't sure why everything Maureen said put her on the defensive, but she could already feel her hackles rising.

Maureen shrugged. "Think about it, Carole," she said as if she were speaking to a four-year-old. "Are you telling me you actually believe that Max— overworked, overcautious Max—is going to have any interest at all in taking on some kind of pathetic problem horse? No way. Not a happening thing."

"You never know," Carole protested. "And the

mare sounded good." She shot a glance at Denise, waiting for her to back her up. How could Maureen totally dismiss a horse she hadn't even seen? And how could she know what Max would or wouldn't do?

"I don't know, Carole," Denise said dubiously. "This horse—Jinx?—really doesn't sound like he'd make a good lesson horse to me, either. And if this lady will really only let them go together, well . . ." She shrugged expressively.

Carole frowned. "Whatever," she muttered, a little annoyed that the stable manager was taking Maureen's side. And as for Maureen herself . . .

Okay, I've been trying to give her a chance, Carole thought as she mumbled an excuse and escaped from the office. *But honestly, I don't know how I'm ever going to work alongside someone as annoying as her!*

As she emerged into the entryway, she saw Ben walking into the indoor ring. He didn't see her, and she almost called after him. Ben would understand, if anyone would. He would want to at least give Jinx a chance, too, before totally dismissing him.

But she stopped herself. After all that had happened, she felt weird about confiding in Ben.

Anyway, it doesn't matter, she thought, turning and heading toward Starlight's stall. *Max is the one who gets to decide what to do about this one. Not me, not Ben, and certainly not Maureen Chance.*

Callie tapped her fingers on the coffee table in the living room, debating whether to go to the stable or not. *I should go,* she told herself. *I should really go. What am I so scared of, anyway? It's not like I even actually saw George yesterday.* She shuddered, remembering her panic at the sight of his mother's car. *Not up close, anyway.*

No matter how many times she told herself there was nothing to fear, though, she couldn't seem to make her body believe it. The very thought of going back there—walking across the stable yard, entering the building, going to the tack room—made her palms sweat and her stomach flutter nervously.

She decided to try a different tack. *Anyway, so what if I run into George?* she thought. *It's not like I can avoid him forever. When school starts again, I'll see him every day. I've just got to deal with it, and the sooner the better.*

"Hi there, Number One Daughter," her father said with a smile, walking into the room. "What are you up to today?"

Callie forced a smile. "Not much," she replied. "What about you?"

"Oh, I was just thinking how long it's been since my favorite daughter and I played a few sets of tennis." Congressman Forester winked and smiled. "How about it? Feel like beating your old man?"

Callie hesitated. She knew she should ask her father for a rain check. She needed to face her fear. And the only way to do that was to go back to Pine Hollow—now, before too much time passed and she lost her nerve completely.

But Dad's so busy these days, with that new welfare committee and everything, she reminded herself. *It's been a long time since we did the father-daughter thing. And it's been even longer since I played a nice, relaxing game of tennis.*

"Sure, Dad," she heard herself say. "That sounds great. I'll go change."

She hopped up and hurried toward the stairs, knowing she was copping out. But she felt relieved.

I'll figure out how to deal with George, she promised herself. *Just not yet. Not today.*

NINE

"Lisa!"

Lisa turned and smiled. Carole was hurrying down the stable aisle toward her. "Hey!" Lisa called. "There you are."

She was surprisingly relieved to see her friend. After her disappointing visit the day before, when she hadn't even ended up riding, she had been hesitant to come back to the stable again that day. Still, she couldn't stand to hang around her empty house all day, either, and so there she was.

Carole skidded to stop in front of her. "What are you up to today?" she asked breathlessly. "Did you decide what to wear to the wedding yet?"

Lisa smiled, deciding to answer the second question first. "No, I haven't really thought about what to wear," she said. "I guess I'll find something before tomorrow. What about you?"

"I don't know," Carole admitted. "I've been so busy thinking about Cam's gift that I sort of forgot to think about anything else—including my pathetic wardrobe—until just now."

"Want to go on a quick trail ride with me?" Lisa said. "We could talk over your outfit choices then."

Carole glanced at her watch. "I'd better not," she said.

"Oh, right," Lisa said. "Curfew?" She guessed that Carole didn't want to mess up on what could be the second-to-last day of her grounding.

"No, not really." Carole turned, wandering toward the stable entryway. "It's just that I want to have plenty of time at the mall this afternoon—I was just on my way out when I saw you, actually. Oh! But guess what. Someone called wanting to sell Max some horses a little while ago. . . ."

She went on to describe the phone call, and Lisa did her best to nod in all the right places as she kept pace beside Carole. But she was only half listening to the story. *Why does it seem like nobody has time for me all of a sudden?* she thought with a flash of self-pity. *I mean, you'd think my friends would want to spend time with me just as much as I want to spend time with them. Don't they realize this could be our last chance to hang out together for a long time? Shouldn't that be more important than, well, shopping?*

". . . so anyway," Carole was saying as Lisa tuned back in to her tale, "I just ran into Max, and he promised he'd set up an appointment to look at the horses after New Year's. *Both* of them."

Carole looked strangely triumphant at that last comment, but Lisa didn't bother to wonder why. She had just spotted Stevie turning the corner.

"That sounds great," Lisa told Carole hurriedly. "Good luck shopping, okay? I'm going to go see if Stevie wants to go for a ride." That was the good thing about having two best friends, she reminded herself. When one of them blew you off, you could always turn to the other one.

"Okay, see you." Carole waved to Stevie and then hurried off in the opposite direction, toward the exit.

When Stevie reached Lisa, she glanced at her watch. "Hey, Atwood," she said. "Did you just get here?"

"Uh-huh." Lisa put on her best beseeching smile. "And I'm dying to go on a nice, long trail ride."

"A long trail ride?" Stevie looked pleased. "That sounds like a fantastic idea."

"Great!" Lisa's heart soared. "So how about it? Ready to go now?"

"Me? Oh, sorry, I can't make it today," Stevie said, looking at her watch again. "Gotta go."

"What?" Lisa frowned, her heart sinking back into her boots. "Why not? Where are you going?"

Stevie shrugged. "Oh, it's nothing really. Errands. You know."

"But couldn't you just squeeze in one short little ride?" Lisa said, feeling a bit desperate. "We wouldn't even have to hit the trails. We could just hop some poles in the ring or something."

"I don't think so." Stevie glanced over her shoulder, seeming distracted. "Anyway, if you're just going to do that, you can go ahead and ride by yourself."

Lisa frowned. She was sure her friend didn't mean to be insensitive, but she couldn't help feeling hurt. She had been spending too much time by herself lately as it was. And most of that time was spent dreading the move. So why did it suddenly feel as if she were already gone?

"Whatever," she muttered. "See you later. Maybe."

Stevie nodded. "Okay, bye then. Have a nice ride, okay?"

Lisa didn't bother to respond, which was just as well, since Stevie was already hurrying off without a backward look. *Okay, so much for happy friend time at the stable,* Lisa thought sourly. *Maybe I should just go for a ride by myself like Stevie oh-so-tactfully suggested. Might as well start getting used to flying solo.*

"Lisa?"

Lisa turned and saw Scott emerging from the

locker room. She swallowed hard, caught off guard by his sudden appearance. It had been a few days since she'd seen him, and she'd almost managed to forget how handsome he was.

"H-Hi," Lisa said. "What's up?"

Scott shrugged, not taking his eyes off her. "Just hanging out," he said. "You?"

"Same."

They were silent for a moment. Lisa felt decidedly awkward. She and Scott had gone out a few times—he'd made no secret of the fact that he was interested in her. However, he knew her history with Alex, and a few days earlier, he'd announced his intention to step aside until she'd made up her mind what to do about that relationship. She guessed that he was just being polite by saying hello—that he would now move on, go off to drive Callie home or whatever. He had promised to give her some space, and she knew that was the best way to handle their friendship right now until she settled things with Alex. It was the right thing to do. The smart thing to do.

But suddenly, she just couldn't stand the thought of spending another long afternoon alone. "Hey," she blurted out. "I was just thinking of going on a trail ride. Want to come?"

Scott looked surprised, but he nodded immediately. "I'm in."

For a second, as she saw the spark of pleasure and interest in Scott's blue eyes, Lisa regretted the impulsive invitation. *It's no big deal,* she told herself uncertainly. *He knows things are still up in the air with me and Alex. He understands. And at least he's always a distraction.*

She realized she was rationalizing, but she didn't care. At that point she would have ridden with just about anyone for the company.

Of course, I'd much rather ride with Scott . . .

She cut off that thought quickly. "Okay, then," she said, doing her best to cover her seesawing emotions. "Let's go find out which horses are free."

A few minutes later she was leading out Checkers, a roan quarter horse gelding that loved the trails. Scott was waiting by the mounting block with a school horse named Windsor, leaning against a fence post as the burly bay gelding grazed on the few meager blades of grass left after December's frosts. The familiar activity of grooming and tacking had helped Lisa relax, and she had almost managed to convince herself that what they were doing wasn't such a big deal after all.

It's a nice day, she thought, glancing at the clear sky. *And Scott's a nice guy—a good friend. That's all there is to it.*

As she approached Scott, Lisa suddenly realized that he wasn't alone with his horse after all. Maureen was lounging against the fence nearby, nearly hidden from Lisa's view by Windsor's body.

Lisa grimaced slightly. She wasn't sure why, but Maureen rubbed her the wrong way. Maybe it was the way her eyes seemed to glide right past most girls and women and zoom straight in on just about every guy she encountered. Just like they were zooming in at that very moment, for instance.

"Hi," Lisa said a little too loudly, interrupting something Maureen was saying about her apartment. "Ready to go, Scott?"

Scott immediately glanced at her with a nod and a smile. "Let's do it."

"Have a good time, you two," Maureen said lazily. "But not *too* good." She winked at Scott and grinned.

Lisa gritted her teeth as Scott chuckled politely. Turning her back on Maureen, she led Checkers toward the mounting block and quickly settled herself in the saddle. Moving her horse ahead a few paces, she bent and busily checked her girth and stirrups just to avoid having to make any further conversation with her.

"Need some help there, Scott?" Maureen said, stepping forward as Scott swung into Windsor's saddle. "Your stirrups look a little uneven. Let me help you with that."

Lisa glanced over her shoulder just in time to see

Maureen put her hand on Scott's thigh, pushing gently to move his leg out of the way so that she could adjust his stirrup. Lisa rolled her eyes. *Gross!* she thought. *Does she have to flirt with every guy she meets? I mean, Scott is at least four or five years younger than she is. What's next—is she going to start trolling for dates at Pony Club meetings?*

Lisa also noticed that Scott didn't really seem to mind Maureen's behavior. He was smiling and joking with her even then, as she patted his leg again to move it back into place, seeming unperturbed by the close contact.

I guess that's the way he is, Lisa reminded herself. *Friendly. Maybe a tad too friendly sometimes.*

She thought about how Alex might have reacted in the same situation. First of all, he wouldn't have let Lisa out of his sight long enough to fall into conversation with Maureen. And if there was a problem with his stirrups, he would have fixed it himself—he hadn't been riding for long, but he knew the basics. Or he would have asked Lisa for help.

"Ready?" Scott's voice interrupted her thoughts as he walked Windsor up beside her.

Lisa blinked, realizing that Maureen was already walking away toward the stable building. "Oh!" she said, feeling a bit guilty for her previous thoughts. She had promised herself she wouldn't compare

Scott and Alex, and she wanted to stick to it. "Sure. Um, did you touch the lucky horseshoe?"

"Sure did." Scott winked at her as they started across the stable yard at a walk. "You were so firm about that rule the last time we rode together, I'll never be able to forget."

Lisa blushed slightly. She guessed that to someone like Scott, the Pine Hollow tradition of touching the battered old horseshoe nailed to the wall near the doorway might seem a little bit silly. But to every rider who had learned to ride there, it was almost unthinkable to ride out without at least brushing the worn metal with a fingertip. The tradition went that no rider had ever been seriously hurt out on the trails or in the ring after doing so, and Lisa figured there was no sense in taking any chances. Besides, she liked Pine Hollow's traditions. They were part of what made the stable so homey and familiar. And they were part of what she would miss when she left.

"Come on," she said, veering off that topic before she started feeling depressed again. "I was thinking we could try the creek trail today."

"Sounds good," Scott replied amiably. "Lead the way."

They rode in silence for a few minutes. The farther they got from the stable building, the more Lisa felt herself relaxing. It was amazing to her sometimes, even after so many years, how riding could improve her mood, her self-confidence, her whole outlook on life. For the first time in days, she managed to push all her worries about the future to the very back of her mind and focus on the here and now.

"Wow. Nice day, huh?" Scott commented.

Lisa nodded, realizing it was true. Sometime that afternoon the weather had reversed itself. The cold wind had completely died down, and with the sun shining brightly in the cloudless sky, it felt more like October than late December. It was so warm that Lisa realized she had never bothered to zip her jacket after leading Checkers out.

"We got lucky," she said. "There aren't too many good riding days like this around this time of year."

"I hope Windsor is enjoying himself." Scott leaned forward to give his mount a pat on the neck. "He's blowing a little already."

Lisa glanced at the big gelding. Unlike the horses at the stable that would be competing in shows over the winter and were kept at least partially clipped, Windsor had been allowed to grow a full, shaggy winter coat. Sure enough, he was starting to look a little warm, even though they'd only been riding for a short time. "He should be okay," Lisa said. "He always heats up faster than most of the horses—Max is trying to take some weight off him to help with that. But I guess we ought to keep them at a walk or a slow trot most of the way."

Scott nodded agreeably. "That's fine with me," he said. "You know I don't ride much, and I'd hate to have this guy gallop off with me and dump me in a ditch somewhere."

Lisa smiled at the image of sedate, proper, well-mannered Windsor taking off over hill and dale, bucking like a bronco. "Don't worry," she said. "Windsor canters slower than most horses trot. And I'm not sure I've ever seen him gallop, even when he's out in the field with the other horses."

"What's the difference between a canter and a gallop, really?" Scott asked. "I mean, I know a gallop is faster—"

"Right," Lisa said. "Also, a canter is a three-beat gait and a gallop is a four-beat gait." She glanced at him with a smile. "Do you mean to tell me you don't know all this already, after living with Callie all your lives?"

Scott grinned and shrugged. "I usually just tune her out when she starts talking horses," he said. "It's easy to do that when it's your sister, you know? But somehow it's all a lot more interesting when it's coming from . . . someone else."

Lisa blushed. "Anyway," she said quickly, "you would know it if your horse started to gallop.

It's a lot harder to ride than a canter—that's why you see jockeys up in two-point when they ride."

"Two-point?" Scott repeated blankly.

"Like this." Lisa adjusted herself into two-point position as Checkers ambled along. "It means there are two points of contact between yourself and the horse, your legs and your hands. You can also call it a half seat. When you're riding like this"—she lowered herself back into her normal position—"there's a third point of contact, the seat."

"I see." Scott raised one eyebrow. "Personally, I like having plenty of contact with the seat."

"Right," Lisa said, wondering if they were still talking about riding. "Anyway, we really don't gallop the horses out here. It's too risky—they could stumble or step in a fox hole or something. The only time they get to gallop is when we do a hand gallop in the ring."

Scott glanced down at his hands. "Okay, and that is . . . ?"

"It's more like a fast canter than a real gallop. You know, not exactly racehorse stuff—they can ask for it in some hunter competitions. But people who aren't into showing don't really ever need to gallop at all."

"Uh-huh." Scott pursed his lips and shot her an amused look. "So I guess you're saying it's only for people who don't mind going fast. What about you, Lisa? Do you like going fast?"

Something about the way he asked it made Lisa think he definitely wasn't talking about riding. "Look, there's the path into the woods," she said, feeling flustered. "We can ride this down the hill and across the creek. It's pretty over there, even in the winter."

"Okay," Scott said. "My seat and I are right behind you."

Lisa smiled weakly, trying not to think about Scott's seat or the comments he was making. She knew he was just joking around, but it still made her uncomfortable. It certainly wasn't making it easy to stick to her idea that this was just a casual trail ride for a couple of casual friends.

"The trail is single file here," she said. "I'll go first for a while if that's okay—Checkers is pretty forward on the trails, and Windsor likes to take his time. Especially if he's hot."

"Sounds like a true gentleman," Scott commented. "Just be careful not to leave me too far behind. I'd hate to be stuck out here all alone."

"I won't," Lisa promised, thinking back to her beginner days when she had worried quite a bit about such possibilities. She turned slightly in the saddle so that she could smile reassuringly at Scott. "But don't worry. If you ever did find yourself out here alone, your horse could take you home. They all know the way."

Scott smiled. "That's good to know. But if you don't mind, I'd kind of like to stick with you for today."

"I don't mind," Lisa replied, quickly turning around to face front again. She didn't want Scott to see that she was blushing again.

"Good," Scott said. "I mean, no offense to old Windsor here or anything." Lisa could hear Scott patting his horse on the neck. "But he's not really the one I'd want to be lost out in the woods with."

"Oh, he might be a little slow, but he would be able to—oh!" Lisa said, cutting herself off as she belatedly realized what Scott was saying. "Um, look, there's the creek up ahead. Since it's not too cold today, let's just go ahead and cross here instead of following it downstream to the narrow crossing. Is that okay with you?"

"Absolutely," Scott said. "You're in charge here; Windsor and I are in your hands."

"Really?" Lisa couldn't resist the opening. "Hmmm. I know I can control Windsor. I'm not so sure about you."

When she glanced over her shoulder, Scott was grinning. "All it takes is plenty of positive reinforcement," he said.

Lisa had to return her attention to her horse as

the trail leading down to the water grew steeper. The creek was very wide and shallow at that point, and Lisa had crossed it many times on horseback and a few times on foot. "Windsor should be okay with the water," she called back to Scott, trying to remember if the big gelding had ever balked at that particular crossing before. "Anyway, Checkers will be fine, so if you stick close to us going down, Windsor will probably just follow along with no problem."

"Don't worry, I plan to stick close," Scott replied.

Lisa decided to assume that he was talking about riding—or at least to pretend she did. Letting the comment pass, she clucked to Checkers, leaning back as he negotiated the last few feet of steep bank and then splashed into the creek without hesitation. Soon the roan gelding had crossed and was climbing the opposite bank. Lisa halted him at the top. Taking a few deep breaths and wetting her lips, she sat there and waited for Scott to join her, keeping her back to him so that he wouldn't see her expression.

Okay, this is getting a little out of hand, she thought. *Scott and I both know we're not supposed to be doing this. Acting like this. Flirting. What was I thinking, coming out here alone with him? What did I expect to happen?*

"Hey, is it okay to let him drink?" Scott called.

Lisa glanced over her shoulder briefly. Windsor had stopped in midstream and was stretching his neck toward the water, pulling Scott slightly forward in the saddle.

"It's okay. You can just wait and move him on when he's finished," she called back, turning to face forward once again.

"Okeydoke," Scott said.

Lisa leaned forward to pat Checkers, who was standing calmly on a loose rein. She could hear splashing behind her and knew she probably only had a moment or two until Windsor had slaked his thirst and Scott joined her on the bank.

And then I have to figure out how to deal with him, she thought.

"Uh, Lisa?" Scott called. "Lisa!"

She turned and glanced over her shoulder again, wondering why he sounded so frantic. Windsor was splashing at the water with one forefoot.

"Oops," she said, suddenly realizing what the horse was up to. "Move him!" she called to Scott. "Give a kick and—"

She cut herself off, seeing that she was too late. Windsor splashed himself on the belly once more, then buckled his knees and lowered himself laboriously into the rushing stream. Scott clung helplessly to the horse's mane for a few seconds, but as the icy water of the creek hit his legs, he yelped and hopped off to one side.

"Give him room!" Lisa called, already kicking her feet out of the stirrups and sliding out of the saddle, remembering that Checkers was reliably trained to ground tie. Then she hurried down the slope toward the water. "Get out of his way—he's probably going to roll!"

Scott jumped aside, looking alarmed. Unfortunately he was so focused on Windsor's feet that he wasn't watching his own. He stepped on something that gave way beneath him, sending him flying to one side. Lisa winced as he landed on one elbow in the icy water.

"Scott!" she yelled, even as she raced the edge of the water. "Are you okay?"

"I'll live." Scott smiled weakly as he climbed to his feet and splashed his way toward the bank.

Lisa held out a hand to help him clamber out of the water. "Sorry about that," she said, feeling guilty. "I should have warned you that horses sometimes do that. If they finish drinking and start splashing around, they may be thinking of taking a nice little bath. I just never thought Windsor would do something like that in the middle of winter."

"Don't worry about it." Scott didn't release her hand as he smiled down at her. "You're still my favorite trail guide ever."

"Thanks." Lisa knew she should pull her hand away, but she couldn't quite bring herself to do it. She looked up at Scott, smiling tentatively in sheer relief that he was okay. He smiled back, then squeezed her hand gently and began tracing a pattern on the back of it with his thumb.

Lisa gulped, realizing how badly she wanted him to lean down and kiss her. How much she wanted to kiss him. She knew it wouldn't be a wise move, but just at that moment, she couldn't remember why. From the look in Scott's eyes as he took a half step closer, she guessed he was thinking the same thing.

A loud snort from the direction of the creek interrupted the moment. Suddenly remembering Windsor, Lisa blinked and yanked her hand out of Scott's grasp.

"I'd better grab him before he decides to head home without you," she said, already moving toward the water. The gelding had finished his dip and was on all four feet again in the middle of the creek, glancing from one side to the other as if deciding which direction to go.

"Wait, I'll go." Scott grabbed her gently by the shoulder, stopping her just before she stepped into the water. "No sense both of us getting soaked."

Before Lisa could protest, he stepped into the creek and splashed over to Windsor, talking soothingly to the horse. Lisa watched him. Her hand was still tingling, as well as her shoulder where he had just touched it.

Okay, I guess it's time to admit it. There's definitely something going on between Scott and me. No two ways about it. She bit her lip as Scott took hold of Windsor's reins, blushing as she thought about how close she'd come to kissing him, right then and there, with two horses waiting for them and Scott's feet probably going numb inside his wet shoes. *If I'm not careful, things could get out of control really fast. And that can't happen. Not until I decide what to do about Alex.*

Alex. How long had it been since she'd actually spoken to him? She wasn't sure, but she knew it was much longer than at any time since they'd first fallen in love. It was a strange thought. Just weeks ago, Alex had been a big part of her daily life. And now? Now she was so occupied with the idea that she might be moving soon that she hardly thought about him, let alone figured out what to say to him when they did talk next.

And of course, having Scott around doesn't help my concentration much, Lisa admitted as Scott came toward her, leading Windsor.

Not wanting to risk another steamy moment just then, Lisa smiled at him encouragingly and then turned to hurry up the hill toward her own horse. The rational, logical part of her mind was taking over once again, telling her that she had to stay in control. Getting in any deeper with Scott right then would be a mistake. Not only because she might be moving soon, making it all sort of pointless, but also because of Alex.

New Year's Eve is tomorrow, she reminded herself. *That's when Alex and I agreed to talk again and figure out where to go from here.*

Stevie had mentioned that Alex was planning on coming to Red and Denise's wedding, so Lisa figured the two of them would have a chance to talk sometime during the evening. Her stomach flipped over nervously as she wondered what he would say. Would he want to get back together? What would she say if he did? What did she want to happen?

She had no idea, and seeing Scott leading his horse up the hill toward her wasn't helping her decide. "Everything okay?" she called, trying to keep her voice steady.

"Could be warmer," Scott replied with a wry smile. He stopped the horse and swung back into the saddle, which let out an audible squish as he sat down. "Not to mention drier. But I think we'll both live."

Lisa nodded and remounted. "We'd better head back," she said, both relieved and disappointed at having to cut the ride short. "I don't want Windsor to get chilled. Or you, either."

Scott smiled but didn't reply. For some reason that made Lisa blush yet again.

A flash of movement caught her eye on the trail ahead. She turned and saw a rider coming toward them at a trot. Squinting, she saw that the horse was a gray.

"Look, I think that's George," she said.

Scott glanced up the trail and nodded. "Wonder what he's doing out here all alone?"

Lisa shrugged, though she wasn't as surprised as Scott seemed to be to find George riding solo. George wasn't exactly a social butterfly—in fact, now that Lisa thought about it, she wasn't sure he had any real friends at all, especially now that Callie had dropped him.

George had already spotted them. He waved and brought Joyride down to a walk as he approached them. "Hi, you two!" he called. Apparently noticing Scott's wet clothes, his smile turned to a frown of worry. "Uh-oh. What happened?"

Scott smiled sheepishly. "Windsor decided to take a bath. Unfortunately, he failed to inform me first, so I ended up taking it with him."

"Are you okay?" George glanced anxiously from Scott to Lisa and back again. "It's awfully cold for that sort of thing."

"Tell me about it," Scott said with an exaggerated

shudder. "We were just about to head for home to dry off."

George nodded. "I was heading back to the stable myself," he said. "I'll ride with you."

Lisa felt a flash of annoyance at the way George had just bumbled along and inserted himself into their ride, completely clueless as usual about the fact that he might not be welcome. But then she reminded herself that George's presence was probably a blessing in disguise.

Having him along means Scott and I aren't alone, she thought as the three of them turned and headed down the trail toward the narrow crossing. She let her reins go slack and slumped slightly in the saddle, letting Checkers follow along at the end of the line. *And not being alone means I don't have to deal with whatever is going on between us. At least not today.*

TEN

Carole paused and glanced in the window of a men's clothing store, briefly wondering how Cam would look in the suede jacket on the mannequin. Then she shook her head.

No matter how desperate I am, there's no way I could afford that, she reminded herself, moving on down the mall. *Anyway, I don't even know if Cam would like something like that. I have no idea what he would like. Aargh!*

She chewed her lower lip as she reached the next store, a card shop. New Year's Eve was the next day, and she was no closer to finding the perfect gift for Cam now than she'd ever been. Glancing into the store, with its shelves full of knickknacks and discounted Christmas items, she sighed.

Then she perked up as she realized she had almost reached The Saddlery. "Of course!" she said aloud. "I'll get him something there."

Smiling self-consciously at a couple of older

women who were staring at her curiously, she moved on. *So this is what it's come to,* she thought with a secret smile. *I'm so desperate to find Cam a gift that I'm reduced to wandering around the mall talking to myself.*

She hurried into The Saddlery, breathing deeply as the intermingled smells of leather and liniment met her nose. Rubbing her hands together eagerly, she glanced around, wondering where to start. Would Cam like a new pair of breeches? Or maybe a riding video or something?

Walking up and down the aisles, she checked out one item after another. She decided the breeches were a bad idea. For one thing, he had been riding in jeans and didn't seem to mind it. Besides, she wasn't sure of his size.

She also rejected the possibility of getting him a riding book or video, since she wasn't really sure what discipline he might be interested in, if any. Since he didn't have his own horse anymore, it seemed silly to even consider buying him a piece of tack or a turnout sheet or some grooming equipment. And a new helmet cover or riding crop didn't exactly make the sort of lavishly romantic statement she was looking for.

Okay, maybe not, she decided at last, heading for the exit. *There's plenty of stuff here that I would love to buy, but Cam's not quite as involved with riding as he used to be. I have to remember that. If I want to show him how special he is to me, I have to get him something he'll truly appreciate, not something that I want him to appreciate.*

She sighed as she emerged into the mall once again, dodging out of the way as a small boy went racing down the aisle in the direction of the food court. Carole turned and headed the same way, deciding it was time to stop for something to drink and for some fast thinking. After ordering a soda at the closest stand, she glanced around for a table. The mall was crowded, though not as crowded as it had been before Christmas, and she soon spotted an available seat.

Setting her purse on the table, she pulled out her chair and sat down heavily. *All right,* she told herself sternly. *You're out of time, so think. How can you show Cam how glad you are he came back into your life?*

Carole sipped her soda and thought hard about that. What could she give Cam that would express all that? What mere gift could sum up how she felt about him?

Hoping for some inspiration, she took another sip of soda and then reached for her purse. She'd stuck a couple of the best photos from the batch she'd picked up Friday in her wallet. She pulled them out, staring at them thoughtfully.

Then, like a miracle, inspiration struck. *I've got it!* Carole thought, gazing at the photo of her and Cam smiling for the camera. *Part of what's so special about being with Cam now is remembering how special he was to me back when we first met. Maybe I could make up a sort of photo history of that—Cam and me, then and now.*

She chewed her lip, wondering if that would be special enough. When she glanced at her watch, she realized it would have to do. She was almost out of time—her father was expecting her home in less than an hour.

Quickly gulping down the rest of her soda, she headed back toward the card shop. Soon she was browsing through their wide selection of picture frames. She found a nice brass one with two spaces and picked it up, glancing at the price. Just as she was about to turn away, she spotted a beautiful silver frame. It was very simple in style; perfect for a guy's room. The only trouble was, it had space for three photos rather than two.

Nice, Carole thought, picking up the frame and running her thumb over its gleaming surface. *I bet Cam would love this one. But what could I put in the third slot without ruining the past-and-present theme?*

Suddenly it clicked. What was the logical addition to a display showing the past and the present?

The future, she thought with a gulp. *I could leave the third space blank, and write a note explaining that it was where Cam could put a photo of us taken in the future—like on our one-year anniversary. The whole thing will be the perfect way to let Cam know how much his friendship has always meant to me, how happy I am that we're together now, and how much I hope we'll stay together for a long, long time.*

It made perfect sense. And more than that, it added the special, personal, romantic touch she'd been looking for.

But could she do it? Could she open herself up like that, let him know how much she really cared? Let him know that she wanted her future to include him, wanted his future to include her? They had grown very close over the past weeks, but even so, it felt like a big step. Could she take it?

"Yes," she whispered, staring at the frame. She would do it. Cam was worth the risk. Besides that, she had a pretty good feeling about Cam's response. He had told her he loved her after only a couple of dates. He would be sure to appreciate exactly this sort of gesture.

Carole smiled and turned toward the register, which had a long line of customers, most of whom seemed to be returning or exchanging holiday gifts. Taking her place at the end of the line, Carole hugged the silver frame to her chest. She couldn't wait to see the look on Cam's face when he opened it the next day.

It will be great, she thought. *I can see it now: He'll be so overwhelmed with emotion that he'll be speechless for a moment. Totally overcome with love and with happiness that I feel the same way he does. Then he'll get down on one knee and give me his gift—a giant, ninety-five-carat diamond engagement ring. He'll explain that he's wanted to pop the question since our first date, and in fact the whole plan for Red and Denise to get married was just a big ruse. It will actually be our wedding that will take place this New Year's Eve! And then he's going to sweep me off to, like, Paris or someplace for our honeymoon. No, maybe Vienna, so we can ride some of those Lipizzaners at the Spanish Riding School. And then we'll live happily ever after, and I'll never have to return to high school again. . . .*

She giggled, bringing curious glances from several of the other shoppers. Pursing her lips and trying to control herself, she smiled and amended her daydream slightly.

Seriously though, he'll probably realize what I'm trying to say right away, she thought with a shiver of anticipation. *I won't even have to say a word to ex-*

plain. He'll just take me in his arms, kiss me, and everything will be even more wonderful than it already is. Now, and in the future.

Mrs. Atwood looked surprised when she opened her front door. "Stevie," she said. "Hello. If you're looking for Lisa, she's not in at the moment."

"I'm not looking for Lisa." Stevie took a deep breath, willing herself onward. This plan had seemed so simple back at the stable; but now, looking at Mrs. Atwood's sour, slightly dismissive expression, she wasn't so sure it was going to work after all. Still, she did her best to stay positive. "I'm looking for you, actually," she went on. "We have to talk."

Mrs. Atwood blinked. "Pardon me?"

"You and me," Stevie replied. *Was that right?* she wondered. *Or should I have said, "You and I?"* Doing her best to put that aside, she cleared her throat. "That is, I need to speak to you about this idea of moving to New Jersey."

"I really don't think there's anything to discuss," Mrs. Atwood said stiffly. "Now, if you'll excuse me—"

"Wait!" Stevie said desperately before Lisa's mother could close the door on her. "Please. Can't I just come in and talk to you for a second?"

Mrs. Atwood sighed and glanced at her watch. "I don't know, Stevie," she said. "I'm very busy."

"Please!" Stevie hated to beg, but she was feeling desperate. All she needed was a few minutes alone with Mrs. Atwood. She was sure that if she could just get her to listen, she could make her understand why making Lisa move away from her home, especially in the middle of her senior year, was completely and utterly nuts. Of course, she was planning to put it a little more tactfully than that. That was the whole idea behind her plan—to follow Phil's suggestion and try to be mature and reasonable. To talk to Mrs. Atwood, adult to adult, and convince her to change her mind.

"Well . . ." Mrs. Atwood hesitated.

That was all the opening Stevie needed. She stepped inside and smiled. "Great," she said. "Come on, why don't we sit down?"

Mrs. Atwood frowned, and Stevie wondered if she'd broken some major rule of etiquette. Lisa's mother was a real stickler about stuff like that. *Oops,* she thought. *I guess since it's her house, maybe she should have been the one to say whether we should sit down.*

Still, there was nothing she could do about that now. Pasting a cheerful, mature smile on her face, she followed Mrs. Atwood into the pristine, formally furnished living room and perched on the edge of a chair.

"All right, then," she said briskly. "I won't waste your time. I just want to explain why it's so important for you guys to stay right here, in Willow Creek."

Mrs. Atwood cleared her throat. She was still standing, her arms crossed over her chest as she gazed down at Stevie. "I don't see how you have any input into that decision, Stevie." Her voice was just as stuffy and formal as the surroundings. "That's a choice that Lisa and I must make for ourselves."

"But that's just it," Stevie explained. "You're not including Lisa in the decision making. She wants to stay here. She needs to stay here. It's best for her."

"I think I'm a better judge of what's best for Lisa than you are, Stevie," Mrs. Atwood replied, her frown deepening the lines around her mouth and the corners of her eyes. "I am her mother."

Stevie took a deep breath, staring at the woman in front of her. Lisa's mother. It was strange, but now that Stevie was there, she couldn't remember ever having an actual conversation with Lisa's mother before, even though Stevie had been in and out of the Atwoods' home on a regular basis for years. It wasn't that Stevie had trouble communicating with adults—on the contrary, she had warm, caring relationships with Carole's father and both of Phil's parents, as well as with Max and Deborah, several neighbors and former teachers, and any

135

number of others. She was even on friendly terms with Lisa's father, though she hadn't seen much of him since he moved to California.

But Mrs. Atwood was different. She had never seemed very interested in getting to know Lisa's friends. Even now that they were all approaching college, she still treated them very much as she had when they were all giggling junior-high kids.

So maybe this is hopeless, Stevie thought with a slight grimace. *If she thinks of me as barely out of diapers, she's not going to listen to anything I say. And if she thinks of Lisa the same way, it's no wonder she's not that interested in hearing about what she wants.*

Still, all she could do was try. "Okay," she said anxiously. "But please, just hear me out for a minute." Gathering her thoughts, she did her best to present the ideas she'd thought out so carefully that morning. It had all made sense at the time, but now that she heard the words coming out of her mouth, they sounded weak and unconvincing, even to her. *You shouldn't move. Lisa only has one more semester of high school. She needs to focus on getting ready for college, not on adjusting to a whole new high school. She won't be able to get in-state tuition at NVU if she lives in New Jersey. Carole and I will miss her.*

When she'd come up with her plan, Stevie had

pictured herself sort of as an intrepid journalist, laying out the facts and letting others draw their own conclusions. But what if a person didn't want to read what a journalist wrote? What happened then?

The whole system breaks down, that's what, Stevie thought grimly as she stood up and meekly followed Mrs. Atwood to the door. *A journalist can't do any good if nobody reads what she writes.*

But a good journalist would at least try to make a difference. That's what Stevie had done. It was all she could do, really.

"Thank you for listening," she told Mrs. Atwood as politely as she could manage. "Please think about what we've talked about, okay?"

"Good-bye, Stevie." Mrs. Atwood didn't wait for further response before swinging the door shut in her face.

Stevie stared at the closed door for a long moment. Then she sighed. "Man," she muttered. "How in the sweet green world did Lisa turn out as normal as she did with that for a mother?"

She turned and made her way slowly down the front path to the sidewalk. *Maybe I would have been better off going with one of those wacky plans we were talking about before,* she thought, kicking at a stone on the walk. *It couldn't possibly make things any worse.*

Had what she'd just done made things worse? There was no way of knowing. But at least she had tried. She would just have to try to find some comfort in that, no matter how things worked out in the end.

ELEVEN

Callie yawned as she walked into the kitchen the next morning. She hadn't slept well—what else was new—and she was feeling groggy.

"Good morning, sweetheart. Happy New Year's Eve!" Callie's mother looked up from her coffee and newspaper with a smile. "Want some breakfast?"

"It's okay," Callie mumbled. "I'll make myself some toast."

Mrs. Forester lowered her paper. "Are you sure?" she asked with concern. "You're going to have a busy day today, what with that wedding and everything, and it's sure to be a late night. You'll need your energy."

"I said it's fine!" Callie snapped. "All I want is toast." She took a deep breath as she noticed the startled look on her mother's face. "Sorry," she mumbled. "Um, thanks anyway."

She turned away quickly and started rummaging in the refrigerator for the butter and orange juice, hoping that her mother wouldn't push it. When the rustle of the newspaper told her that her mother had returned to her reading, Callie closed the refrigerator door and stuck a couple of pieces of bread into the toaster. Taking a few deep breaths as the coils heated to bright orange, she tried to remain calm and act normal so that her mother wouldn't notice anything was wrong.

But while Callie managed to hold it together on the outside—her hand was almost completely steady as she poured herself a glass of juice—she couldn't make herself relax on the inside. Her mother's mention of the wedding had broken through her sleepy haze and brought back all her anxiety about the coming evening, deep and sharp. Her stomach churned as she imagined sitting in the same room with George. And what if he wanted to sit with her? Talk to her? What if he actually asked her to dance or something?

The toast popped up with a clang of springs, making Callie jump. Shooting her mother a glance, Callie was relieved to see that she hadn't noticed her consternation. She grabbed the toast, tossing it onto a plate as it burned her fingertips. After slapping some butter on the hot surface, she grabbed the plate and her juice and escaped from the kitchen.

Soon she was back upstairs in her bedroom, sitting cross-legged on her unmade bed as she ate her breakfast and tried to figure out how she was going to survive the next twenty-four hours. *I can't do it,* she thought as she chewed mechanically on a bite of toast. *I can't go to this wedding. No way.*

"Callie? There you are." Scott yawned as he strolled into the room, still in his pajama pants and T-shirt.

Callie frowned. "Do you mind?" she said testily. "You might try knocking."

"The door was open." Scott blinked at her curiously. "What's the matter with you?"

"Nothing," Callie muttered, feeling sullen. She really wasn't in the mood for Scott's usual cheerful morning chatter. And she definitely didn't want to get into some big debate with him about her own bad mood.

To her surprise, he didn't push it. Instead he wandered over to her dresser, picking up a hairbrush and staring at it for a second. Then he set it down and picked up the lipstick that was next to it.

"What are you doing?" Callie asked. "I don't think that one's your shade."

"Huh?" Scott glanced up, then hastily set down the lipstick. "Oh. Nothing." He walked over to her bookcase and stared at her trophies for a moment, then turned and headed back over to the dresser, seeming restless.

What's his problem? Callie thought. *He hasn't acted this weird since he was about to break up with that girl he met at Dad's inauguration party.*

With that, it clicked. "Hey," she said. "Isn't today the day when Lisa and Alex decide if they're getting back together?"

Scott glanced at her. "Yeah," he said, his shoulders slumping. "Any inside track on what she's thinking?"

"Sorry." Callie shrugged. "If she's talking about it, it's not to me."

"Right. Well, I guess we'll all know soon enough." Scott bit his lip and stared at himself in the dresser mirror. "Soon enough."

"I guess so."

Scott sighed loudly and shot Callie a sidelong glance. "Would you think I'm a horrible person if I told you I hope they decide to call it quits?"

"No," Callie said. "I'd think that was perfectly normal. I know you like her. And you don't have much of a shot if she and Alex get back together, so of course you'd hope they break up for good. Sounds normal to me."

"I know," Scott said. "But still, I mean, Alex is a great guy. And he and Lisa have a history. It's always sad when two people outgrow each other, and—"

"Oh, get over yourself," Callie interrupted impatiently. "It's okay for you to want her for yourself.

It's not like you had anything to do with them deciding to take this little break in the first place."

Scott brightened slightly. "That's true." Then his shoulders slumped again. "On the other hand, I'm sure I haven't exactly helped Alex's cause by asking Lisa out so often."

Callie frowned, wishing he would go away and leave her alone. She had her own problems to deal with, and they were a lot more serious than a hopeful crush. "Well, if it makes you feel any better, I'd say Nicole Adams hasn't helped the cause much either. She and Alex are practically attached at the hip these days. So stop obsessing."

Scott sighed again, looking so pathetic that Callie softened toward him. "Look," she said. "Sorry. I'm a little distracted. I've got stuff on my mind."

"Really? What is it? You're not having trouble with your horse, are you?"

Callie hesitated. Her brother was looking at her with real concern. Should she confide in him about what had really happened out there with George? It was awfully tempting. Scott could be a little shallow and clueless sometimes, but when it came right down to it, he had a good head on his shoulders. Maybe he could help her figure out how to deal with what had happened.

"It's not that," she said slowly. "Actually, I haven't really told anyone about this yet. But . . ."

"What is it?" Scott must have sensed something in her voice, because he took a couple of steps closer, his face serious.

At that, the floodgates opened. As Scott listened quietly, Callie poured out the whole story, from the moment George had appeared way out there in the middle of nowhere—and more or less admitted he'd tailed her there—to several tense minutes later when Scooby had kicked out nervously, knocking George into a tree.

". . . and so when I realized he was unconscious, I hightailed it out to the road and flagged down a car, and the driver called the paramedics on his car phone," Callie finished at last. "I borrowed the phone to call Red, and he came out and picked us up in the stable van, and the rest is history. Ever since then, I've been totally freaked out. That's why I've hardly been to the stable for the past week."

Scott remained silent for a moment. "Wow," he said at last, shaking his head. "That's really something. I had no idea."

"I know." Callie picked up her toast, which was cold by then, and stared at it. "Like I said, I haven't told anybody what really happened."

"Um, but what do you think George was doing out there?" Scott looked uncomfortable. "I mean, I can totally understand why you, um . . ." His voice trailed off helplessly.

"Why I freaked?" Callie asked bluntly. "Can you really? Because if I hadn't been there myself, I don't think I would. I would think I was nuts. I sort of do as it is," she added quietly.

Scott cleared his throat. "Okay," he said. "I mean, I don't think you're nuts. If you felt threatened, that's real enough for me, you know?"

"Sure. Thanks." Callie forced a smile. She could tell that Scott wasn't sure what to think—an unusual situation for him.

He probably thinks I'm exaggerating, she thought, picking a crumb off her bedspread. *He probably figures George came across my route map and got some kind of idea about hacking around with me, and then got clumsy with the shoe and the phone and all the rest of it because he could tell I was angry about him being there.*

She couldn't really blame her brother. Wasn't that exactly what she'd been trying to convince herself had happened? Didn't she think she was exaggerating what had happened, too? The trouble was, she couldn't seem to stop herself.

"Don't worry, though," Scott said. "I'll definitely run interference for you tonight if you want."

"Tonight?" Callie repeated blankly.

"The wedding," Scott reminded her. "It's tonight, remember?"

"Oh, right," Callie muttered. "Actually, I'm not sure I'm going to go."

Scott looked shocked. "Not go?" he said. "But you have to go! You can't let George stop you from celebrating with Red and Denise and the rest of our friends. That would be like letting him win."

Callie hadn't thought of it that way before. "I guess," she said reluctantly. "But I just don't know if I can deal with it. Seeing him, I mean. It's too soon."

"Listen." Scott stepped forward and put a hand on her arm, his blue eyes concerned. "You have to do what you have to do. But for what it's worth, I think this might be one of those situations where it's better just to get right back on the horse. So to speak. And it doesn't have to be so terrible. I meant what I said. I'll keep George away from you tonight if you go. Scout's honor."

Callie smiled weakly at her brother. "Thanks," she said. "And maybe you're right. I can't let this keep me locked in my room forever." She took a deep breath, trying to banish her fear once and for all. "Okay, then. If you'll play guard dog, I guess I'll go."

Stevie reached for the syrup bottle, which was in the middle of the kitchen table beside the butter dish. "So I'll bet you don't get food like this for breakfast up there at college, huh?" she asked Chad, who was sitting across from her, steadily shoveling an enormous stack of pancakes into his mouth.

Chad glanced up at her, chewed, and swallowed. "No way," he replied. "The dining hall at NVU believes in recycling. As in, recycling old tennis shoes into something resembling food."

Stevie laughed. "This from the guy who once ate dirt as a protest when Mom served us liver," she teased. Covering her mouth to hide a slight burp, she reached for the glass of orange juice at her elbow.

She glanced up as Alex walked into the room, yawning. "Morning," he muttered, heading for the refrigerator.

"Morning?" Stevie said with a grin. "It's practically afternoon. And I thought *I* slept late today!"

Alex didn't respond. He pulled out a carton of orange juice and poured himself a glass, then took a long drink before topping it off again.

Chad stabbed another tower of pancake pieces with his fork. "Yo, Alex, you'd better grab some pancakes now before Stevie gobbles them all. Dad made them like an hour ago, so they're a little cold." He shrugged. "But hey, that's what microwaves are for, right?"

"No thanks." Alex took another sip of orange juice. "I'm not hungry."

Stevie made a big show of shaking her head and

cleaning out her ears. "What?" she said. "Am I hallucinating? Because I would swear I just heard one of my bottomless-pit brothers say he wasn't hungry."

"Bottomless pit?" Chad grinned. "Hey, I resemble that remark!"

Alex didn't laugh. "Whatever," he muttered. "I'm just not hungry, okay? Drop it."

Stevie opened her mouth to continue her teasing, but she clamped it shut again. It had just dawned on her why Alex was acting so weird. Sleeping until after ten. Not wanting breakfast. Dragging around like the walking dead.

She cleared her throat. "Hey," she said in a gentler tone. "So, um, when do you think you'll talk to Lisa?"

Alex shot her a suspicious look. "What?"

"You know," Stevie prompted. "Isn't today the deadline? The day you guys talk about, you know . . ." She let her voice trail off.

Alex looked decidedly uncomfortable. "I guess," he muttered, putting his empty glass in the sink. "Not that it's any of your business."

Stevie winced. Judging from Alex's demeanor, he wasn't looking forward to his talk with Lisa. What did that mean? Was he just nervous about how the talk would go? Was he worried that she wouldn't take him back? Did he think Scott was going to steal her away? Or—Stevie could hardly force herself to consider the last possibility—was he dreading telling her that he didn't think they should get back together?

He wouldn't be that stupid, Stevie told herself, shooting her twin a sidelong glance. *Would he?*

She really wasn't sure of the answer to that. A few weeks earlier, she wouldn't have expected him to ask out a bimbo like Nicole Adams, either, let alone bring her home to meet Mom and Dad.

Stevie opened her mouth to ask him more questions about his plans, but Alex hurried out of the room.

Chad blinked after him. "Wow," he mumbled through a mouthful of pancake. "What's with him?"

Stevie sighed. "Today's the day he and Lisa decide what's up with them," she explained. "They decided that on New Year's Eve, they'd talk and figure out where they want to go from here. As in, whether they'll stay broken up or get back together."

"Ah." His curiosity satisfied, Chad returned his attention to his plate.

But Stevie stared off in the direction her twin had gone, her appetite suddenly gone. What was Alex thinking right then? What was he feeling? She wished she were a mind reader so that she could know.

But I guess I'll just have to wait until tonight and find out along with everybody else, she thought, anxiety twisting her overfull stomach into a sort of bloated knot. *In the meantime, all I can do is hope that the wedding and everything will be so totally romantic that it will bring Alex and Lisa to their senses and make them realize that they belong together.*

TWELVE 12

Carole smoothed the skirt of the red dress she had just zipped up, turning this way and that in front of her dresser mirror. The bold color looked nice against her cocoa-colored skin and dark hair, but Carole wasn't sure she had the guts to wear it. The full skirt was shorter than she was used to, and the fitted bodice emphasized her slender figure in a way that made her feel self-conscious. Still, both her best friends had sworn that the dress was perfect on her. They had talked her into buying it despite her doubts, and now she was trying to decide whether she dared to wear it to the wedding that evening. Would Cam like it? Or would he think she looked silly, like a little girl playing dress-up in her mother's clothes?

He'll probably like it, Carole told herself uncertainly, twisting again to get a view of her back. *He likes everything I wear. At least he says he does. Of course, I've never worn anything quite like this for him before. . . .*

Deciding she needed a second opinion, she hurried downstairs to the living room, where her father was sitting at his desk paying bills. "Hey, Dad," she said. "How do I look? Is this dress better than the other one I had on?"

Colonel Hanson looked up and smiled. "You look beautiful, honey," he said. "And you looked beautiful in the other outfit, too."

Carole rolled her eyes. "Big help," she muttered. "Seriously, Dad. I need to know. Which one should I wear tonight? Which one do you think Cam will like better?"

"The one you have on is great," her father replied firmly, still smiling. "You have to forgive me for being a little indecisive. This is kind of a new experience for me, you know."

"What is?" Carole was still distracted by worrying that the dress was too tight. "What do you mean?"

Her father shrugged. "Hey, if you were asking me which one of your ratcatcher shirts showed the fewest wrinkles, or which shade of breeches looked best with your navy show jacket, I'd be in my element. But getting dressed for boys instead of horses?" He spread his hands helplessly. "That's something I don't know too much about."

Carole blushed. "Stop it," she said sheepishly. "This is serious, you know."

"I know, I know." Colonel Hanson grinned. "I'm sorry, sweetie. I just can't resist a little teasing. But you really do look lovely in that dress. I'm sure Cam will love it."

"Do you really think so?" Carole twirled around once, making the skirt flounce out. Then, feeling a bit foolish, she stopped. Her father was right. It really wasn't like her to get so obsessed with what she was wearing unless she was entering an important horse show and needed to be dressed properly for the judges. And that was different. Carole knew what she was doing there. While she might be more comfortable in old worn-in breeches and a sweatshirt, she knew how to do herself up in full formal hunter dress when necessary.

Thanking her father for his help, she headed back upstairs to her room. Slipping off the dress, she hung it carefully over the edge of a chair. She had a few hours to think about what to wear to the wedding that evening. In the meantime, she had her reunion and gift exchange with Cam to look forward to.

I can't wait, she thought with a shiver as she slipped back into her jeans and sweater. *I just hope he likes his present.*

She walked over and picked up the neatly wrapped package sitting on her bedside table. She had chosen a tasteful maroon paper with a small-dot pattern and a matching maroon ribbon. Now she couldn't help admiring the gift—it looked classy and masculine, perfect for Cam.

"Okay," she murmured. "Now all I have to do is survive the wait until Cam calls."

She glanced at her watch. Cam had sent her an e-mail from his relatives' house the day before, telling her that he expected to get home by two o'clock. It was almost two now, and Carole wasn't sure she could stand it if she had to wait much longer.

With an impatient sigh, she flopped onto her bed and picked up the book she'd left lying there. It was a new hardcover about training jumpers, and she had been looking forward to reading it ever since she'd first heard about it. Still, as she flipped through the pages, she couldn't seem to focus on it at all. Every time she looked at a photo of a rider flying over an obstacle, she started picturing how Cam would look performing the same move. Whenever she came to a chapter or paragraph that seemed interesting and started to read it, she would quickly come across a word or a phrase that somehow reminded her of Cam.

This is ridiculous, she told herself, tossing the book aside and leaning back against her pillow. *I can't just sit around waiting for him to call. That's too pathetic, even for me.*

As she was debating whether to go downstairs and try to find something to distract her on TV, the phone rang. "Cam!" Carole breathed.

She leaped off the bed so fast that her legs got tangled in the bedspread. With a grunt, she flew headfirst to the floor. She caught herself with her hands, but one knee connected solidly and painfully with the edge of her bedside table.

"Ow!" she moaned, grabbing her knee as tears sprang to her eyes. Blinking them back, she rubbed the sore spot gently and then climbed carefully to her feet. Her knee throbbed and she could already tell she was going to have a monster bruise, but she would live.

Hobbling out into the hall, she realized that the phone had fallen silent after a couple of rings. Pausing at the head of the stairs, she glanced down uncertainly.

"Carole?" her father's voice came a moment later. He appeared at the bottom of the stairs. "Oh, there you are. Phone for you." He winked and smiled. "It's you-know-who."

"Thanks, Dad," Carole said with a rush of relief. She grabbed the phone from the hall table and dragged it into her room, shutting the door behind her. Then she took a deep breath and put it to her ear. "Cam?"

"Hi, beautiful," Cam's familiar voice greeted her. "I'm back!"

"Welcome back," Carole said softly. "I—I missed you."

"I missed you too. Like crazy." Cam's voice was low and husky. "I thought if I didn't see you soon, I'd go totally mental. So when can I see you?"

"Right now," Carole replied. "I mean, you know. As soon as humanly possible. How about if we meet at Pine Hollow?" She figured that way, after they'd exchanged gifts and snuggled a bit, they could take a ride and catch up. It would be a nice way to spend some quiet time together before the crowds and excitement of the wedding that night.

Cam hesitated. "Actually," he said after a moment, "I was thinking maybe you could come over here."

"Where? You mean your house?" Carole was surprised. "Um, are you sure? I mean, I thought the stable would be—"

"Please?" Cam said. "It's just that my dad borrowed my car because his is out of gas, so if I want to meet you anywhere else, I'd have to wait for him to get back. And I have no idea when that will be."

"Oh. Well, okay then." Carole was in no mood to protest. She could go to Pine Hollow anytime. If Cam wanted to see her so badly that he couldn't even wait until his car returned, who was she to argue? "I'll be there in fifteen minutes."

Lisa picked up the remote control and flipped channels again. "Another how-to show," she muttered, rolling her eyes as an earnest-looking woman began to explain how to use old Christmas ribbons to decorate a picture frame. "Great."

She had already spent most of the afternoon looking for something to distract herself from worrying about what to say to Alex. Cleaning her room hadn't done the trick; nor had catching up on her back-to-school reading. And now the television seemed to be letting her down, too. The daytime programs hadn't yet made way for New Year's Eve specials, and the soap operas and talk shows didn't interest her.

With a sigh, Lisa hit the power switch and the TV screen went black. Stretching her arms above her head and propping her feet up on the polished cherry coffee table, she allowed her gaze to stray to the phone on the end table beside the couch.

Should I just call him, get it over with already? she wondered, lowering her arms and slumping back against the cushions. *I mean, we didn't exactly say when on New Year's Eve we'd talk. Maybe he's just sitting around waiting for me to get in touch.*

Somehow, though, she doubted that. Alex was

planning to attend the wedding that evening, just as she was. She was sure the two of them could find a private moment to talk during the festivities. Surely he was thinking the same thing.

It makes sense, she thought. *It will definitely be better to do this in person rather than over the phone.*

That much was true. But as Lisa pictured their meeting, her stomach churned nervously. What would they say to each other? What would Alex want to do? What did she want to do? She still had no idea, although she was starting to realize that there was no way they would be able to go back to what they'd had before. Not after everything that had happened.

But did that mean they should just throw it all away? Should she just give up on the first guy she'd truly loved and move on to someone else? Start dating Scott and just forget that she and Alex had ever meant the whole world to each other?

Scott. He would be at the wedding, too. "How weird will *that* be?" Lisa muttered, feeling herself flush slightly as she remembered their trail ride the day before. As far as she could remember, she'd never been in the same room with both Alex and Scott since she and Alex had decided to take a break from their relationship. How would she handle seeing them both?

Then she realized that it probably wouldn't be an issue, except perhaps in her own mind. This wasn't a movie, where Scott was going to stride up and punch Alex out or challenge him to a duel for her hand. No, Scott knew exactly where he stood. Lisa was sure he'd be watching her and Alex with great interest, but she was equally sure that he wouldn't interfere, no matter what happened.

So I guess that leaves it all up to me, she thought uneasily. *I just have to decide what I want to do, and then hope that Alex wants the same thing. After that, I can deal with Scott.*

Before she could think about that anymore, her mother bustled into the room. Lisa hastily removed her feet from the coffee table, bracing herself for the usual stern lecture on comporting herself like a proper young lady rather than an ill-mannered child. To her surprise, though, her mother didn't even seem to have noticed.

"Lisa," she said distractedly, running a hand through her short, graying hair. "Have you seen today's newspaper? I thought I left it in here."

"No, I haven't seen it," Lisa replied.

Mrs. Atwood sighed loudly. Then she stared around the room, seeming lost. "I just don't know where it is," she remarked.

Lisa gazed at her mother curiously, forgetting about both Alex and Scott for the moment. *Mom has been acting kind of weird since she got back from New Jersey yesterday,* she thought with a flash of worry. *I wonder if there's something she's not telling me? Like maybe she put an offer in on some house in Aunt Marianne's neighborhood and the moving vans are arriving tomorrow.*

"Mom?" she said uncertainly as her mother continued to stare into space. "Are you okay? Is something going on that I should know about?"

Mrs. Atwood blinked and looked at her. "What is it, Lisa?"

"Never mind." Lisa decided it wasn't worth delving into just then. If something was happening with the move, she would find out all too soon anyway. Besides, knowing her mother, her strange behavior could mean nothing at all.

She's probably in a snit because somebody looked at her funny on the plane, she thought wryly. *Or maybe the flight attendant served her the salt-free kosher vegetarian meal by mistake, and Mom's just trying to figure out whether or not she can sue.*

Finally Mrs. Atwood wandered out of the room, still mumbling about the missing newspaper. Leaning back with a sigh, Lisa put the whole encounter out of her mind. She could deal with her mother after the wedding. Until then, she had more immediate things to think about.

"Carole!" Cam smiled as he swung open the heavy oak front door of his family's house. "Come on in. You look amazing!"

"So do you," Carole replied shyly, stepping over the threshold and allowing him to envelop her in a hug. "Welcome home."

"Thanks." Cam loosened his grip, then stepped back to look at her. He smiled. "Man, did I miss you this past week." His fingers caressed her arm just above the elbow, making that whole side of her body tingle. "I couldn't think about much else other than getting back here and kissing you."

Feeling bold, Carole tilted her head back. "What are you waiting for, then?"

With a smile, Cam pulled her close. They kissed for a long moment that almost made Carole forget where she was. But finally, feeling a little embarrassed, she pulled away and glanced over her shoulder at the still open door. "Um, okay," she said with a sheepish chuckle. "I guess we just gave your whole neighborhood a show."

Cam grinned. Pushing the door closed, he gestured for her to follow him. "Come on. Let's go get more comfortable."

"Okay." Carole followed him down the hall. "So where's your mom? I haven't even had a chance to say hi to her since you guys moved back."

"Mom?" Cam shrugged. "She's out shopping. You can say hi later if you want."

"Shopping?" Carole repeated blankly. She glanced around, suddenly realizing that the house was very quiet. "Um, is your dad still out with your car?"

Cam didn't answer. Instead, he put his arms around her and pulled her close again. "Yeah," he murmured, with his lips brushing hers. "And if you don't mind, we could stop discussing my parents now. I'm more interested in me and you."

Carole gulped, feeling nervous, though she told herself she was being silly. *This is perfect,* she thought. *Now we'll have all the privacy we want to do our gift exchange. And then maybe we can go over to Pine Hollow in my car, even if Cam's folks aren't home yet.*

"Um, so aren't you curious?" she asked abruptly, interrupting his kiss.

He blinked and pulled back. "What?"

Carole smiled and held up the wrapped gift, which she'd almost forgotten she was holding. "Your Christmas present," she said. "Don't you want to see what I got you?"

"Oh. Of course." Cam massaged her shoulder with one hand as the fingers of his other hand traced the line of her jaw. "Later." He moved in, kissing her gently on the cheek, then on the lips.

"Come on, Cam." Carole pushed him away before she got lost in his kisses again. "I thought we were going to exchange gifts now." She didn't want him to know how nervous she was about what he would think of the framed photos, so she forced a playful smile. "Aren't you curious about what's in here?"

"Sure, I guess." Cam finally stepped back, looking slightly flushed. "Okay, then. Let's have it."

He took the package and perched on the bottom step. Carole held her breath as he ripped through the paper and ribbon to the cardboard box underneath. Soon he was pulling out the frame and examining the two photos in it.

"It's sort of like a history of us," Carole explained anxiously, praying she hadn't made a huge mistake. "Read the card."

Cam did so, then glanced up with a smile. "Carole, this is great," he said huskily. "I love it. And I love you. Thanks."

"You really like it?" Carole asked as he stood and kissed her on the cheek. "For real?"

"Absolutely. It makes me feel so close to you." Cam stood and wrapped his arms around her waist. "It makes me want to be even closer."

Carole wasn't sure what he meant by that, but she couldn't help laughing with relief. After all the agonizing she'd done over what to get him, it was wonderful to see the appreciation on his face.

"What?" Cam asked expectantly, rubbing her back and smiling down at her. "What's so funny?"

"Nothing," Carole said, not wanting him to

know how nervous she had been about his reaction. She felt foolish and unsophisticated enough as it was sometimes just trying to figure out what being in a relationship meant, when Cam already seemed to know exactly how to go about it. He never intentionally made her feel that way, of course, but nonetheless, she figured it was better if he didn't know just how clueless she felt at times. "Um, so how about it?" she added hastily to cover her thoughts. "Don't I get to open my present now?"

"Absolutely." Cam brushed a strand of hair off her face. "It's up in my room."

"Okay." Carole stepped back and waited, expecting him to go upstairs and get it.

Instead, Cam took the first couple of steps and then paused, looking back at her. "Well? Aren't you coming?"

Carole gulped. It hadn't occurred to her to follow him upstairs. Suddenly she was once again very aware of the silence in the empty house. *He wants me to go up to his bedroom with him?* she thought uncertainly, feeling uncomfortable. *Why? Why can't he just bring my present down here?*

Cam was still watching her. "Well?" he said again. "Come on, you said you wanted to open it. So let's go."

Looking into his familiar face, Carole did her best to shake off her nerves. *What am I getting so stupid about, anyway?* she thought. *This is Cam I'm talking about here. He loves me. I love him. I trust him. So what's the big deal about hanging out in his room for a while? What am I scared of?*

"Coming," she said, doing her best to sound normal.

She followed him up the stairs to the second floor. Cam headed for a door near the end of the hall, swung it open, and then gestured for her to preceed him inside. "After you, beautiful," he said with a smile.

Carole forced a smile in return, hoping that he couldn't hear the nervous pounding of her heart. As she stepped into the room, she glanced around. The white-painted walls were covered with posters of basketball and football players. A bookcase between the two large windows was crammed with sports trophies and autographed baseballs.

"Have a seat," Cam said as he headed toward the closet. "I'll get it."

"Okay." Carole perched gingerly on the edge of a wooden chair near the door.

Cam rummaged in the closet and emerged a moment later with a small box wrapped in gold foil. When he saw her, he smiled. "That doesn't look too comfortable," he said teasingly. "Come on over here and sit down." He sat on the edge of his bed and patted the spread beside him.

Carole laughed nervously. "Oh. Okay." She got up and walked across the room, sitting carefully on the bed a couple of feet away from Cam.

"That's better." Cam slid closer and handed her the package. "Here you go. Merry Christmas." He folded his hands in his lap.

"Thanks." Carole immediately felt foolish. What was she so nervous about? Eagerly ripping off the gold paper, she uncovered a small white gift box. She lifted the lid and gasped. Nestled inside on a bed of white cotton was a necklace. The thin, delicate silver chain held a gleaming silver pendant shaped like a pair of running horses.

"Do you like it?" Cam was watching her face expectantly.

"Oh, Cam!" she breathed, looking up at him. "I love it! It's so beautiful! Thank you." She leaned over to kiss him.

He met her kiss eagerly, his hands slipping around her. Nervous again, Carole broke away after just a few seconds. "Um, I want to put it on," she said, jumping to her feet and hurrying toward the small mirror hanging on the wall near the door.

Cam followed her. "Here, let me." He took the box from her. Then, as she stared into the mirror, he lifted her hair aside and slipped the necklace around her neck, fastening the clasp and then reaching around to gently straighten the pendant at her throat.

Carole gulped as his hand lingered there, his eyes meeting hers in the mirror. He was so handsome, so caring. . . .

"I'm thirsty," she blurted out. "Um, can we go downstairs and get a soda or something?"

"Not now, okay?" Cam whispered, gently taking her by the shoulders and turning her around to face him. "I just want to show you how much I've missed you."

He kissed her again. Carole kissed him back, not wanting to hurt his feelings. She'd missed him, too—she'd missed him like crazy. And it was so nice to be in his arms again, knowing that he loved her.

"Carole," Cam murmured as his lips left hers and began to explore her chin and neck. "Carole, you're so amazing." He tugged gently on her arms, his lips never leaving her skin as he pulled her back away from the door.

Carole's heart was pounding as she realized he was steering them back toward the bed. She tried to speak up, to insist that they go back downstairs. But Cam covered her mouth with his own once again, even as he lowered them both onto the edge of the bed.

"Cam, wait," Carole mumbled, trying to figure out the best way to tell him they had to stop. She wasn't ready for this, any of it. Her heart still beating like a drum, she tried to gather her thoughts.

She was very aware that Cam's left hand was wandering down her body, tugging gently at the hem of her shirt.

"Carole," Cam replied huskily, pushing her back against the pillows at the head of the bed. "Carole, you don't know what you do to me. I can't get enough of you." He leaned over her, pressing her into the mattress as he bent to kiss her again.

Carole closed her eyes as Cam kissed her deeply. Both his hands were exploring now in places they'd never been before, but she couldn't seem to gather her will to stop him. She knew it was too soon, she wasn't ready, but she didn't know how to—

"Cam!" a woman's voice broke in suddenly.

Cam leaped to his feet, elbowing Carole in the stomach in the process. "Mom!" he exclaimed, his voice cracking slightly. "What are you doing home so soon?"

Carole blinked and came to her senses as she glanced over and saw a tall, slender woman standing in the doorway in a winter hat and coat, staring at her and Cam with a frown. Cam's mother.

Carole's face turned beet red. "I, uh, I have to go," she mumbled, sitting up fast and straightening her disheveled clothes. "I have to go."

She stood up and raced toward the door, not daring to look at either Cam or his mother. She wasn't sure she'd ever felt so humiliated and flustered in her entire life. What did Cam's mother think of her, catching her in Cam's bedroom—on Cam's bed!—like that? How could Carole have let things get so out of hand?

Mrs. Nelson stepped aside, and Carole rushed past, heading straight for the stairs. She was vaguely aware of Cam calling her name, but she didn't stop. She couldn't face him or his mother just then. She had to get outside, into the clean, cold winter air, and clear her head.

Within seconds she was sitting in her car and strapping on her seat belt. She put the vehicle in gear and backed out of the driveway as fast as she could, barely avoiding dinging Mrs. Nelson's car, which was parked beside her.

She didn't relax until she was on the highway heading back toward Willow Creek. *Whew!* she thought, slumping down in her seat. *That was pretty weird back there.*

She gripped the steering wheel tightly as she remembered how helpless she had felt to stop what was happening. What was wrong with her, anyway? She should have known better than to let things go so far. Why hadn't she just spoken up and asked Cam to cool it? He would have understood. He cared about her. He wouldn't want her to do anything that made her uncomfortable. He wouldn't want to rush her.

Realizing that made her feel a little better. *I'll just have to talk to him about this tonight at the wedding,* she told herself, hardly seeing the cars on the road around her. *I'll explain that I need to take the, um, physical side of our relationship a little slower, at least for now. He'll understand.*

She smiled slightly, feeling better still. Cam *would* understand, she was sure of it. Her smile faded and her face started to burn again as she remembered the shocked look on Mrs. Nelson's face.

Yes, Cam would understand. Nevertheless, Carole planned to stay out of his mother's way for a *long* time.

THIRTEEN

"**W**ow!" Stevie let out a whistle as she and Phil walked into the Regnerys' house that evening. "Is this really the same old grungy living room I remember?" She winked at Phil and glanced over her shoulder at Alex, who had followed them inside.

Max gave her a sour look. "Welcome, Stevie. I think."

Stevie grinned at the stable owner apologetically. "Seriously, Max," she said. "This place looks totally fabu. I mean it. You and Deborah did great."

Max nodded brusquely, then smiled. "Thanks, Stevie," he said. "In that case, you can stay."

He turned away to greet some more newcomers, and Stevie dragged the two guys farther into the spacious room, looking around in genuine amazement. She had been kidding in saying the living room was usually grungy. In fact, Deborah's good decorating taste meant that the large space, which

171

had been created by knocking down most of the walls on the first floor of the house, was cozy and inviting. That evening, though, it looked downright amazing. Most of the furniture had disappeared, replaced by tables laden with food and drink and candles. Small, twinkling white Christmas lights were strung from the rough-hewn wooden beams overhead, setting off the fresh flowers that decorated every available surface. A plush red carpet led the way from the bottom of the turned oak staircase across the room and down an aisle created by two columns of folding chairs. A wooden arch, which Stevie recognized as one that had until recently decorated Deborah's herb garden, stood at the head of the aisle, draped with white ribbons and still more flowers.

"Wow," Stevie said again, impressed. "When Max and Deborah throw a wedding, they really go all out, don't they?"

"Come on, let's grab some seats," Phil suggested as he shrugged off his coat and turned to catch Stevie's as she took off hers. "We want a good view."

"Definitely." Stevie surveyed the crowd. About a dozen people were already seated, while the rest milled around the room talking. "Look, there's Lisa." Stevie waved to her friend, who was seated near the front and had just turned and spotted them.

"I'm thirsty," Alex said abruptly. "I think I'll grab a soda before this thing gets started."

Stevie glanced at him anxiously, wondering what he was thinking. "Okay," she said. "We'll save you a seat if you want."

"That's okay." Alex didn't meet her eye. "I'm sure I'll be able to find one."

Stevie nodded and sighed, then grabbed Phil's hand. "Come on, let's go sit with Lisa," she said. "But remember, not a word about, you know, my little errand yesterday."

"Don't worry, I'm a vault." Phil squeezed her hand.

Stevie smiled at him gratefully. He was the only one she'd told about her awkward little visit with Mrs. Atwood the day before. She wasn't sure she wanted Lisa to know about it at all—after all, it probably hadn't done any good—but in any case, the last thing Stevie wanted to do was distract her tonight, right before her big talk with Alex.

As they reached Lisa's row, she stood up. "Hey," she greeted them. "You guys look great."

"You're looking pretty spiffy yourself," Stevie replied, taking in the shimmering green silk dress that Lisa was wearing.

"Thanks." Lisa glanced down at herself shyly. "Um, could you save my seat for a second? I want to . . . I'll be right back."

"Sure." Stevie smiled blandly as Lisa stepped past her and made her way quickly up the aisle. Then she turned to Phil and poked him in the shoulder so hard that he jumped and yelped in pain. "Check it out," she whispered, her eyes following Lisa across the room. "She's going to talk to Alex. It won't be long now until they're back together."

"Or split apart for good," Phil reminded her gently.

"Right," Stevie said shortly, not allowing herself to consider that possibility too much. "Or that."

Lisa caught up with Alex. "Hi," she said softly to his back.

He turned and nodded somberly. "Hi."

Lisa gulped, her mind suddenly blank. It was weird being face to face with Alex again after so long apart. She ran her eyes over the familiar planes and angles of his face, feeling as if the last few weeks had been some kind of bizarre dream. Had they really decided to stop seeing each other? It just didn't quite seem real.

There was a long, slightly tense moment of silence as they stood there staring at each other. The spell was broken when Deborah clapped her hands loudly from the foot of the stairs, just a few feet away from where Lisa and Alex were standing.

"Thank you all for coming!" Deborah said loudly

as conversation hushed around the room. "We're so glad you all could be with Red and Denise on this very special night. We'll be getting things under way shortly, so if you could all please take your seats . . ."

"I guess we'd better go sit down," Alex said.

"Right," Lisa agreed. She glanced at him, gathering up her courage. "Um, but maybe we should meet up right after the ceremony. You know, to talk."

Alex nodded quickly. "Okay."

"Okay, then." Lisa cleared her throat. At that very moment, the front door opened and Scott strode in with a loud laugh and a hearty greeting for Max, who had let him in. Callie was beside her brother, but Lisa hardly noticed her. She gulped, feeling herself blush at Scott's grand entrance. "Well, I'll see you afterward, then," she told Alex hastily, scurrying off toward her seat.

I hope he didn't notice the way I totally overreacted right then, she thought.

It wasn't until she was sitting down beside Stevie that she realized she wasn't sure which "he" she meant—Alex or Scott.

Callie glanced around nervously as she followed Scott into the room, hardly noticing the decorations. She still wasn't sure she'd done the right thing by coming. What was she going to do when she encountered George? How would he act when he saw her?

She didn't have long to wait before she found out the answer to that last question. "Callie!" a familiar breathless voice exclaimed from the direction of a small knot of people near the stairs.

Callie gulped. She barely had time to turn her head and look before George was barreling toward her. He was dressed in a navy suit for the occasion but still managed to look pudgy and sweaty and slightly unkempt. His blond hair was slicked back with some kind of gel, but a few pale tufts stuck up just above his high forehead.

"Callie! I'm so glad you're here!" George exclaimed brightly. "I've been looking for you at the stable for days, wanting to thank you."

"Th-Thank me?" Callie repeated helplessly. Beside her, she was aware of Scott gulping anxiously: He seemed just as startled as she was and didn't say a word.

George smiled. "Uh-huh," he said. "You know—for getting help when I tripped and knocked myself out last week. I don't know what would have happened if you hadn't been there!"

If I hadn't been there, you wouldn't have been there, either, Callie thought, though she didn't say it out loud. Her heart was pounding so fast she wasn't sure she could speak if she wanted to. Whatever she had expected of her first encounter with George after the accident, this wasn't it.

"Anyway, I really appreciate it," George went on, clearly oblivious to Callie's discomfort. "Also, thanks a bunch for looking out for Joy while I was out of commission. She's pretty high-strung sometimes, and I hate to think what might have happened to her if you hadn't been there to take her out. She would've scratched up her legs or tossed a shoe at the very least."

Callie winced at the mention of George's horse's shoes. How could he keep babbling on, thanking her for helping him, without so much as mentioning the way he'd practically wrenched Scooby's shoe off? That was what had caused all the problems in the first place. Didn't he remember that?

"Seriously," George continued, hardly seeming to notice that Callie hadn't responded, "if there's anything I can do for you, Callie, anything at all, just ask. I really owe you one, and I'm not going to forget it."

Finally Scott seemed to recover from his surprise and remember his earlier promise to Callie. "Hey, George, buddy," he said jovially, patting George on the back. "You must've been to Max's house before. Want to give me a little tour? This is my first time, and I don't want to bother Max or Deborah."

"Sure!" George said immediately. "Come on. Callie, you'll come, too, won't you?"

Callie gave him a tight smile, the best she could

manage under the circumstances. "Thanks, but I'd really like to go say hi to, um"—she scanned the crowd quickly, looking for a familiar face—"uh, Carole. She's right over there. But you two go ahead."

George blinked, then shot Callie a slightly disappointed look. "Um, okay," he said to Scott. "Follow me."

As the two guys made their way across the room toward the kitchen at the back of the house, Callie slumped against the wall with relief. But that emotion soon changed to anger. How dare George act as if nothing terribly unusual had happened out there in the woods—that it had all been some sort of ordinary, understandable accident? How dare he think that they could possibly still be friends, or even friendly acquaintances, after what he'd done?

Carole smiled shyly as Cam stepped aside to let her enter the row of folding chairs. She sat down, smoothing the skirt of her yellow dress. "Thanks. This place looks great, doesn't it?" She glanced forward at the graceful wooden arch at the head of the aisle, imagining how beautiful Denise would look standing beneath it in her wedding gown. She shivered slightly in anticipation.

"Yeah, it's amazing," Cam agreed as he took his seat beside her.

Carole shivered again as the sleeve of his dark suit brushed her bare elbow. She still felt strange about what had happened earlier, though Cam hadn't so much as hinted at it.

Maybe that means it wasn't as big a deal as I thought, Carole told herself hopefully. *Maybe he understands already. Maybe he realizes why I acted the way I did without my even having to tell him.*

She shot a glance over at Cam, liking that idea. After all, Cam knew that she hadn't dated much before him. He had to realize that she wasn't very experienced compared to a lot of people their age. . . .

Her thoughts trailed off as her eye wandered past Cam toward the door. Ben Marlow had just entered. He was removing his coat, nodding at something Deborah was saying to him.

Carole winced. Ben looked so uncomfortable it was almost painful to watch. Why had he come, anyway? She knew he was friendly enough with Red and Denise, but it wasn't as though the couple would be heartbroken if he didn't show up. Carole doubted they would even have noticed.

And it's not as if Ben's very good in social situations, she thought. Any *social situations.* She grimaced slightly as she remembered the one brief kiss they had shared at that horse show back in the autumn. Thinking of that confusing encounter—when Ben had spent five minutes acting as if he really cared about her and then the next several weeks pretending he barely noticed she was alive—still made Carole's face flush slightly with humiliation. But then Cam turned to smile at her, and she felt a little better immediately.

I'm really lucky to have him, she thought, touching the silver pendant at her throat as she returned Cam's smile. *And I should probably just stop worrying about what happened this afternoon. It really wasn't that big a deal—I should be able to tell that just by the way Cam is acting tonight. He's being his usual wonderful self.*

She continued to smile at Cam gratefully. He blinked. "What?" he asked, looking slightly worried. "Why are you looking at me like that?"

"Oh, nothing much." Carole reached over and took his arm in hers. "I was just thinking what a lucky girlfriend you have."

"That's funny," Cam replied, putting a hand on her knee and squeezing. "Because I happen to think that your boyfriend is the luckiest guy in the world."

Carole leaned her head on his shoulder, too happy to speak. *I was right,* she thought. *I really shouldn't make a bigger deal than I need to out of little problems and misunderstandings like the one this afternoon. Cam and I can work things out, because we love each other and know how to communicate.* She tilted her head slightly, catching another glimpse of Ben as he hung up his coat in the closet near the door. *Unlike some other people I could mention.*

She pushed all thoughts of Ben out of her mind as she spotted Callie coming toward them. Sitting up straight, she waved at her friend. "Hi!" she called. "Long time no see."

Callie took a seat in the row ahead of Carole and Cam. "Hi, you two." She smiled at them, though Carole couldn't help noticing that she looked sort of tired. "Having fun?"

"Absolutely." Cam slung an arm around Carole's shoulders and gave her a hug. "How about you, Callie?"

"Sure," Callie said shortly, though she seemed to be looking at something over Cam's right shoulder.

Carole blinked, wondering if something was wrong. She had noticed a few days earlier that Callie hadn't been spending much time at Pine Hollow lately, which was very strange for her in general, but even stranger for someone with a brand-new, much anticipated horse.

She bit her lip, wondering if she should ask Callie if everything was okay. What if she was having problems with Scooby or was doubting herself or her horse? Callie wasn't exactly a blabbermouth—Carole hated to think that her friend could be suffering in silence because she was too proud to share her problems with anyone. Still, Carole hesitated. She had tried to speak to Callie when she'd first noticed that she wasn't acting quite like herself, and Callie had made it perfectly clear that she wasn't interested in discussing it. Why should Carole think that anything had changed?

Before Carole could decide whether or not to say anything, Stevie and Phil hurried over to them. "Yo!" Stevie said with a grin. "What are you guys doing over here on the bride's side? We were saving seats for you on Red's side."

"Red's side?" Carole repeated blankly, not sure what Stevie was talking about and still a little distracted by her earlier thoughts.

"You know, sweetie. Usually at weddings, the bride's family and friends sit on this side of the aisle, and the groom's people are over there," Cam explained, gesturing first at their own seats and then at the ones across the way. Then he turned to Stevie. "But I don't get it. I thought you guys were tight with both bride and groom."

Stevie shrugged. "Yeah, I know," she said. "But we've known Red longer. Plus, Denise has all her friends from grad school here, and poor old Red hardly has anyone."

Carole grinned, imagining what Red would say to that if he were close enough to overhear. "I don't know if I'd go that far," she said, glancing around the crowded room. The seats on both sides of the aisle were filling fast. "But I'm sure Red would totally appreciate your loyalty."

Stevie and Phil took the empty seats beside Carole. "Hey, by the way, what's the deal?" Stevie murmured as Cam started chatting with Phil about some sporting event they'd both watched on TV earlier that day. "I thought you were going to wear that hot little red number tonight."

"Um, I—it had a spot on it," Carole lied, feeling uncomfortable. She hated fibbing to her friend, but there wasn't time to go into the real reasons just then. Especially since Carole wasn't even sure what the real reasons were. Somehow, she just hadn't been able to bring herself to put that dress back on. Not after what had happened that afternoon at Cam's house.

That was totally stupid, though, she thought, a little annoyed with herself for being such a baby. *Cam would have loved that dress.*

Still, she was glad that she'd ended up wearing her familiar, comfortable old yellow dress to the wedding instead. That way she was able to just relax and enjoy herself without worrying that her skirt was riding up too far or her buttons were about to pop.

"Look," she said, pushing all thoughts of her clothes, that afternoon's misunderstanding, and Callie's possible problems out of her mind as she spotted Red walking toward the flower-bedecked arch, looking handsome and a little nervous in his tuxedo. "I think they're just about ready to start."

FOURTEEN
14

"It really was a lovely ceremony, wasn't it?" Lisa said politely, smiling at the woman in the peach pantsuit standing in front of her. She wasn't completely sure, but she thought the woman might be Red and Denise's landlord. She had a vague memory of being introduced before the ceremony, but she'd been a little distracted at the time. Actually, she'd been distracted during the entire evening so far, thinking about what she had to do before the night was over.

Spotting Alex hovering nearby, Lisa took a deep breath. It was time.

"Excuse me," she told the woman. "I need to go say hello to someone."

She walked toward Alex, who was watching her with an unreadable expression on his face. "Hi," she greeted him when she reached him.

"Hi," he responded softly. "Um, it's not too cold out tonight. Want to take a walk?"

185

"Sounds good. I'll get my coat."

Lisa headed toward the closet near the door, with Alex at her heels. This was the moment she'd known was coming for the past few weeks, the one she'd been dreading, mostly because she hadn't known what she was going to say when it came. She hadn't even been sure what she wanted to say.

But all of a sudden, she did. She knew exactly what she needed to say. And for the first time, she was ready to say it.

". . . and then she said 'I do,' just like he said," Maxi said excitedly. "It was just like on TV, when Princess Peabody got married to Prince Pepper. Except they both said it at the same time."

Carole grinned. She had no idea which TV show the little girl was referring to, but it didn't seem to matter. "Oh, really?" she asked. "That must have been a nice wedding, too. But I thought this one was very romantic, didn't you?"

"What's *omantuck* mean?" Maxi asked.

Cam, who was standing beside Carole, sighed loudly. "You'll learn about that in school someday," he said abruptly. "Carole, want to go grab some sodas or something?"

"In a minute." Carole leaned closer to Maxi. "*Romantic* means, well, 'romantic.' It's like when you really, really love someone, and you love being with them. It makes everything seem wonderful and special. That's romantic."

"Oh." Maxi thought about that for a second, pushing a strand of hair out of her eyes. Her mother had put the little girl's hair up in a bun for the occasion, but somehow, between Maxi's entrance before the ceremony and the present time, most of her silky auburn hair had made its way free, leaving just a few strands tucked up beneath a pink ribbon. "Then I guess I think Mulligan is romantic."

Carole laughed. "Your puppy? No, no, that's different," she said. "Puppies are wonderful and special, too. But in a different way."

"Carole," Cam muttered. "Come on. I'm thirsty."

Carole blinked and shot him a surprised look. Was it her imagination, or did he sound a little grumpy? She realized that not everyone their age liked hanging around with little kids, but Maxi wasn't just any little kid. She was one of Carole's favorite people, five years old or not. Besides, this was Maxi's first wedding—it was no surprise that she was excited and eager to talk over every detail.

"The wedding was fun," Maxi said confidently, not seeming to notice Cam's comment. "But Mommy says the next part is even funner. She says that next comes the exception."

"I think she probably meant 'reception,'" Carole corrected gently. "That means—"

"Carole!" Cam interrupted, sounding impatient. "I really think we should go down and check on the horses now. Don't you?"

"Oh." Carole flushed, realizing just how antsy Cam really was. She guessed that Maxi had been prattling on longer than she'd realized, and he was eager to get on with enjoying the reception. "Um, okay. Excuse us, please, Maxi. We have to go for a few minutes. Why don't you go say hi to Stevie? She's right over there, and I know she really wants to talk to you." She pointed out her friend, who was nearby chatting with Scott and Callie as the three of them helped themselves to refreshments.

"Okay!" Maxi said cheerfully. With a wave, she skipped off toward the others.

Carole turned to face Cam. "Sorry about that," she said. "But Maxi is so cute, I just had to see what she thought of the wedding."

"Yeah, okay." Cam smiled beseechingly. "But certain other people want a little of your attention, too."

Carole smiled back, feeling warm and flattered. It was nice to have a guy so eager to spend time with her that he couldn't think about anything else. This was the first time in her life that she'd ever felt so desirable, and it was a pretty nice feeling most of the time.

Of course, it would've been nice to spend a few more minutes hanging out with Maxi, she thought a bit resentfully. *I haven't seen much of her lately.*

She did her best to shake off the thought, though. "It looks like Maxi's pretty well distracted," she commented, glancing over to where the little girl was racing off toward the kitchen. "Want to grab those sodas now?"

"I've got a better idea." Cam took her hand and tugged gently, leading her toward the front door. "Let's be true to our word and go check on those horses."

"Okay," Carole agreed with a slight blush, figuring that he just wanted to step outside so that they could be alone for a moment.

The memory of how she'd felt that afternoon in his room—nervous, helpless, overwhelmed—swept over her briefly. But she put it out of her mind. Sneaking a few smooches on Max's front porch wasn't anywhere near the same sort of thing. Besides, hadn't she just been thinking how glad she was that Cam understood how she'd felt about that, that she could trust him?

Soon the two of them were stepping outside into the bracing winter night. But instead of stopping, Cam continued across the porch and down the steps. "Wait a minute," Carole said. "Where are we going?"

Cam blinked at her. "The barn," he said. "That's where they keep the horses, remember?"

"Oh! You mean we're really going to check on them?" Carole said uncertainly. "Um, I just thought—never mind. But shouldn't we wait a little while? I mean, the reception just started, and we haven't even had a chance to congratulate Red and Denise yet."

Cam smiled. "Don't worry, they'll still be here when we get back. They can wait a little while for our official congratulations." He put his arm around her and pulled her close. "But I'm not sure I can wait any longer to be close to you."

"Oh." Carole didn't know what to say to that. She was eager to spend more time alone with Cam, too, especially after being apart for a week. But did it really have to be in the middle of good friends' wedding reception?

She almost immediately felt guilty for that thought. How could she nitpick about Cam's timing? He wanted to be with her, that was all. He wanted it so much that he couldn't think about anything else. Shouldn't she feel the same way? Wasn't she being silly in worrying so much about missing a few minutes of the reception?

"Okay," she said, glad that it was dark so that he couldn't see her blushing. "I mean, me too." Slipping her hand into Cam's, she glanced down at the darkened stable building. "Let's go."

Stevie glanced up from the punch bowl just in time to see Cam open the front door and usher Carole through. "Wonder where they're going?" she muttered.

"Huh?" Phil followed her gaze. Then he smirked. "Do you really have to wonder?" he teased, slipping an arm around her waist. "I never realized you were so naive, my dear. Want to go upstairs and take a look at my etchings?"

"Very funny," Stevie said, making a face at him. But she realized he was right. Cam had returned from his trip only that day. Naturally he and Carole would want to steal a few private moments to get reacquainted, especially after such a romantic ceremony.

I just hope it had the same kind of romantic effect on a certain other couple—or rather, ex-couple—I could mention, she thought. That reminded her that she hadn't seen Lisa since they'd all gotten up from their seats a few minutes earlier. She glanced around the room, but there was no sign of her. There was also no sign of Alex.

Stevie gulped. This was it, then. The big conversation was probably taking place at that very moment.

As she glanced around, trying to make certain that she wasn't missing something—that Lisa wouldn't suddenly appear from the direction of the powder room, or Alex become evident leaning over the refreshments table and stuffing his face—she noticed that someone else was scanning the room as well.

Uh-oh, Stevie thought. *Looks like maybe Scott just noticed that Lisa and Alex are both missing, too.*

She was sure that Scott wouldn't do anything to get in the way of anything that might happen between Alex and Lisa, one way or the other. Pretty sure, anyway.

"Hey," she said, grabbing Phil's jacket sleeve and almost making him drop the cheese he was layering on a cracker. "There's Scott. Let's go say hi."

Phil gave her a suspicious look. "Any particular reason you're feeling the urge to talk to him all of a sudden?" He popped the cracker into his mouth.

Stevie shrugged and grinned. Phil knew her too well. There was no point in trying to cover up what she was thinking. He knew how worried she was about the fate of Alex and Lisa's relationship, and he also knew how interested Scott was in that very same topic. "Oh, I just thought it might be a good idea to distract him right about now." Keeping her hold on Phil's arm, she dragged him off in Scott's direction.

It wasn't until they had almost reached him that

Stevie noticed that, in addition to Callie, he was standing with Ben Marlow. She blinked, surprised. As far as she had ever been able to tell, Scott and Ben got along about as well as oil and water. For some reason, Scott's easy, smooth charm just seemed to rub Ben the wrong way. And Ben's taciturn, sometimes sullen manner tended to turn off most of the people he encountered, and Scott was no exception.

She didn't waste much time worrying about Ben, though. "Hey," she greeted the trio. "Quite a wedding, huh?"

"It was really nice," Callie said, glancing over her shoulder and frowning slightly.

Stevie cocked her head, wondering why Callie looked so weird—almost nervous. But she forgot about that when she noticed Scott staring toward the front door. "So!" Stevie said, a little too loudly. "What did you all think of Denise's dress?"

Meanwhile, she noticed out of the corner of her eye that Ben was sidling away from the group. When he caught Stevie looking at him, he cleared his throat. "Horses," he muttered. "Better go check on them." Without another word, he turned and hurried toward the door.

With a shrug, Stevie returned her attention to Scott. "Did you hear me?" She poked Scott in the shoulder. "Denise's wedding dress. Huh? Pretty, isn't it?" She gestured vaguely toward the bride, who was standing across the room talking to some of her grad-school friends.

Scott raised an eyebrow. "Denise's dress?" he repeated, glancing in the bride's direction. "Sure, it's nice. Since when are you so interested in bridal fashions, Stevie?" He waggled his eyebrows at Phil. "You two don't have any announcements to make, do you?"

"Ha, ha." Stevie grinned weakly. She glanced at Callie for help, figuring that Scott's sister must be aware of how he was probably feeling at the moment, and of what Stevie was trying to do.

But Callie didn't seem to be paying attention to the conversation. She was hunched up against the nearest table, her eyes darting here and there and a nervous-looking frown on her pretty face.

What's wrong with her? Stevie wondered. *Doesn't she like weddings? Or is something else going on that I don't know about?*

She opened her mouth to ask, but before she could, Scott scowled. "Incoming," he whispered to his sister.

"Huh?" Stevie said, glancing over her shoulder. When she saw George Wheeler hurrying toward them, she realized what Scott must have meant.

Uh-oh, she thought. *Callie's been trying to let George down gently for ages. And now that he's telling everyone who'll listen how she practically saved his life last week, it must be harder than ever to do that.*

Still, Stevie wasn't prepared for Callie's reaction to Scott's warning. "E-Excuse me," she murmured. Then she took off, literally running for the hallway leading past the kitchen to the powder room.

Stevie blinked. "Callie?" she called, but her friend was already gone. Stevie turned toward Scott. "What was that all about?"

Scott didn't answer. He just shook his head sadly as George reached them, huffing and puffing as if he'd just run the Kentucky Derby on foot.

"Hi!" George said breathlessly. "Wasn't Callie here a second ago?"

Scott nodded shortly. "She had to go."

"And so do I," Stevie put in, suddenly concerned. Something was going on with Callie—something more than an attempt to avoid an annoying crush. And Stevie intended to find out what it was. She glanced at Phil. "Back in a sec."

Without waiting for a response, she hurried off in the direction Callie had gone. Soon she was in the narrow hallway, which was relatively quiet compared to the noisy and crowded main room. Stevie approached the powder room door, which was closed.

"Callie?" She knocked gently. "It's Stevie. Are you in there?"

The door opened so abruptly that Stevie jumped back in surprise. Callie's tearstained face looked out at her. "Get in here!" she whispered with a sob.

Stevie obeyed. Seconds later the door was shut behind her. Callie locked it and then backed away, huddling against the sink. Her hands and shoulders were shaking uncontrollably, and her face was as pale as Stevie had ever seen it.

"Callie!" Stevie was more than concerned now; she was downright scared. What could possibly have happened to make her friend—usually so confident and together—break down like this? "What's the matter? You can tell me. . . . Obviously something's really gotten to you, and I want to help. Please, what is it?"

"Why don't you mind your own business, Stevie?" Callie snapped. "I wouldn't have let you in if I thought I'd be getting the third degree."

Stevie winced slightly. Despite her pathetic appearance, Callie's tone was nasty. But Stevie wasn't about to be scared off by a few insulting words. "This *is* my business," she told Callie. "You're my friend, and you're in trouble, or hurting, or something. That makes it my business. Now what's wrong?"

"It's stupid," Callie muttered, wiping her eyes with the back of her hand. "I'm an idiot."

Now they were getting somewhere. Stevie stepped over and took Callie's free hand. "No, you're not," she said firmly. "Whatever's going on, I really do want to help. Now spill it before I have to whup you upside the head."

That actually earned a wan smile. Callie took a deep breath. "All right, I'll tell you. But you have to promise not to think I'm a total loser, okay?"

"That's a promise I know I can make." Stevie crossed her heart.

Callie sighed loudly and reached for a tissue, dabbing at her face. "Okay, then," she said, her voice trembling. "I guess you might as well know the truth. Not that you'll believe it anyway—I barely believe it myself sometimes."

By now, Stevie couldn't even imagine what Callie was about to tell her. But she knew there was only one way to find out. She stepped across the small room and perched on the closed toilet seat, making herself as comfortable as possible. Then she gazed at Callie somberly. "I'm listening."

"Okay, then," Callie said again. She bit her lip. "It all started last week, when I decided to take

Scooby way out in the woods for a good training session. . . ."

Nearly fifteen minutes had passed since Carole and Cam had left the Regnerys' front porch. The night was clear and not too cold, and it had just been too tempting to stop a few times to look up at the countless stars twinkling overhead. There was no moon, and the warm yellow light pouring out onto the frostbitten grass made the darkness beyond seem deeper and more private than ever. Carole's fingers and toes were cold, but her face was warm from Cam's kisses.

"This is nice," Cam murmured as he brushed his lips over her chin.

Carole giggled. "I know," she said. "But don't you think we should try to get to the stable soon? My toes are starting to freeze."

"Uh-oh!" Cam's face registered mock concern. "I think we'd better do something about that."

He grabbed Carole, lifting her right off her feet. "Yikes!" she yipped in surprise, grabbing his neck for balance. "Are you crazy? You're going to give yourself a hernia or something!"

"I would carry you to the ends of the earth," Cam replied gallantly, kissing her on the tip of her nose. "Luckily, though, I won't have to. We're almost there."

Glancing over her shoulder, Carole realized that the stable's rear entrance was just a few yards away. "So we are," she said lightly as Cam stepped forward into the dim patch of light coming through the nearest window. "Does this mean we can head inside and warm up?"

"Sounds like a plan." Cam nuzzled her neck, then lowered her gently until she was back on her own two feet.

Soon they were inside. Carole had always loved the hushed, peaceful, private feeling she got from being in the stable at night. There were no screaming beginner riders, no radio playing in the office, no banging of metal pitchforks or gurgling of hoses. The only sounds were made by the horses—their breathing, chewing, and gentle snuffles and snorts. Being a witness to that was always special, but being there with Cam that night felt even more so.

"Isn't this amazing?" Carole's voice automatically lowered to a whisper as she breathed in the smell of hay and warm horseflesh. She glanced at the nearest stall, where one of the stable ponies was snoozing contentedly, and smiled.

Cam stepped up to her and rested his hands on her shoulders, looking down at her. "Uh-huh," he said. He glanced toward the entryway, where the overhead light was on, casting dim light and gentle shadows down the stable aisle where they were standing. "So is that like a night-light for the horses?"

"Not usually." Carole shrugged, her mind more on the horses surrounding her than on the light. "I guess someone must have forgotten to turn it off. Or maybe Max is planning to come down after the . . ." She let her voice trail off as she realized that Cam wasn't listening. Instead, he was staring intently into her eyes.

"Carole," he said in a low, husky voice, "you are so beautiful. You do know that, don't you?"

"Um." Carole wasn't sure how she was supposed to answer that.

Before she could figure it out, Cam pulled her toward him with such force that she gasped out loud. He kissed her, and for a long moment she forgot everything else.

A loud snort, accompanied by the dull thud of a hoof meeting a wooden wall, interrupted the moment. Carole blinked and pulled away. "What was that?" she wondered aloud, glancing down the aisle.

"Never mind," Cam murmured, caressing her cheek.

Carole stared toward the stall nearby where Geronimo, Pine Hollow's only stallion, was kept. Like all stallions, he could be fractious at times, and he'd been known to kick a few stall doors in his time. But Geronimo was gazing lazily in their direction, his ears relaxed as he surveyed the darkened aisle.

The thud came again, and this time Carole thought she could pinpoint its origin. "Oh," she said. "It's probably Firefly. She's that new filly we're training—well, actually, she's not that new anymore, but sort of. Anyway, she can be a little— What?" she interrupted herself as Cam sighed.

"Oh, nothing," he said, stroking her hair. "It's just that I was hoping this would be the best place to come for us to be alone, with no distractions." He smiled ruefully. "I guess I should have known better. There's no place more distracting for Carole Hanson than a stable."

Carole immediately felt a little guilty. Was Cam insulted? She supposed he might have some reason to be. How flattering could it be, after all? He'd been kissing her, and she'd been distracted by a horse kicking its stall. "I'm sorry," she said.

"Don't be." Cam smiled. "But listen, why don't we find someplace we can be more comfortable? You know, so we can really relax and talk."

"Okay." Carole thought that sounded like a great idea. Now that she thought about it, she and Cam really hadn't had a chance to do much real talking since his return. "How about the office? There are chairs in there."

Cam glanced up toward the ceiling. "Actually, I was thinking maybe we could try the hayloft," he said. "It would be cozy up there—you know, with that great hay smell and all."

"Oh." Carole was a little surprised at the suggestion. She loved Pine Hollow's spacious hayloft and had spent many happy hours up there gossiping with her friends and spying on the people and horses below. Still, it seemed like an unlikely choice at the moment. "Um, okay. Are you sure?"

"Absolutely." Cam took her hand gently in his own. "Come on, it'll be perfect."

Carole followed as he led the way toward the wooden ladder leading to the loft. He stepped back, allowing her to climb up first. She did so, feeling a little self-conscious—as far as she could remember, she'd never climbed into the loft while wearing a skirt. Or if she ever had, there certainly hadn't been a handsome guy right behind her.

But when she glanced down, Cam had his eyes averted. She breathed a sigh of relief, feeling slightly foolish. Cam wasn't some five-year-old boy on a playground somewhere, peeping up girls' skirts while they played on the jungle gym. He was a classy, mature guy who knew how to treat a girl and make her feel special.

Up in the loft, Carole glanced around. Only a little of the light from below seeped through the floorboards, and it was pretty dark. As she surveyed the bales stacked neatly all around her, she automatically found herself estimating the number and trying to decide how long they would last before it was time to reorder. Then, as Cam swung himself up off the top of the ladder, she snapped back to reality, feeling another twinge of guilt. She wasn't working—she was there with Cam. Why did she keep getting distracted? He never seemed to be distracted from her.

He certainly seemed to be totally focused on her at the moment. As she turned toward him, he stepped forward and took her in his arms. "Alone at last," he whispered as he bent to kiss her.

Then he led her toward a low section of hay bales, sinking down onto the nearest one and pulling her down beside him. Carole felt the scratchy hay prick her slightly through the thin fabric of her dress and pull at the nylon of her stockings, but she didn't pay much attention to that. She was much more concerned with what Cam was doing. He was leaning into her, pressing her back against a taller stack of bales behind them. His hands, which had started at her waist, were already sliding upward.

Uh-oh, Carole thought, doing her best to block his hands with her elbows. *I guess I was wrong. It doesn't seem like Cam really got the message this after-*

noon after all. Maybe he just thought I was embarrassed because his mother walked in on us.

This time, Carole knew there was no chance of Cam's mother walking in and interrupting. They were alone in the stable, late at night, with nobody around at all. If anyone was going to stop things from going too far, it was going to have to be her.

But do I really want to stop it? she wondered faintly as Cam nudged her elbow aside and continued to explore, still kissing her at the same time. *I mean, what am I so afraid of, anyway? Cam and I are in love. It's no big deal, not really.*

Somehow, though, she couldn't quite make herself believe that. It just didn't feel right—not so soon, not just like that, with no discussion or anything. And she knew that Cam would never want to make her do something she didn't want to do. She just had to explain things so that he would understand. "Stop," she gasped, shoving at him so hard that he let out a grunt of surprise. "Please, Cam. Wait. We have to talk."

"What's the matter?" Cam sat up straight and looked at her in alarm.

Carole sat up, too, doing her best to catch her breath and get her runaway heartbeat under control. "I—I don't think I was clear enough, um, earlier," she said, thinking of that afternoon. She was doing her best to be loving but firm so that Cam would understand what she was saying without feeling rejected. The last thing she wanted to do was hurt his feelings. "You know I, um, haven't really dated all that much. So I'd rather we just, you know, take things kind of slow. You know, physically."

"What's the matter?" Cam looked hurt. "I'm just trying to get close to you, Carole. Don't you like being close to me?"

"Of course!" Carole said immediately. "It's not that. You know I love being with you. It's just that I'm a little nervous about . . . you know."

"Don't worry," Cam crooned, leaning in to place a series of small kisses along her jawline. "There's no need to be nervous. Not when you're with me." His hands traced their way up her arms and across her collarbone.

Carole pushed him away. "No, you don't understand," she said. "I just can't do this right now. I'm really sorry."

Cam frowned. "I guess I didn't understand," he said. "I thought you were saying you love me."

"I do!" Carole protested. "I just—"

"I don't know, Carole," Cam interrupted. "If you loved me as much as I love you, you would want this as much as I do. I guess I was wrong about your feelings, that's all."

"No, you weren't," Carole protested, grabbing his hands and squeezing them. "I *do* love you."

Cam leaned toward her. "Really?" he said, loosening one hand from her grip and gently touching her cheek with his fingers. "Then I don't understand. I mean, it's natural for you to be a little nervous, since you don't have much experience. But I thought we were having fun."

"We were," Carole replied uncertainly, her cheek tingling slightly. "Um, I just don't think we should have *too* much fun right away, you know?"

Cam picked a piece of straw off her shoulder. "It's just that I hoped this could be sort of an extra holiday gift, you know, to each other." He stroked her arm gently, making her skin tingle all the more. "I mean, what better way for us to show each other how much we really care? Please let me show you, Carole. I promise you won't be sorry."

Carole bit her lip, feeling her resolve waver. When he put it like that, it really did make sense. She'd spent much of the past week trying to figure out a way to show Cam how much she cared about him, and this was one way she could do it—a way he'd appreciate a lot more than a few pictures in a frame.

"No," she said after a moment. "I'm sorry, Cam. I really want to make you happy, but I can't do something that makes me uncomfortable. It has nothing to do with how much I love you, it's just

that I don't feel right about it. I hope you understand."

Cam frowned. "I'm starting to think you're serious about this," he said slowly. "You're sure you
won't change your mind?"

"I'm sure," Carole said, relieved. Maybe now
they could go back to the party—dance, have a
good time with their friends, and forget all about
what had just happened.

But when she smiled tentatively at Cam, his
frown deepened. "I see," he said coldly. "I guess I
was wrong about you, Carole. I thought you cared
about me, like you said. I thought you were mature
enough for a serious relationship. But if you're going to act like a kid, maybe I shouldn't waste any
more of my time."

Carole gasped, hardly believing her ears.
"What?" she cried. "No, Cam! Please tell me you're
joking. I do love you! More than anything!"

His face softened immediately. "Really?" he said,
sliding closer and taking her in his arms again. "Oh,
Carole. I'm so happy to hear you say that. Do you
really mean it?"

"Of course I do," Carole replied with relief. She
relaxed into his arms as he began kissing her face.

Whew! That was close, she thought. *Cam really
freaked out there for a second. But I should have*

known we could work through it. I guess maybe his male ego was just a little hurt by—

She froze, suddenly realizing that Cam's hands were fumbling with the zipper at the back of her dress. "What are you doing?" she gasped.

"Hold still," he whispered. "Just a second. . . ."

Carole felt the zipper sliding down, first a few inches, then halfway down her back. She still seemed to be frozen in place, her body and mind unable to respond to what was happening. Only when she felt Cam's warm hands begin caressing her back did she snap out of it.

"Stop!" she cried, jumping away and grabbing at the back of her dress, trying to pull the zipper back up. "What do you think you're doing?"

Cam stared at her in surprise. "What do you think?" he asked. "I thought we'd covered this. I thought you said you loved me."

"I do!" Carole exclaimed again, feeling flustered as the zipper caught on her hair. "But that's what I was trying to say. I love you, but I'm not ready. I'm sorry, Cam."

Cam scowled. "Whatever. Then I suppose I *am* wasting my time." He stood up and brushed off his pants. "I thought we'd worked this out."

"So did I," Carole said, not really understanding why he looked so upset.

Cam crossed his arms over his chest. "You said

you loved me more than anything," he said coolly. "But you don't seem to be willing to prove it. That's answer enough for me. Good-bye, Carole."

Carole blinked, her jaw dropping as she tried to figure out what was going on. Who was this angry stranger standing in front of her? It wasn't the Cam she'd grown to love over the past few weeks, that was for sure. "B-But wait," she stammered. "I don't understand."

Cam didn't respond. He spun on his heel and stalked toward the ladder, disappearing down it without another word.

"Whew! I'll be right back," Stevie told Phil breathlessly, fanning her face with her hand. "I'm going to get some fresh air."

"Okay." Phil grinned, his face hot and flushed. "Want a soda? I'll grab you one."

"Thanks."

Stevie elbowed her way off the dance floor, humming along with the song playing on the stereo. She and Phil had been dancing nonstop for the past half hour, and she was beat. The room was still crowded with wedding guests, and it was getting a little warm and stuffy.

Making her way to the front door, Stevie glanced around the room. Callie and Scott had left a little while earlier, claiming family obligations—though

Stevie was pretty sure that George's presence had a lot more to do with it.

I wonder where everyone else is, though? Stevie thought as she opened the door and stepped through it into the chilly night air. She checked her watch. Only half an hour until midnight. *If they're not careful, they're all going to miss out on the big New Year's moment. Of course, I might forgive Alex and Lisa if they're tucked away in some private spot, making up. . . .*

She nearly jumped out of her skin as she stepped out onto the porch and realized she wasn't alone. "Eep!" she cried as a figure shifted on the porch swing. "Oops, sorry. I didn't realize anyone else was—Lisa?" She peered more closely at the figure. "Is that you?"

"It's me." Lisa's voice was soft and sounded slightly sheepish. "Sorry to scare you. That's what I get for sitting around in the dark, I guess."

Stevie walked over and sat down beside her friend. Lisa was huddled at one end of the swing, wrapped in her winter coat. "So?" Stevie said.

"So." Lisa sighed. "Alex and I broke up. For good this time."

Stevie winced. "Really?" she said carefully. "Um, I'm sorry. I really am."

"I know." Lisa smiled at her, though her expression in the dim light was melancholy. "I'm sorry, too. But it's for the best."

What does she mean by that? Stevie wondered. *It almost sounds as if she's just given up—on her relationship with Alex, and, just maybe, on her whole life here in Willow Creek.*

Still, she didn't quite dare to ask Lisa to explain. She hated the idea that Lisa seemed to be giving up without a fight. But when she thought back to her little chat with Mrs. Atwood, Stevie couldn't quite muster up her former optimism. Could this really be the beginning of the end?

Lisa turned to glance at the window. "Hey, check it out," she said, her voice suddenly returning almost to normal. "I think something's happening in there."

Looking inside, Stevie saw Deborah waving her hands for attention. Max was standing beside her, and Red and Denise were behind him, looking flushed and happy. "Looks like the happy couple might be getting ready to go," Stevie said. "Maybe they want to miss that post-midnight traffic on the way into town."

"Let's go in and help see them off," Lisa suggested, already climbing to her feet.

Suddenly realizing that she was freezing—she'd come outside without a coat, not planning to stay so long—Stevie shivered and nodded. "Right behind you."

Sure enough, as they entered the house, Red and Denise, hand in hand, were addressing the crowd of well-wishers, thanking them for coming. "And most of all," Red added, glancing over at his hosts, "we want to thank Max and Deborah. Their generosity made this whole magical night possible."

Stevie joined enthusiastically in the cheers, clapping and stomping her feet as the newlyweds made their way through the crowd, heading for the back door. As Stevie glanced around the room, looking for Phil, she noticed the front door opening again, admitting a slightly disheveled-looking Carole.

I guess she was down checking on the horses or something, Stevie thought, noticing a few pieces of hay in Carole's hair.

She squinted at her friend, suddenly concerned. Carole often had hay in her hair, but that wasn't really the point. When she'd left the party with Cam earlier, she had looked great—hair and makeup neat and pretty, clothes perfect, expression happy. Now she looked as though she'd spent the past half hour wrestling bales out of the hayloft. She also looked more than a little upset.

I wonder . . . Stevie thought worriedly. Before she could finish the thought, she noticed Ben standing nearby, his gaze trained in the same direction as hers had been. *Hmmm, I wonder when he turned up again?* Stevie thought, vaguely remembering his departure sometime earlier. *And why's he staring at Carole like that?*

She blinked curiously. Ben was watching Carole's entrance closely, an odd look on his face. His expression was usually so guarded that Stevie couldn't help studying it now—it was sort of sad, or maybe worried.

Wondering if Ben could possibly know something that she didn't, Stevie glanced back at Carole. Her friend was alone—that was strange in itself. Stevie was getting accustomed to seeing Cam practically glued to Carole's side most of the time.

Stevie was about to go over and see what was going on when Phil tapped her on the shoulder. "Care to dance?" he said with a gallant little bow. "In case you didn't notice, they're playing our song."

Stevie gasped, realizing he was right. Someone had just switched the CD player back on and a slow song was playing. It was an old song, the one that she and Phil had first slow-danced to way back in junior high, and it brought back a flood of memories, almost all of them wonderful. Sometimes it was easy for Stevie to take her relationship with Phil a little bit for granted—they had been together so long, knew each other so well. But at other times, it really came home to her just how lucky she was to have him. How lucky they both were to have found each other and managed to stay together, through ups and downs, good times and not-so-good ones. Managed to fall in love and stay there, while other couples crashed and burned all around them. For a second, as the music swelled, Stevie almost felt as though she might cry.

Instead, she smiled at her boyfriend. "I'd love to dance," she said, momentarily forgetting about Carole and Ben and Lisa and Alex. As Phil swept her into his arms and onto the makeshift dance floor, the two of them might as well have been the only people in the world.

Carole felt shaky and nauseous and very, very alone, even in the crowded room. In some ways she felt as if she were a completely different person than the one who'd left some hour and a half earlier. The one who'd left with Cam.

How could he do this to me? she wondered bleakly, her eyes staring sightlessly at the happy dancing couples just a few yards away. *Why didn't I see it coming?*

She had spent the last hour huddled in an empty stall, thinking about those questions and many more. Finally, when her fingers and toes had started to go numb, she'd reluctantly returned to the party. A glance at the parking lot was all it took to let her know that Cam had left, which meant she needed to find another ride home. Otherwise, it would have been tempting to just slink off into the dark Virginia night and never come back.

Cam certainly wouldn't miss me if I took off, she thought with a touch of bitterness. *He's a completely different person than the guy I knew years ago. I know that now. He never loved me—he was just using me all along. And I was the big fool who believed every stupid line he fed me.*

She felt tears welling up again. Not sure she could hold them back, she turned to head for the door again, figuring she'd try to regain her composure out in the peaceful darkness of the front porch.

But before she'd taken two steps, she spotted Ben coming toward her, dodging past several slow-dancing couples. She stopped short, startled to see him. She'd forgotten he was even at the party to begin with, and she found it hard to believe he had stuck around for so long.

Even more surprising than that, though, he was looking directly at her. For once his dark eyes didn't glance and then skitter off, as if trying to avoid all contact. He kept his gaze locked on hers, and while his expression was as stoic and unreadable as ever, she would have sworn she saw concern in those eyes.

To her further astonishment, he walked right up to her and stopped. "Uh, hi," he mumbled, his gaze finally faltering. Staring over her left shoulder, he shrugged. "So, um, do you want to dance?"

The last five words were muttered so quickly that for a second Carole wasn't sure she'd heard them right. "D-Dance?" she stuttered uncertainly.

Ben nodded. Then he held out his arm.

Carole just stared at it for a moment, perplexed. Then, realizing that he was waiting for her to respond, she gulped and nodded mutely, not knowing what else to do. She stepped forward and placed a hand tentatively on his shoulder, feeling his hand touch down lightly at her waist.

They danced. Ben's steps were slightly awkward and off the beat, but Carole didn't mind. She also didn't mind that he didn't say a word through the entire song.

And after a while, it seemed only natural for her to turn her head slightly, resting it on his shoulder. She still felt sad and weird and confused. But also, all of a sudden, she felt just a little bit less alone.

FIFTEEN

Lisa stroked the Appaloosa gelding on his smooth cheek. "Good boy, Chip," she murmured, feeling a little sad. Chip had always been one of Alex's favorite horses at Pine Hollow. It seemed strange that Lisa would probably never help Alex tack up the gelding again. She smiled wistfully, recalling how Alex had jumped the first time he'd tried to tighten Chip's girth by himself, not realizing that the gelding always nipped the air when he felt the strap tightening around him.

Alex thought Chip was trying to bite his arm off, Lisa thought. *It was so funny, I thought I'd never stop laughing. . . .*

She sighed, gave Chip one last pat, and moved on. This was no time to dwell on the past. She and Alex had talked it out—they had both agreed that this was the best thing to do. She had been a little surprised at first to discover that Alex was trying to work up the nerve to tell her the same thing she was trying to work up the nerve to tell him. But maybe she shouldn't have been. After all, they had always seemed to read each other's minds and agree on almost everything.

You'll always be special to me, he had told her, blinking back tears. *I mean it. I'll never forget what we had, Lisa.*

Me too, she had agreed, her voice sounding as though it came from somewhere very far away. *You were the first guy I ever really loved.*

Alex had bitten his lip then, perhaps taking note of the way she'd used the past tense. Then he had nodded. *Good luck, Lisa*, he'd said. *I hope you'll always be happy. And I hope we'll still be able to be friends.*

She had nodded, not trusting herself to speak. Somehow she doubted the two of them would be spending much time hanging out together as friends, though she supposed that as long as he was Stevie's brother and she was Stevie's best friend, they would see each other regularly. It wouldn't be the same, though. It could never be the same as it was—not with Alex, and not with any other guy. That made her as sad as anything, that feeling. It was sort of like the feeling she got when she reached the last page of a really, really great book. The knowledge that it was over and that she could never recapture the feeling. Even if she read the book a second time, it wouldn't be the same.

Lisa blinked and took in a deep breath, letting it out in a whoosh as she did her best to shake off the memories of the previous night. After all, she had as much reason to be happy as she did to be sad, and she preferred to focus on the happy part for a while. Smiling as she imagined what her friends would say when she told them her latest bit of news, she started down the stable aisle.

She found Stevie in Belle's stall, picking out the mare's feet. "Hey," Lisa greeted her, leaning on the half door. "Going for a ride?"

Stevie glanced up and smiled. "Hey yourself," she replied. "Happy New Year. And nope, I'm too beat to even think about anything as strenuous as hoisting a saddle."

"Really?" Lisa cocked her head to one side. "But what about our tradition?" For as long as they'd been riding at Pine Hollow, she and Stevie and Carole had done their best to go on a trail ride together every New Year's Day.

Stevie brightened. "Oh! I almost forgot about that," she said. "With all the excitement and everything this year . . ." She shrugged. "Speaking of which, I forgot to ask you last night. What did you think of the wedding?"

"It was great." Lisa smiled, remembering how

happy Red and Denise had looked as they'd promised to spend their lives together. "Very romantic. I'm glad Max and Deborah insisted on throwing it for them instead of letting them go down to the town hall or whatever."

"Me too." Stevie sighed happily.

Lisa glanced at Belle, who was standing quietly at Stevie's shoulder. "So how about that trail ride?" she prompted. "Is Carole here?"

"Nope, haven't seen her." Stevie checked her watch. "Maybe she's off somewhere making up with Cam."

"I hope so." Lisa had been too distracted to pay much attention to Carole and Cam the previous evening. But she had seen Carole leaving with Maureen instead of Cam, and then Phil had mentioned that he'd heard they'd had a fight. "What happened between the two of them, anyway?"

Stevie lifted one shoulder slightly. "I'm not sure." She tossed her hoof pick lightly from one hand to the other. "I only talked to Carole briefly—she just said it was over and she didn't want to talk about it. But you know how that goes. When you have your first fight, you always think it's over. But I'd bet my dressage saddle that they're together again by the end of today."

Lisa nodded, figuring she was right. Carole and Cam would work things out. In the meantime, she had bigger and better things on her mind. "By the way," she said, carefully keeping her voice casual. "I had an interesting talk with Mom this morning."

"Oh?" Stevie said cautiously.

This time Lisa couldn't hold back her grin. "Uh-huh," she said. "She told me she changed her mind. We're not going to move!"

"*Yee-hah!*" Stevie shrieked so loudly that Belle tossed her head and stepped back, startled. Stevie opened the stall door and leaped out into the aisle, practically bowling Lisa over with her hug. "You're staying! That's great! I guess your mom was listening to me after all."

"Thanks," Lisa replied breathlessly, laughing at her friend's enthusiasm. "I'm pretty happy about it myself." She blinked, suddenly realizing what Stevie had said. "Wait. What do you mean, my mom listened to you? When did you talk to her?"

Stevie released her, grinning sheepishly. "Well . . ."

"Spill it," Lisa demanded suspiciously. "What have you been up to?"

Stevie shrugged. "Okay, you know me," she said. "I couldn't just sit back and do nothing while your mom dragged you halfway up the East Coast. Um, so I was thinking about some of those plans we were talking about a while back—you know, like paying my little brother to take your place or whatever."

"Yes?" Lisa chuckled, remembering that conversation. She had been so upset then, but looking back, it really had been kind of funny. Then she frowned slightly, realizing what Stevie was saying. "Wait a minute. Don't tell me you actually tried any of those ridiculous plans?"

"No, no," Stevie said hastily, stroking Belle as the mare cautiously returned to the front of the stall. Pushing Belle back a step or two, Stevie swung the door shut to keep her from wandering out into the aisle. "Like I said, I was sort of thinking about it. But Phil talked me out of trying anything crazy like that."

"Thank goodness."

"He also said something that started me thinking," Stevie went on. "He said I had to start acting mature, or something like that. Which is kind of ironic if you think about it, since he actually seems to think that World Wide Wrestling is, like, actual entertainment for grown-ups, not to mention how he still eats that cereal with the bunny on the box—"

"Focus," Lisa broke in. "I'm still waiting to hear how you ended up chatting with Mom."

"Oh, yeah." Stevie smiled apologetically. "I was just getting to that. See, I started thinking about how maybe being mature and logical and everything might just work. I mean, it's probably what you would have done in my place."

"What would I have done?" Lisa was feeling confused.

Stevie patted Belle on the nose. "I went and talked to your mom," she said. "You mentioned she'd be coming home from her trip on Monday, so as soon as you turned up here at the stable, I figured that was my chance. I hightailed it to your house so that your mom and I would have some quality time alone."

"Really?" Lisa thought back, remembering how upset she'd been when Stevie had blown her off that day. She was surprised and touched to learn the real reason she'd done it. "Wow. I had no idea. What did you say to her?"

"Oh, I just presented the facts," Stevie replied. "Like the fact that none of us here in Willow Creek could possibly live without you."

Lisa smiled and reached out to hug her friend again. "Thanks," she said. "It means a lot to me—that you cared enough to do that. I hate to tell you, though, but I'm afraid that isn't what did the trick."

"That's okay. I don't care what did it as long as you're really staying." Stevie hugged her back, then turned to push away Belle, who was nosing at her jacket pocket. "No more carrots for you, you big pig," she told the horse firmly. Then she returned her attention to Lisa. "Just out of curiosity, though . . ."

"It was her trip to New Jersey." Lisa sighed, remembering her mother's grim face as she'd related the details of her trip. "It seems it didn't go quite as well as she'd hoped. I guess she'd been picturing it as some kind of perfect place, where she would get to hang out with her sister all the time and be happy. Sort of like when she went up there this past summer. She had a ball during that visit, but this one was totally different." Lisa grimaced, feeling bad about her mother's disillusionment, though there really wasn't much she could do to help. "When she got there this time, it was snowing a little. Apparently she thought that was great at first. But after two solid days of flurries, making the roads slippery and the sidewalks slushy, it got kind of old."

Stevie nodded. "I don't know how those people up north do it," she agreed. "A little snow once in a while is nice, but it does get old fast. Especially when you're dying to go on a trail ride and you can't do more than walk because the footing sucks."

"I know," Lisa said. "And Mom's not the type to pull on snow boots and make the best of it, you know? But also, when she thought about living there, I think she realized that she would be leaving our nice, quiet, tree-lined neighborhood, with our big yard and everything, and moving to someplace where you're lucky if you have space for a decent-sized shrub." Lisa pulled up a mental picture of her aunt's home. "I expect she also noticed how noisy and crowded it is around there, with all the traffic and long lines at the stores." She shuddered, realizing how close she had come to having to deal with all that herself. "But the biggest thing—at least this is what she says now—was the real estate prices. When she started looking around, she found out that there was no way we could afford anything even close to being as nice as our house here."

"Really?" Stevie stroked Belle's nose. "Expensive, huh?"

"Brutal," Lisa said. "Mom didn't go into a whole lot of detail this morning, but from what she did say, it sounded like we probably couldn't afford to buy a house at all, or even rent anyplace decent. So the only other options would be to rent a small apartment, which Mom couldn't stand." She winced, thinking how true that was. Her mother was very appearance-conscious, and living in a three-room apartment would probably kill her. "Or else we would have to move in with Aunt Marianne and Uncle William for a while until she saved up enough money for a down payment."

"Yikes," Stevie said succinctly.

"That's what I said. For a second, I actually thought she was telling me that was what we were going to do." Lisa shuddered at the thought. "Luckily, Mom seemed to find the idea just as horrifying as I did, which makes me think maybe she and Aunt Marianne got on each other's nerves a bit during this visit."

"So just like that, the big moving plan is scrapped?" Stevie asked. "You're definitely staying?"

"It looks that way." Lisa smiled, still hardly daring to believe it. "What a relief."

"I'll say," Stevie agreed. "This is fantastic news, and you know what we do when we get fantastic news."

"What?"

Stevie grinned and slapped Belle on the neck. "We go for a trail ride!"

Lisa smiled. "I thought you were too tired to hoist a saddle," she teased.

"Forget it. I just got my second wind," Stevie declared, already turning down the aisle. "Now come on, let's hit the tack room."

"What about Carole?"

Stevie stopped short. "Oh, yeah," she said. "I can't believe she's not here by now. After all, this is supposed to be the first day of the end of her grounding."

Once Lisa had sorted out that sentence, she nodded. "That's right. Besides, I was hoping to give her my big news in person. You're the first one I've told." She smiled as she imagined sharing the news with Carole, and then with her other friends, like

Callie and Scott. Banishing the image of Scott's possible reactions, she turned to Stevie. "For all we know, though, she may be spending the whole day with Cam. Maybe we should just head out. We can leave a note in the office in case she gets here and wants to ride out and find us."

"Sounds like a plan," Stevie agreed immediately. "Let's go!"

"Oh! There you are, sweetie," Colonel Hanson said breathlessly, rushing into the kitchen while tying his necktie. "Did you just get up?"

"Uh-huh," Carole said listlessly, though she had actually been awake for more than three hours. She just didn't feel like going into detail at the moment. "Where are you going?"

Her father glanced at her briefly, though his expression was distracted. "I have that charity auction today, remember? I'll probably be late, so you're on your own for lunch and dinner." He smiled. "But that shouldn't be so bad, right? Especially since your punishment officially ended at midnight." He grinned. "Congratulations, honey. You survived. And you're off the hook."

"Really?" Carole did her best to feign the happiness and anticipation that she should have felt at that announcement. "I can go back to riding full-time? And back to my job?"

"Yes," her father replied. He held up one finger. "I do still expect you to keep your grades up, though. And when you go back to work, not quite so many hours, okay? Otherwise we'll be right back where we started."

"Don't worry, Dad," Carole said. "I've learned my lesson."

He smiled again and rushed off toward the hallway, and she slumped back in her seat, poking distractedly at her barely touched English muffin. She had learned her lesson, all right, but not only the one her father knew about.

I still can't believe it wasn't just some horrible nightmare, she thought, her throat constricting as she thought of Cam. *But I know it couldn't have been. You don't have nightmares if you can't fall asleep.*

She grimaced, remembering the way she'd tossed and turned all night, trying to come to terms with what had happened. Somewhere around four-thirty in the morning, she had finally been forced to face the awful truth once and for all. She had been a fool, a stupid, naive fool. The Cam she thought she knew—the kind, caring guy who sincerely loved her and wanted her to be happy—had been an illusion, created out of her own hopes and dreams and insecurities and fueled by her memories of their younger days together. But a kind, caring, loving guy wouldn't do what Cam had done to her. There were no two ways about that.

I must be the world's biggest loser to have fallen for his lines, Carole thought morosely, pushing her plate away. *And I fell for them, all right, hook, line, and sinker.*

She blinked back the tears that were threatening to spill over. Now that she knew what a cad Cam was, why did it still hurt so much to think about him? How could she still, even now, care about him?

I guess I really am the world's biggest loser, she thought, resting her elbows on the table. *It's no wonder guys aren't lining up for me.*

At that, the image of another guy popped into her head. Ben. What had that been about? She had just about fallen over in surprise when he'd asked her to dance.

That was so weird, she thought, feeling her cheeks grow warm. For a few minutes there, she had almost forgotten about Cam as she'd relaxed in Ben's arms. *It was like he knew, somehow, what had happened with Cam and wanted to, like, comfort me or something. Help me through it. Be a true friend.*

It had been a nice feeling. Neither of them had said much when the song had ended and they had parted ways, but Ben had smiled at her tentatively and muttered something about seeing her soon. It really was as if they'd connected somehow, in a different way than ever before. Become closer. Would he acknowledge it when she saw him next? Or would it be just like that kiss all over again, where he pretended it never happened?

Oh, well, she thought, pulling her plate toward her again. Picking up her muffin, she took a small bite. *I guess I'll just have to wait and find out.*

Callie lay on her bed, flipping idly through a magazine, though she hardly saw the glossy images in front of her. *I know I should feel better today,* she thought with a frown. *After all, I saw George last night, he spoke to me, and nothing horrible happened.*

She winced as she remembered fleeing to the bathroom. Okay, so that hadn't exactly been a high point in her life. But it wasn't as if George had followed her there and broken down the door with an ax.

I've just got to get a grip on myself, she told herself firmly, resting her chin on her hand as she stared into space. She had been busy that day—her father had dragged the whole family to a boring political New Year's Day reception, as usual—and she hadn't had much time to think about George at all. That had been somewhat of a relief, though she hadn't been able to completely stop the vision of his face from popping into her mind at odd moments, whether she was shaking hands with a senator or smiling politely at a wealthy campaign contributor. *This is all in my head,* she reminded herself. *I'm the only one who can fix it. Starting now.*

Her stomach flipped nervously as she remembered the resolution she'd made at midnight as she and Scott had toasted each other with grape juice in the living room. She still felt a little guilty about making him leave the wedding reception/New Year's Eve bash early—he had obviously been having a good time, even while he was worrying about Lisa and Alex. That was just the way Scott was. He loved a party.

But I'm going to follow through on my resolution, she thought, pushing aside her guilt about Scott. He would get over it. *I'm not going to let George—or my own fears—keep me away from Pine Hollow. I'm going back into training, starting first thing tomorrow, and that's all there is to it.*

Despite her determination to do just that, she felt as though she might cry. And she didn't want to do that. She didn't want to allow George to have that kind of an effect on her. To distract herself, she tossed her magazine aside and headed for the door, planning to fix herself a bedtime snack.

Downstairs, she flipped on the kitchen light and then dug through the refrigerator until she located a strawberry yogurt and some grapes. Thanks to her mother's latest diet, there wasn't much else in there aside from assorted condiments and two gallon jugs of springwater.

"Oh well," she muttered, collecting a spoon and a glass of water and setting the whole collection on a tray. "This will have to do."

Popping a grape into her mouth, she picked up the tray and headed for the living room. Maybe the TV could distract her for a while.

She was picking her way carefully across the darkened living room—her parents had gone out for the evening, and Scott was upstairs, so the downstairs lights were off—when a sudden movement caught her eye. Glancing over at the large picture window, she saw a round, pale face pressed against the glass.

Callie screamed. Her hands went numb, and the tray slipped out of her grasp, landing on the floor with a crash. The face disappeared so quickly it was as if it had never been there.

"What?" Scott raced into the room, a startled expression on his face. "Callie, what's wrong? Did you scream?"

Callie covered her mouth with her hand, her eyes still fixed on the spot where she'd seen the face. Unable to speak, she pointed.

Scott glanced at the window. He had obviously relaxed a little as soon as he'd seen that she was still in one piece, but he looked worried. "What is it?" he asked. "Did you see something?"

Callie nodded. Finally finding her voice, she said, "Out there. Someone—Someone looking in."

"You mean like a Peeping Tom?" Scott frowned and took a step toward the window, glancing out at the dark yard. "Could you tell who it was?"

Callie hesitated. She had recognized the face. Absolutely, without a doubt. But she couldn't bring herself to say the name. "Um, no," she lied. "It was—It was so quick, I—"

"Okay." Scott didn't let her finish. He was already heading for the door, pausing just long enough to grab his jacket and a flashlight out of the front hall closet. "Sit tight. I'll take a look." He shot her a comforting glance as she followed him toward the door. "Don't worry, it was probably just a kid goofing around or something."

"Probably," Callie said, pretending to agree. As Scott strode out of the house, she had to return to the living room and sit down. Carefully averting her eyes from the window, she did her best to keep her mind blank, not think too much about what she had just seen. But she couldn't stop shaking.

First the stable, she thought. *Then school. Now my own home. Isn't there anyplace I can feel safe anymore?*

ABOUT THE AUTHOR

BONNIE BRYANT is the author of more than a hundred books about horses, including the Pine Hollow series, The Saddle Club series, The Saddle Club Super Editions, and the Pony Tails series. She has also written novels and movie novelizations under her married name, B. B. Hiller.

Ms. Bryant began writing The Saddle Club in 1986. Although she had done some riding before that, she intensified her studies then and found herself learning right along with her characters Stevie, Carole, and Lisa. She claims that they are all much better riders than she is.

Ms. Bryant was born and raised in New York City. She still lives there, in Greenwich Village, with her two sons.

More *Romantic Times* Praise For Connie Mason!

THE LAIRD OF STONEHAVEN
"[Ms. Mason] crafts with excellence and creativity . . . [and] the added attraction of mystery and magic."

LIONHEART
". . . Upholds the author's reputation for creating memorable stories and remarkable characters."

THE DRAGON LORD
"This is a real keeper, filled with historical fact, sizzling love scenes and wonderful characters."

THE BLACK KNIGHT
"Ms. Mason has written a rich medieval romance filled with tournaments, chivalry, lust and love."

THE OUTLAWS: SAM
"Ms. Mason always provides the reader with a hot romance, filled with plot twists and wonderful characters. She's a marvelous storyteller."

THE OUTLAWS: RAFE
"Ms. Mason begins this new trilogy with wonderful characters . . . steamy romance . . . excellent dialogue . . . [and an] exciting plot!"

GUNSLINGER
"Ms. Mason has created memorable characters and a plot that made this reader rush to turn the pages. . . . *Gunslinger* is an enduring story."

BEYOND THE HORIZON
"Connie Mason at her best! She draws readers into this fast-paced, tender and emotional historical romance that proves love really does conquer all!"

BRAVE LAND, BRAVE LOVE
"An utter delight from first page to last—funny, tender, adventurous, and highly romantic!"

To my readers who have deluged me with fan mail.
To newspaper editors Don Holmes and Ann Dupee
for putting me in their pages.
To Clermont Pulix Manager for always making room
for several cases of my books.
To all my family and friends for their support.

Other books by Connie Mason:

A TOUCH SO WICKED

VIKING WARRIOR

THE PRICE OF
  PLEASURE

HIGHLAND WARRIOR

A TASTE OF PARADISE

A KNIGHT'S HONOR

GYPSY LOVER

THE PIRATE PRINCE

THE LAST ROGUE

THE LAIRD OF
  STONEHAVEN

TO LOVE A STRANGER

SEDUCED BY A ROGUE

TO TAME A RENEGADE

LIONHEART

A LOVE TO CHERISH

THE ROGUE AND THE
  HELLION

THE DRAGON LORD

THE OUTLAWS: SAM

THE OUTLAWS: JESS

THE OUTLAWS: RAFE

THE BLACK KNIGHT

GUNSLINGER

BEYOND THE HORIZON

PIRATE

BRAVE LAND, BRAVE
  LOVE

WILD LAND, WILD LOVE

BOLD LAND, BOLD LOVE

VIKING!

SURRENDER TO THE
  FURY

FOR HONOR'S SAKE

LORD OF THE NIGHT

PROMISE ME FOREVER

SHEIK

ICE & RAPTURE

LOVE ME WITH FURY

SHADOW WALKER

FLAME

TENDER FURY

DESERT ECSTASY

A PROMISE OF
  THUNDER

PURE TEMPTATION

WIND RIDER

TEARS LIKE RAIN

THE LION'S BRIDE

SIERRA

TREASURES OF THE
  HEART

CARESS & CONQUER

PROMISED SPLENDOR

WILD IS MY HEART

MY LADY VIXEN

Connie Mason

Tempt
the
Devil

LEISURE BOOKS NEW YORK CITY

A LEISURE BOOK®

September 2009

Published by

Dorchester Publishing Co., Inc.
200 Madison Avenue
New York, NY 10016

ISBN 10: 0-8439-6316-6
ISBN 13: 978-0-8439-6316-8
E-ISBN: 978-1-4285-0728-9

Visit us online at www.dorchesterpub.com.

Tempt the Devil

Chapter One

London 1715

It was a terrible day to die—was there ever a good one? Swirling mist and dense fog blocked out the sun. Defiant and proud, he stood on the hastily erected scaffold, his lip curled in a sardonic smile as his silver gaze swept over the jostling crowd making merry at his expense. A heavy black beard concealed the deep dimple in his left cheek. If it hadn't, his dark, demonic features would have been transformed instantly. His roguish good looks were enough to bring many a young maid swooning at his feet.

He stood tall and imposing, almost regal, a noose around his neck, hands tied behind his back, prepared to pay the devil his due. There'd be no more bargaining—nay, he'd traded his soul long ago. Yet lust for life spurted hot and fierce through his veins. Was this how it would all end? He supposed it must, given the life he had led. There was little he regretted, though in his estimation his evil reputation far surpassed his deeds. Still—it was a terrible day to die. . . .

The coach moved cautiously through the throngs of people lining the waterfront on Tilbury Point. Few paid heed to the crest emblazoned on the door or the liveried footman trying to clear a path for the lumbering vehicle. The grand spectacle soon to take place drew people from all walks of life, and amidst the teeming mobs dukes rubbed elbows with bakers and earls with beggars, with nary a complaint. It was a pickpocket's paradise, more lucrative than a country fair or market day.

Inside the coach the rotund Lord Harvey Chatham, Earl of Milford, stuck his head out the window for a better view as his coach neared the waterfront. All around him ragged peasants jostled for position with well-dressed shopkeepers, lawyers, and doctors. Ladies waved scarves as their serving maids scurried to keep up with their mistresses.

Drummers had been ordered out for the occasion, and were pounding out a staccato rhythm. Behind them a line of dragoons held the masses of humanity in some semblance of order. More dragoons carrying muskets stood at attention. Suddenly flutists joined the drummers and their music trilled through the fog-shrouded air. Though it was nearly noon, the weather was dismal for mid-July. A chill mist dampened the air but not the spirits of the crowd. Shouts, catcalls, and raucous singing emerged from the mob as well as from windows above the street level packed with spectators. The noise was deafening, the spectacle as colorful as a circus, the hoopla splendid for such an awesome occasion. At exactly high noon the Thames was between ebb and flow tide.

"Damn me, we're almost too late," muttered the earl, a frown drawing his pleasant features into a scowl. "'Tis the crowds, m'dear, damn annoying. Not even this foul weather has dampened spirits on this auspicious occasion. You'd think the man was a hero instead of a notorious pirate."

"I wish you hadn't made me come along, Father. It's . . . it's so . . . bizarre."

"You're not turning squeamish on me, are you, Devon? You look so bloody pale all of a sudden." Concern colored the earl's words as he searched his daughter's lovely features. "'Twas Winston who suggested I bring you today. Thought you might enjoy it."

Devon fixed her father with an austere look. "Enjoy seeing a man hanged? Really, Father, both you and Winnie know me better than that. I think the custom barbaric."

"You should hate the man as much as I do, m'dear," Lord

Chatham opined. "Diablo has cost me hundreds of pounds in lost cargo. I've invested heavily in shipping only to have most of my vessels plundered by Diablo and his kind. Winston's father lost nearly his whole fortune." This wasn't entirely the truth, for Winston's father, the Duke of Grenville, was a notorious gambler who had squandered most of his inheritance, but Lord Chatham did not burden Devon with that knowledge for the man was on his deathbed.

"Diablo," Devon mused. "I wonder if the man is Spanish. The good Lord knows the Spanish have caused us enough grief in recent years."

"Pirates owe allegiance to no one but themselves, m'dear."

Devon remained thoughtful, regarding the jabbering crowd through the coach window. Suddenly the coach ground to a halt, and against her will Devon's wide blue eyes were jerked toward Tilbury Point and the scaffold standing stark and forbidding against the leaden sky.

"We can go no further, Your Grace," the driver called down to the earl. "The road ahead is all but impassable."

"Drat!" Lord Chatham said, exasperated. "Well, no help for it, m'dear, we'll have to go the rest of the way on foot. I mean to see the devil breathe his last."

"I'm not moving, Father," Devon demurred. "I've no stomach for such goings on. If I hadn't agreed to meet Winnie here I'd have stayed home."

"And miss the excitement?" Lord Chatham asked, piqued by his daughter's lack of enthusiasm. "Your fiancé is to accompany us to Lady Mary's musicale after the hanging. Do you see Winston anywhere?"

"In this crowd?" Devon scoffed, shaking her splendid mass of golden curls. Piled elegantly atop her well-shaped head, Devon's hair was the color of ripened wheat. Combed out, it reached below her waist in a riot of rippling waves and spirals.

"Well then, I'm off, m'dear," the earl said, waving gaily as he stepped down from the coach. "Peters and Hadley will remain here to see that no harm comes to you. A festive occasion like this deserves a proper viewing."

Devon watched as her father's stocky figure was swallowed up by the mass of humanity crowding Tilbury Point. The only child of Lord Chatham, Earl of Milford, nineteen-year-old Lady Devon was considered the catch of the season. Tall and slender, her body was curving and regal. Her waist was slim, her hips tapered into impossibly long legs. Numerous men courted her, as much for her seductive beauty and grace as for her generous dowry. But for some reason Devon had chosen to accept the proposal of Viscount Winston Linley, the son of the Duke of Grenville. His pretty speeches and outward devotion as well as his blond good looks had won her hand, and they were to be married in six months, after Winston's resignation from the navy.

Following in his father's footsteps—he had been a naval officer before the dukedom fell to him with the disappearance of the young heir to the title—Winston had purchased a commission in the Royal Navy and had recently taken command of the *Larkspur*. Devon cared little that Winston's father had squandered the family fortune—she had enough money for both of them. Though she felt no great stirrings over Winston, Devon knew that he was a man who would not try to control her. Accustomed to being her own woman, she could not tolerate the thought of a marriage bogged down by restrictions and rules demanded by most men of this day and age. Winston had been a compromise, for he presented no threat to her independence and his devotion could not be faulted.

A loud cheer forced Devon's attention to the scaffold where Diablo stood, flanked by two burly guards. Did they expect him to escape with his hands tied behind his back and a rope around his neck, she thought disgustedly. She could see him clearly as she leaned out the window, succumbing to some perverse need to view the devil known only as Diablo.

Diablo faced death with a steadfast courage that Devon couldn't help but admire. A slow smile curved his lips with ironic humor despite the jeering crowd waiting for his untimely end.

A riptide of emotion surged through Devon as she peered up at the black-bearded pirate. The sea breeze tousled his raven hair, blowing errant strands across his forehead. The deep tan of his face sharply opposed the gaping, dirty white shirt that strained across his massive chest. The tight breeches hugging his narrow hips and muscled thighs took her thoughts in a wantonly sensual direction, and a guilty tinge crept up her neck. Reluctantly moving her wide blue eyes back to his dark, brooding face, Devon could not tell the color of his eyes from where she sat but noted the touches of humor hovering around his generous mouth. She was amazed at his ability to find amusement in his desperate situation. But then, what could one expect from a man who found joy in killing, raping, and robbing?

Diablo fixed his smoldering silver gaze on no one in particular, roving over the hundreds of revelers gathered for his hanging like vultures waiting to pick his bones. He squared his broad shoulders and smiled, determined to meet his fate with the same raw courage with which he had conducted his life. Diablo was aware of the stir he created among the women in the crowd, and with the arrogance of one fully cognizant of his virile male appeal, winked roguishly at a comely maid standing nearby. Her delighted squeal gave him little joy.

Then he directed his gaze farther afield to the line of vehicles clogging the street, finally settling on one coach where a ravishing blonde leaned out the window. If he had to die, he reflected, he'd find nothing more pleasing to take to his grave than the image of the enticing blonde. She was sheer perfection, from the golden ringlets curled on her forehead to the tempting fullness of her red lips.

Over the heads of the rowdy, exuberant crowd, their eyes met, clung, and Devon felt the world fade away around her. Instinctively she knew Diablo's eyes would be a clear, piercing gray. She no longer saw the hordes of people, nothing stood between her and Diablo. He was stunningly virile, with a power that coiled within him, exuding total masculinity. He was dark, dangerous, and devastatingly handsome—beard and all. And unscrupulous, barbarous, and obviously without remorse for his heinous deeds. The devil was well named.

It was all Devon could do to drag her eyes from the commanding figure sentenced to die a horrendous death. After he was dead, his body was to be hanged a second time on a gibbet placed in the Thames for all entering and leaving London Harbor to see. His head would be encased in a metal harness and his body strapped in a cage to hold the bones together once the flesh began to decay. Turning away, Devon tried not to feel pity, but her tender heart defeated her.

Sighing regretfully, Diablo watched the beautiful woman in the coach turn aside, fully aware that his rather colorful life was about to be snuffed out at the age of twenty-eight. There were still so many things left to experience, he reflected sadly. He had never known true love, or the joy of seeing a child of his loins brought into the world. And he had not righted a grave injustice done to him when he was a child, one that had irrevocably changed his life.

Diablo watched warily as the hangman approached bearing the black hood. He shook his head, refusing to face death as a coward. He much preferred dying with his dignity intact. He had already faced hell and conquered it, so dying held no fear for him. The hangman shrugged and looked to the dragoon captain for the order to pull the lever controlling the trapdoor. Diablo tensed, bracing himself for the endless drop into eternity. Then, amazingly, he opened his mouth and his rich, ribald laughter rolled over the crowd, the sound a derisive mockery of death.

His laughter sent a shudder through Devon's slender frame. The man was mad. Did he respect nothing? If imminent death didn't frighten him, obviously nothing did. Vaguely she wondered what it would take to bring a man like Diablo to his knees, then promptly dismissed the thought. A man with no scruples, one who laughed in the face of death, would bend before neither man nor God.

The drums struck a sharp tattoo and the fifes began a mournful wail. At the same moment Devon's attention was diverted by a disturbance in the crowd. Women screamed, men swore, many joining in the melee. Within minutes people everywhere were either engaged in combat or scrambling to get out of the way. To Devon it looked as if the solid sea of humanity was in motion, the noise deafening and frightening. She thought of her father somewhere in the midst of all this madness, and fear seized her. Her first inclination was to find him herself, but she soon realized the folly of her thinking. Her meager strength would be of little help in the crush of bodies. Leaning out the window, she called to the coachman and footman, bringing them swiftly to her side.

"Perhaps we should leave, my lady," Peters advised, alarmed at the turn of events.

"Not without Father," Devon protested, shaking her head vigorously. "I'm safe enough here. Take Hadley and find Father. Hurry, please."

Reluctant to leave but realizing that their employer could be injured by the ugly mob, the two men did as they were bid, soon losing themselves in the crowd. Devon watched apprehensively as the dragoons left their posts and plunged into the midst of the fighting in a vain attempt to maintain order. Devon wondered what had happened to change the course of events from a celebration to an all-out riot. Unbidden, her eyes flew to the scaffold where fate had seen fit to grant Diablo a temporary reprieve.

A gasp left Devon's throat and she blinked in disbelief. Was she the only one out of hundreds who saw what was taking place? A giant of a man, wielding a wicked-looking cutlass, leaped to the deck of the scaffold in one lithe motion. Dressed in wide pantaloons and a vest that bared his massive chest, he dealt handily with the guards flanking Diablo. He moved so swiftly that Devon barely saw the downward slash of the cutlass as it severed the ropes binding Diablo and removed the noose encircling his neck. Devon watched in stunned disbelief as the two men dropped down into the midst of the mob and were soon lost in the teeming masses.

Devon waited with bated breath for the cry of discovery, troubled by the jolt of elation surging through her. Though the devil inspired fear in her, she could not help but admire his courage and daring.

Then suddenly Diablo appeared at the edge of the crowd, somehow arriving unscathed and undetected, his huge rescuer protecting his back. Almost at the same time four disreputable-looking ruffians appeared from different directions, all gravitating toward Diablo. And horror of all horrors, they were headed directly for her coach!

Just as Devon gathered her wits and prepared to flee, Diablo flung open the door and leaped inside, landing squarely atop Devon's slim form. The air left her lungs in a loud whoosh, and a terrible fear assailed her. She struggled in vain against the weight pressing her into the squabs, but just then the coach took off with a jerk and she felt the almost sensual massage of Diablo's hard body grating against her own softness.

Devon raised her eyes to find him watching her. His silver eyes—she knew they'd be silver—gleamed with appreciation and amusement as he gave her an audacious wink.

"Well met, my lady." His voice was velvet-edged and rich with an underlying warmth that Devon found oddly disconcerting. "How fortunate I am to find refuge in the bosom of a beautiful woman." Slowly and seductively his gaze slid over her face to rest on the swell of her heaving breasts.

Devon gasped in dismay, angered at the suggestive tone of Diablo's voice and puzzled by the ripple of excitement he created in her. "Get off me you . . . you devil!" she blasted, pounding ineffectually on his broad chest. "And stop this coach immediately. My father will have your head for this. He's the Earl of Milford!"

"I saw the crest on the door from my—er—lofty perch," Diablo returned lazily. "That's the reason I chose this coach. That and the stunning lady I saw leaning out the window." The teasing laughter was back in his eyes and a seductive huskiness lingered on his voice.

"You won't get away with this," Devon hissed, hating the way this pirate had captured her senses.

"I already have," Diablo chuckled, the sound a low rumble in his chest. "And you, my lady, will see that I escape with my hide intact."

"I'll do no such thing!" Devon disagreed strongly.

A hue and cry went up behind them, and Devon realized that Diablo's daring escape had finally been discovered. Diablo also heard and reluctantly levered himself off Devon to peer out the window.

"Bloody bastards," he muttered as a company of mounted dragoons thundered after the purloined coach.

Devon swiveled to lean out the other window and was heartened to see that both her father and Winston had somehow found mounts and were riding with the dragoons. She turned to Diablo, gloating. "My father and fiancé are hard on our heels, and when they catch you you'll wish the hangman had done his job."

"Bloodthirsty little minx, aren't you?" Diablo grinned cheekily. "But then, you wouldn't have been at my hanging if you weren't. Sorry to disappoint you, my lady, but I've grown quite fond of my neck and this worthless life."

"A vicious, despicable life," added Devon. "Your vile deeds are legend. Murder, robbery, rape, every crime attributable to mankind. You're a . . . a . . . devil!"

"Aye, they call me devil," Diablo admitted, his expression turning grim. The clear silver of his eyes changed to murky gray, his sensuous mouth hardened, and suddenly Devon knew real fear. "I freely admit to thievery, even murder, but I've yet to commit rape. Do not goad me, my lady, or I might be tempted."

Devon recoiled from the bearded apparition, wishing she could melt into the cushions. She should have realized she couldn't reason with the devil.

Diablo turned away to concentrate on the dragoons pounding behind the coach. He was fairly certain they wouldn't be fired on as long as he had the earl's daughter for a hostage. The lovely lady was his ticket to freedom. He slid a speculative glance in Devon's direction, finding himself oddly curious to learn her name. Just then the coach lurched and Devon flew across the seat, landing in Diablo's lap.

A mischievous smile turned Diablo's eyes to a predatory silver. Instinctively his arms tightened around Devon's soft womanly curves and a groan left his lips. Nothing had ever felt so good. "What is your name?" he asked.

Mesmerized by Diablo's compelling gaze and deep-timbred voice, Devon answered instantly. "Devon. Lady Devon Chatham."

"Devon," Diablo repeated slowly. His eyes roamed appreciatively over her face and hair. "Damn, but you're a tempting morsel!"

Then, before Devon had a chance to gather her wits, his mouth slanted across hers hungrily. The kiss was surprisingly gentle, sending a shockwave through her entire body. But as it deepened, Devon felt his tongue trace the soft contours of her lips, then plunge inside to explore the moist inner recesses.

Shock sent her senses whirling. No one, not even Winston, had kissed her like that. When Diablo's hand came up to cup her breast, Devon regained her wits. But before she had the opportunity to protest, there came a banging on the coach roof. Diablo jerked upright, setting Devon on the seat next to him just as a wiry little man lowered himself through the window. Devon gaped as two more men quickly followed, crowding into the cramped confines of the coach.

"Well done, lads," Diablo congratulated heartily. "Where's Dancy?"

"On the driver's bench with Akbar," one of the men replied. "You all right, cap'n?"

"I am now, Squint. You lads arrived in the nick of time. A few minutes more and I'd be fish bait."

"You can thank Kyle and Akbar for that." Squint grinned. "We only followed orders. 'Course we didn't know for sure it would work, but we couldn't let you hang." He stared at Devon. "Who's the wench?"

"The lady is our luck, lads. Meet Lady Devon. Her father, the Earl of Milford, will make certain the dragoons let us board our ship without mishap. Where is the *Devil Dancer* moored?"

"She's anchored in a little cove near the mouth of the Thames," another of the pirates piped up.

"Excellent, Fingers," Diablo grinned. "Mayhap tonight we'll have a party and you can play us a tune." Named for his ability to play the reed flute, Fingers was tall and thin, his mismatched clothes hanging loosely on his lanky frame. He carried his flute with him everywhere.

"What about her?" asked a third man sourly, pointing to Devon. He was as fierce-looking a man as Devon had ever laid eyes on, with heavy dark brows, a permanent scowl, and wild black hair sticking out from under his wool cap.

"Lady Devon will be released unharmed once she's served her purpose, Rooks," Diablo explained.

"The shore battery will fire on us before we leave the Thames," Squint predicted glumly. " 'Twill take some fancy maneuverin' to escape their bloody cannon."

"They won't fire on us with Lady Devon aboard," Diablo said confidently.

Finally Devon found her tongue. "What? Surely you don't mean to take me aboard your pirate ship! I won't go."

"You have no choice, my lady," Diablo pointed out. "But I give you my word no harm will come to you."

"The word of a pirate? You're asking me to trust a man known for his ruthlessness?"

For some reason Diablo found Devon's fury amusing, and a grin overtook his features. "You'll do as I say, my lady."

"The dragoons are gainin', cap'n," Fingers called out, hanging out the window.

"How much farther?" Diablo asked sharply.

"Ten minutes," Squint estimated, "if we keep up this pace."

They were traveling so fast that Devon knew she'd be black and blue from banging against the side of the coach. Diablo was only partially successful in protecting her with his own muscular form.

Behind them the dragoons were indeed gaining on the speeding coach. Both Lord Chatham and Winston Linley had managed to keep up with the soldiers, so when the dragoon captain drew his pistol and prepared to give the order to fire, the earl screamed out in protest.

"Stop, you fool! My daughter is in that coach. I'll have your head if she's hurt."

Shaking his head in disgust, the captain stayed his order. No matter how badly he wanted Diablo, he hadn't the nerve to contradict the wishes of an influential earl. Besides, he knew Lady Devon personally and would hate to see her come to harm at his hands.

"We're nearly there, Diablo," Squint called out. "There's the longboat waitin' in the shoals."

When Lord Chatham saw the coach skid to a halt on a point of land overlooking the mouth of the Thames, his heart sank to his well-shod feet. Then he saw a longboat waiting a short distance off shore, and fear for his daughter's safety twisted his gut. He turned to Winston and barked, "Use whatever means necessary to keep the shore battery from firing." Winston nodded grimly and thundered off.

Before the dragoons reached the place where the coach had stopped, five men including the huge, bald pirate called Akbar, quickly scrambled down the bank and waded out into the water where the longboat bobbed in the surf. Only when the dragoons slid to a halt a short distance away did Diablo step from the coach, dragging Devon behind him.

"Don't shoot!" Lord Chatham warned.

He dismounted, advancing a short distance, hoping to reason with the vicious pirate. "Let my daughter go, Diablo," he called out as Diablo pulled Devon relentlessly toward the shore. "Name your price."

"I have no need of your gold, milord," Diablo answered. "Nor will I harm your daughter. When I am safely away she will be set free and escorted safely home. More than that I cannot promise."

"Have you no compassion? Devon has caused you no harm. She is but an innocent victim."

"Aye, milord, and I'm sorry for it, but you have my word, I'll keep Lady Devon safe."

By now Diablo had reached the edge of the water. Bending, he scooped Devon up in his arms and dashed for the boat bobbing in the surf a short distance away. He placed her inside and scrambled after her while his men took up the oars and began rowing. Afraid to fire for fear of hitting the earl's daughter, the dragoons stood helplessly on the riverbank and watched the longboat round the point, hugging the shore as it made its way unerringly to where the *Devil Dancer* was moored.

"Father!" Devon screamed as the shore drew farther and farther away. "Father—" The word ended in a sob as she realized the futility of her plea.

But Devon was not one to give up so easily. She jumped to her feet and tried to leap into the water, certain she could make her way safely to shore. But Diablo was too quick for her. He seized her waist and forced her down beside him. Struggling for her very life, Devon flung herself out of Diablo's restraining arms, and hit her head against the side of the longboat. The last sound she heard as she slid into darkness was her name on Diablo's lips.

Chapter Two

"Her breathing is regular, Diablo, I doubt that she's badly hurt. A slight concussion, perhaps. Who is she?"

The man who spoke was tall, nearly as broad and imposing as Diablo, with flaming red hair and midnight blue eyes. He was dressed in pirate regalia of baggy pants and blouse with a wide red sash wound about his slim waist. His clothes were surprisingly clean for a pirate and his fingers gentle as he carefully probed the purpling bruise marring Devon's temple.

Diablo's silver gaze slid over the reclining form stretched out enticingly on his bed. "She's Lady Devon Chatham, daughter of the Earl of Milford."

"Saints preserve us," the redhead intoned, rolling his eyes heavenward. During times of stress his Irish brogue was more pronounced than usual. "You aim high, my friend. What are you going to do with her? The men won't be too pleased having a woman aboard the *Devil Dancer.*"

"The lady serves a purpose, Kyle," Diablo informed his lieutenant and second in command.

Kyle O'Bannon was the only man who knew Diablo's secret. He acted as doctor and treated the sick and wounded on the *Devil Dancer* when the need arose. He had become a fugitive after aiding his fellow Irishmen in a conspiracy against the crown while in medical school. He fled school, became involved in smuggling on the Cornish coast, and joined Diablo's crew while helping unload contraband from the *Devil Dancer.* From the moment the two men met they became fast friends.

"But for Lady Devon we would not have made it back to

the ship," Diablo continued. "The lady's father was instrumental in keeping the dragoons from firing on us. Her being at the hanging was a stroke of good fortune. Already we are past the shore patrol and out of danger. Your plan to create a diversion at the hanging was absolute genius, Kyle." Diablo grinned, clapping his friend on the back.

"The lass is a real beauty," Kyle said wistfully, "so young and innocent. You won't hurt her, will you? I won't allow it."

"Relax, Kyle, Lady Devon will be set ashore on the Cornish coast and our friend Cormac can see her safely home," Diablo assured him. "I promised her father she'd not be harmed and I mean to keep my word. You're sure she's all right? She seems to be sleeping deeply."

"Aye, she'll be fine," Kyle said, relief coloring his words. If Diablo meant the girl harm, he was prepared to do battle with his captain. Though Diablo wielded more authority than most pirate captains, every man aboard had a say in ship rules and the disposal of booty. And the girl was definitely booty. "Let Lady Devon sleep, it's the best thing for her right now."

"Aye," Diablo agreed. "You go on, I've a few things to attend to here before I join you. Fix a course for Land's End. We'll go in at dark and row the lady ashore."

After Kyle left the captain's spacious quarters in the ship's stern, Diablo lingered behind, his eyes returning time and again to the golden-haired beauty lying in his bed. She was somewhat taller than the average woman; slender, willowy, with jutting breasts, fine hips, and shapely thighs. Her facial bones were delicately carved, her mouth full and temptingly red. Long, sooty lashes lay curled against the creamy texture of her cheeks like two butterfly wings. Diablo thought Devon the most ravishing creature he'd ever seen and would have given his soul to learn the secrets of her luscious body.

Was she a virgin? Diablo wondered, his hands itching to

test the smoothness of her flesh. Or had Devon's fiancé already savored the pleasure she had to offer? A surge of hatred jolted through Diablo at the thought of Devon's nameless, faceless fiancé bedding the gorgeous wench. Diablo's eyes fell on Devon's slipper-clad feet. Both her shoes and stockings were sopping wet from being dragged through the surf. He bent to the task of stripping off her shoes and stockings before she caught her death of cold.

Diablo groaned aloud when he reached beneath Devon's skirt to untie the ribbons holding up the sheer white stockings on her long, slender thighs. The skin beneath his questing fingertips quivered slightly as he slowly rolled the wisp of silk down one shapely leg. Never had he felt anything so soft or temptingly exquisite. It took all his willpower to keep his hand from straying upward to the beckoning nest of warmth pulling at his senses.

Devon's eyes flew open as Diablo's hand lingered on the inside of one thigh. Though she was nearly paralyzed with fright, her temper flared when she awoke to find Diablo taking liberties with her body.

"What are you doing!"

Diablo chuckled, the smile in his silver eyes a sensuous flame that ignited something deep inside Devon. "Removing your shoes and stockings, my lady," he replied, his voice tinged with amusement as he bent to his pleasurable task. "They're wet and you'll rest more comfortably without them."

"Take your hands off me!" Devon spat, swatting his hands away. "I'm not so helpless that you can ravish me at will."

"Ravish you, my lady? While you are unable to enjoy what I do to you? Never! If and when I make love to you, you'll know it."

Devon paled. No one—absolutely no one—had ever talked to her like that. "Why, you . . . you barbarian! Satan! If you lay a hand on me I'll . . . I'll . . ."

Diablo threw back his head and roared with laughter. Devon thought he resembled the devil with his jet black hair and beard and those strange silver eyes. Yet there was something magnetic about the man, a sensuousness revealed in the hard lines of his face and the depth of his eyes. His muscular strength was awesome, his bold features frightening. But what was most surprising to Devon was Diablo's humor. It was so out of character, contradicting all she'd ever heard about the man.

Beneath Diablo's thick black beard Devon could make out the fine bones of a face that might be called aristocratic if one didn't know what he was. It was a well-known fact that pirates in the year 1715 came from all walks of life. Could Diablo possibly be from a noble Spanish family fallen on hard times?

"If I wanted to bed you, Lady Devon, I would do so with or without your permission, regardless of what you think of me."

Devon pushed herself to the farthest corner of the bed, expecting Diablo to pounce on her at any moment. She tilted her chin defiantly, determined not to give in without a fierce fight. "Don't come near me!"

"Feisty wench, aren't you? Rest easy, Lady Devon, I'm too tired right now to do you justice. How's your head?"

Since the moment she opened her eyes to find Diablo fondling her leg, Devon was aware of her pounding head. She winced when she found the bruise on her temple. "It hurts, no thanks to you. Why didn't you leave me behind?"

"Had I been stupid enough to do that we'd have been blown out of the water by the shore cannon."

"What are you going to do with me?"

"As I said before, you'll be set ashore."

Devon searched Diablo's face, wanting to believe him but afraid to trust his word. No woman was safe with him, and she'd be a fool to drop her guard where Diablo was concerned.

Sensing Devon's misgivings, Diablo added, "You're safe enough in my quarters. No one will harm you here."

"Does that include you?" Devon challenged boldly.

Diablo did not answer immediately, staring at Devon strangely, his silver eyes taking in every inch of her charmingly disheveled form. His admiring glance was blatantly sexual, freezing the breath in Devon's throat. When he finally spoke, his voice, deep and sensual, sent a ripple of awareness through her.

"I'd be lying if I said I didn't want you, Devon. You're a damn tempting morsel to a man who's accustomed to seizing what he wants."

Mesmerized, Devon could not move when Diablo pinned her to the bed, his mouth devouring hers hungrily. Vaguely she felt the roughness of his beard scraping across the tender skin of her face, the heady sensation sending the pit of her stomach into a swirl. She tried to throttle the dizzying current racing through her, but when Diablo deliberately outlined her lips with the tip of his tongue and then plunged inside, she jolted in response. As the kiss deepened, Devon felt her body ignite in a way she never thought possible. The male hardness of his virile form left an indelible print on her own softness, his desire for her a hot lance between them.

He was slowly and completely demoralizing her, eroding her will to resist. But she had more moral fiber than that blackguard gave her credit for, Devon reflected, marshaling her strength. When Diablo renewed the attack on her senses, she broke free.

"Nay, don't!"

"Are you afraid of me, Devon?"

"Aye, I admit it. I . . . I'm afraid of what you'll do to me."

"I won't hurt you."

"You already have hurt me by taking me away from my father."

"And your fiancé?" Diablo prompted. "Have you forgotten him?"

"Of course not," Devon refuted, her eyes stormy with anger. "He's probably worried sick. If you had any compassion at all you'd turn around and take me back."

"Compassion? I am the devil, and devils have little compassion. I could easily ravish you here and now and no one would say me nay. But I won't." Diablo sighed regretfully. "I promised your father you'd be returned unharmed."

"A devil with a conscience, how refreshing," Devon bit out sarcastically. "However, I am grateful for not having to suffer your despicable attentions."

"I admire your courage, my lady." Diablo smiled, his eyes as keen as silver daggers. "Most men fear me."

"I am not a man."

"I've noticed." He raked her slim form appraisingly. "I only allow beautiful women in my bed. But alas, I fear I must forego the pleasure right now. But if you insist, I will find time later," he grinned, finding amusement in Devon's gasp of outrage.

"Get out of here!"

Diablo levered himself to his feet, his tall, lean form looming above her. "I'll be back," he drawled lazily. "Don't try to leave if you value your hide." Devon watched warily as the handsome rogue sauntered from the room with the rolling gait of one accustomed to balancing on the deck of a tossing ship.

Devon thought he looked every bit as evil as his reputation, except for his eyes. How could those silver mirrors portray such teasing humor when everyone knew the acts of depravity he was capable of? Were there two men lurking inside that attractive body?

The thought that Diablo intended to return galvanized Devon into action. When he entered the cabin again, she intended to be armed with more than words. There had to be some sort of weapon in the room. Diablo wouldn't have an easy time subduing her, if that was his purpose. No indeed, Devon smiled deviously, that miserable blackguard wouldn't find her meekly awaiting his pleasure.

Diablo grinned all the way to the quarterdeck. The spirited wench occupying his bed was a tasty morsel he'd give his right arm to possess. But even a fool could tell she meant trouble. For her own sake as well as his, he had to get her off the ship as soon as possible. Already his men were casting lustful glances in the direction of his cabin. His crew were loyal only up to a point, and some couldn't be trusted out of his sight. Normally pirates elected their captain from among their own. That's how he had come to possess the *Devil Dancer*. Over the years he had hand-picked his crew until he felt reasonably certain his orders would be strictly adhered to. But Diablo was no fool. Lady Devon was too beautiful, too enticing, to be exposed to his crew for any length of time. Besides, women on board were considered bad luck and he had no intention of flaunting tradition.

"The course is set, Kit, we should reach our destination day after tomorrow."

Diablo's brow furrowed. "How many times have I told you not to call me Kit within hearing distance of the crew, Kyle?"

"No one's around, Diablo," Kyle gestured. "Besides, your name means nothing to them. You've been Diablo too long now to make any difference."

"I suppose you're right," Diablo allowed, wondering if there was anyone on earth who really cared who or what he was. "Just the same, except in the privacy of my cabin, I prefer you call me Diablo."

"What about the lass?" Kyle asked, adroitly changing the subject.

"She's fine. She woke up shortly before I left the cabin."

"I hope you didn't scare the lass too badly—or hurt her," Kyle added sharply. "The poor thing has probably led a sheltered life and is unprepared to deal with the likes of you. Your ugly, bearded face would frighten even the hardiest soul."

Diablo tilted his head back and laughed richly. "The *poor* lass was upbraiding me furiously when I left the cabin. She displayed neither fear nor awe of my ferocious features. Believe it or not, Kyle, I didn't touch the girl, though it took considerable willpower to keep from ravishing her. Who knows, she might have enjoyed it." He shrugged eloquently; his silver eyes held a hint of longing Kyle did not miss.

Just then Akbar approached on silent feet, his incredible bulk surprisingly nimble. A wide smile split his fierce features as his black eyes raked Diablo from head to toe. Crossing his arms across his massive chest and wagging his bushy eyebrows, he said, "You look no worse for your stay in Newgate. Mayhap the beard is a trifle more unruly than normal."

"I'm rather fond of the beard," Diablo replied, stroking the luxurious growth with long, supple fingers. "It suits me."

"Wear it in good health, my friend," Akbar boomed, "and thank Allah you've still a neck to support it."

"I've you and Kyle to thank for that," Diablo replied, turning serious. "I must admit I was becoming rather nervous standing on the gibbet with a rope around my neck."

"We provided the distraction, but you're the one who got us all away safely," Akbar reminded him. "Some of the men are wondering about the girl. They think you should share her."

"The girl stays with me," Diablo said, his features hardening. "She'll be set ashore at Land's End. Spread the word that I'll defend my right to keep her for myself."

Akbar nodded but said nothing. He was astute enough to realize Diablo would not back down on this.

"A mite possessive of the lass, aren't you, Diablo?" Kyle

questioned, looking somewhat puzzled. "What's so special about her?"

"Dammit, Kyle, you know I've never willingly turned over women captives to the crew unless they were whores to begin with and willing. Nor have I ever resorted to rape."

"What about all those lasses who shared your bed before they were set free or ransomed?"

Flashing a roguish grin, Diablo said, "I've forgotten nothing. I have a reputation to maintain, and the women were willing. But Lady Devon is—I don't know—perhaps she reminds me of another life."

"It's still not too late to return to that life."

"There's a hefty price on Diablo's head. No country in the world would welcome me, including England."

Akbar stood silently by, listening. His massive bulk towered over Kyle and Diablo, both large, powerfully built men. With his bald head covered with a colorful scarf and a gold hoop dangling from one ear, Akbar looked every bit the fierce, unprincipled pirate he was. He waited for the conversation to lag before speaking.

"We're in for a blow, Diablo," he warned, eying the lowering sky with misgiving. The day that had begun dismal and rainy now looked threatening as the rising wind whistled through the sails.

"So much the better," Diablo returned, pleased with the way things were working out. "The English navy won't be so anxious to give chase with a storm in the offing. It will provide ample time to put Lady Devon ashore. Cormac, our contact in Cornwall, will see that she reaches London safely.

"Warn the crew, Kyle, and see that the ship is prepared to ride out the storm. I'll be in my cabin if you need me."

The two men watched as Diablo turned and retraced his steps to his quarters. "Diablo appears anxious to return to the woman," Akbar said with a knowing grin.

"Aye," Kyle agreed, not quite as amused as Akbar. "He

seems fair taken with the lass, and I don't like it. She's trouble, my friend, big trouble. She's the daughter of the Earl of Milford. Need I say more?"

"Allah help us," Akbar muttered. "Diablo aims high. Does he intend to bed the woman before he puts her ashore?"

"He wants to, but whether he does remains to be seen."

"A quid says Diablo has her before he sets her ashore," Akbar wagered.

"I'm betting on the lass," Kyle countered, "and expect to be a quid richer for it."

Methodically Devon searched Diablo's cabin, carefully examining the contents of every drawer in the map-strewn desk. Finding no hidden weapon, she turned to the sundry articles of clothing hanging on hooks from the bulkhead, but to no avail. The only thing she found that remotely resembled a weapon was a dull letter opener, and that certainly wouldn't scare a man like Diablo. Then her eyes fell on the sea chest across the room. Scrambling to her knees, she began rummaging through its contents, finding an assortment of clothes, papers, and keepsakes. She was on the verge of giving up in despair when her fingers found what they were looking for lying at the very bottom. Her hand closed around cold steel as she drew a small-caliber pistol from the chest.

Devon noted that the pistol wasn't loaded and returned to the chest to look for ammunition. To her delight she found bullets along with all the paraphernalia needed to load and prime the weapon. Carefully following the process taught her by her father, Devon prepared the pistol for firing. Then she closed the lid of the chest, slipped the pistol into her pocket, and sat down on the bed to wait.

A smile lingered on Diablo's lips as he paused outside his cabin, thinking about the girl inside. She was keen-witted, feisty, had a tongue as sharp as a knife, and was far too great a temptation. Just looking at her set his blood to boiling. Most women would be quailing in fear, but he was sure that Devon was pacing the cabin and cursing him. He'd sell his soul to the devil to have her in his bed, willingly, for one glorious night. The thought produced a jolt to his loins as he slowly turned the handle and entered the cabin.

Devon sat on the bed, her eyes watchful as Diablo approached. "I've ordered some food," he said, his eyes roaming freely over her trim form. "It won't be what you're accustomed to, but nourishing nevertheless."

"I'm not hungry," Devon responded warily.

"Then you can watch me eat, I'm famished. Prison fare leaves much to be desired." He lowered himself into the only chair in the room, stretching his long-muscled legs out before him. A tense silence ensued.

Devon grew restive under Diablo's avid scrutiny and wished he would say something—anything. She felt more secure with verbal fencing than being the object of his lustful admiration. She squirmed like a mouse caught in a trap and felt in her pocket for the comfortable weight of the pistol. The tray of food that arrived a short time later was a welcome relief, and Devon relaxed somewhat as Diablo turned his attention from her to his dinner.

"Are you sure you won't join me?" Diablo asked, popping a slice of salted beef in his mouth.

"Nay," Devon sniffed haughtily, turning up her nose.

"Suit yourself. But I'd think you'd want to fortify yourself for—later."

"Later?" squeaked Devon in dismay. "Wha—what do you mean? You said I wouldn't be harmed."

"I have no intention of harming you," Diablo grinned, his eyes flashing with silver lights.

Diablo knew he shouldn't bait Devon so relentlessly, but she was so charmingly innocent he couldn't resist. Was it an act or was she truly untouched? he wondered, finishing the meal. He shoved the tray aside and sat back, replete, thoroughly enjoying himself. It wasn't often he found the opportunity to associate with women of the upper class. Not that he lacked female companionship. On the contrary, women came easily to him. Women like Scarlett flocked around him like bees to honey. He could have her and those like her whenever he wanted. But Devon was different, and it pleased him to toy with her.

"You—still intend to let me go, don't you?" Devon asked, her bravado slowly disintegrating. Only the solid weight of the pistol against her thigh kept her from panic.

Diablo nodded slowly, a lazy smile hanging on the corner of his mouth. "A friend in Cornwall will see you safely to London. But that still leaves us with two long nights in which to become better acquainted," he said with sly innuendo. "I'd like to know every inch of you intimately."

"I know everything about you that I care to know," Devon responded, his erotic words creating a strange, uncomfortable emotion in her. She could feel the magnetic charge emanating from him and wondered if he still meant to ravish her.

Undeniably Diablo was a handsome devil, beard and all. He was dark as a Spaniard; his powerful, well-muscled body moved with easy grace. He looked tough, lean and sinewy. A humorous mouth set in a rugged, severe, albeit attractive face was strangely at odds with his profession. Devon doubted there was another man to compare with him and wished she was anywhere but in his intimidating company. The urge to be held by him unnerved and frightened her.

Diablo uncoiled his lean length from the chair and approached Devon with lazy grace. His body ached with the need to make love to her, but he wouldn't do it unless she invited him to, and that appeared unlikely. He sat down beside her, and she immediately leaped off the bed, pressing herself against the wall.

"Don't touch me!"

"You're beautiful, my lady."

"And you're a devil."

"Aye, a devil who'd trade his soul to attain heaven in your arms."

"You're mad!" Devon blasted, the determined look in Diablo's eyes fueling her fear. She had hoped to be spared the need to defend her honor, but Diablo was pressing her too assiduously. She was left with no recourse.

Diablo's silver eyes sparkled mischievously. He couldn't remember when he'd taken such delight in a woman. He knew he was treading in dangerous waters but couldn't resist. He admired Devon's spirit and thought her remarkably brave for one unaccustomed to the cruelties of life. He thought to steal a kiss, or two, to merely sample her sweetness, but Devon failed to recognize his teasing manner. He was brought up short by the sudden appearance of a pistol in Devon's shaking hand, pointed at his heart.

"I told you not to come near me." Her voice was slightly breathless despite her best efforts to be calm.

"I seriously doubt you could kill a man, Devon," Diablo challenged, advancing slowly. "Besides, the gun isn't loaded. I recognize it as one I keep stored in my sea chest."

"I loaded it," Devon gloated. "Do you think me stupid?"

"Nay, far from stupid, my lady. Now give over the gun before you hurt yourself. You have my word you won't be harmed. You'll be set ashore just as I promised, in the same condition in which you arrived."

Devon eyed Diablo dubiously. "I don't trust you."

"Give me the gun, Devon," Diablo said, "before someone gets hurt." He stretched out his hand, palm up.

"Nay." Devon's chin tilted at a stubborn angle, warning Diablo that his words had fallen on deaf ears.

Then Diablo made a move that nearly proved fatal. He lunged forward to seize the weapon from Devon's shaking hand. His strong fingers clamped around her frail wrist, causing an involuntary reaction in the finger poised against the trigger. Whether Devon would have pulled the trigger of her own accord was moot as the gun exploded in her hand. Diablo's eyes widened in shock and pain as he staggered backward, stumbled, then fell heavily, slamming his head against the corner of the marble-topped desk. Devon stared in stunned fascination at the red stain blossoming against Diablo's white shirt. He lay so still and white at her feet that she feared she had killed him.

The door to the cabin flung open, admitting Akbar, followed closely by Kyle. Devon recognized the huge Turk as the man who had cut Diablo from the gallows but did not recall Kyle, who had remained with the ship. Kyle paled, stunned by the sight of Diablo lying still as death with Devon standing over him holding the smoking pistol.

"Sweet mother Mary," Kyle whispered, shock rendering him motionless. "You've killed Diablo!"

A howl of rage exploded from Akbar's throat as he shouldered past Kyle to kneel at Diablo's side. His face was a mask of outrage and hatred as he swiveled to glare at Devon.

"I—I didn't mean . . ." Devon swallowed painfully, her sentence trailing off when she realized that nothing she could say would make any difference to Diablo's faithful crew. If he were dead, she fully expected to follow soon.

"Kyle, Diablo needs you," Akbar growled, jerking Kyle from his frozen stance.

Kyle hesitated but a moment, asking, "What about the lass?"

"Leave her to me," Akbar returned, fixing Devon with a baleful look.

"Don't—" Kyle's words were left unsaid as his attention was captured by Diablo, who picked that moment to groan. Kyle dropped to his knees, Devon all but forgotten.

But she was not forgotten by Akbar, who seized her

roughly and dragged her from the room, thrusting her into the arms of two burly pirates. "Throw her into the hold," Akbar ordered curtly. "If Diablo lives he can decide what's to be done with her. If he dies . . ."

There was no need for him to continue. Devon held no illusions about her fate should Diablo die.

Chapter Three

Sometime during the night the threatening storm struck with all its fury. Deep in the bowels of the ship Devon huddled in a miserable heap. Cold, hungry, wretched, she curled up on a damp bale, terrified of the furry creatures that brushed against her legs. Her greatest fear was of dying under such deplorable circumstances far from her loved ones. Hours had passed since she was thrown into the hold, abandoned and utterly alone and forgotten in a world totally foreign to her. Did Diablo still live? she wondered dismally. Dear God, she hoped so. She never meant to kill him, just protect her honor in the only way she knew how. Truth to tell, she wasn't certain she could have pulled the trigger of her own accord. But Diablo had taken that choice from her.

Suddenly the ship tilted dangerously and Devon slid off the bale, landing with a splash in the ankle-deep water seeping into the hold. For a timeless interval she thought the beleaguered ship wasn't going to right itself, certain she would be consigned to the deep forever. It was a terrifying thought, and she recited every prayer she'd ever learned. Then slowly the ship began an upward sweep, only to heel over in the opposite direction. And so it continued throughout the long night and next day as the wind and rain wreaked havoc on the *Devil Dancer*.

"How is Diablo?" The door to the captain's cabin opened and Akbar was literally blown inside, dressed in raingear and dripping wet.

"The wound isn't serious," Kyle replied. "The bullet passed

through his side cleanly, without damaging anything vital. He was damn lucky, the bleeding was minimal."

Akbar scowled, his fierce features becoming even more forbidding. "Why is he still unconscious? It's been nearly twenty-four hours."

"'Tis his head," Kyle explained. "A concussion, is my guess. He'll come around in good time." For his own safety during the storm Diablo had been lashed to the bunk.

Akbar grunted, his mind somewhat eased. He and Diablo had been friends since Black Bart captured the Turkish brigantine on which Akbar served. Because of his extraordinary size and strength, Akbar had been pressed into Black Bart's service. Though Diablo had been a lad at the time, he had saved Akbar's life during a storm when high seas threatened to wash his unconscious body overboard. Akbar had been struck by a falling timber and would have been swept over the side but for Diablo's quick thinking; he had lashed them both to the broken mast. An unlikely friendship had existed since then between the two men. When Diablo led a mutiny against Black Bart and seized the *Devil Dancer*, Akbar was at his side.

"Tend Diablo well," Akbar grunted as he turned to leave.

"How goes it topside, Akbar?" Kyle asked.

"We're riding it out well enough. The *Devil Dancer* is as trim and fit as any ship afloat."

"Aye, she is that. What about the lass? Where—"

The sentence died in his throat as the ship shuddered, followed by a loud crash.

"Allah help us," Akbar intoned, preparing to rush back out into the raging elements. When Kyle made to follow, Akbar shook his head. "See to Diablo, my friend." Then he was pushing through the door, his head bent against the howling wind and pelting rain.

"What's happening?"

Kyle whirled to find Diablo's eyes open, though he was still somewhat confused. "You're awake!"

"Obviously. Why am I tied to the bunk?"

"The storm. It's for your own protection."

Just then the ship lurched to the starboard, then righted itself, tossing like a cork on the towering waves. "Release me, Kyle, I'm needed topside."

"You're staying right where you are, Kit. Your wound is healing and obviously your concussion is mending, but you're still too weak to battle the elements. Akbar has things well in hand."

Diablo's brows furrowed. "I . . . what happened? What wound?"

"Don't you remember?"

"Nay . . . well . . . not everything. Was I shot?"

"Aye, I was hoping you could tell me how it happened. Do you recall Lady Devon?"

A slow smile transformed Diablo's face. "Who could forget that little wildcat?" His eyes made a quick survey of the room. "Where is she?"

"She shot you, you know."

"Not purposely, Kyle. I'm certain she wouldn't have pulled the trigger if I hadn't goaded her. True, she threatened me with the pistol, but I more or less deserved it." A horrible thought suddenly came to him. "What have you done with her?"

Kyle looked decidedly uncomfortable. "I . . . I'm certain the lass is fine, Diablo."

"You're . . . certain? God's bones, Kyle, don't you know?"

"I was occupied with seeing to your injuries and thought little about her at the time. Akbar handled it, but I've not had the opportunity to question him for the storm struck shortly afterwards."

"How long have I been out?"

"Twenty-four hours."

Diablo cursed violently, working his arms free and attacking the knots that held him captive. The activity earned him a stab of pain followed by a wave of dizziness. Defeated, he fell back against the pillow, too weak to continue. "Damn you, Kyle, and damn Akbar if he hurt the girl."

Kyle thought his captain far too distressed for his own good and abruptly whirled, busying himself at the water pitcher. "Here, drink this," Kyle offered, ignoring Diablo's threats as he turned and held a cup to his captain's lips.

"What is it?" Diablo asked, his eyes narrowed suspiciously.

"Just water," Kyle said, his eyes not quite meeting Diablo's.

Grunting, Diablo drank deeply, then sputtered, slapping the cup from Kyle's hands. "God's bones! Laudanum! I thought I could trust you."

"You can. Now quit blustering and rest. I promise to check on the lass the first chance I get."

"Tell . . . Akbar . . . I'll have . . . his head if . . . she's been harmed," Diablo said, finding it difficult to concentrate.

"I will, my friend," Kyle vowed. I only hope it's not too late, he thought.

As luck would have it, Kyle found no opportunity to speak with Akbar until the next morning. The storm finally blew itself out with the coming of dawn, and the huge Turk immediately set the crew to repairing the mainmast and damaged rudder. A reading showed they had been blown far off course and were now floundering somewhere in the Atlantic. Until another sighting was made no one knew exactly where they were.

Before Diablo awoke, Kyle had released him from his bonds, then went to fetch a hot meal for himself and his captain, their first in two days. While he was gone, Diablo stirred, tested his limbs, and staggered somewhat unsteadily to his feet. He found himself able to stand despite the jolt of pain in the vicinity of his wound and could move about freely if he ignored the dull ache in his head. Setting his teeth against the stab in his side, Diablo proceeded to bathe and dress in clean clothes. Except for his grumbling stomach and worry over Devon, he felt remarkably able to cope with his duties.

Damn that Akbar, he silently upbraided. The man was far too zealous in wanting to protect him. He didn't think Akbar would take it upon himself to punish Devon, but one never knew about the fierce Turk. Diablo decided it was time he took over his own ship and proved to his crew he was fit to command.

Just then the object of his angry ruminations entered the cabin without knocking, coming up short at the sight of Diablo standing on his own two feet and looking none the worse for wear.

"Allah be praised. Twenty-four hours ago I thought you at death's door."

"And before that I was close to having my neck stretched," Diablo grumbled. "Mayhap I should change my name to El Gatto, the cat, for surely I have been blessed with nine lives." Then his lips turned downward into a fierce scowl. "Where is she, Akbar?"

At first Akbar looked puzzled, then comprehension dawned. "The girl! I've been too involved with the storm and saving the ship to give a thought to her."

"You forgot? You haven't harmed her, have you?" Diablo flared, his silver eyes kindling with anger. "Exactly where is Lady Devon?"

"Confined in the hold," Akbar said somewhat sheepishly. "In all the excitement I completely forgot about her."

"God's bones, man, that was two days ago!" Diablo thundered. "Has no one checked on her? Has she been given food and water?"

"I told you, the storm—"

"I want her out of there—now!"

"Aye," Akbar grumbled, turning to do his captain's bidding. "I'll see to it." He went out muttering dire predictions about women aboard pirate ships and trouble.

Deep in the belly of the ship, Devon was unaware that the storm had ended. Nearly comatose, she lolled in sodden misery atop the bale in which she had ridden out the storm. Covered with filth, her golden tresses a snarled nest, she had been sick many times during the past two days and was now dangerously dehydrated from lack of water. She felt herself near death—wished for it, actually. So when the hatch opened, allowing in the first light Devon had seen in two days, it proved too much for her. The terrifying figure looming like a huge ogre above her seemed like something out of her worst nightmare, sending her spinning into a deep, dark void.

Diablo raged furiously when Akbar entered his cabin carrying an incredibly dirty and unconscious Devon. He leaped to his feet, sending a plate of food flying. "Put her down on the bed," he barked, "and send Kyle in here."

Diablo wrinkled his nose, all too aware of the stench of vomit combined with dampness and mold clinging to Devon's clothing, and he spit out a string of curses. Devon's pale little face filled him with fear, as did the white line around her pinched lips. Without a moment's hesitation he stripped the reeking rags from her body and tossed them out the door. Then he drew a sheet over her and left hurriedly to fetch hot water. He returned shortly, and using clean linens from his sea chest, set himself to thoroughly cleansing Devon's body of accumulated filth. Only when he finished did he allow his eyes to feast upon the arrestingly beautiful charms of her perfect body.

Lightly he trailed his fingertips from her collarbone to the tip of one breast, mesmerized when the nipple hardened beneath his touch. The breath exploded from his chest in a painful jolt. Never had he felt anything so velvet soft, so exciting or tempting as Devon's white skin. Cresting the symmetrical mounds of her breasts, which were full yet not overly large, were coral tips puckered into tight buds. They seemed to be pouting for the touch of his mouth, and Diablo forced his wayward thoughts elsewhere as his gaze continued downward.

Diablo's loins swelled and his silver eyes widened appreciatively as they came to rest on the golden nest of tangled hair between Devon's smooth thighs. Beads of sweat popped out on his forehead and he knew a moment of panic. Some sixth sense that never failed him told him that this woman had the power to change his life. Even as he scoffed at the ridiculous thought that this woman—any woman—could mean more to him than brief sexual satisfaction, Diablo's eyes continued their sensual journey, devouring Devon's long, slim legs, shapely thighs, and trim ankles. Even her feet were narrow and dainty. In fact, everything about Devon pleased him. But she wasn't for him—he knew it and accepted it.

Whores, doxies, and widows of easy virtue were what he was accustomed to, not a lady bred and born. They belonged behind manor walls producing children for their aristocratic husbands. Once Diablo might have belonged to that world, but now it was too late. He had been cruelly thrust into a pirate's life and later freely embraced the profession, choosing to live and operate outside the law in the tradition of piracy.

Diablo and men like him were considered enemies of mankind. They owed allegiance to no one, claimed no country. Ships from any country could seize a pirate ship, bring it to port, try all the crew regardless of nationality, and hang them. Like his brothers, Diablo sailed the Pirate Round—a route stretching from North America around the tip of Africa—to pillage the eastern seas and return home—in this case Nassau—with their holds filled with booty.

Pirates were a barbarous lot, yet among themselves they passionately advocated a rude sort of democracy, with a high regard for justice and the rights of individuals and distaste for tyranny and abuse of power. They could be generous toward those they liked and trusted, often bestowing rich gifts. Shipmates losing eyes or limbs were allowed to remain aboard and earn a half-share of the booty.

Though a strict disciplinarian, Diablo was a fair man who treated women captives better than most pirates did. He recalled those days long ago, had fate been kinder to him, when his life might have taken a different course. And as he gazed longingly at Devon, he knew he couldn't take her cruelly no matter how he yearned to invade that tempting body. Were he offered the opportunity he'd not ravish her but would make leisurely love, bringing her gently to womanhood. With a sigh of regret, Diablo pulled the sheet over Devon's nude form, feeling strangely like a traitor to his profession. Not one of his acquaintances, save for Kyle perhaps, would deny himself a woman he wanted as badly as he wanted Devon.

"I'm sorry, Kit, I thought the lass was confined to a cabin," Kyle apologized as he stepped into the cabin. "I'd never knowingly allow her to be placed in the hold. How is she?"

"I hoped you could tell me, Kyle. And damn it, man, call me Diablo."

"Sorry, Diablo," Kyle muttered. "Move aside so I can have a look."

Diablo obeyed, watching closely as Kyle examined her. "She's dehydrated as well as exhausted," he pronounced at length. "Force liquids down her and let her rest and she'll be fine. You're aware, of course, that we've blown off course and there's no possibility now of putting the lass ashore at Land's End."

Diablo nodded grimly. "I suspected as much. Have you taken a reading yet?"

"Aye, we're roughly five hundred miles due west of France. It would be too dangerous now to return to English waters."

"What about damage?"

"The rudder was damaged and we've taken on water, but Akbar has the men working on the problem. Men are also mending the sails and fashioning a new mast. We'll be under way sometime tomorrow. What course should I set?"

Diablo was silent a long time, his eyes straying to Devon, who remained blissfully unaware of his dilemma. A man of his word, he had promised Devon he would set her ashore, but fate had intervened and willed otherwise. Deep down, Diablo felt relieved that the choice had been taken from him, for his instinct was to keep Devon with him until she came to his bed willingly.

"We sail for Nassau," he said, reluctantly tearing his eyes from Devon's still form. "There's booty in the hold and the lads need time ashore. Besides, the ship could use a good careen and it wouldn't hurt to remain invisible for a spell."

"What about the lass?"

"Needless to say, she'll remain under my protection for the time being."

"What?" Devon had been awake for several minutes, listening. Now, hearing Diablo's words, she reared up in angry indignation, unaware she was nude beneath the sheet.

Both men turned as one, Kyle's loud gasp echoing Diablo's groan. Two pairs of eyes fastened on Devon's heaving breasts. Only then did Devon realize what was happening. Glancing down at herself, she shrieked in outrage, yanking the sheet up under her chin.

"Sons of Satan! Murderers! Rapists! Both of you. Where are my clothes? Why am I nude? Who are you?" This last question was directed at Kyle.

"Lady Devon, may I present Kyle O'Bannon, my lieutenant and right-hand man," Diablo said with a flourish. "We've done you no harm, my lady. Your clothes were wet and filthy. I couldn't in good conscience leave you in them."

"I thought I killed you," Devon said sourly, unwilling to reveal her relief at seeing him alive.

"Are you disappointed? I was lucky, the bullet passed through my side. 'Tis bloody uncomfortable but far from life threatening. I've suffered worse."

"Too bad," Devon muttered, clutching the sheet tightly. "I demand you give me my clothes and put me ashore as you promised."

"Your clothes were ruined and I had them thrown overboard, but you'll be provided with others," Diablo replied, smiling guilelessly. "As for the other . . ." He shrugged expansively. "I fear I'm forced to break my promise. You'll remain with me for the time being."

"I should have known you'd not keep your word, you lying blackguard."

"Look, Devon—"

"I'll leave you two alone," Kyle interrupted, swallowing a knowing grin. "I've work to do. I'm glad you're feeling better, my lady." Then he was gone, thinking he wouldn't trade places with Diablo for a captain's share of the booty. The lass had a tongue sharp enough to slice a man to pieces and obviously wasn't afraid to use it.

Kyle chuckled all the way to the quarterdeck. Diablo had his hands full with the lass, and Kyle didn't envy him. Once the crew learned that Devon was to remain aboard, trouble was sure to follow. It had been some time since the lads had been ashore, and Devon was too great a temptation for men starved for female companionship. Kyle hoped they'd reach Nassau before all hell broke loose.

Alone with Diablo, Devon fumed in impotent rage. Raking long fingers through his raven locks and looking decidedly disgruntled, Diablo said, "I'd strongly advise, my lady, that you act with caution where I'm concerned. You're in no position to make demands. Insulting me or my men will gain you damn little. You've already tasted a sample of Akbar's justice and should thank God that I survived your attack."

"Akbar! Is that the name of the barbarian who threw me in the hold? I expect no less from bloodthirsty scavengers," Devon flung out. "You should know that both my father and my fiancé will follow you to the ends of the earth. No one will rejoice more than me when you're finally swinging from the gallows."

"Ah, my lady, you wound me grievously," Diablo taunted, clutching his heart in mock pain. "And as enjoyable as sparring with you is, I have a ship to run. I'll see that food, water, and clothes are brought to you, but I wouldn't leave this cabin if I were you. My men are a rough lot who haven't had a woman in some time."

After delivering that thinly veiled threat, he sketched a rather clumsy bow due to the painful throbbing of his head, smiled beguilingly, and left the cabin.

Staring at the closed door, Devon was puzzled by the strange attraction that existed between her and the pirate. Deep in her heart she sensed that he wouldn't harm her and knew it was in her best interest to remain inside the cabin. Devon hadn't the slightest doubt that Diablo could be as ruthless and cunning as his name implied. Nonetheless, she experienced an odd lack of fear.

What would happen to her? Devon wondered dismally. Would she ever see her father or Winston again? She knew her father would move heaven and earth to find her and assumed Winston felt the same. Even now they could be aboard the *Larkspur* searching the ocean for her. That thought brought a measure of comfort to her.

A short time later a grizzled pirate limped into the cabin on a crudely carved wooden leg carrying a tray of food and drink. Famished, Devon ate and drank ravenously of the dismal fare as if it were the finest feast. She had just downed the last morsel when a trunk arrived filled with expensively fashioned women's clothing, and Devon spent considerable time sorting through the attractive array of garments. Vaguely she wondered what had become of the lady who owned the clothes, but the thought was so distressing she quickly put it from her mind.

Finally making her selection, Devon donned a modest gray daygown, the plainest of the lot. She had no wish to incite the lust of Diablo or his crew in any way. She wanted to be a little gray mouse unworthy of attention. She failed miserably. The fine silk gown molded her young curves to perfection. The high neck served to emphasize the bold thrust of her breasts, define the slim turn of waist, and outline gently swelling hips. White silk stockings, ruffled garters, and low-heeled slippers completed the demure outfit.

Next Devon attacked the tangle of golden curls swirling about her waist with a brush she found in the chest. She brushed until the heavy mass flowed down her shoulders and back in brilliant, silken waves. Then she explored the cabin, discovering, much to her relief, a chamberpot, and little else. Then she sat down to wait, pondering her fate and attempting to analyze the man known as Diablo.

After a time Devon grew bored and gingerly approached the door. Testing the knob, she found that it opened easily beneath her hand. Her first instinct was to rush headlong from the cabin, but Diablo's warning came back to haunt her. Yet the urge to examine her surroundings and learn exactly what she was pitted against was too great a force within her. Gingerly she eased open the door, noting that the stern cabin opened directly onto the main deck. She stood poised uncertainly in the doorway for several long minutes, blinking in the bright sunlight.

From all quarters Devon noted signs of vigorous activity.

One group of men worked on the mainmast, which had been snapped in two, while others sewed on the huge sail laid out on deck. Still more men scurried back and forth engaged in various duties of repairing their ship. Neither Kyle nor Akbar were anywhere in sight, but Devon soon located Diablo standing on the bridge overseeing the progress. His hands braced on the rail, he bent to call something to one of his crew, and Devon's eyes roamed appreciatively over the muscles bunched beneath his white, open-necked shirt.

Why would a man like Diablo turn to piracy? Devon wondered, her eyes lingering on his face fringed with thick black hair. He looked quite ferocious with the luxurious growth, and Devon couldn't help thinking that he would be outrageously handsome without the beard, though with it he was still devilishly attractive. Bold, strong, stubborn, arrogant. Each of those words could be used to describe Diablo's unique features. Add to those, ruthless, demanding, and cruel.

Intuitively Devon realized it would be folly to venture forth among these rapacious pirates—men who respected nothing and no one. Greed ruled them and lust drove them. Devon silently turned to make a hasty retreat, but fate intervened.

"Ho, lads, 'tis Diablo's whore!"

Suddenly one of the pirates loomed before Devon, blocking her path. "Old Pegleg weren't lyin' when he said she be a beauty."

The man was short, stocky, and incredibly dirty. He wore an eyepatch over his left eye, and what was left of his hair clung to his neck in dirty limp strands. He grinned at Devon as if he could eat her up in one gobble as he reached out to fondle a blonde curl.

"Don't touch me, you cur!" Devon spat, wishing she had listened to Diablo and remained safely hidden.

"Yer too ugly fer the likes o' that fancy piece, Patch," one of the bystanders taunted crudely. "She's the cap'n's private whore."

"Ain't we always shared alike on the *Devil Dancer,* Davy?" Patch replied, impaling Devon with his good eye. "How can the cap'n object if we vote to pass the wench around?"

All work stopped as dozens of pairs of eyes swiveled to where Devon stood quivering like a cornered doe. She squealed in protest when Patch seized her around the waist and dragged her into full view. Her pounding fists had little effect on Patch's massive chest, her feeble protests earning her a cuff to the head that sent her reeling. Several of the men looked nervously toward Diablo, who had yet to notice the commotion for he had left the bridge to inspect the work being done on the rudder.

"Me first," Patch said, claiming Devon and swinging her high in his arms as he carried her to where the sail lay spread out on the deck. Suddenly Devon found herself flat on her back with Patch crouching above her.

Finding courage in the intensity of her anger, Devon scrambled to her knees while Patch paused to unfasten his clothing. From the corner of her eye she saw Diablo turn around, finally aware of the ruckus, and she knew instinctively that her salvation lay with him. He was a pirate, true, but she sensed no threat in him as she did in these other desperate men who would cruelly rape her. She watched expectantly as Diablo approached the circle of men surrounding her, at the same time keeping a wary eye on Patch who at that moment lunged for her.

Rising to her feet, Devon reacted instinctively, aiming a well-placed kick at Patch's privates. The man reared back, howling in pain, and Devon took to her heels, scrambling through the stunned crowd while screaming Diablo's name at the top of her lungs. Patch was still bending over clutching his groin when Devon reached the safety of Diablo's open arms. As his arms closed protectively around her, she was amazed at her sudden lack of fear.

"What are you doing out here?" Diablo asked, jerking

Devon around to face him. "You foolish child! Didn't I warn you what would happen if you showed yourself on deck?"

"I . . . I thought . . ." Devon stammered, quailing beneath Diablo's hard glare.

Giving her a little shake, Diablo placed Devon behind him, then turned to confront Patch, who hadn't yet recovered from Devon's vicious blow. "What do you mean by this, Patch? Didn't you hear me claim the lady for myself?"

"I heard, Diablo, but it ain't fair," Patch complained bitterly. Several of the crewmen nodded in agreement. "Ain't none of us had a woman since them two French whores we took off that French sloop near Barbados. Why're ya bein' so damn selfish when ya never cared before?"

"I don't need to explain myself," Diablo bit out. "You signed the articles. You know the rules. The crew get their share of the booty after the captain and officers take their cut."

"Women ain't included," grumbled Patch sourly, appealing to his mates for support. "What say you, Davy, Leech, Snake? How about it, lads?"

The men named shifted nervously from foot to foot. Though they wanted to agree with Patch, they feared Diablo and his ferocious Turk too much to side publicly with him.

"It looks like this is between you and me, Patch," Diablo said with quiet menace. "The woman is mine. Do you want to challenge me for her? I've already offered to split my share of the booty with the crew to compensate for the loss of the wench, but I'm ready and willing to defend my exclusive right to her."

Patch seemed to have second thoughts about confronting Diablo. The captain was a powerful and cunning man, a fierce fighter and superb leader, fair and protective of his men. Yet he could be a harsh disciplinarian when the need arose. Under his able command they had taken many prizes and shared equally in the booty. Patch knew when he should back off and prudently decided to bide his time. Diablo couldn't be with the wench every minute of the day and night, and he'd find her alone sooner or later. It didn't bother Patch in the slightest that once he'd finished with Devon he would be forced to kill her in order to keep her from talking.

"Keep the wench, Diablo, and use her in good health," Patch said at length. "Your share of the booty will buy me more wenches in Nassau than I can handle." Abruptly he turned and swaggered away. The rest of the crew drifted back to their duties, the flurry of excitement ended before it really began.

Only Kyle and Akbar remained at Diablo's side, each positioning himself to reinforce their captain during the brief encounter. Had they been needed they would have fought staunchly beside Diablo.

"I knew the woman meant trouble," Akbar muttered, eying Devon balefully. It was apparent that the huge Turk had little use for women, finding them all unworthy of Diablo, whom he considered superior to any man alive.

"I should have locked her in," Diablo observed sourly. "I won't make that mistake again. Escort the lady to my cabin, Kyle, and lock the door." His silver gaze pierced Devon like twin blades of flashing steel.

Kyle nodded, grasped Devon's arm firmly, and half-led, half-carried her into Diablo's cabin. "You did a foolish thing, lass," he said, scowling. "You should have listened to Diablo. Locking you in is for your own protection."

Devon searched Kyle's attractive features carefully. Of all the men aboard the *Devil Dancer* he looked the least like a pirate. Tall and broad, red-haired and clean-shaven, he appeared more trustworthy than any of them, including Diablo. Surely such a man had some redeeming qualities, Devon reflected. The thought occured to her to appeal to him for help.

"Protection!" Devon scoffed derisively. "What kind of protection could I expect from a blood-thirsty scavenger?"

"You'd be surprised." Kyle smiled thinly. "You haven't been harmed yet despite the fact that you nearly killed Diablo. That alone should speak well for Diablo's intentions."

"Where am I being taken? Diablo promised to set me ashore."

"The storm blew us too far out to sea to make that possible, lass. You'll have to seek answers from Diablo." He turned to leave.

"Kyle—that is your name, isn't it?" Kyle halted, turned back to Devon, and nodded guardedly.

"Aye."

Devon licked her suddenly dry lips, hoping she hadn't misjudged Kyle's character. "Please, won't you help me? You know Diablo kidnapped me. Ask him to set me ashore anywhere and I can make my way back home. I'll see that you're handsomely compensated for your trouble."

"Ah, lass, I can't be bribed," Kyle said regretfully.

Devon looked so appealing he wished he could help her. But he'd not go against Diablo for anything. Though Diablo was a notorious pirate and could be ruthless and even cruel at times, few knew of the gentle side to the man. Kyle felt reasonably certain Devon would not be harmed.

"Then I'm wasting my time," Devon snapped waspishly. Deliberately she presented her delectable backside to Kyle. Grinning in obvious appreciation, Kyle left the cabin, locking the door according to Diablo's instructions.

Devon paced the cabin, venting her famous temper. Somehow she'd get out of this, she predicted, and when she did, Diablo would rue the day he set eyes on her. No matter where he took her, Winnie and her father would follow. When they caught up with that miserable blackguard, he would finally meet his destiny.

Chapter Four

An unappetizing meal was provided Devon later that day. Pegleg brought it in to her, then promptly left without uttering a word, locking the door behind him. When it grew dark, Devon lit a lamp and awaited Diablo's next move. She had no way of knowing he had decided to share Kyle's cabin, for he was still too angry with Devon to be in the same room with her. She had sorely tried his explosive temper, and he feared he would wring her pretty neck once they were alone. Finally Devon fell into an uneasy slumber, curled up fully dressed in the oversized bunk.

Immersed in a world of dreams, Devon did not hear the scrape of the lock or squeal of hinges as the cabin door was carefully inched open. The lamp Devon had lit earlier still burned, and Patch grinned evilly as his one good eye easily found her.

It had taken some doing to get the key to the cabin, but Patch considered himself smarter than most of his fellow pirates. It just so happened he'd been standing nearby when Diablo entrusted the key to his cabin to Pegleg so that the one-legged sailor might bring food to Devon. Because Pegleg was an old man, Diablo trusted him not to molest his property. Patch couldn't believe his ears when he heard Diablo tell Pegleg he was sharing Kyle's quarters tonight. That evening, Patch had only to invite Pegleg to share a bottle of rum he had stashed away and purloin the key when the old sailor was too drunk to notice.

Patch waited until everyone was sleeping. He was more than a little contemptuous of Diablo's sleeping arrangements. Perhaps his captain's wound prevented him from enjoying the woman as fully as he might wish, Patch theorized, and he preferred to wait to bed her.

Patch eased inside the cabin, silently closing the door behind him as he drew the dirty scarf from around his neck. He planned to stuff it in Devon's mouth to keep her from crying out. His steps carried him to the bunk, where he paused to admire the entrancing sight.

Devon stirred uneasily. Something disturbed her slumber. Something menacing. Had Diablo finally returned to punish her for disobeying him? she wondered groggily. Slowly she opened her eyes and caught sight of the filthy one-eyed man looming above her. She opened her mouth to scream.

Diablo awakened with a start. He tried to rise, clutched his wounded side, then fell back against the pillow. Several agonizing minutes passed before he gathered the strength to lever himself to his feet. A ray of errant moonlight fell on Kyle's sleeping form. Nothing amiss here, Diablo mused, wondering what had roused him from a deep sleep. Then he remembered. Somewhere from inside his head came a silent plea for help. Devon! Was he so attuned to the little wildcat that he knew the moment danger stalked her?

Arming himself with cutlass and pistol, Diablo stealthily made his way along the moon-drenched deck to the stern, speaking briefly to the watch, who assured him all was well. He thought to return to his rest when he stumbled upon Pegleg lolling in a drunken stupor. At first he thought nothing of it. Then a terrible premonition seized him. With the agility of a jungle cat, Diablo whirled, moving lightly on the balls of his feet toward his cabin. His heart thumped wildly inside his chest and every instinct screamed of danger.

Diablo opened the door, the roared in outrage when he saw Patch reaching down toward Devon. Her eyes were wide and staring, her mouth gaping open in a silent scream.

"Touch her and you're dead," Diablo said with quiet menace, brandishing his cutlass in a widening arc. "It seems I arrived in the nick of time."

Patch spit out a stream of obscenities, cursing the fates that brought Diablo to Devon's rescue. He thought the man well named, for something more than luck had brought him here at this moment. Had Diablo indeed sold his soul to the devil as everyone claimed? Sliding Devon a look of intense longing, Patch stepped away from the bunk, ruing the day he ever sailed on the *Devil Dancer*. This wasn't the first time he'd clashed with Diablo nor would it be the last. Only the next time he'd win.

"I weren't gonna hurt her none, Diablo," Patch whined obsequiously. "You shoulda shared the wench like always."

"You know the rules, Patch, and the punishment. Akbar!" he called out, knowing the huge Turk would be nearby, waiting for his call. Little happened on the ship without Akbar's knowledge.

Sure enough, within minutes Akbar stepped inside the cabin, a cutlass dangling from his fingertips. "I am here, Diablo." Not a muscle in Akbar's stern face revealed his thoughts as he stared forbiddingly at Patch, then shifted his disapproving gaze to Devon.

"Throw this scum in the hold. The first order of business tomorrow morning will be to administer punishment. Twenty lashes should suffice."

"Aye," Akbar agreed, herding Patch toward the door. When Patch hung back, a prick of Akbar's cutlass sped him onward.

Seventy curious men milled about on deck when Patch and Akbar appeared. Though those closest strained their necks to see inside the cabin, they found the door slammed firmly in their faces. But it soon became apparent what had happened and news spread through their ranks like wildfire. Patch had violated the rules and had earned himself a flogging.

"Did he hurt you?" Diablo asked Devon, his face set in grim lines. Though his stern visage did not relax, he approached the bunk slowly, fearful lest he frighten Devon more. But he needn't have worried, for Devon was made of sterner stuff than her fragile appearance suggested. She was more angry than frightened.

"That repulsive toad did me no harm." The shiver that swept over her slim frame belied her brave words.

Diablo swallowed a grin. He had to admit the feisty wench had courage—more courage than sense. Actually, he admired everything about her, and obviously so did his crew. In the future he would have to take precautions, even if it meant sleeping beside Devon each night, if only to protect her, torture though it might be.

"I think it's time I explained your position aboard the *Devil Dancer*, Lady Devon," Diablo began, stifling a chuckle as he imagined her response to his words.

"My—position?"

"Aye, so that there'll be no question in the future in the minds of my crew, or any misunderstanding between us concerning your place here. I made a mistake by leaving you alone tonight, but I won't do so again."

"Just what is my position, Diablo? You're aware, of course, that my father will pay handsomely for my safe return. Turn around and take me back home," Devon pleaded earnestly.

"There's my crew to think of, my lady. Seventy lives depend on how well we evade the English navy, as well as eluding other ships bent on our destruction. I was stupid enough to get caught once, but it won't happen again. I promise you'll be sent home when I find a way to do so without endangering our own lives. In the meantime you'll serve as my mistress."

Suddenly the need to touch Devon was so intense that Diablo couldn't resist the urge to reach out and lightly brush his fingertips across the high ridge of one cheek. Devon sucked in her breath, his caress tender yet erotically provocative. The look in his eyes told her he was aroused by her, and she fought against the sizzling attraction that quivered to life between them.

"You're crazy if you think I'll be your mistress," Devon snorted derisively. Her blue eyes blazed with defiance, and Diablo thought she never looked more adorable. Unconsciously she sent forth a heady blend of innocence and simmering passion, a volatile combination Diablo longed to savor.

"You have no choice in the matter, my lady." His voice was slow and lazy and subtly sensual.

Devon stared dumbly, fully aware that she should not succumb to the handsome rogue.

"I'll fight you every step of the way," she warned, her voice taut with a new kind of fear. Would he give her to his crew to enjoy if she defied him?

"We'll discuss it tomorrow, Devon," Diablo said wearily, surprising her. "Go to sleep, I'll not bother you tonight. My side aches abominably and I'm exhausted."

"Where will you sleep?" Panic colored her words.

"Right here beside you." Then he treated Devon to that beguiling smile that had the power to render her witless.

"I'll sleep on the floor," Devon demurred. She leaped off the bunk and began pulling the blanket from the bunk.

Diablo stayed her hand, drawing her roughly up against him. "You'll sleep in the bunk, beside me, even if I have to tie you down."

"You—wouldn't!"

"Try me, my lady. You've succeeded in wearing my patience thin. You know what I'm capable of, so I strongly suggest you leave off goading me."

Diablo meant only to frighten Devon, but she felt so damn good in his arms he yearned to kiss her, to taste the sweetness of her mouth, partake freely of everything she had to offer. A muffled protest died in her throat when his lips captured hers. The kiss was slow and lazy, and amazingly innocent. Something Diablo intended to remedy immediately.

"Open your mouth," he whispered against her lips.

Then his lips brushed over hers softly and he lifted her chin to deepen contact. She trembled, and some perverse imp inside her made her open her lips. His tongue slipped inside, touched hers. She quaked in his arms as they tightened about her, feeling the entire length of him molded to her softness. Something huge and hard pressed relentlessly against her belly.

Devon froze. Never had anyone kissed her in such a suggestive manner. Winnie would never presume to insult her in so demeaning a manner, but she expected no less from this son of Satan whose viselike embrace was squeezing the breath from her. Yet she could not deny her body's need to respond to his kiss with an answering heat. Then abruptly she found herself gently set aside. Stepping back, Diablo stared at her strangely, his thick black brows quirked quizzically.

"That was an amazing kiss for an innocent."

"You forced me!"

"If I were a gentleman, I'd agree. Unfortunately . . ." He shrugged with exaggerated eloquence, leaving Devon to draw her own conclusions. Then he calmly stretched out on the bunk, making room for her with overstated courtesy. Deliberately he closed his eyes, but Devon knew from the tenseness of his body that he was alert and waiting.

Gingerly she perched on the edge of the bunk, eying Diablo warily. When he made no threatening move, she lay down, as close to the edge as she dared. Her body was as taut as a bow string, but gradually, when she realized Diablo offered no immediate threat, she relaxed, and at last drifted off to sleep. Diablo was not so lucky.

Lying beside Devon was sheer torture. Diablo had only to

reach out and—no—not that way, he cautioned himself. One day soon he'd have Devon, but it wouldn't be rape. He wanted her—God, how he wanted her—willing and responsive. He figured he had plenty of time to wear down her resistance. On his island, in his home, there'd be no one for her to turn to but him.

Diablo realized that returning Devon to England at this time would be pure folly, for he assumed that by now her father and fiancé had the entire British navy combing the seas for her. And he damn well wasn't going to be caught again, or operate with the fleet breathing down his neck. Besides, the men had been at sea a long time and could use a spell in port, and the ship needed careening. There was plenty of booty to divide, so Diablo was reasonably certain the crew wouldn't grumble about being set ashore for a time.

Diablo groaned aloud when Devon turned in her sleep, seeking his warmth as she pressed full length against him. No matter how hard he tried, he couldn't prevent himself from slipping an arm under her head and drawing her into the curve of his body. With a will of its own his hand sought the soft rise of her breast. When she didn't awaken or protest, Diablo sighed, intensely grateful for that one small concession, and closed his eyes, finding surprising comfort in touching her.

Devon awoke with a start. Bright sunlight streamed through the two long windows and she blinked repeatedly. Her heart pounded with trepidation as she half-turned, expecting to find Diablo's lean length stretched out beside her. But to her immense relief he was gone. Nothing remained but the indentation where his head had lain on the pillow beside her.

Rising, Devon found water in the pitcher and washed thoroughly, keeping a wary eye on the door. She had just finished brushing her long blonde hair when Diablo returned bearing a tray. He looked freshly bathed and shaved and even more attractive than she remembered. His white shirt, festooned with yards of lace on the cuffs and down the front, was open at the neck and spotlessly clean. Tight black pants hugged muscular thighs, and left Devon no doubt concerning his masculinity. Curiously, he wasn't smiling that maddening smile she had become accustomed to.

"Eat, Devon, it's nearly time." He placed the tray on the desk and motioned her forward. Devon eyed the food with cool disdain, then turned her nose up at the unappetizing mess.

"Time? Time for what?"

"Have you forgotten so soon? The flogging, what else? Everyone aboard the *Devil Dancer* is required to be present at Patch's punishment."

"Flogging?" Devon repeated stupidly. "The custom is barbaric. Surely you don't expect me to watch."

"You're the reason the man is being flogged," Diablo reminded her. "The crew will expect you to be there. Besides, I fully intend to flaunt you as my mistress so in the future no one will doubt that you're mine."

"But I'm *not* yours!" Devon protested vigorously. "Nor will I ever be a man's possession."

"Oh, you will be mine, Devon." Diablo smiled ruthlessly. "Sooner than you think. Hurry, now, the crew is already gathering on deck."

Glaring at him murderously, Devon wolfed down her food without tasting it, then rose reluctantly to her feet. "I'm ready, but I'm not going to enjoy this."

As Devon moved toward the door, Diablo's critical silver gaze swept the entire length of her from head to toe. "Where did you find that drab dress?" Before she could form a reply, he ordered curtly, "Change it."

"Change it? But why? All the others are far more revealing."

"Just change it. I'll be back in five minutes." He stomped out the door without the courtesy of an explanation.

Fuming in impotent rage, Devon was grateful at least that Diablo allowed her to change in privacy. Rummaging through the chest of clothes put at her disposal, she chose an attractive gown fashioned of turquoise silk that shimmered with iridescent silver threads. The narrow waist pushed her breasts up until they threatened to spill out of the gown. Under different circumstances Devon would think nothing of wearing such a daring creation, but aboard this devil ship it seemed far from appropriate. Idly she wondered why Diablo insisted on such an ostentatious display. At the last minute she placed a lace scarf over her shoulders and felt somewhat reassured.

"That's much better," Diablo commented dryly when he reappeared moments later. His mouth quirked in amusement when he noted the concealing scarf, but he said nothing, allowing her that small concession.

Within minutes Devon found herself standing beside Diablo on the main deck of the *Devil Dancer*. Patch was already lashed to the whipping post, his back bared to receive the promised twenty lashes from the tarred rawhide whip nearly an inch thick. The crowd opened ranks, allowing Diablo and Devon to approach the condemned man. Evidently Akbar was to mete out the punishment for, naked to the waist, he stood over Patch, the rawhide whip held loosely in one huge hand.

"Oh, God," Devon gasped, pulling back. But Diablo was relentless.

"You started this, my lady, and you will see it to the finish. Begin, Akbar."

Flexing his enormous muscles, the giant Turk brought the first stroke whistling down on Patch's exposed back. The howl of agony that followed sent a chill down Devon's spine.

The next strokes fell in quick succession, with no mercy, no respite allowed the screaming pirate. Patch made no visible effort to stifle his cries, and Devon's hands flew up to shield her ears. After ten strokes she could take no more.

"Stop! Please stop! You're killing him."

"He'll live, my lady," Diablo said tightly. "He'll live to think twice about flaunting my authority. Discipline is everything aboard a ship. If I relent now, my crew would no longer respect me and I'd find myself quickly replaced. Believe me, Devon, this is the only way. Continue, Akbar," he commanded, ignoring Devon's distress.

Patch's back looked like raw meat, and Devon felt herself grow weak with revulsion. Her knees buckled, and she was grateful for Diablo's support as he placed a strong arm around her, pulling her close. Otherwise she would have disgraced herself dreadfully by falling flat on her face.

"Steady, my lady," Diablo whispered as the whip rose and fell with relentless regularity. " 'Tis nearly over."

Then it truly was over. Someone doused Patch's back with a bucket of salt water and he was half-carried, half-dragged to a place where Kyle could tend his wounds. Silently the crew melted away, leaving no man doubting that the lady belonged solely to Diablo and the devil would demand his dues from any unfortunate soul who coveted what Diablo considered his private property. It was exactly the response Diablo had hoped for.

Sickened by what she had witnessed, Devon did not object when Diablo turned her in the direction of his cabin. Only when the door was firmly closed behind them did she speak.

"That was the most heinous act I've ever seen!"

"Maintaining discipline is vital on my ship. You have no idea what these men are like or what they're capable of. Pirates are a breed apart. Some are deserters from the British navy; some were taken from crews of captured merchant-men and forced to join us, though a married man is never forced to join the brotherhood. They can be cruel, sadistic, and ruthless beyond your wildest imaginings.

"If I relented with Patch I would eventually lose control of my crew. I've worked too hard for my position to relinquish it at the whim of a woman."

"You say pirates are a breed apart," Devon challenged. "Where do you fit in? Are you a deserter? Were you captured and forced? From what country are you?"

"A long time ago I was forced," Diablo said, a faraway look in his eyes. "But later I embraced the profession freely and willingly. Does that answer your questions?"

"All accept for your nationality."

"I am from the sea." It was a stock answer given by pirates when asked where they were from.

"You're not uneducated and you speak well," Devon mused thoughtfully. "I suspect there's much you're not telling me. Why the mystery, Diablo? Your name is Spanish—have you been banished from your homeland or disinherited by your family?"

"Inquisitive little imp, aren't you?" Diablo chuckled. "Suffice it to say I do what I do because I enjoy the adventure— and the rewards." There was no mistaking his meaning, for his silver eyes sparkled with appreciation as they roamed freely over Devon's entrancing face and figure.

His look was so blatantly sensual, so charged with sexual innuendo that even an innocent like Devon reacted instinctively to the power of his personality. And she feared her reaction. Self-preservation forced her steps backward, only to have Diablo follow relentlessly.

"Don't touch me."

"You're my mistress, I can do as I please."

"I'm not your mistress. I have a fiancé. I'm to be married in a few weeks."

"Who is he, some aging earl willing to squander his fortune on you?"

"Not that it's any of your business, but he's young and a viscount. I don't need his money, I've plenty of my own."

"Only a viscount?" Diablo taunted, wagging a shapely black brow. "Perhaps he's marrying you for *your* money."

"He loves me," Devon defended stoutly.

"Has he bedded you?"

Devon looked so startled that Diablo felt reasonably certain no man had ever touched her, including the virtuous fiancé.

"Does he kiss you?"

"Why—why, of course," sputtered Devon, by now totally confused. "Why are you asking me all these crude questions?" Devon definitely didn't like the way things were going. In fact, she hated the way her body responded to Diablo and his special magnetism.

"Does he kiss you like this?" Diablo took her in his arms, pressing tiny, teasing kisses on her mouth, eyes, and cheeks. Then he concentrated solely on her lips, his hand cupping the back of her head, tilting her face up to his mouth. He stopped long enough to whisper, "Or like this?"

This time his kiss was hard and deep and hungry. The fury of his kiss forced open her mouth and his tongue slipped inside, brazenly tasting her. Her eyes were closed, the trembling golden lashes poised upon her flushed cheeks like velvet butterfly wings. The shocking evidence of his arousal was like a rock between them, and panic seized Devon. Who did this odious pirate think she was? A woman of loose morals? She was Lady Devon Chatham, the daughter of an earl, educated, refined, and smart enough to know that she was on the brink of losing her precious virtue.

Suddenly she was free of those steel bands confining her, and her eyes blinked open. She was startled to find Diablo staring down at her with a smile that was arrestingly wicked. "You liked that, didn't you, Devon? I think you'll enjoy being my mistress. I know I will." His outrageous teasing sent her senses reeling, and she adroitly changed the subject.

"What about ransom? My father will pay you anything you ask for my safe return."

Breathlessly she awaited Diablo's answer, thinking that everything about the man was a contradiction. Not one blessed thing she'd ever heard about him made sense when one considered all that had happened since she'd had the misfortune to meet Diablo. Though she constantly provoked him, he hadn't harmed her. He could have easily brutalized her but had displayed amazing restraint. He might have done to her what men did to woman (she suspected what it might be but had no firsthand knowledge of it) yet had not ravished her except for a demanding kiss or two. He wanted her for his mistress yet appeared willing to give her time to adjust to his request.

"Nay, I want no ransom. I have riches enough."

"You promised to let me go," Devon reminded him, growing desperate.

"Aye, so I did." He smiled wolfishly. "Did you not know pirates were notorious liars? I've become quite taken with you, my lady. If I must spend time ashore I'd prefer to spend it with you. When I take to the sea again I'll see that you're returned to England."

"But not in the same condition in which you found me, I'll wager," Devon challenged.

His silver-gray eyes roamed her figure with wicked delight. "I'll do you no harm, if that's what you're worried about. But I mean to have your maidenhead, if it exists."

"You'd rape me?"

"I think not," he claimed with cool assurance.

Then he was kissing her again, his thick, wiry beard harsh against the tender skin of her face and neck. His lips moved restlessly over her eyes, cheeks, the end of her nose, before slanting hungrily over her mouth, the tip of his tongue probing along the line of her lips until they parted. He plundered ruthlessly the sweetness she sought to withhold, taking pleasure in the shudder passing through her slender form.

Traveling downward over Devon's tiny waist and generous hips, Diablo's big hands grasped the firm mounds of her buttocks, pulling her so close that hardly a breath remained between them. Desire was a hard knot inside him, and Diablo seriously doubted that he could withdraw without doing serious damage to his sanity. But he didn't want to rape Devon, or hurt her in any way no matter how badly he wanted her. He had all the time in the world to seduce her gently into his bed—she wasn't going anywhere but to Paradise, his very own island where his word was law. The thought of eventually having Devon warm, willing, and responsive beneath him was all the inducement needed to control his ardor.

"I have duties, my lady," he said, his breath rasping between his teeth. "You've won a reprieve for the time being. One day soon," he promised, his eyes turning to smoldering ash, "the devil will have his due."

Devon collapsed on the bunk the moment Diablo's virile form disappeared through the door. Evidently he still didn't trust her for she heard the scrape of the key turning in the lock. Or was it his mates he didn't trust? Either way, she was a prisoner on a devil's ship, the innocent pawn of a man who intended to use her well before discarding her. Never! Devon silently vowed.

Diablo was still smiling when he reached the quarterdeck, still aroused but glad he had decided against forcing the feisty little wench. Paradise was a beautiful island, highly conducive to seduction. Meanwhile, he'd work on Devon's senses, accustom her to his touch and slowly erode her fear and defiance.

"Don't you think you were a wee bit hard on the lass, Diablo?" Kyle asked. He had watched Diablo approach and did not miss the triumphant grin plastered across his face. "Forcing her to watch the flogging was cruel."

"The lady is tougher than you think, my friend," Diablo advised, eyes twinkling merrily. "Besides, it was necessary. You know as well as I how quickly the crew can turn against us. I can't afford to relax my guard. For the time being the men respect and trust me, and I want to keep it that way. Are the repairs completed?" he asked, changing the subject.

"Aye, Akbar is awaiting the order to raise the sails. I've set the course for the Bahamas."

"Nassau first, Kyle. We're to wait there for Le Vautour. When last we met he offered to sell our loot to the governor of New York in the American colonies. He and Le Vautour are great friends, and the Frenchman will get us a good price."

"Le Vautour—the vulture—can you trust that wily bird?" Kyle asked skeptically.

"As much as anyone in our profession," Diablo said with a shrug, though not really convinced. "I had hoped to visit the colonies myself to partake of their hospitality, but I think it unwise at this time, though it would be refreshing to visit a port and be welcomed with open arms."

"Aye," Kyle was quick to agree. "Boston and New York are renowned ports of call for pirates the world over. And when the brotherhood visits Philadelphia they act as if they own the place, and no one disputes their right. The American governors support us, give us provisions, crews, protection, and even hospitality."

"The colonies make a profit out of piracy, Kyle. They provide a market for our booty and sometimes give us fake sailing papers. For them, sheltering pirates is a blow against the British rule they abhor."

"The lass stays with you, I suppose," Kyle said dryly, once again bringing Devon into the conversation.

"I won't abandon her in a foreign land, if that's what you

mean. I've decided to keep her as my mistress," Diablo revealed.

"Saints preserve us," Kyle muttered, shifting his eyes heavenward. "Are you daft, Kit? Isn't Scarlett enough for you? Why tempt the fates? There are beautiful women aplenty, both in Nassau and on Paradise."

"I've already decided, Kyle. No amount of argument will change my mind. Lady Devon intrigues me. I want her, dammit, and I'll have her! I've taken women captives to my bed often enough in the past, my friend, so why should one more bother you?"

"Tell me the lass is willing and I'll say no more."

Diablo had the grace to flush beneath his concealing beard. "She will be," he promised with male conceit.

Somehow Kyle doubted it. "What about Scarlett? You know how hot-tempered that she-devil can be."

"I'll handle Scarlett when the time comes. Say no more. My mind is made up. For the time we're ashore Lady Devon will be my mistress, and she'll be willing." Suddenly a devilish gleam lit Diablo's eyes. He always did enjoy a game. "I'll make you a wager, my friend, seeing how interested you are in the lady's fate. My share of the booty says the lady will come to my bed willingly before we set foot on Paradise. Either way, I promise she'll be sent home unharmed when the *Devil Dancer* sails again."

"I accept," Kyle agreed, knowing the feisty lass would lead Diablo a merry chase before she gave in—if she gave in. "If I lose, my share is yours."

Chapter Five

Diablo returned to take supper with Devon that night. Lines of fatigue etched grooves around his mouth and he was definitely favoring his right side. A pang of remorse for the pain she had caused him sliced through Devon, but only for a moment. She considered it just punishment for the way he had ruthlessly kidnapped her.

Supper was a sorry affair, the food barely palatable. Diablo said little, staring at her in a disconcerting manner. Once he asked why her face appeared reddened and chafed, almost as if it had been bruised. She promptly replied that his wiry beard had damaged the tender skin, unaccustomed as it was to his rough use. At first Diablo seemed startled, then he turned thoughtful, occasionally fingering his luxurious growth as they ate.

Kyle arrived later to change Diablo's bandage. Devon busied herself with cleaning up the remains of their supper while Kyle worked over Diablo's torso. She wasn't certain she could trust herself to look objectively upon the smooth bronze skin stretched so tautly across the pirate's impressive frame. He was too tempting, entirely too virile and imposing to suit her.

Once his wound was dressed, Diablo left the cabin, and during the interval Devon hastily prepared for bed. She was about to crawl into the bunk fully dressed when Diablo returned. He took one look at her and said, "There are plenty of nightclothes in the chest I sent you."

"I—I'd rather not."

"I insist. You can't be comfortable like that." His silver eyes took on a predatory gleam as he opened the chest, lifting out a voluminous white garment made of linen and hardly conducive to seduction. "I'll help you."

"N—no! I can manage," Devon cried, snatching the gown from his fingers. "Turn around."

"I've seen you before and I must admit it only whet my appetite."

"Diablo, don't do this."

"Do what, my lady? Surely you must agree that I've been remarkably patient with you. I'd be laughed out of the brotherhood if it got out that I've yet to bed you."

"I won't tell anyone," she promised hopefully.

Diablo tilted his head back and laughed heartily. "Well said, my lady. Now get undressed so we can both get some sleep."

Surprisingly, he turned away, went to his own sea chest, and began assembling various paraphernalia. Hurriedly Devon pulled the gown over her head and stripped away the clothes underneath. When she finished she stood there uncertainly, still refusing to move to the bed.

"Get in bed," Diablo ordered tersely, aware of her every move though his back remained turned.

"I intend to put up a fight," Devon advised, lifting her chin defiantly. "I'll resist you every step of the way. Rape is the only way you'll have me."

Diablo sighed tiredly. "Get in bed, Devon, you're safe tonight."

Standing rigidly, Devon perched on the horns of a dilemma. If she wasn't so frightened of this handsome devil she would find humor in the situation. No, she corrected, she wasn't exactly frightened, merely intimidated by the aura of power surrounding him, and threatened by his virility.

Coming to a decision, Devon moved woodenly to the bed, sank down on its comfortable surface, and scooted as far to the opposite side as she dare. Diablo said nothing, just continued with what he was doing. Devon eyed him narrowly as he placed several pieces of equipment on the wash stand, turned up the lamp, and set to work. Dismay widened Devon's blue eyes when she realized what he was about.

"You're shaving!"

"Aye."

Totally absorbed, Devon watched in rapt fascination as more and more of Diablo's handsome face was revealed with each stroke of the razor. Firm, square jaw, full, sensual lips; his features spoke of power and ageless strength. What Devon thought most amazing was the way his mouth curled on the edge of laughter. But what really entranced her was the deep dimple hovering at the corner of that wide, mobile mouth. No wonder he wore a beard, was Devon's initial reaction, for without it no one would have believed that such a classically handsome face lurked beneath the beard of this fierce pirate whose very name inspired fear in the hearts of the bravest of men.

Only one word came to mind. "Why?"

"Because it pleases me," came his cryptic reply. "And I hope it pleases you as well. I'd not have your tender skin damaged on my account."

"Me? It matters little to me how you look, for it doesn't change what you are. Too bad you didn't slit your throat while you were at it."

Diablo shook his head, then burst out laughing. "You're priceless, Devon, truly priceless. I look forward to the day when I will know all the secrets your body possesses."

Before he snuffed out the light, Devon was treated to a fleeting glimpse of that devastating dimple in his cheek. Then she heard the rustle of clothes, and the bed sagged to accept his weight. When his warmth settled beside her, she started in spontaneous reaction.

"Lie still, Devon, and go to sleep."

Sleep! How could she sleep with Diablo's hard frame

pressed so intimately against her? When he turned and pulled her into the curve of his body, she gulped convulsively and held her breath, preparing to do battle. But to her relief—or disappointment—he did no more than stroke the outer curve of her breast. Still, it was more than she was willing to allow.

"Don't touch me!" Inadvertently her elbow jabbed into his wounded side.

"Umph! Blast it, Devon, do I have to tie you down? That hurt."

"Good. Keep your hands to yourself."

"Hellion," he muttered, turning over. After making that stupid promise to Kyle, he hoped to slowly accustom Devon to his touch until she came to accept him naturally and willingly. He had hoped to create a need in her, one only he could assuage. But if tonight was any example, it looked as if he'd soon be parted from his share of the loot.

Devon sighed contentedly, serene and warm in her cozy nest. She felt safe, protected, and oh so comfortable. Something soft nuzzled her neck. Then a teasing, bristly sensation irritated the tender skin of her face. She frowned in her sleep but did not waken. Her breasts tingled, her long legs shifted restlessly beneath a caressing warmth she could not identify.

"Sweet, so sweet." The words, whispered in her ear, brought Devon fully awake.

Diablo was bending over her, covering her face and neck with teasing, nipping kisses. His hands, those large, rough hands, were under her nightrail, exploring the smooth texture of her flesh . . . her belly, her legs, tracing a hipbone with one calloused finger, tenderly fondling her swelling breasts. Then she felt a rush of air as her gown was raised and Diablo bent his dark head to touch his tongue to her aching nipples. He groaned once, then took the pouting bud into his mouth and began suckling with ever increasing vigor.

Devon's body jolted with the shock of it. "Stop it!"

"Ah, you're a ripe piece, sweetheart. See how your body responds to me? Let me make love to you. Let me teach you to enjoy all I can do for you."

"I want nothing to do with you or your kind," Devon resisted. The urge to lie back and let Diablo impose his will on her was so great she had to bite her lip to keep her sanity intact. "I'll never submit to you willingly."

"And I'll have you no other way," Diablo muttered beneath his breath, levering himself from the bunk. "It's growing late and I've a ship to run. I'll return later to take you for a stroll on deck." He flashed her a grin before rising in all his naked glory, unashamedly displaying the need she created in him.

Before she turned away from the entrancing sight, Devon caught a glimpse of long-muscled legs, firm-fleshed buttocks, slim waist, and impossibly wide shoulders. A flush crept up her neck when she tried to concentrate on anything but the virile length of that part of him she tried so hard to ignore.

It amazed Devon that she hadn't thought of Winston or their marriage in days. Not since Diablo came into her life like a swirling whirlwind to scatter her wits. What was the matter with her? she chided herself.

"Come along, my lady, the sun will do you good."

Diablo grasped Devon's waist firmly and guided her out the door onto the sun-drenched deck. It was a glorious day, and the crew scurried about their chores stripped to the waist, their bronzed torsos glistening with sweat. A few followed the slow progress of Diablo and Devon along the deck, but most, recalling Patch's fate, kept their gaze carefully averted, at least while Diablo guarded his mistress so zealously.

"You look radiant today, my lady," Diablo complimented as he eyed her choice of apparel.

Devon had chosen an attractive blue day dress, its deep oval neckline and sleeves lavishly embellished with lace. It hugged her supple curves to perfection, bringing attention to her tall, lissome form. She chose to ignore his compliment, pretending fascination in the ship.

Noting her keen interest, Diablo said, "She's a sloop, Devon. See her rapierlike bowsprit? She's fore and aft rigged, swift and nimble," he pointed out proudly. "She weighs one hundred tons and can do eleven knots under favorable winds. She carries a crew of seventy-five, fourteen cannon, and four swivel guns. Her shallow draft—less than eight feet—allows her to navigate shoal waters and hide in remote coves when necessary. Damn handy when being pursued. She also maneuvers well in channels and sounds."

Though Devon knew little about ships, she found herself listening raptly to Diablo's description, captivated by the deep timbre of his voice. "Have you always been her captain?" she dared to ask, intrigued by the man and the life he had chosen.

"Nay," he answered quickly enough. "She belonged to Black Bart and was called the *Marauder*, but I renamed her when I took over."

"What happened to Black Bart?"

"A mutiny, my lady. Needless to say, he no longer has need of his ship."

Wisely, Devon did not pursue the subject. Instead, she asked, "How did you come to be captured by the English, away from your ship and crew?"

"Curious, aren't you? But I see no harm in telling you. I was betrayed." His eyes turned murky, causing a shudder to ripple through Devon's body.

"Betrayed? By whom? Why?" It seemed highly unlikely that anyone would dare betray him.

Diablo stared out across the sparkling blue water, his eyes shuttered. "If it takes the rest of my life I'll learn the man's name, and his reason. He'll never find me so careless again.

"We were hidden in a cove at a remote spot along the Cornish coast. Our hold was filled with French brandy and I was to meet our contact, a man I would trust with my life. I took but six men ashore with me in a longboat, and we had no sooner stepped on dry land than we were set upon by a company of dragoons. It was a trap. Kyle saw what was happening from the bridge of the *Devil Dancer* and immediately took her out to sea. He was following my standing orders in such a situation, to retreat with the loot and ship intact. Thus only a few men and I were carted back to London and tried for piracy. I later learned my message to Cormac had been intercepted and he knew nothing about our meeting. Luckily I used a code name and the authorities never learned who serves as our contact in the area."

"Whoever betrayed you must hate you," Devon observed.

"A pirate makes countless enemies, for reasons that need no explanations. Come along, sweetheart, it's time to take you back."

But Devon was reluctant to return to her dreary prison. "What made you turn to piracy?"

Abruptly Diablo's good humor vanished. "That, my lady, is none of your business. Shall we go?" He tightened his hand on her arm, unaware he was causing her pain until she cried out in distress. Only then did his expression lighten and his grip relax. "God's bones, sweetheart, my background would bore you."

Somehow Devon doubted it. The man was an enigma. A dark, unfathomable mystery that defied logic. Devil or man? Gentleman or rogue? Killer? Devon sensed that the answer lay in his dim past. Who was Diablo really? What terrible event in his shrouded background had turned him to piracy?

* * *

The days passed with surprising regularity. Though Devon felt in no way threatened by Diablo's absolute authority, she feared the erotic power he held over her senses. Each night he undressed and climbed into bed with her as if it were the most natural thing in the world. He still continued to caress, fondle, and kiss her, but made no further assault upon her virginity. She held on to the hope that she might still go to the altar as Winston's virgin bride. If she had overheard the conversation between Diablo and Kyle after Diablo had shaved his beard she would have revised her thinking.

"Dear Blessed Mother!" Kyle exclaimed, dismay coloring his words. "What happened? Did the lass snatch your chin bald?"

"I shaved," shrugged Diablo. "'Tis time."

"You *are* smitten with the lass, aren't you?"

"Nay," the devil denied. "'Tis only that I'm not overly anxious to part with my share of the booty." His eyes sparkled wickedly, belying his rather simple explanation.

"Have you won then, Kit? Do I lose my share?"

"Nay, your booty is safe—for the time being. But soon, lad, soon."

"The game has just begun, Diablo, I'm still wagering on the lass."

"The prize will be mine," Diablo predicted arrogantly.

Devon was standing on deck with Diablo when the first of the Bahamas came into view. The islands were like a bracelet of shining jewels set in a background of dazzling turquoise. Devon was enchanted with their clear sparkling water, coral reefs swarming with hundreds of varieties of fish, and white sand beaches.

"A brigand community thrives in Nassau on New Providence Island. Over a thousand pirates dwell there now," Diablo informed her.

"Are there no settlers?" Devon asked.

"No more than four to five hundred families, and they give us no trouble. The snug harbor is perfect for our needs. Too shallow for large men-of-war, but deep enough for the shallow draft craft favored by buccaneers. And the high coral hills afford a hawk's-eye view of approaching enemy or potential prizes."

He told her that the reefs abounded with conch, fish, and lobster. Fruit and vegetables grew in abundance, and freshwater springs were plentiful. There were also wild pigs and pigeons to feast upon. The Bahamas provided a refuge perfect in every way.

"What about the governor?" Devon asked dubiously. "What does *he* think of the Bahamas being a pirate's haven?"

"All the governors have welcomed us," laughed Diablo, "and shared in the booty. We'll stay in Nassau but a short time before continuing on to Paradise."

"Paradise?"

"Aye, a small, secluded island where I built a house and live when not prowling the seas. Few know of it in this maze of islands and keys, but I have everything there I need. Some of the men keep women on the island, and there are even a few children."

Devon wondered if any of the children belonged to Diablo but thought it better not to ask. Shortly afterwards she was escorted back to the cabin and had to content herself with watching the proceedings from the long stern windows of Diablo's quarters. It was late afternoon when Diablo entered the cabin and advised Devon to pack a bag. At dusk they were rowed ashore.

"Where are we going?"

"I'm meeting someone in Nassau. We'll stay at the Wheel of Fortune Inn until he arrives."

Devon grew excited. An inn meant people, and perhaps someone willing to help her escape this devil's lair. Soon the longboat bumped against the shore, and Diablo lifted Devon out with a flourish, setting her on her feet at the water's edge. Devon surveyed her surroundings, and was shocked by what she saw.

A steamy tent town festered the white sand beach and coral outcroppings near the harbor. Hardly a permanent building existed anywhere, except for taverns where pirates drank and fought. As she and Diablo picked their way through the tent city, Devon saw men lolling inside with prostitutes, some coupling openly on the ground. Others gathered outside the tattered sail tents gambling away fortunes. Devon had no way of knowing, but Nassau supported the greatest concentration of pirates in the New World. Besides the thousand living on the island, at least another thousand lived aboard ships scattered throughout the harbor. It was a pirate's paradise, with no laws except that of fist and cutlass.

"Not a pretty sight," Diablo admitted, gesturing at the shantytown and the lawless men inhabiting it. "Perhaps I should have left you aboard the *Devil Dancer*, but I wanted you where I can keep an eye on you. Once it's known you're my woman you won't be bothered. Even pirates have a code of honor they respect."

"I'm not your woman!" Devon denied hotly. "Nor will I ever be."

"The subject is debatable," Diablo said and grinned, flashing the dimple previously hidden by his beard. "For your own sake I suggest you act like my mistress. We'll work out the details later."

Devon was forming a scathing reply when Diablo halted before a rambling wooden structure a short distance from the harbor. A wooden sign hanging askew proclaimed it to be the Wheel of Fortune Inn.

"We're here," Diablo said, guiding Devon inside.

Devon halted abruptly just inside the door, certain she

had stepped through the gates of hell. Only Diablo's arm about her waist kept her from turning and fleeing.

The huge common room exploded with people—mostly men. Men of all sizes, descriptions, and shapes. Tall, short, fat, thin, young, old. Most were ugly, grotesque even, but a few could be called pleasant looking. None were ordinary. They wore an odd assortment of clothes, mostly dirty and ragged, some colorful. They wore enough weapons collectively to outfit an army.

"Ho, look yonder, lads," a man brandishing a tankard of ale called out. "See what the wind blew in. If me old eyes ain't deceivin' me, 'tis the devil himself."

"Aye, and the devil's lady," added another. "Who's the wench, Diablo? Last we heard ye was waitin' ta git yer neck stretched. Thought we seen the last o' ya. Ye look a mite naked without yer beard."

"Greetings, lads!" hailed Diablo. "As you can see, death holds no fear for the devil. He'll not meet destiny till he's good and ready." At that remark cheers erupted in the crowded room. "As for the beard, I'm prettier without it, don't you agree?" His words brought forth a ripple of laughter.

"The wench, Diablo! Who's the wench?"

"I'll tell you this much, lads, she's mine and none's to touch her or they'll have me to deal with."

"To the devil's lady," toasted one of the pirates, raising his tankard in salute.

"Aye," echoed the combined assemblage. "To the devil's lady! May she melt the devil's heart!"

There wasn't one among the motley group of the most despised men in the world that didn't envy Diablo his beautiful prize. Nor was there a prostitute in the room who didn't envy the lady, for not a man on the island could compare with Diablo.

Devon was in a virtual state of shock. The multitude of armed, vicious-looking men and painted, gaudily dressed women assaulted much more than her senses. How in the world was she to find someone to help her escape in this assortment of scum? They were the dregs of humanity, men and women unfit to mingle with polite society. A wail of despair left Devon's trembling lips.

Alerted by her cry, Diablo tightened his arm around Devon's quaking shoulders. "Don't fret, my lady, no one will harm you while you're with me. Besides, we'll only be here until Le Vautour shows up."

"Those men, they're looking at me as if—as if—" Her words faltered, unable to describe the way the pirates' lustful, hungry eyes made her feel.

"Can you blame them? You're a damn beautiful woman."

While Devon stood frozen by her surroundings, Diablo had bespoken a room and was now guiding her up the stairs. The room assigned them was pleasant enough with large windows affording a magnificent view of the harbor. The furnishings were spartan but sufficient; the curtains and counterpane covering the bed somewhat ragged but reasonably clean. Devon supposed pirates weren't overly fussy, and she wondered what the bed linens looked like.

"I'll leave you now, Devon," Diablo said, interrupting her silent inspection of their quarters. "We'll have supper when I return. I think you're smart enough to know now not to leave the room, but for your own safety, lock the door behind me. I'll have a bath sent up."

Devon thoroughly enjoyed the bath, donning a lightweight linen frock suitable for the hot weather, which she found oppressive compared to England's cool, damp climate. She vigorously brushed her long blonde tresses until they glistened like silk, then tied it all back with a ribbon at her nape, opting for coolness instead of style. Then she sat down to wait for Diablo.

He returned shortly, followed by a pair of servants who carried in a tub of bath water and removed her dirty water.

The moment they left, Devon realized that Diablo meant to bathe while she was in the room.

"Surely you don't mean for us to share this room," she said with cool disdain.

"Did you see anyone downstairs you'd prefer to share it with, my lady?" Diablo mocked, quirking a dark brow. With a deft motion he peeled off his white silk shirt. Flashing Devon an infuriating grin, he moved his fingers to the fastenings on his trousers.

"Wait! I—it's not decent."

"We've shared the same room for weeks, Devon, so why the sudden burst of shyness now? Soon we'll be as close as two people of the opposite sex can be." There was no mistaking his meaning.

"Why waste time on someone who doesn't want you?" Devon challenged. "Surely there are women in Nassau more willing than I to bed you."

"Undoubtedly," Diablo agreed amiably as he sat to remove his boots. "But a blue-eyed blonde has captured my fancy and none other will do." First one boot and then the other hit the floor. Then he stood to strip the final piece of clothing from his splendid form. "You can scrub my back, sweetheart."

"When hell freezes over!"

Deliberately Devon turned her back on Diablo's blatant display of pure masculine virility. His deep chuckle brought a flush of anger to her cheeks. She suffered through the humiliating experience of Diablo's bath with as much aplomb as she could muster, staring out the window while her mind tried to block out thoughts of his nude body.

"You can turn around now, sweetheart, I'm dressed." His voice held a hint of laughter. "I'm starving. This place isn't much, but the food is excellent."

Devon couldn't help but admire Diablo's figure resplendent in tight black pants and ruffled white shirt. Wide-top black boots and red sash added dash to the outfit. A black coat and a cutlass at the waist made him the most imposing man Devon had ever had the misfortune to meet. With his beard gone, he didn't look quite so ferocious, and she was struck anew by the mystery surrounding him.

He led her downstairs to a small table in the common room where the dinner he had ordered was being served. Just as Diablo predicted, the food was delicious, many of the dishes containing unrecognizable ingredients. The array of fruits stunned Devon, and she wasn't satisfied until she sampled them all, much to Diablo's delight.

The Wheel of Fortune Inn was even more crowded and boisterous than earlier in the day when she arrived, and Devon hated the way the drinking, carousing men stared at her. She wondered how Diablo, a man of obvious refinement, could tolerate living amongst men who behaved like animals. She watched warily as two more pirates staggered through the door, dressed in an odd assortment of clothes and armed to the teeth. One of them spotted Diablo and nudged the other. Then both headed directly for their table. Devon nearly choked on a large bite of fish when they halted before them.

"I knew they wouldn't hang ye with that big Turk lookin' out for ye," the shorter of the two said in greeting. "Ye surely are a sight for sore eyes, Diablo. What happened to yer hair?" One dirty finger pointed at Diablo's smooth chin. "Ye always were a handsome devil, but now ye're even prettier."

"Annie! Where in the hell did you blow in from? Is Calico Jack here, too?"

Annie! Surely she misunderstood, Devon thought. The pirate couldn't be a woman! But amazingly, it was true. A closer inspection revealed the outline of breasts beneath the wrinkled shirt, and rounded feminine hips nearly concealed by baggy pants.

"Aye," Annie said with a grin, "Jack be here. We arrived just today after sellin' our booty in the American colonies.

Did ye know Mary is sailin' with us now?" Annie eyed Devon with interest but said nothing.

"Good to see you again, Mary," Diablo greeted the second pirate.

Though she tried, Devon couldn't disguise the look of amazement crossing her features. Two women pirates! And Diablo treated them as if lady pirates were a common occurrence instead of a rarity.

"I hardly recognized ye, Diablo," Mary smiled, revealing a mouthful of yellowed teeth. "Who's the wench? Is she the reason ye shaved yer beard?"

"Methinks my lady prefers me clean-shaven." His glance slid to Devon, who looked on the verge of apoplexy. "Sweetheart, meet Anne Bonny and Mary Reed, they sail with Calico Jack. Ladies, this is Lady Devon Chatham, my— er—companion." Devon merely nodded in acknowledgment, too stunned to speak.

"Lady, ha!" snorted Anne, a notorious pirate with a price on her head. "What would a lady be doin' with the likes o' you?"

Mary Reed apparently found that remark hilarious, for she burst into raucous laughter. "Aye," she heartily agreed, "yer doxy might look like a lady and have a fancy name, but she still earns her keep on her back. She's a rare beauty, though. I'll wager plenty have offered to take her off yer hands when ye tire of her."

By now Devon was over her shock, and the women's crude remarks left her seething with anger. "Doxy!" she sputtered, ready to explode. "I'll have you know I'm—"

"There's Calico Jack," Anne said, rudely interrupting Devon and waving her hands wildly at the flamboyantly dressed pirate who had just entered the inn. "Take care o' yerself, Diablo, ye're far too vital to swing from a gibbet." She turned to leave.

"Aye," chimed in Mary, nodding at Devon as she joined her friend. Soon they were lost in the crowd.

Devon frowned, staring at their departing backs with growing dismay.

"What do you think of my friends," Diablo asked teasingly.

"They're crude, vulgar, and in no way resemble ladies," Devon answered without hesitation. "Whatever would possess a woman to take up piracy?"

"Who knows?" Diablo shrugged. "I strongly suspect they do it for much the same reason a man embraces the brotherhood: adventure, money, greed."

"Is that why you turned to piracy?"

Diablo grew silent, his face inscrutable. During his pensive introspection, disappointment, bitterness, and soul-wrenching loneliness fleetingly crossed his face. The expressions spoke eloquently of anguish he had endured and burdens he bore. Devon seriously doubted she would ever know what was in Diablo's heart, for he guarded it too zealously. Obviously he had no intention of answering her question, for he rose abruptly, bringing their meal to an end.

"I'll see you to your room, Devon. I'm needed aboard the *Devil Dancer* this evening, but tomorrow I'll take you on a tour of the island."

Profound relief surged through Devon, elated that Diablo didn't intend to force himself on her tonight. True to his word, he left her at the door, admonishing her to keep it locked until he returned later tonight. Needless to say, Devon had no intention of venturing alone anywhere in Nassau. She seriously doubted that any of these lawless creatures would help her escape. She would be jumping from the frying pan into the fire by taking her chances with this disreputable lot.

It was very late when Diablo returned and awoke her to unlock the door. He did no more than undress and slide into bed beside her, rolling her into the curve of his body and falling immediately asleep. The next morning he was gone before she awoke.

Later that day he appeared to take Devon on a tour of the island. If one overlooked the shantytown on the beach and the hulls of rotting wrecks littering the harbor, the island was a beautiful, sun-drenched land with regal palms and brilliant flowers bowing gracefully beneath cooling sea breezes.

"How long will we stay here?" Devon asked absently.

"Until Le Vautour arrives. Shouldn't be too many days."

"Then what?"

"Then we sail to Paradise. Some of the crew will remain in Nassau, but those with women on Paradise will join me."

"Where is your island?" Devon dared to ask.

"Not far from here on one of the unnamed keys. The natural harbor is too shallow for men-of-war, and a coral reef surrounds it and protects us from unwanted visitors. Only those who know the way in can enter."

"Diablo, I'm begging you again, please let me go. You know I'll never willingly consent to become your mistress." While he was in a mellow mood, Devon had to try one more time to reach his conscience.

The deep dimple flashed in Diablo's cheek, warming her all over. She hated the way this man made her feel, despised the responsive chord that thrummed to life when he smiled at her so beguilingly. She had to get away before his persistence eroded her willpower to the point where she would agree to anything he suggested—even to becoming his mistress. And that must not happen. She belonged to Winston. No man had the right to take what rightfully belonged to her fiancé.

"Sweetheart," Diablo said, his voice low and strident, "I haven't forced you, nor harmed you in any way. But that's not to say I won't. You know what I am, what I'm capable of." He reached out to caress her cheek, his touch oddly tender in the light of what he had just threatened. "I've been remarkably patient, but I can't say how long I will continue to indulge you. Damn the bet, willing or not, I intend to bed you!"

"Bet? What bet?"

"It's not important, sweetheart." They had arrived back at the inn and Diablo saw her to their room. "We'll discuss this later tonight."

Devon primped before the mirror. She wore a becoming dress of shimmering blue-green silk that daringly bared her shoulders and the tops of her breasts. She'd brought only three dresses from the ship and this one hadn't been worn yet. Servants had just carried out her dirty bath water, and Devon turned to lock the door as Diablo had instructed, but before she could turn the key the door burst open with a resounding bang.

"Who in the hell are you?"

The woman who spoke had hair the color of living flame, long trouser-clad legs, and a face so breathtakingly beautiful that Devon could only stare in wonder. "Where's Diablo?" the woman asked, sweeping the room with eyes that resembled brilliant emeralds. They were hard and cold and utterly ruthless.

"He's not here," Devon replied warily.

"I was told this is Diablo's room," the redhead claimed, eyeing Devon with cool disdain. "Who are you and what are you doing here?"

"I—this is my room."

Suddenly comprehension dawned. "You're his whore! How dare Diablo bring a fancy woman here with him. That blackhearted devil! Next time he'll think twice before flaunting his new mistress before me. A bit of fluff like you can't possibly satisfy him. He needs a real woman like Scarlett Defoe."

"I assure you, Miss Defoe, I'm not Diablo's mistress."

"What are you doing in his room?"

Devon bit her lower lip in consternation. It did indeed look damning. "I had no choice. I'm Diablo's prisoner."

"His prisoner! Ha! Likely story," Scarlett snorted derisively. "The door was unlocked when I came in, and Diablo would hardly be that careless were you a prisoner. Who are you?"

"Lady Devon Chatham."

"English?"

"Aye."

"Well, my lady," she mocked, "I'm Diablo's woman. And I don't share my men. Pack your things and get out of here."

"But—"

"Now." With slow deliberation Scarlett drew the cutlass strapped to her slim waist, brandishing it in Devon's face.

"Believe me, Miss Defoe, you are more than welcome to Diablo. I want nothing to do with that devil."

"You're lying," Scarlett scoffed. "Women are always panting after Diablo. Why should you be any different?"

"Not this woman. I wish only to return home."

"Then do so, and hurry it up. Find yourself another protector. I'll wager you'll have little difficulty doing so. Leave Diablo to me."

Devon would have liked nothing better than to leave, but not this way. Not throw herself on the mercy of cutthroats and brigands. At least she knew what to expect with Diablo.

Not one to be intimidated, Devon ordered, "Get out of my room, Miss Defoe. I'll leave when I'm good and ready and not before."

Scarlett's full red lips turned down sourly and her green eyes flared with sudden anger. She stalked menacingly toward Devon, sleek hips and long shapely legs moving with feline grace. Tight black pants hugged her curves like a second skin, her green silk shirt gaping at the neck and showing

the tops of full unfettered breasts. Angered, she was magnificent, and Devon was surprised that Diablo could even
consider another woman with Scarlett willing—nay, eager—
to bed him. As Scarlett advanced, Devon suddenly realized
her danger. The woman was armed, vicious, and apparently
intent on murder.

Scarlett Defoe was a product of the Paris slums who had
clawed her way out of degradation and into the position of
being considered one of those fearless breed of women pirates as ferocious as any man. She had started her career as a
sailor's doxy, then was heartlessly sold to a smuggler. The
smuggler's ship was attacked by pirates and Scarlett was
claimed by the captain. During a later battle the pirate captain was killed, and Scarlett, supported by a group of follow-
ers, took over the ship, which she renamed the *Red Witch*.
Soon the crew came to respect her courage and daring, and
none disputed her right to become their captain.

When Scarlett met Diablo she experienced her first stirrings of love, aware that it was all one-sided but willing to
take what little of himself he offered. They became lovers,
meeting mostly on Nassau and less frequently on Paradise.
Until now Scarlett had managed to maintain her tenuous
hold on Diablo's affections by banishing the competition,
employing whatever method necessary.

Seeing Devon standing before her cloaked in youthful innocence and beauty made Scarlett realize that her undis-
puted position as Diablo's woman was reaching its conclusion.
Devon was everything Scarlett wanted to be but was not.
Devon was young, lovely, and appeared to be a lady. Perhaps
the biggest insult to Scarlett's senses was Devon's obvious innocence. She advanced on Devon with deadly deliberation,
the tip of her cutlass pressed menacingly into the soft skin of
Devon's white neck. A drop of blood appeared at the site of
the tiny wound.

Too late Devon realized the danger Scarlett presented,

and regretted so many things. Her life was about to end without her ever having experienced love and fulfillment.

Suddenly a tall figure loomed in the doorway, and Devon's mouth formed the silent word with a joy that shocked her. "Diablo."

Chapter Six

"What in the hell is going on here?"

Scarlett's green eyes narrowed, but the blade pressing against Devon's throat did not waver. "I'm going to dispose of your doxy."

"God's bones, Scarlett, are you daft? Release Devon at once!"

"Nay, Diablo, you can't bully me. I know why you've brought the wench here and I won't have it."

"You've nothing to say about it, Scarlett, we made no promises to one another," Diablo said with quiet emphasis. He knew well Scarlett's volatile temper and genuinely feared for Devon's life unless he was able to defuse the situation. If Scarlett harmed Devon in any way he'd kill the brazen bitch on the spot.

Undaunted, Scarlett flicked the blade tip to draw yet another drop of blood, bringing a gasp of pain to Devon's lips. That tiny red droplet drove Diablo to fury as he drew his own cutlass, slashing it upward until it came to rest at Scarlett's breast.

"Lay down your weapon, Scarlett, you'll not hurt Devon." There was a hard edge to his voice, a deceptive calm that often preceded violence, and Scarlett was astute enough to recognize it instantly. It was that very quality that inspired fear in the hearts of his enemies. She knew if she angered him excessively Diablo would skewer her without a moment's regret.

Scarlett decided that killing Devon wasn't worth dying over. Reluctantly she lowered her cutlass, her face a mask of rage.

"Who is the wench, Diablo, and what's she to you?"

"The lady's name is Devon Chatham. Her father is the Earl of Milford."

"She claims she's your prisoner, though we both know why you brought her here," Scarlett hinted slyly.

"Aye, I suppose you could say that."

Scarlett's fierce scowl eased somewhat. She could understand holding an heiress for ransom—she'd done it herself a time or two. "Have you bedded her?"

"That's none of your business. I've never asked who you've bedded. You could have slept with your entire crew for all I cared. Now get out of here before I forget the friendship that existed between us."

Scarlett whirled, eyes blazing green fire as they raked Devon insolently from head to toe. "Have joy of her then, Diablo, until her ransom arrives. But I seriously doubt the pale little thing will satisfy you for long. What we shared was more than mere friendship. You know where to find me when you have need of a real woman."

With deceptive calm she jammed her cutlass inside her sash, aimed a seductive smile at Diablo, and strolled from the room, hips swaying with tantalizing grace. Diablo slammed the door behind her, then turned to Devon, a frown worrying his wide brow.

"Sweetheart, are you all right? I'm sorry about Scarlett. I didn't know she was in Nassau."

With more gentleness than she thought possible, Diablo drew Devon's quaking form into his arms. Taking a spotless white handkerchief from his pocket, he dabbed tenderly at the drops of blood surrounding the small puncture on her throat caused by the prick of Scarlett's blade. Then, to Devon's shock, he gently laved the wound with the moist tip of his tongue. Devon drew her breath in sharply, his gesture highly erotic and totally unexpected.

Somehow finding her voice, she said, "Scarlett is your

mistress." Why did it have to sound like an accusation rather than a question, Devon reflected, exasperated with herself for caring.

"Nay, sweetheart," Diablo denied. "She was merely someone to help fill my lonely hours ashore. We are two of a kind and understood one another."

Against her will Devon melted into Diablo's embrace, welcoming his comfort, accepting his protection. But when his tongue touched the sensitive skin of her throat it ignited a fire that burned its way into every part of her body. His lips naturally gravitated from that vulnerable spot upward to her mouth, slightly parted with dismay. Diablo accepted the invitation, slipping his tongue into the moist opening, tasting, exploring to his heart's content.

Emotionally drained, Devon swayed dangerously, and Diablo's arms tightened around her supple curves, his hands roaming with seductive slowness from waist to buttocks to breasts where he paused to savor those delightfully full mounds. Devon sighed, knowing she should resist, but with his touch too tantalized to care. Winston's tepid kisses and tame caresses were nothing compared to this man's touch.

"I want you, sweetheart." His raspy breath tickled her ear, sending a ripple of awareness through her tense body. "I've wanted you from the moment I laid eyes on you, so prim and proper, yet more beautiful than words can describe. If it wasn't for that damn bet . . ."

"Bet?" murmured Devon, the word reaching deep into her subconscious to snatch her back to reality. "What bet?"

"It's nothing, sweetheart, nothing to concern yourself over. Just concentrate on what I'm doing, how beautifully your body is responding to my touch." Deliberately his thumb drew circles through the cloth of her dress around her nipples, and when the buds tautened, he pulled gently at them with the tips of his fingers. The effect was devastating to both of them. "God's bones, Devon, let me love you. I want to be the man to lead you into womanhood."

Nothing in Devon's previous knowledge prepared her to deal with a man like Diablo whose wide experience made him irresistible to women. She directed a look filled with panic into his passion-glazed face, caught in the tingling enchantment of his passion. Though every nerve ending screamed for surrender, she resisted the need to give herself to Diablo. The man was a pirate, a thief, and a despoiler of women, no matter how handsome or desirable, and Devon could not forgive him for snatching her from her loved ones. By now her poor father must be distraught, not to mention Winston's anguish over her abduction.

"Nay, don't, Diablo. I know nothing of what you're talking about."

The smile in his eyes contained a sensual flame that sent a jolt of fire sizzling through her veins. "Let me teach you and I swear you'll enjoy it."

His monumental conceit succeeded only in destroying the euphoria she had experienced from the moment Diablo's lips and hands had claimed her. Shrugging free of his arms, she hissed, "I want nothing to do with you or your loving. Because of you I was nearly killed by that red-haired witch. Don't expect me to fall into your arms like all those loose women you're accustomed to."

"I knew from the moment I laid eyes on you that you were like no other woman I've ever known, sweetheart."

It was true, Diablo reflected soberly. She had fire and mettle and refinement and beauty. She was an arresting mixture of hoyden and lady, without the simpering dullness of so many well-bred young women. Throughout her ordeal she had defied him at every turn, well aware that he had absolute power over her. He sighed and plowed distracted fingers through his hair. No matter how courageous or defiant, he still wanted her. Unaccustomed to self-denial, Diablo felt that he was losing the tenuous hold on his senses. He would have to seduce her soon or lose his mind.

All restraint fled as Diablo reached for her, dragging her back into his arms. Passion was thick and molten within him. His eyes slid over her lazily, his voice seductively sensual. "I want you, sweetheart. I promise I won't do anything you don't want me to do."

Devon stared at him with a desperate mixture of hope and disbelief. She knew she could not stop him if he decided to take her without her permission, but his words promised a chance, albeit a slim one, to prevent him from having his way.

"You mean it? You'll stop when I ask? You won't—hurt me?"

"Hurt you?" His voice assumed the same wickedness as his smile. "The last thing I want to do is hurt you. True, I want to hear you cry out—but in pleasure, not pain."

Then Devon felt his hands on the bodice of her dress, unfastening each tiny button with great expertise. When he brushed the material aside and tugged the ribbon holding together her chemise, a shudder, not entirely of fear, passed through her. Diablo sucked in his breath, awestruck. Her breasts, pale as alabaster, were crowned with impudent pink nipples, taut and wetly tempting to a man who had been starved for so long.

Reverently he touched one fleshy bud, smiling when it puckered delightfully. He responded by playing with it, first pulling and squeezing lightly, then rolling it between his fingers and thumb, teasing it mercilessly with his feather-light touch. The thick pebbly texture fascinated and aroused him, producing a clamor deep in his loins.

While his fingers were busy with one nipple he bent and ran the tip of his tongue around the other. First he dragged the tip of his tongue across the bud, then lashed it with light, teasing strokes, finally pulling it into the wet cave of his mouth. He suckled gently as his tongue continued its fiery dance.

Devon reeled drunkenly, dismayed at the magnitude of the response he evoked in her. Blood pounded in her brain, leapt from her heart, and made her knees tremble. How could a vile pirate affect her like this when a decent man like Winston failed to inspire her with little more than indulgent fondness? Then all thought fled as Devon felt the rest of her clothing leave her body, and she stood gloriously nude before Diablo's hot, probing eyes.

"God's blood, Devon, you're like a beautiful masterpiece, fragile yet flesh-and-blood real. Every other woman pales in comparison. I think—I think if any other man tried to touch you I'd kill him."

Sweeping her into his arms, he placed her on the bed, bending to strip her of shoes and stockings. Then he stretched out beside her, fully clothed. Intuitively he sensed the awakening embers he roused within her and rejoiced, wanting to fan them into hot flame to match his own. Gently his hand outlined the circle of her breast, then slid across her silken belly. His touch was light and teasing, and to her dismay, Devon found herself welcoming the sweet agony of full arousal.

"Do you want me to stop?" Diablo asked. "I always keep my word." His tongue trailed a path of liquid fire down her ribs to her stomach while his hands searched out all her pleasure points.

Devon moaned softly, lost in a sensual fog where nothing mattered but the way Diablo made her feel, all warm and melting inside.

"Tell me, sweetheart," Diablo prodded relentlessly, "should I stop?"

A tiny puff of air lodged in Devon's throat as his bold caresses took him to the soft burning core of her, that forbidden place that ached for his touch. Another breath caught on a gasp as his fingers found her moistness and became more insistent, his watchful eyes never leaving her face.

Devon wanted to resist, tried desperately to voice a protest that would stop this exquisite torture, but having Diablo desist now would be tantamount to plunging off the face of the earth into darkness. Against her better judgment she was succumbing to Diablo's masterful seduction and his will was becoming hers.

"I understand, sweetheart," Diablo murmured, flashing his dimple. "You don't have to say anything, just relax and let me love you."

He left her for a moment, and when he returned Devon felt the hairy roughness of his chest rasp against her sensitive nipples. He buried his face in the fragrant silk of her hair, thinking how small and fragile her body felt in his arms, yet her breasts were womanly and full against him. All his senses were intoxicated with the taste and smell of her, and he fought against the overwhelming urge to take her swiftly and love her voraciously until his enormous hunger was appeased.

Suddenly Diablo was desperate to remove his restrictive trousers and he shifted, sliding them down over muscled thighs and legs. Then he kicked off his boots, his undergarments quickly following. His manhood, now thick and throbbing, surged against her. Before Devon squeezed her eyes tightly shut she caught a glimpse of that huge male part of him. She thought him magnificent; just looking at him made her mouth go dry.

"Open your legs, sweetheart," he urged, his voice quivering with excitement. He felt like a lad with his first woman.

Looming above her, his leg insinuated itself between her thighs and he guided himself into the moist cleft. His warm sex nudged the opening and Devon tried to jerk away, shocked out of her sensual haze. Surely she was too small for him.

"Diablo, no! You can't! It's not possible."

He brought her back hard and thrust forward while his arm wrapped around her waist so there was no escaping him. "Trust me, sweetheart, it's not only possible but thoroughly enjoyable. You'll see, just relax, I don't want to hurt you."

She resisted fiercely for a moment, then, seeing no hope, relaxed as he suggested, not once considering asking him to stop. He had brought her too far for that. His initial thrust brought a cry of pain as she felt herself fill and stretch with his hugeness. Her whimpers served only to inflame him as he pressed harder, deeper, into that virgin passage. Then he felt the membrane give beneath his relentless prodding, and thrusting forcefully, entered her fully, delighting in the moist heat that contracted around him to hold him snugly.

"It's done, sweetheart, I won't hurt you again," Diablo said gently, remaining motionless to allow her time to adjust to his size. "God's bones, you're so tight and warm it's all I can do to keep from exploding."

Devon felt as if she were being torn apart. She had expected some pain, if girlish gossip could be believed, but nothing like this. Just when she felt certain she would die, the pain began to recede, replaced by an unfamiliar sensation that began at the place of their joining. It grew with each passing moment, causing her to move her hips experimentally. Yes, the pain was definitely gone, and she looked at Diablo questioningly, as if to ask, what now?

Diablo groaned, his control slowly disintegrating. "Now— comes the—pleasure," he gasped disjointedly, sensing her question.

He rocked her gently at first, teaching her the rhythm. She gloved him so tightly with her moist heat that every thrust brought a friction so exquisite it bordered on pain. "You're wonderful," he mouthed in her ear. "It's as if I've waited all my life for you." Deliberately he quickened his pace, rejoicing in the wonder visible in her sky-blue eyes.

"Diablo!" she cried, unprepared for the floodtide of sensations bombarding her with lightninglike jolts of pure rapture. Not knowing what to expect next frightened her.

"Kit, call me Kit," he urged, desperate to hear his name on her lips.

"Kit! I feel so—I don't know what's happening and it scares me."

"Let me come, sweetheart, don't rush it. Ride with the storm, flow with it, you'll know when the time is right. I can't believe you're so wonderfully responsive. Don't think, just feel."

Right? Right for what? Devon wondered, urgency driving her toward the center of the storm Diablo described.

Suddenly Diablo's thrusts became frenzied, and instinctively Devon rose up to meet him, abruptly aware that he was the storm and she was riding it to some distant pinnacle of discovery. His body was covered with a fine sheen of sweat, his breath harsh and panting. He hated leaving her behind but could hold back no longer.

He needn't have worried, for Devon was with him every step of the way. "Kit! Kit! I think—oh, God!" Waves of ecstasy shuddered through her, her pleasure pure and explosive. That which she struggled to reach came to her in a rush of sweet agony.

Diablo knew by the fluttering contractions that enveloped and stroked his manhood the very moment when rapture seized her and sent her soaring. Only then did he allow his own passion to gallop to a thundering climax. Then he collapsed, taking care to rest the bulk of his weight on his elbows. His eyes were silver pools of wonder and delight.

"You're amazing," he said smiling, his voice a breathless shudder. "I kidnapped a lady and discovered a wildcat."

Still awed by what had happened, Devon struggled to control her own breathing. "I—didn't know," she whispered wonderingly.

"How could you?" Diablo replied, finally finding the energy to flip to his side. "I was the first."

A slow flush crept up Devon's neck and she attempted to cover herself.

"Nay, I want to look at you. Your skin is so soft and white, like the purest alabaster. Your breasts just fit my hands and your nipples—ah, sweetheart, your little pink nipples were made for my mouth." As if to prove his words he bent over and took one pouting bud into his mouth, suckling gently.

The action seemed to release Devon's frozen senses, and she stared at Diablo with something akin to horror. What had she done? How could she give up so easily that which rightfully belonged to another man? "Don't touch me!" she gasped, pushing him away.

Stunned, Diablo scoffed, "A little late for that, isn't it?" His thick eyebrows angled upward, lending him a devilish look.

"You—you raped me! You took advantage of my innocence despite your promise."

"I heard no protests," Diablo refuted. "I made love to you, sweetheart, and you enjoyed it. It will be even better next time for there'll be no more pain."

"Next time! There will be no next time," Devon denied hotly.

She closed her eyes, vividly recalling those magic moments when nothing existed but the ecstasy they shared. It must never happen again. For Winston's sake and their future together she must resist the pirate's considerable charm and seductive prowess. Diablo was a contradiction of every rule. Bold, ruthless, blackhearted. Tender, charming, loving. Which was he?

Suddenly a vague memory stored away in a chamber of her brain prickled her conscience. "Who is Kit?" Her question brought a scowl to Diablo's face.

"I know no one named Kit!"

"You asked me to call you Kit. Did you think me too addled to remember? Is Kit your real name?"

A strangled sigh escaped Diablo's lips and he rolled to his back, placing his forearm over his eyes in an oddly vulnerable gesture. "Only Kyle knows me as Kit, but he's forbidden to use the name. If I revealed the name to you it was in a moment of weakness. I must ask you not to use it—except in the privacy of our bedroom," he added wickedly.

"Then I shall never use it," Devon pledged. "Now, please, let me up. Are you not satisfied at having your way with me? What more can you want?"

"Do you really need to ask?"

With agile grace he slid his weight atop her, fully aroused again. It truly stunned Diablo to think a mere woman could produce such conflicting emotions and swift arousal in him.

"Nay, Diablo, not again," Devon resisted, pushing against his chest. "I told you I—"

"*Mon ami*, are you in there?"

The heavily accented voice accompanied by a pounding on the door did exactly what Devon's protests failed to do to Diablo's ardor. "God's bones," he groaned as if in pain, "why now?"

"Open the door, Diablo, tis Le Vautour. We've business to conduct."

"Aye, I'm coming," Diablo answered crossly, none too pleased at the untimely interruption. "Cover yourself," he growled at Devon as he shrugged into his pants.

Scooting downward, she pulled the sheet under her chin, her eyes wide and questioning. "Who is it?"

"The man I've been waiting for," came his terse reply. Then conversation ceased as Diablo padded barefoot to the door.

"It's about time, *mon ami*," the visitor boomed in a commanding voice the moment the door opened to him.

Before Diablo could protest, the man pushed his way inside. "Don't tell me you're abed at this early hour," the Frenchman guffawed, staring deliberately at Diablo's bare feet and equally bare chest. His eyes sparkled with mirth until he spied Devon curled up in bed, her tousled blonde curls poking out from under the sheet. The entrancing sight sobered him immediately.

"Ah, *mon ami*, I have intruded upon your amusement, no? Introduce me to your *chère amie*. An enticing piece, from what little I can see of her. Perhaps I can persuade you to share her."

An enraged yelp left Devon's lips as she flung the sheet over her head.

"Wait for me downstairs, Le Vautour," Diablo said tightly. "The lady belongs to me, I'll share her with no one."

"Ah, so that's how the wind blows," Le Vautour remarked, casting covetous glances at Devon's delectable form outlined beneath the sheet. "It does my heart good to see you tied in knots over a bit of fluff." He laughed heartily, slapping his well-muscled thigh.

Le Vautour, the vulture, an apt nickname for a man who looked every bit the bird of prey he was named after. He was tall and thin, his beaked nose a perfect fit for his long, not unhandsome features. Somewhat of a dandy, he dressed exceptionally well for a pirate, carefully choosing fashionable clothing made in France, his native country. Sly and crafty by nature, Le Vautour instilled trust in few of his comrades. He was known to be cruel and heartless in his dealings with captives and peers alike. His eyes, jet-black, fathomless pits, were hooded like those of a hawk, making it impossible to know what he was thinking.

"Get out of here, Le Vautour," Diablo repeated, herding him toward the door. "I'll be down in fifteen minutes."

"I insist that you and your *chère amie* join me for supper," Le Vautour invited eagerly. "I'd like to meet her under— um—more appropriate circumstances."

Silver lightning flashed in Diablo's eyes as he slammed the door behind Le Vautour. Damn! he seethed impotently, why should Le Vautour seeing Devon anger him so? He was acting like a jealous husband. Husband! God forbid! He threw up his hands in disgust, turning toward Devon who was peeking over the edge of the sheet.

"Le Vautour has arrived. Hurry and dress, Devon." Just thinking about Le Vautour's disparaging remarks about Devon made his voice harsher than he intended. "We've been invited to supper."

Devon gasped in dismay. "Surely you don't mean for me to join you!"

"I'm afraid so, sweetheart," Diablo said, his voice gentling. "The man won't be appeased until his curiosity is satisfied. I don't trust him, but circumstances force me to deal with him. It's best if I don't anger him or give him cause to back out of our agreement."

The common room of the Wheel of Fortune Inn buzzed with activity. Pirates of all description laughed, talked, fought, and consorted with prostitutes everywhere Devon's gaze took her in the crowded room. She toyed distractedly with her food while Diablo and Le Vautour talked business. But Devon was not fooled. Though Le Vautour appeared engrossed in planning the joint venture with Diablo, his black gaze swept over her again and again. His look was lazily suggestive, and Devon tried hard to ignore it. Besides, she knew by his stiffening shoulders and clenched jaw that Diablo saw it, too, and liked it as little as she did.

When Diablo was momentarily distracted by a friend who called to him from across the room, Le Vautour seized the opportunity to wink provocatively at Devon. Flushing, she lowered her head, concentrating on the congealing mess in her plate. Then Scarlett swaggered through the door and a hush descended over the room. Everyone present knew how it was between Diablo and Scarlett and wondered what the she-devil would do now that Diablo was openly courting another woman. It was obvious a rousing row was eagerly anticipated, and all eyes turned to watch Scarlett's slow, sensual progress across the room. Unerringly her steps took her to where Diablo sat with Devon and Le Vautour.

Hoping to avoid another nasty confrontation and spare Devon further shame, Diablo rose abruptly, excused himself, and hurried to head off the flame-haired virago.

"At last," Le Vautour sighed, impaling Devon with his piercing black eyes. "I thought we'd never be alone, *ma petite*. You do not seem too happy about your arrangement with Diablo. Now that I've seen more than the top of your head I find myself yearning to know you intimately. I can offer you much more than Diablo, and I'm a better lover. What do you say, *ma chère*, will you be my mistress? I'll arrange everything."

Devon's mouth flopped open. It rankled to know that everyone thought her the kind of woman who could be easily bought and sold. She hated Diablo for bringing her so low. She'd do anything to escape him—anything. Perhaps she could even use Le Vautour to help her escape this hellhole. Not that she would ever agree to become his mistress. But perhaps he was greedy enough to accept the promise of money to carry her away from Diablo and the strange power he had over her. Never would she forgive him for seducing her so thoroughly and making her enjoy it. It was something that couldn't—wouldn't—happen again.

Diablo breathed a heartfelt sigh of relief when he managed to prevent Scarlett from creating a scene. Only when he promised to come to her aboard the *Red Witch* so they might talk in private did Scarlett agree not to vent her displeasure at Devon in public. After tossing a venomous glance in Devon's direction, the leggy redhead joined a group of friends seated around a table relating lusty tales of daring deeds and misdeeds.

Diablo's silver eyes glinted with dangerous lights when he saw Le Vautour leaning intimately toward Devon, speaking earnestly. So engrossed were the two they failed to hear Diablo approaching. But Diablo's hearing was keen. He distinctly heard Le Vautour ask Devon to be his mistress. And by the thoughtful look on Devon's face it appeared she was actually considering the offer.

"Devon isn't free to accept or decline your offer, Le Vautour," he informed the Frenchman curtly.

Startled, Le Vautour looked up, a bland smile appearing on his dark, intense features. "Ah, *mon ami*, you cannot fault a man for trying. Mademoiselle Devon is an enchanting creature, but so is Scarlett. Even a fool could see that Scarlett is none too happy about being replaced and I merely offered Mademoiselle Devon my protection should she desire it. Why should you have a monopoly on beautiful women?"

"As I said before, Devon cannot possibly accept your insulting offer."

Le Vautour searched Devon's face with slow perusal. "Let the lady speak for herself. I meant no insult."

"Devon's not free to make a decision," Diablo repeated tightly. "I'm holding her for ransom."

"You mean she's your prisoner as well as your mistress?" Le Vautour asked, astounded.

Suddenly Devon came alive, her eyes ablaze with angry fire. "I'm no man's mistress! When I'm returned to my father, he'll see that you and your kind are wiped off the face of the earth."

Leaping to her feet, she pushed her way through the crowd and up the stairs to the privacy of her room, collecting her dignity around her like a regal mantle.

Chapter Seven

Devon longed to lock the door behind her but Diablo had the key. Being forced to associate with men like Diablo and Le Vautour sent her into a frenzy of wrathful indignation. But she'd show them, she silently vowed. She was a match for any man. Using cunning and guile she'd escape Diablo somehow and one day marry Winston, if he'd still have her.

Her thoughts were scattered when the object of her rage burst into the room. "I love the way you look when you're angry," Diablo drawled lazily. "You please me so well, sweetheart, I may never let you go."

"You wouldn't dare keep me against my will! Father will search the world over until he finds me."

"And your fiancé? Will he join in the search?"

"Of course. He loves me."

"They'll not find you, sweetheart, until I'm ready for them to find you," Diablo assured her confidently. "And after what we shared together in this room, that might never happen. It was exciting, Devon. *You* were exciting. I could—"

"Stop it!" Devon shouted, covering her ears. "I won't listen to this. You forced me! It will never happen again."

"It will if I say it will." He reached for her but she deftly evaded him. "You've created a hunger in me that needs constant feeding."

"Go find Scarlett and gorge yourself on her."

Diablo laughed with wry amusement. He found her wit and spunk highly entertaining, and her body wildly sensual and responsive. She could protest all she wanted, but he knew she wasn't immune to him. He had brought rapture to her virginal body once and longed to do so again. But given her state of mind Diablo decided not to press her further tonight. Besides, he promised Scarlett he'd meet her aboard the *Red Witch* and it was time he left. He only hoped he could convince the red-haired vixen that their association had run its course and it was time to move on.

"Perhaps I *will* find Scarlett," he taunted, turning to leave. "For your own safety I'm locking you in. I won't be back till morning. Be prepared to leave when I arrive."

"Leave? Where are you taking me?"

"To Paradise." Then he was gone, leaving Devon with a new worry. How would her father and Winston ever hope to find her on a hidden island protected by a natural barrier that kept out unwanted visitors?

"I'm surprised you were able to tear yourself away from your doxy," Scarlett flung out disparagingly. "She's not your type, Diablo. You'd do well to stick with your own kind."

"The only reason I'm here is to settle this between us. I've made you no promises about our future. We simply enjoyed one another when we chanced to meet. And in between times I've not been celibate, nor do I imagine have you."

"True," Scarlett agreed, "but this is the first time you've brought a woman to Nassau. Do you intend to take her to Paradise? To my knowledge, I'm the only woman you've ever brought there to share your bed. What is this woman to you besides a hostage? I don't like sharing my men."

"And I don't like bossy, possessive women," Diablo countered, his temper flaring. "I told you before I'm holding Devon for ransom. I'll take her wherever I damn please."

"Does that include your bed?" Scarlett asked with a derisive toss of her fiery head. "She doesn't look the type to enjoy it, not like I do. I need you, Diablo. Stay aboard the *Red Witch* with me tonight and I'll show you how much. Remember how good we were together?"

Scarlett didn't begrudge Diablo an occasional woman, for

she was no saint herself. What she didn't like, wouldn't stand for, was another woman coming to mean something more to him than a warm body or a moment's solace. And astutely Scarlett sensed that Lady Devon Chatham was a woman who could easily replace her permanently in Diablo's affections. Not only would Scarlett miss his expert loving, she would earn the contempt of her peers for losing Diablo to another woman.

Her hips swaying provocatively, Scarlett approached Diablo, running the back of one hand over a clean-shaven cheek. "I miss the beard," she purred. "It chafed me most erotically in delicious places. But I suppose I can grow accustomed to seeing your handsome face exposed."

Grasping him behind the neck, she pulled his face down to hers until their mouths touched. Greedily she seized his lips, kissing him with all the passion and longing that mere words failed to convey. Her fingers went to his shirt and eagerly began working the buttons through the button-holes. Diablo groaned, his body reacting spontaneously to Scarlett's kiss and to her body molding his from thigh to breast. The sudden rise of his flesh brought a delighted grin to Scarlett's red lips.

"You want me, Diablo. By damn, I know you do!"

"You're an enticing wench, Scarlett, and as you well know I'm not made of stone."

Thrilled by his response, Scarlett pressed closer, certain that once Diablo was in her bed he'd have no further need for another woman. She was confident of her ability to make him desire no one but her. But Diablo had other ideas. Though his body might have reacted spontaneously to Scarlett's seduction, his mind rejected her utterly. Having tasted Devon's sweetness mere hours ago and been gloriously sated, he refused to soil the unique experience by bedding Scarlett. He had enjoyed Scarlett thoroughly while it lasted, but it was over.

Deliberately removing her busy fingers from his shirt front, Diablo set Scarlett aside and stepped back. "Behave, Scarlett. Don't debase yourself by begging. You're a beautiful woman and can have any man you want."

"I want *you*," Scarlett said with bitter emphasis. "What happens after you ransom the little slut? If you reject me now, don't expect to be welcomed back with open arms once she's gone. My pride won't allow it. If you leave me tonight, my devilish love, I'll never forgive you. You'll find I make a better lover than enemy."

Diablo searched Scarlett's face, his eyes narrowed to slits. He held no illusions about Scarlett, she would indeed make a formidable foe, but he felt certain he could handle any threat she presented. The simple truth, one that surprised him utterly, was that he no longer desired Scarlett sexually. Since he had met Devon, all women paled in comparison, and if he couldn't have Scarlett as a friend he didn't want her at all.

"So be it," he intoned, his smile fading. "I had hoped we could remain friends even though I no longer want to be your lover."

"Go then!" Scarlett spat. "Get out of my sight. Just remember what they say about a woman scorned."

Overjoyed to be allowed on deck, Devon watched the islands and cays that made up the Bahamas slip by. She had been escorted aboard the *Devil Dancer* early that morning by Diablo, who hadn't returned until dawn to the room they shared.

Some islands looked like bright jewels set in brilliant aqua circled by snow white. Others were mere rocky formations surrounded by barrier reefs separated from land by a wide lagoon. On one island, which Diablo said was Andros, the vivid pink of hundreds of flamingos captured her attention. The water was so clear and blue she could see thousands of tropical fish beneath its surface.

Devon could easily understand why the Bahamas were a pirate's fiefdom and the Caribbean a pirate's lake. There were many nooks, crannies, creeks, shallows, rocks, and reefs for a ship to hide in. And from what she gathered from bits of overheard conversation, the appointed governors were ineffectual in routing pirates from their shores. In fact, pirates like Charles Vane, John Thurber, Black-beard, Stede Bonnet, and Calico Jack found the Bahamas a virtual paradise. No wonder Diablo chose to make his home in these hospitable islands.

Thinking of the devil must have conjured him up, for Diablo appeared as if by magic at Devon's side. They had had little opportunity to speak privately since he had escorted her aboard.

"Beautiful," he said softly. Though he spoke of the passing scenery, his eyes never left Devon's face.

"Are the islands inhabited?"

"There are a handful of settlers on one or two of the larger islands, but for the most part they remain uninhabited."

"What about Paradise? Do you own it?" Devon questioned.

Diablo laughed, pleased by her interest. "Believe it or not, I do own Paradise. It was granted to my family years ago, and I doubt that any of my living relatives even remember it."

"Your family? Tell me about them."

Diablo's eyes became hooded and a remote sadness settled over his handsome features. "I have no family," he refuted. "Look to the starboard!" Adroitly he turned her attention away from his personal history.

Devon looked to where Diablo pointed, seeing a large land mass lush with vegetation, a wide lagoon with pure white sand forming a beach, and high coral hills at its center. No sign of life was visible, and Devon assumed it to be another uninhabited island.

"Welcome to Paradise." From all of Diablo's glowing descriptions, Devon had expected something extraordinary. But Paradise looked much like any of the other lovely islands and cays surrounding it.

Sensing her disappointment, Diablo smiled a mysterious smile. "Look below the waterline and you can see the coral reef I spoke of. It completely surrounds the island, making it impossible to approach if one does not know where to find the hidden break in the reef. Only ships with drafts five to eight feet can safely negotiate the treacherous shallows."

Devon turned her attention to the sparkling water below. She gasped when she saw the jagged coral that had the power to rip a ship's hull apart.

"It's time I took the wheel," Diablo said. "Few of my men are capable of navigating through the narrow gap in the reef without doing damage to the hull. If Kyle were here he could do it, but I sent him with Le Vautour to protect our interests."

"I don't trust that Frenchman. I never know what is going on in his devious mind and I refuse to tell him the secret of my island. I've made arrangements to meet Le Vautour and Kyle in Nassau after our booty is sold to collect the profits. Afterwards I'll return to Paradise with Kyle."

Devon's avid gaze followed Diablo as he sprinted across the deck, secretly admiring the play of muscles across his back and the flexing of his taut buttocks. With each step he took, the ripple of corded sinews reminded her of the unleashed strength of his whip-cord lean body. Though she tried not to remember, nothing could make her forget how tenderly, how passionately he had made love to her. He made her feel adored and protected. How could it be possible for a pirate to make her feel cherished? she wondered distractedly. How could a man of his calling bring her the kind of happiness she had never known existed? Was it likely that Winston could fulfill her in the same way? Somehow she doubted it.

Devon's musings came to an abrupt halt when she realized the ship had turned toward shore and was riding in on a brisk breeze. She held her breath, listening for the scrape of coral against the hull. But Diablo handled the trim craft as masterfully as he did women, clearing the reef with only inches to spare. The air left her lungs in a whoosh, only to be drawn in again when she realized they were still traveling full speed with no order given to trim the sails. At their speed they would soon slam into the surf and become beached in the soft white sand.

Bracing herself for the crash, Devon aimed a desperate glance at Diablo. To her utter amazement he seemed completely at ease, as if wrecking a ship were something he did every day. The shore loomed ahead with alarming speed and Devon closed her eyes, gripping the railing with all her meager strength. When the expected impact did not come, she opened her eyes tentatively.

She was amazed to find that they were entering a hidden river just wide enough to accommodate the *Devil Dancer*. Lush vegetation at the shoreline obscured the mouth from all who were not aware of it. Unless the exact location was known, one would never know it existed. They sailed slowly up the channel for some distance until they entered a wide lagoon rimmed with a crescent of white sand. She could hardly believe her eyes. Not only had a dock been built in the lagoon, but neat rows of huts and warehouses basked lazily beneath the hot afternoon sun. She could see people rushing out of their houses and crowding the beach to greet them. Most were women and old men, but a few children could be seen scampering beside their mothers.

Devon looked at Diablo, who was squinting into the sun to check the trim of the sails. "Too much canvas," he called out to Akbar, who relayed his orders to the men on deck and aloft. "Shorten the main topsail. Sails fast to yards. Larboard bank! Anchor at ready." With practiced ease Diablo maneuvered the *Devil Dancer* to her berth beside the wharf.

Devon heard the anchor cable rattle over the side, then the splash as the big iron hook crashed into the deep lagoon. Diablo strolled to where Devon stood by the rail.

"You could have warned me," she accused. "I thought sure we'd crash into the shore."

"Do you trust me so little?" Diablo teased. His dimple flashed and Devon deliberately turned her eyes away from the entrancing sight.

"I don't trust you at all," she argued. "I should have known you'd make your home someplace that's totally inaccessible. Does anyone know your secret?"

"Damn few," Diablo allowed. "Only those I completely trust."

"I know," Devon whispered shakily. Her eyes grew round as saucers when she realized what that meant. Either Diablo trusted her with his secret or he never meant to let her go. It could also mean he would kill her when she was of no further use to him.

A frown knitted Diablo's dark brow. As Devon had so aptly pointed out, he had failed to consider the fact that bringing her to Paradise was foolhardy, placing scores of lives at her mercy, mostly innocent women and children. He was exposing more than his own vulnerability, and he hoped he'd not live to regret it.

Soon the gangplank was in place and Diablo guided a reluctant Devon onto the dock and through the jostling, happy crowd waiting to greet their men. Only those men who kept women on Paradise had come on the *Devil Dancer*, except for Akbar who rarely left Diablo's side. Those free of responsibilities or entanglements had remained in Nassau to drink and wench until the ship was careened and the wood infected with teredo worms replaced. Then she'd return to Nassau to collect the crew and return once again to piracy.

Curious eyes followed Devon's progress along the beach.

Some called out greetings to their chief, welcoming him home after his sojourn in an English prison. Others, nudging one another in delight, made lewd speculations about Devon and her relationship to the handsome pirate. By the time they left the crowd behind, Devon's cheeks were burning. What truly rankled was being referred to time and again as "the devil's lady."

Studying her surroundings carefully and storing the information for later use, Devon noted that Diablo was leading her down a dusty track past warehouses and crude huts that comprised the village, then up a slight rise. By the time she reached the top she was breathless and perspiring. She had no bonnet to shade her from the sun, and her golden hair clung damply to her neck and cheeks. The charming sight made it difficult for Diablo to concentrate.

God's bones, he wanted her! Once had but whet his appetite for the gorgeous wildcat. The way he felt now, a hundred times wouldn't be enough. What in the hell had possessed him, he wondered, to bring Devon to Paradise. The consequences could be far-reaching and devastating. Though he hated to admit it, the little vixen had entranced him from the beginning. He knew he should have released her as he had promised, but when the storm conspired against his plans, taking Devon to his island seemed the natural thing to do. There was only one way to flush her out of his system and that was to sate himself with her sweet flesh.

At the top of the rise, Devon came to an abrupt halt. Hidden from the beach by a copse of tall trees that provided shade from the relentless sun stood an imposing house. Devon hardly expected to find a magnificent dwelling after seeing the crude buildings in the village on the beach.

Built entirely of wood, the rambling two-story dwelling was surrounded by a wide veranda, its numerous windows opened to admit gentle sea breezes. Tall, graceful columns supported the upper-floor veranda that stretched across the front of the house. The exterior had mellowed to a pale tan, and though not so grand as the stately Chatham House, its clean lines and simplicity charmed Devon.

"I know it's nothing like you're accustomed to," Diablo said anxiously. For some reason he wanted Devon to love his home as much as he did. "But you'll find it comfortable and well staffed. You'll want for nothing while you're my guest."

"It—it's more than I expected," Devon admitted shyly. "Actually, it's quite grand. Do—do you keep slaves?" Her nose wrinkled in distaste, for she had little use for slavery. "It must take many people to maintain the island. Do you grow a crop? Or keep animals?"

"I raise sugar cane," Diablo said and smiled, pleased by her interest. "But I hire Arawak Indians from neighboring islands to work the fields and staff the house. I keep no slaves. I find the Arawaks quite dependable, and the arrangement works well. Rum is distilled on the island and sold to the American colonies."

Once again Diablo's answer surprised Devon. She would have thought him the type to keep slaves to do his bidding, picturing him as a cruel taskmaker. Must he destroy every preconceived idea she had of him, forcing her to view him as a humane being rather than a ruthless despoiler of people and property?

"Come along, sweetheart, I'm sure Tara has a cool drink waiting us."

"Tara?" Devon asked curiously. Who was Tara? Another of Diablo's women? There must be scores of them roaming the face of the earth.

As if on cue a tall, slim woman stepped through the front door. A wide, welcoming smile tilted the corners of her full lips. Smooth tan skin stretched tautly across high cheekbones beneath huge sloping eyes as black as midnight. Delicately sloped brows lent her a fragile beauty that Devon found fascinating. Her hair was long and black as ebony, worn simply behind her ears and held in place by a spray of fresh flowers. A colorful sarong skimmed her lithe, willowy figure without being blatantly suggestive, leaving bare tan calves and slender ankles. Devon thought her quite lovely though somewhat past the first bloom of youth. She appeared to be in her late twenties. Somehow the thought that this beautiful woman was Diablo's mistress aroused an anger in Devon, one she was unprepared to deal with.

"There's Tara now." Diablo quickly closed the gap between himself and the native woman, sweeping her into his embrace, much to Devon's consternation. Her laughter, a lovely tinkling sound, set Devon's teeth on edge.

Tara wriggled free of Diablo's arms, slapping at him playfully. "Welcome home," she said, smiling enchantingly. "I feared we would never see you again when I heard you were in prison, though in my heart I knew you were resourceful enough to escape the hangman."

"Then you knew more than I did, my lovely Tara. I truly thought I was being dispatched to hell to meet the devil. But at the last minute a beautiful lady saved my life." One long arm reached out to draw Devon to this side.

Tara's delicate brows arched quizzically above slanting black eyes as she stared at Devon.

"Devon, Tara is my housekeeper." Then to Tara. "This is Lady Devon Chatham, your new mistress. You are to obey her every whim while she is here as my guest. She is to be denied nothing—except the right to leave until I allow it."

Devon impaled him with a murky stare, barely suppressing her anger. How dare Diablo dictate her life! Then, remembering her manners, she nodded politely to Tara, wondering about the woman and her relationship to the handsome pirate.

Seeing Devon with Diablo shocked Tara. She had been employed by Diablo for several years, being somewhat older than Devon gave her credit for, and in all that time he had never installed a woman in his home as mistress, though Tara knew that many women, Scarlett included, would kill for that honor. Now, out of the blue, he brings home a mistress. Granted, Devon was a raving beauty, and clearly an aristocrat, but what use did Diablo have for such a woman? Sensing that Diablo was waiting for her approval of Devon, Tara made the only response available to her.

"Welcome, my lady. Please come inside. I'm sure you'd like to freshen up while I prepare something cool to drink. If everything isn't to your liking you've only to tell me."

Pleased by Tara's words, Diablo took Devon's hand and led her inside, pride in his home written all over his expressive features. And the moment she entered the house Devon knew why. The rooms were large, light, and airy. A gentle breeze wafted through the open windows, setting the lacy curtains in motion. The furnishings were exquisite, and Devon wondered how many ships Diablo had plundered to obtain them. Mostly they were of French design, with several good English pieces strategically placed for effect. A staircase rose majestically from one side of the central hall.

"Show Devon to the front guest room," Diablo said, "and order a tub for both of us. Her trunks are being brought up by cart."

"Of course." Tara nodded agreeably. "Follow me, my lady."

Devon hesitated, unwilling to place herself in the hands of Diablo's mistress. "Go on, sweetheart," Diablo urged, giving her a gentle push. "Tara will take good care of you."

Before Devon turned to follow Tara, she said, "Your home is lovely, Diablo."

"I want you to be happy here, Devon. This setting was created solely to enhance your beauty."

Embarrassed that Tara should be privy to Diablo's flowery words, Devon returned curtly, "I don't expect to be here long enough to fully appreciate your island." Whirling, she followed a somewhat shocked Tara up the stairs.

The room assigned Devon contained everything she could possibly want or need. What truly surprised her was that it was obviously decorated with a lady's taste in mind. A canopy bed hung with pale blue curtains dominated the large, airy room filled with delicate white and gold French furnishings. Lacy blue curtains blew lazily in the breeze, fluttering against walls hung with gold and blue wallpaper. A thick Turkish carpet beneath her feet cushioned her steps. Devon noted that two doors led from the room and wondered if both were dressing rooms.

"Does it suit you, my lady?" Tara asked in a lilting voice.

"It's lovely," Devon allowed.

"Diablo will be pleased."

"I don't care if Diablo is pleased or not."

"I—don't understand," Tara said, puzzled. Diablo's woman didn't appear overly enthusiastic about being on Paradise. Didn't she know it was an honor to be chosen by Diablo?

"Nay, I don't suppose you do. Are you Diablo's mistress?" Devon asked bluntly, her curiosity too great for verbal sparring.

The heavy black lashes that shadowed Tara's cheeks flew up as she was caught off guard by Devon's rude assumption. "Is that what Diablo told you?"

"Diablo told me you were his housekeeper, but I'm neither blind nor stupid."

Consternation marred Tara's lovely brow. "You have nothing to fear from me, my lady." Had Diablo hinted that they were lovers? Tara wondered. Until she found out just what Diablo wanted Devon to know, she decided to divulge nothing. At least not until she had spoken with her enigmatic employer.

"Perhaps Diablo can best answer your question," Tara said cryptically. "I'll see to your bath."

* * *

The bath felt wonderfully refreshing, the scented water deliciously wicked as it slid over Devon's satiny skin. She sighed contentedly and closed her eyes, resting her head against the rim of the tub. The trunk containing her clothes had arrived shortly before the bath, and Tara worked efficiently at putting them away while Devon lolled in the tub. Suddenly Tara glanced toward one of the doors that Devon had yet to explore, nodded, and quietly left the room.

"Hand me the bathsheet, Tara," Devon said, holding out her hand but too lazy to open her eyes. When the soft material touched her fingertips she reluctantly cranked her eyes open and rose gracefully to her feet. She sensed his presence long before he spoke.

"It's a damn shame to cover all that radiant beauty."

A gasp left Devon's throat. "Diablo! What are you doing here? Where's Tara?"

"Gone. I dismissed her."

"What must she think? How dare you invade my privacy."

"It matters little what Tara thinks," Diablo confided. "I pay her well to follow my orders and she's completely loyal to me. This is my home and no doors are locked against me. I go where I want, when I want."

Devon shook with impotent rage, holding the bathsheet against her breasts as a shield. Diablo's grin widened as he snatched the sheet from her fingers and held it outstretched. "Step out, sweet-heart," he urged. "Cook has a light lunch waiting for us."

"I'm perfectly capable of drying myself," Devon sniffed haughtily. Her attempts to snatch the sheet from his hands proved futile.

"You're compelling me to use force," Diablo sighed with mock regret, seizing Devon around the waist and lifting her from the tub with ease.

Setting her on her feet, he spent several leisurely minutes

carefully perusing her nude form while she slowly burned with embarrassment. "Everything about you is perfect," he proclaimed with slow relish.

Tiny drops of glistening water clung to the creamy surface of her skin, dripping off the coral tips of her breasts. The thick thatch of golden hair between her legs curled in tight ringlets, hiding the treasure beneath that Diablo longed to explore. Heaving a tremulous sigh, he stepped forward and slowly began drying her with the soft bathsheet. Not an inch of flesh was left unattended as Diablo lavished loving attention on her quivering form.

The simple chore was nearly too much for him, and he closed his eyes against the wealth of feelings assailing him. The sweet, tantalizing fragrance of her rose up to taunt him. His heart thundered in wild acceleration, and his hands shook with the effort.

To her chagrin, Devon was not entirely immune to Diablo's slow perusal or the warmth of his hands on her body. A soft melting pervaded the core of her, turning her bones to liquid. He was freshly bathed and shaved, and the scent of him tantalized her senses. The tangy odor of spice and tobacco combined with his own natural masculine aroma to draw her further into his web of seduction. Mesmerized, Devon offered no resistance when Diablo lowered his mouth to hers. His lips were hard and searching, his thrusting tongue seeking her sweetness. Crushing her to him, he showered tiny nipping kisses around her lips and along her jaw. A low moan left Devon's throat as she melted inside, ready and willing to do his bidding.

"God's bones, Devon, I can't seem to get enough of you," Diablo breathed raggedly. "Since that night at the Wheel of Fortune I've thought of nothing but loving you again. I want you, sweetheart, and your response tells me you want me just as badly." His words had the effect of dashing cold water in her face.

"No, don't touch me!" Instead of clinging, her arms shoved ineffectually against his massive chest. "I don't want you. I'll never let you do *that* to me again. Only my husband has the right."

"How will you stop me?" Diablo's lips stretched upward in a predatory grin. "I made you want me once, I can do so again. Forget that fiancé of yours and concentrate on pleasing me."

"You'll find me not so willing next time," Devon asserted firmly. "I'm not the innocent I was, easily seduced by smooth words."

Diablo's answer was to swoop Devon off her feet, carry her to the bed, and toss her down onto the soft surface. Kneeling above her, he pinned her to the bed with his considerable weight. "Give over, sweetheart," he urged raggedly. "I'll have you no matter what you want."

"Then go ahead," Devon challenged, going limp beneath him. "Get it over with."

Diablo went still. No, he wouldn't take her that way, not by force. He'd make her want him, prove to her she needed him as badly as he needed her. He pulled her legs apart and knelt between them. His hands slid hot and sure up her slim calves, over the resisting softness of her thighs. He stroked her breasts, her belly and back down her thighs. Devon caught her breath, commanding her body not to respond and failing miserably.

He devoted loving attention on her breasts, rubbing his thumbs over her nipples, then kneading the soft fleshy mounds before using his mouth to draw on the taut nubs. Kneeling between her parted thighs, Diablo's face hardened with determination, his eyes a haunting shade of gray, cold as steel and just as merciless. Suddenly Diablo was a man Devon didn't recognize, a frightening man who stirred something primitive and foreign in her.

"Kit, no . . ." Devon did not realize she had used that forbidden name. She tried desperately to close her legs against him, but he was holding them open, gently stroking her soft warm center.

"Shh—I won't hurt you," he said gently, finally finding the response he sought. But he wanted more—much more than mere response.

Devon jerked violently when he dipped his head and kissed her between her legs, the heat and wet pressure of his mouth against her creating a fiery need she never knew existed until now. "Nay—you mustn't!"

Shock at what he was doing sent her to the edge of sanity. His mouth was a brand, his intimate caress a torment, and she was a living flame, but still she fought against his erotic invasion.

Grasping her hips, Diablo brought her closer still, holding her firmly while his tongue continued its gentle massage. Sensing Devon's reluctance and fear, Diablo urged, "Don't be afraid, sweetheart. Give to me." Then he continued his tender torture, his tongue parting, seeking, laving the moist center of her being with practiced thoroughness.

"Kit—!" His name left her in a breathless gasp as ecstasy overwhelmed her and carried her beyond herself to a shuddering release. She regained her senses to find Diablo stripped of his clothes and poised above her, his shaft a hard lance demanding entry.

"Devon, you little witch, what have you done to me? I'm obsessed with you. If I didn't know better I'd think myself in—" His words faltered and an astounded look contorted his features. What he had nearly admitted needed time and serious thought and was better left unsaid.

Then his mind went blank as he probed deep and long within her body. Her moist warmth surrounded him as his loving torment turned frantic, shuddering his tribute, thrusting wildly, his rasping voice calling her name as he took them both to heaven.

Chapter Eight

"Sweetheart, did I hurt you?" Devon's soft sobbing intruded on Diablo's euphoria, injecting a discordant note in an otherwise blissful moment.

"I hate you!" she exclaimed. "I never wanted this to happen again. I promised myself it wouldn't."

"If it makes you feel any better, sweetheart, you never had a chance against me. The devil always wins. He devours innocents like you."

"What must your mistress think?"

"My mistress? To whom are you referring?" A hint of amusement turned Diablo's eyes into sparkling diamonds.

"Do you think I'm stupid?" Devon exploded. "I saw how Tara looked at you. How could you be so callous, so—so—unfeeling?"

Shock followed disbelief across Diablo's face. "You think Tara is my mistress?"

"Isn't she?" Devon challenged.

"Nay. She is my housekeeper, no more. Are you jealous, sweetheart?" The thought of Devon being jealous of other women pleased Diablo immensely.

"But—I thought—"

"There's no woman in my life but you, sweetheart," Diablo said, his voice ripe with emotion and strangely subdued. "With you in my bed I neither need nor want another."

A tremor passed through Devon's slender body. She saw the heart-rending tenderness in his gaze, and her own heart turned over in response. She fought an overwhelming need to remain close to Diablo, to be everything he wanted. Despite his despicable profession, his maddening arrogance, he had released an emotion long held locked within her heart. Why couldn't it be Winston who unleased her passion? The answer was simple. Her fiancé's tepid charm couldn't compare with Diablo's devastating appeal. The very air around him crackled with electrifying magnetism.

Yet deep in her heart Devon knew she would continue to seek her release despite her unholy attraction for the pirate. Her future lay with Winston, one of her own kind, not with a man wanted for committing every crime known to man. It was as inevitable as breathing that Diablo would hang one day, and Devon prayed she'd not be forced to witness it.

"Are you cold, sweetheart?" Diablo asked solicitously. He noted her tremor and hoped it meant he affected her in the same way she affected him. Before Devon could form an answer he fitted her snugly into the curve of his body, his arms protective. "I love the way you feel." His hands began a leisurely journey over the hills and valleys of her soft flesh. "You inspire me with the strength and stamina to make love endlessly. I never seem to tire when you're in my arms."

"Not again!" Devon squawked, dismayed. "You can't!"

"Just watch," Diablo smiled wolfishly. "Nothing you do or say will keep me from you. Nothing!" The fierceness of his words brought a shiver of fear to Devon's breast. It was a promise she was to remember many times in the future.

Desperation drove Devon as the days passed one after another with no mention of her release. Each night Diablo joined her in her bed, making love to her so tenderly it often brought tears to her eyes. The longer she was exposed to his special brand of loving, the more she feared she could never leave him with her heart intact. He was bold, arrogant, fearless, tender—and totally corrupt. Each time he took her, Devon continued to resist, to withhold a vital part of herself. She discovered it was the only way to retain her sanity. Repeatedly she begged to be allowed to return to her father, but Diablo would hear none of it nor promise her anything.

Much of Diablo's time was consumed with duties pertaining to his ship and men. When he was absent he was careful to assign one of his trusted men—usually Akbar—to guard Devon. Yet to all intents and purposes, Devon was mistress of his house, her orders strictly adhered to by all the servants. Tara made certain she consulted daily with Devon about menu choices and mundane housekeeping matters.

Diablo's housekeeper treated Devon with grudging respect after Diablo explained to her Devon's role in his life. Astute as well as beautiful, Tara soon realized that Devon had become more than a mere mistress to Diablo. Never had she known her employer to be so obsessed with a woman. Yet it was obvious to Tara that Devon did not appreciate her exalted position, that she eagerly awaited the day when Diablo would return her to England. But Tara seriously doubted that day would ever arrive, and thought it would prove quite interesting to watch the outcome of the little drama unfolding on Paradise.

Meanwhile, Tara seemed pleased to have the fierce Akbar nearby. She'd always been fascinated by the huge Turk, though he rarely seemed to notice her. Perhaps now she'd learn what made the man so unresponsive to women and attempt to remedy it.

Nearly a month after her arrival Diablo informed Devon that all repairs had been completed on the *Devil Dancer* and it was time to meet Le Vautour in Nassau and return Kyle to Paradise. He had allowed them sufficient time to sell their booty in the American colonies and return.

"Try to miss me, sweetheart," Diablo said wistfully. "I know I'll miss you. The next two days will seem like an eternity."

Surprisingly, Devon did miss the roguish devil who had captured her senses. Her heart was pounding excitedly when he returned to Paradise two days later. He greeted her exuberantly, pleased with the results of his business dealings with Le Vautour, which netted him and his crew a small fortune. He informed Devon that Kyle would be joining them for supper that night.

Wanting to please Diablo, Devon took extra care on her appearance. Exactly why she wanted to look her best escaped her, but two days without Diablo seemed like an eon.

One of the gowns Diablo had presented to her was a lovely turquoise silk that Devon hadn't yet worn. At first she thought it too fancy, but then changed her mind, deeming it perfect for the occasion. Tiny cap sleeves set low on her bared shoulders, a snug bodice, and a wide ruffle along the hem displayed her figure to perfection. With Tara's help her blonde tresses were dressed in a most becoming style. When she walked into the dining room that evening, Diablo was entranced. And so was Kyle.

The meal was a happy and congenial affair, but it was obvious that Diablo had eyes for no one but Devon. His silver gaze devoured her with hot longing, wishing they were alone so he could show her how much he wanted her. Almost regretfully, he asked Kyle to entertain Devon while he saw to a few details involving the dividing of the profits from the booty Le Vautour had sold for them. Then he disappeared into his office, promising to hurry.

"How have you fared, lass?" Kyle asked. His midnight blue eyes seemed to probe into her very soul.

"Well enough," came her terse reply, leaving much unsaid.

"Are you happy here on Paradise?"

"As happy as one can be in prison."

"You look radiant. Obviously Diablo has done you no harm. Has he not mentioned your ransom? Repairs on the *Devil Dancer* are nearly completed and he'll soon return to sea. The crew have had their fill of land and are anxious to ply their trade once again."

"Diablo has said nothing to me about leaving Paradise,"

Devon revealed, her anger flaring. "How long does he expect to keep me prisoner? What will happen to me once he leaves? I want to go home, Kyle! Why doesn't he release me? Or demand ransom? I don't want to be his whore!"

Unbeknownst to Kyle or Devon, Le Vautour stood just outside the open window, eavesdropping. After Diablo and Kyle left Nassau, he had run into Scarlett at the Wheel of Fortune Inn and was forced to listen to her vindictive rantings over Diablo's infatuation with his lovely captive and how he had ruthlessly abandoned Scarlett. The longer he listened, the more convinced he became that with Scarlett as an accomplice he could take Devon away from Diablo and pay him back for killing Black Bart. A devious plan hatched in his mind, and Scarlett eagerly agreed to help.

It didn't take much persuasion on Le Vautour's part to wrest the secret of Paradise Island from Scarlett, or enlist her help in ridding Diablo of his beautiful captive. Le Vautour had hoped, after their joint venture in disposing of the booty, that Diablo would invite him to Paradise. But he knew now that Diablo was far too cautious to divulge his secret to someone he didn't trust. Therefore he'd have to rely on his cunning to defeat the wily Diablo.

Le Vautour sailed from Nassau mere hours after Diablo. Following Scarlett's explicit directions, he found the break in the reef and sailed through with no more than a scrape or two. But instead of steering the *Victory* up the river to the hidden lagoon, he anchored at the mouth and under cover of darkness rowed a small boat to Diablo's village. Concealing the craft in the rich vegetation farther down the beach, Le Vautour used the dark shadows to advantage as he made his way to Diablo's house, again following Scarlett's directions. That's how he came to be eavesdropping at Diablo's window. If his plan worked, he would soon have Devon, leaving Scarlett to Diablo. He didn't divulge the best part of his scheme to Scarlett, for if she knew it would result in Diablo's death she would never have agreed to help him.

Le Vautour heard everything Devon said, and it proved enlightening as well as astounding. He had assumed that Devon was with Diablo willingly, despite Diablo's claim that he was holding the lady for ransom. In fact, Le Vautour seriously doubted that Diablo had ever requested ransom from Devon's wealthy family.

Devon's outburst and damning words proclaiming herself Diablo's whore left Kyle speechless. He had no idea what to say to ease her conscience or alleviate her shame over what Diablo had done to her. He should have known better than to wager his share of the booty on Diablo's ability to seduce Devon, for his hot-blooded friend had proven more than once that women found him irresistible.

He was saved from either condoning or condemning Diablo's behavior when Devon, choking on a sob, turned and fled from the room and out the door into the darkness. Kyle did not follow, remaining inside to confront Diablo with Devon's plight. If Diablo intended to return to sea, it was no more than right that he send Devon back to her family.

From the dark shadows outside the window, Le Vautour watched with gleeful anticipation as Devon fled from the house. It was just the opportunity he had been hoping for. He had heard Diablo take his leave earlier and had seen him enter his study, assuming that Kyle would follow shortly. Le Vautour chortled with glee when Kyle did indeed leave, storming into Diablo's study to confront his chief about his intentions toward Devon.

Devon did not stop when she reached the veranda. Glancing over her shoulder, she was relieved to see that Kyle hadn't followed, and she continued on until she came to the path leading down the hill into the village. Not brave enough to venture further on her own, she came to a halt, breathing heavily from her exertions. Would she never be allowed to leave this place? Did her father think her dead? Or was he searching for her, worrying over her fate instead of taking care of himself? He was no longer a young man, and Devon wondered what her abduction would do to his health.

Devon gazed wistfully at the two ships bobbing at anchor in the bay, bathed in brilliant moonlight. If she ever left here alive, the tranquil beauty of the island was something she'd remember to the end of her days. Entranced by the dancing moonbeams above sparkling water and the swaying palm trees, she failed to hear the soft patter of footsteps behind her.

"An impressive sight, isn't it, *ma chère?*"

Devon started violently. "Le Vautour! My God! How did you get here? Does Diablo know you're on the island? I thought—"

"Forget Diablo. Are you so frightened of him, *ma chère?* I would never treat you so shabbily if you were mine. In fact, you're the reason I'm here."

"I'm not frightened of Diablo at all," Devon contended, recalling how tenderly he had made love to her the night before. If she didn't know better, she'd think he actually cared for her. He made her feel so protected, so cherished, she knew that if she didn't leave soon the tiny bud she harbored in her heart would soon blossom into love and demand recognition. And Devon was determined that would not happen. "What do you mean you're on Paradise because of me?"

"I know you wish to leave Diablo," Le Vautour said boldly.

Devon's mouth flew open in astonishment.

"If you're wondering how I know," Le Vautour said, smiling blandly, "I heard you and Kyle talking a few minutes ago."

"You eavesdropped!" Devon accused.

"Of course," Le Vautour admitted dryly.

"I don't suppose it's exactly a secret that I'm a prisoner here," Devon complained bitterly. "If Diablo means to ransom me, I've heard nothing of it."

"Were you my prisoner I'd keep you tied to my bed forever."

Though handsome enough, this pirate was nothing like Diablo. Devon sensed in Le Vautour a cruelty that was missing in Diablo, a flaw in his character that far surpassed all Diablo's bad traits. Blushing furiously, she turned away from his probing gaze, recalling that this was the man who had found her in Diablo's bed at the Wheel of Fortune Inn but a few short weeks ago.

"Please leave me alone."

"Let me help you, *ma chère*," Le Vautour urged, his voice a husky whisper. "Trust me and I'll take you back to England, if that's what you truly desire."

"Trust you? I hardly know you, so why should I trust you?"

"You want to leave here, don't you?"

"I—yes, of course I do."

"My ship is at your disposal, ready to whisk you away from here. Come with me and I'll see that you reach England safely." Darkness obscured the predatory gleam in his obsidian eyes.

"Leave with you? I couldn't possibly . . ." Her words faltered as she paused to consider Le Vautour's offer.

At first it seemed ludicrous that she leave with the infamous pirate. She would be changing one captor for another. On the other hand, she desperately needed to escape Diablo and his devastating effect upon her before she was lost forever. Though Le Vautour was hardly one to inspire confidence, Devon decided it couldn't hurt to listen to his proposal and learn exactly what he had in mind.

"Why would you help me? What do you stand to gain?"

"Ah, *ma chère*, a great deal if your father is suitably grateful for your safe return. I understand he is quite wealthy."

Devon nodded astutely. "As you well know, my father is the Earl of Milford and I can guarantee he will be extremely generous to the person who sees me safely back to England, unharmed and untouched," she emphasized.

"Why would I harm so beautiful a lady?" Le Vautour refuted breezily. "Especially one who will make me rich."

"And you promise to make no other demands on me?" Devon wanted to know.

"Demands, *ma chère*? I would have you know I am a Frenchman and a gentleman." Highly affronted, he straightened to his full six-feet-three.

Devon seriously doubted that the pirate knew the meaning of the word. "When would we leave?" She glanced toward the beach and saw only the *Devil Dancer* outlined against the moonlit sky. Where was Le Vautour's ship? How had he found Paradise?

"Soon, very soon. Rumor has it that three Spanish galleons recently left Florida, their holds loaded with gold and silver." Only a part of that statement was true. "I mentioned it to Diablo when we met in Nassau, and he expressed a strong desire to claim the treasure for himself. His ship is in top shape and his crew eager to return to sea, while my *Victory* is in no condition to battle the Spanish."

Devon slowly digested Le Vautour's words, wondering how far she could trust him. She knew he thought her attractive, but did his greed exceed his lust? Thus far he had done nothing to cause her concern, merely offering her a way off the island in exchange for money. If he harmed her in any way, she'd make certain her father learned of it and would refuse to reward him for his trouble. Still . . .

"Wipe the uncertainty from your mind, *ma chère*," Le Vautour advised, reading her mind. "I promise to bring you no harm."

"Where is your ship? Do you know another entrance to Paradise?" Her mind whirled in confusion.

"Leave the details to me," Le Vautour advised. "I will be here when the time is right."

"But, how . . ."

"Devon, are you out there?"

"Diablo!" Devon hissed in warning. "You know he'll never willingly let me go."

"Leave everything to me. I must go now, it's best I'm not seen. If you are serious about leaving Diablo, don't mention my being here." With the stealth of a fox Le Vautour melted into the shadows. "I'll be in touch, *ma chère*, be prepared."

"What are you doing out here by yourself, sweetheart?" Diablo asked suspiciously when he came upon Devon standing alone at the crest of the hill. "You *are* alone, aren't you?"

"Of course, unless you count the moon and stars."

"It is a beautiful night, I can't blame you for lingering out here." Sidling closer, he embraced her from behind, resting his chin on her bright head.

"Were your dealings with Le Vautour profitable?" Devon asked idly.

"Better than I had hoped. Of course Kyle was along to see that Le Vautour held up his end of the bargain. Our booty brought a good price, and even after Le Vautour's cut the men will be pleased with their shares."

He did not mention that his share would be enriched by Kyle's cut even though he didn't intend to take all his friend's earnings despite their bet. Kyle had berated him thoroughly for using Devon for his own pleasure without a thought for her tender feelings. Kyle had urged him to return Devon to her father, and that was when Diablo had broken down and admitted that he loved Devon, that he could no more let her go than he could stop eating or breathing.

"Then you found Le Vautour to be trustworthy?" Devon probed, jerking Diablo from his musings. She hoped his answer would ease her misgivings about the French pirate.

"Only so far as it pleases him to give his trust." Diablo frowned, annoyed by Devon's interest in the buccaneer. "Why are you so curious about Le Vautour? I admit he cuts a handsome figure in his fancy clothes."

Realizing her mistake, Devon quickly said, "I don't care a fig about the man. I was merely making conversation."

"With you in my arms, conversation is the last thing on my mind," Diablo said, nuzzling her neck. "Come inside, sweetheart. Kyle is gone and I've thought of nothing but undressing you all evening. Admittedly that gown looks outrageously lovely on you, but my greatest pleasure comes with removing it, as well as all the other fripperies underneath that conceal your beauty."

Devon sucked her breath in sharply. His voice was low and strident, the most sensual she'd ever heard. Time and again she'd vowed to resist his devastating appeal, but her resolutions faded beneath the assault of ragged, spontaneous emotions. When he was near, nothing mattered but the need to touch and be touched. Nothing counted but being loved by this vital man who possessed her with wild abandon and loved her to distraction. Finding herself responding to Diablo's loving with the same wild abandon was reason enough for Devon to leave him. Soon she would be beyond redemption and bound to him forever.

But forever had no meaning where Diablo was concerned. The hangman stalked him wherever he roamed. Involvement with him was too uncertain, too dangerous. It would mean pain and separation and certain death. Not knowing when or where death awaited him was too painful for Devon to contemplate, and so, for her own peace of mind, she must leave him. Still, until she left she could see no earthly reason not to enjoy his loving. One day soon nothing but a vague memory would remain of the man she could easily love.

"Do you know what I'd like, Diablo?" Devon suggested impulsively.

"If it's within my power, it's yours," he promised rashly. "Just don't ask that I let you go. I—can't."

"I'd like for us to make love out here, beneath the moon and the stars, with the cool grass for a bed."

Her soft evocative words turned him instantly hard. When he finally spoke, his voice was spiked with jagged edges. "Just hearing you ask me to love you is more than I ever hoped for." He turned her in his arms, and his mouth covered hers with a scorching passion that singed all her nerve endings.

Anxious to test the texture of his skin, Devon slid her hands under his shirt, delighting in the tempered strength beneath her stroking fingers. The firm flesh and rippling muscles that shifted beneath her touch felt like steel sheathed in velvet, and Diablo groaned in frustration.

Savoring the honeyed sweetness of her kiss, he slowly bore her to the ground, at the same time shrugging out of his shirt to allow her better access. Devon lost all knowledge of time and place as she nuzzled his chest, her lips locating the tiny nubs on his flat male breast. She nipped and sucked with delicious abandon as Diablo jerked in response.

"God's bones, sweetheart, I wish I knew what triggered this burst of unbridled passion. I'd like to think it's due to my great appeal, but something tells me there's more to it than that."

"Don't question my motives, Diablo," Devon purred seductively. "Just enjoy this night."

"And all the nights to come," he added, flashing a devilish grin that exposed the dimple lurking at the corner of his mouth. "I adore you, sweetheart."

Devon knew that his words, spoken in the heat of passion, meant little, but they contributed to the magic of the moment. A moment that might never be recaptured. With efficient haste Diablo disrobed her, her nude body glowing like mellow alabaster in the moonlight. Then a terrible urgency seized him and he could wait no longer. There was no time to remove his trousers, no time for tender words or kisses, only the need to possess her now, here, forever. With shaking fingers he unfastened his trousers, freeing his rigid manhood to seek the ultimate prize.

"Sweetheart, I'm sorry," he gasped raggedly. "I can't wait."

His pulsing staff surged proudly into view as he loomed above her, kneeling between her legs on the soft grass, kissing her flat velvety stomach and then each breast in turn. With practiced ease his hard male body slid into the sweet melting warmth of hers. He buried himself deep—so deep—inside her welcoming heat, eliciting a groan from somewhere in the depths of her soul. She was as ready and receptive as he was eager.

Mindless in his hunger, dauntless in his quest, he thrust, withdrew, then thrust again, his passionate rhythm shared by Devon's fragile, trembling form as she raised herself to meet him. Deliberately pacing himself, he strove to bring her the greatest pleasure possible. Some terrible need inside him drove him, some tiny hidden voice told him that soon this must all end. It was too good to last, his love too one-sided to provide lasting happiness, his life too uncertain. Devon was not his to love.

Then all thought was abandoned when Devon stiffened and cried out. Only when the last tremor left her body did Diablo unleash his own stampeding passions. Afterwards Devon lay contentedly in his arms, England and Winston nothing but a passing thought.

Stroking her soft flesh, his heart pounding in his ears, Diablo gasped, "I never thought I'd find a woman I could love, sweetheart—and then you came into my life. If only . . ."

"If only what?" Devon asked with breathless anticipation. If he told her he was in love with her, she'd never find the courage to leave him.

"Never mind, it's too late anyway. Years too late. Besides, I need to make love to you again, more leisurely this time, in bed." Scooping her up in his arms, he walked slowly back to the house.

"Diablo, wait, our clothes! What will Tara think?"

"She'll think nothing. She's not even here. She's spending the night in the village with her widowed mother."

Finding comfort in his words, Devon relaxed in Diablo's strong arms, unaware of the pair of avid, lust-filled eyes following their progress.

Unbeknownst to them, Le Vautour had remained to witness their rapture. While they made wild love he burned with the need to possess the stunning blonde. Though she had known passion in the arms of Diablo, Le Vautour recognized an innocence about her that fired his desire. He had no doubt that Diablo had taken her maidenhead and no other man had used her sexually. Devon was so refreshingly youthful and untainted that Le Vautour would promise her anything to have her in his bed.

Besides, all indications to the contrary, Le Vautour hated Diablo. He had been waiting years to get close enough to that devil to do him some grave mischief. He had deliberately ingratiated himself with Diablo in order to pay him back for a past injustice done to a man who was more than a friend to Le Vautour. Years ago Diablo had led a mutiny that resulted in Black Bart's death, a man more like a father to Le Vautour than his own. Moreover, Diablo had seized Black Bart's ship, claimed it for his own, and renamed it *Devil Dancer*. Now, at long last, Diablo would learn the true meaning of betrayal. Lady Devon might not know it, but she would be the instrument of her lover's downfall.

Le Vautour chuckled beneath his breath. He knew that the Earl of Milford would pay dearly for his daughter's safe delivery no matter how many men had shared her favors. Once on his ship, Devon would be his despite his promises to the contrary. He'd have it all, Devon's tempting body and her father's money. Lying to suit his own purposes bothered Le Vautour not at all. Men like him—and that included Diablo—were accustomed to using trickery to gain their own ends. What made revenge all the sweeter was the knowledge that Diablo seemed genuinely fond of the lovely Lady Devon. Will he still feel that way when the lady betrayed him?

"Devon, what ails you?" Diablo asked, looking up from his dinner and frowning. "You've hardly touched a bite of food in the past two days. Are you ill?"

Devon jumped at the sound of his voice. "What! Sorry," she apologized sheepishly. "Nay, I'm not sick, just—distracted, I guess."

Actually, she was more than distracted. It had been two days since she'd spoken with Le Vautour about leaving, and the strain of waiting was fraying her nerves. Each day she remained with Diablo, every time he made tender love to her, drove a spike into her heart, aware that she would soon leave him forever. It was as inevitable as life and death that they part; they didn't belong together, no matter what her heart told her. Love is a capricious emotion, it creeps up on you when you least expect it and leaves you devastated when you realize it can never be, Devon reflected.

"I know what will raise your spirits," Diablo hinted, grinning wolfishly. "I don't think I'll ever tire of . . ." His words faltered as loud voices interrupted their intimate meal. Tara rushed into the room.

"What is it, Tara?" Diablo scowled, annoyed by the ruckus. Domestic disputes were best left to the housekeeper, he hated to be disturbed by the staff's bickering.

"It's—"

"Ho, Diablo, is that any way to greet a friend?" Stepping into the room, Scarlett coolly surveyed the intimate setting.

"Scarlett, what in the hell are you doing here?" Diablo jumped to his feet, a scowl darkening his broad brow. "If I recall, we parted on less than friendly terms in Nassau."

"I don't believe in holding grudges," Scarlett returned saucily. "Besides, petty arguments have no place in business dealings."

"True," Diablo allowed, wondering what Scarlett was up to. It wasn't like her to take their split lightly. Knowing Scarlett like he did, Diablo strongly suspected she had some trick up her sleeve, and she wasn't on Paradise to renew old friendships. "All right, Scarlett, tell me, what brings you to Paradise?"

"Not in front of your doxy," Scarlett said spitefully, nodding at Devon.

"If you're speaking of Lady Devon, I suggest you watch your tongue," Diablo warned. "Come into my study, we'll not be disturbed there." To Devon, he said, "Sorry, sweetheart, I'll be back as soon as I find out what Scarlett is up to."

"Don't wait up, my lady," Scarlett taunted after Diablo left the room. "My business will no doubt take some time." Her husky voice hinted that more than business would be conducted behind the closed door.

"Take as long as you like, Scarlett, I'm not Diablo's keeper," Devon returned haughtily.

Devon fumed as Scarlett strutted off after Diablo, her tall figure superb in tight pants, full-sleeved shirt, and colorful vest. From the moment she entered the room Devon realized she was the "friend" Le Vautour had mentioned. Did Scarlett's abrupt arrival have anything to do with Le Vautour and his plan to take her off the island? she wondered.

Admitting to herself that she had grown to love Diablo was the most difficult thing Devon had ever done. But no matter how hard she tried she could no longer deny her feelings for the pirate rogue. Aye, Devon decided resolutely, love him or not, she'd still leave when Le Vautour came for her. She knew that Diablo would only break her heart, while Winston was the kind of man she could depend upon. She didn't need the heartache the pirate would bring to her. Telling herself it didn't matter if Scarlett succeeded in seducing him, Devon retired to her room to contemplate her bleak future with a man she could never love while the hangman's noose awaited the one she did love.

"I'm waiting, Scarlett," Diablo said, thrumming his fingers impatiently on the top of his desk. "Tell me what brings you to Paradise."

With exaggerated slowness, Scarlett took a seat opposite Diablo, crossed her incredibly long legs, and fixed him with the full seductive power of her green eyes. "I have some information that might interest you."

"What kind of information?" Diablo asked shrewdly.

"Did you know there's a substantial reward out for Lady Devon? The earl is quite anxious to recover his daughter, judging from the size of the reward. Stede Bonnet's ship was captured three weeks ago by a navy frigate and instead of being destroyed it was allowed to proceed on its way in order to relay the message to Nassau.

Diablo had already heard the rumor in Nassau when he had gone to meet Le Vautour and Kyle. News traveled fast in the Caribbean. The system worked better than a newspaper as word traveled from ship to ship around the Caribbean and pirates' ports of call.

"Aye, I heard."

"What are you going to do about it? The woman belongs with her own kind. She'll bring nothing but trouble to you if you insist on keeping her. Can't you see she's not for the likes of you? But you and me, we're alike, my friend. Neither of us demands more of each other than we're willing to give.

You're a handsome rogue, Diablo, and the best damn lover I've ever had."

An amused smile hung on the corners of Diablo's lips. "I'm hardly in a position to take Devon back to England."

"The *Red Witch* is at your disposal, Diablo. I'll be happy to take the lady back to her daddy and collect the reward. I'm not as notorious as you, and the price on my head not so great. I can easily get in and out of England to do your bidding."

"Most accommodating of you, but I'm not sending Devon back. Not now, maybe not ever, and certainly not with you."

A red haze obscured Scarlett's vision. Before she fell in with Le Vautour's plan she wanted to give Diablo every opportunity to rid himself willingly of his new mistress. By Devon's own admission she was a reluctant prisoner and anxious to leave Diablo's protection. But what truly dismayed Scarlett was the fact that Diablo appeared smitten with the lady and reluctant to part with her, leaving Scarlett with no alternative. For Diablo's own good she was forced to join Le Vautour in his endeavor.

"Is that all you wanted, Scarlett? It's getting late and—"

"She'll keep," Scarlett bit out, her voice tinged with disgust. "I'm sorry I missed you in Nassau a few days ago, but Le Vautour told me your venture proved quite profitable. Are your men ready to sail?"

"The *Devil Dancer* is ready to go to sea the moment I give the command."

"But you can't tear yourself away from your little whore."

Diablo's eyes turned murky as he regarded Scarlett coldly. "That's enough, Scarlett! Don't judge all women by your own standards. Devon is a lady, an innocent virgin until I stole that from her."

His words served only to intensify her hatred for Devon.

She'd do anything to save Diablo from himself, certain that one day Devon would lead him to the gallows. But he was too damn infatuated to see it.

"What if I told you that three Spanish galleons, their holds loaded with gold and silver, were within striking distance?"

Diablo regarded Scarlett warily. "How do you know that?"

"I saw them with my own eyes not two days ago. I followed them from Florida waters and know exactly where to find them. I'd take them on alone, but they are armed and I don't dare risk my ship and men without help. I'm telling you because I need your aid. Join me and we'll split the booty equally."

Diablo's attention sharpened at the thought of attacking the despised Spanish. Already he could smell the tangy odor of the ocean and taste spindrift on his lips. Spanish galleons! God's bones, he'd give anything to relieve them of their precious cargo. Even after splitting the booty he'd have enough to retire for life. Maybe enough to offer Devon—no, he chided himself. Devon belonged to a different world and one day must be returned to her own kind. Not even his great love for her could leap across the abyss to unite them.

When he first heard rumors in Nassau, Diablo thought it merely gossip, since no one seemed to know for certain or had seen the elusive fleet, but he knew that Scarlett had no reason to lie. Still, something inside Diablo prodded him to caution, despite the fact that buccaneers lived by a code of honor. "Who else have you told about this?"

"No one, do you think me stupid? When I failed to find you in Nassau I came directly to Paradise. You're the only one I'd trust to help me."

"Le Vautour probably knows but his *Victory* is in no shape to give chase. He intends to drydock her for a month in Nassau to make necessary repairs."

"Are you with me then?"

Several tense minutes passed as Diablo gave careful consideration to Scarlett's proposal. It wasn't the first time she had enlisted his help in similar ventures, so why should he refuse now? They had dealt well together before and could do so again. They may have parted in anger in Nassau, but evidently Scarlett regretted her hasty words and approached him now as a way to mend their friendship. His primary objection was leaving Devon on Paradise unattended. He smiled inwardly as a solution came to him. Though Kyle would protest vigorously, he would be left behind to protect Diablo's prized possession.

"When do we leave?"

A wide grin split Scarlett's beautiful features. "The sooner the better, if we want to intercept the galleons before someone else finds them."

"Some of my crew are in Nassau," Diablo replied. "If I sail with the morning tide I can pick them up and rendezvous with the *Red Witch* on the west side of New Providence Island."

"I'll be there," acknowledged Scarlett eagerly. "Don't bother to show me out, I know the way."

Diablo had already buried his head in a ledger when Scarlett slipped from the room. But instead of letting herself out the front door, she sidled up the stairs, keeping carefully to the shadows. Her prior knowledge of the house led her directly to the room assigned to Devon. Not bothering to knock, she turned the knob and stepped inside.

Chapter Nine

Clad in a diaphanous bedgown that Diablo had given her, Devon stood before the windows gazing wistfully into the star-studded night. Light from a single candle outlined her figure beneath the gauzy material, painting it gold to match the bright strands of hair brushing her waist. The click of the latch brought her instantly alert and she whirled, expecting to see Diablo. The welcome died on her lips.

"You! What are you doing in my room? Where is Diablo?"

Scarlett eyed Devon malevolently, aware that this lovely vision awaited Diablo and would soon be decorating his bed, the sole recipient of his ardor. Her hands clenched in barely suppressed anger, and she would have flown at Devon if Diablo wasn't nearby to come to her defense.

"I have something to say to you," Scarlett bit out.

"How did you find your way to Paradise?" Devon asked, moving away from the window.

"I'm no stranger to Diablo's island," Scarlett smirked. "He trusts me."

"Say what you will, then leave," Devon returned shortly.

"Be prepared to leave tomorrow. Diablo sails on the morning's tide, and Le Vautour says to tell you to expect him."

Devon blanched. Evidently Scarlett was privy to her plans to leave Diablo and had been enlisted by Le Vautour to help. What had Scarlett said to Diablo to make him leave so suddenly? Devon trusted Scarlett even less than she did Le Vautour. "I'll be ready."

"I must go before I'm discovered." With the stealth of a sleek cat Scarlett edged toward the door, reached for the knob, then paused. "Why?" she asked curiously. "Why do you want to leave Diablo? Few men are as handsome. I've never known a better lover, and he seems genuinely fond of you. Perhaps you think yourself superior to him."

"You wouldn't understand," Devon said dismissively. Scarlett was not one to invite intimacy, nor did Devon wish to divulge how deeply it would hurt to leave Diablo. That bit of knowledge must necessarily remain buried deep within the chambers of her heart.

With a snort of disgust, Scarlett slowly pivoted and left the room as quietly as she had entered.

Diablo rubbed the back of his neck to ease his tired muscles and looked longingly toward the stairs. After Scarlett left he sent one of the servants to the village with a message for Kyle. A short time later Kyle arrived and Diablo imparted all the information provided by Scarlett about the Spanish galleons. Grumbling crossly, Kyle left to round up the crew and ready the ship for immediate sailing, none too happy about Diablo's request that he remain behind. Though Kyle had protested vigorously, Diablo was adamant, trusting no other man to look after Devon in his absence.

Nothing remained now but for Diablo to join Devon in her bed and make slow, passionate love to her till morning. Taking the stairs two at a time, he entered her bedroom on silent feet. She was not asleep as he expected but was sitting in a chair gazing forlornly out into the black velvet curtain of night.

"Might I hope that wistful look is because you miss me?" Diablo teased.

"Diablo!" Leaping to her feet, Devon went eagerly into his waiting arms. "It's so late. I've been waiting for you."

"Come to bed, sweetheart. The night is nearly spent and I can't leave without loving you."

"Leave?" The right note of surprise and regret entered her voice. "Am I going with you?"

"Not this time, love. This is—business. Kyle will remain behind to keep you amused."

"I don't need to be amused," she replied, dismayed. How could she leave the island with Kyle dogging her steps? "I don't need a watchdog, either. Besides, knowing Kyle as I do, he'll want to be with you."

"Nevertheless, he stays. He'll receive his share of the booty just like the others."

Before Devon could voice another protest, Diablo scooped her into his arms and placed her on the bed. She watched avidly as he shed his clothes, the dim light illuminating the bulging muscles of his magnificent torso. His powerful frame moved with easy grace as he stood before her proud and unashamed. Devon stared in fascination at his tempting physique, acutely conscience of the male aura of sexuality he exuded. That male part of him that gave her so much pleasure sprang forth boldly from the dark forest between his thighs, and Devon reached out boldly to stroke the velvet staff into throbbing life.

Diablo seized her hand. "Nay, sweetheart, I don't want the night to end before it begins. Lie back and let me love you."

Knowing this was the last time she would be with Diablo like this, Devon's own driving need became a living flame within her. She wanted to put her brand on this man so that she'd remain in his memory beyond time and space. "It's my turn, Kit," she said with bold innuendo. "Let me love you."

Before he could protest she pulled him down beside her on the bed, shrugging out of her bedgown while he watched in breathless anticipation. "I'm all yours, sweetheart," he managed to gasp as she slid her body full length atop him.

Putting her hands, lips, and mouth to good use, Devon used everything Diablo had taught her to bring him the greatest pleasure he had ever known. When she straddled his slim hips and took him deep into her moist sheath, he was driven out of his mind with need. She set the rhythm and Diablo eagerly followed until the blood pounded through his veins and desperation seized him. Then he grasped her hips, holding her captive, his impatience growing to explosive proportions as he thrust wildly—deeply.

Devon groaned in sweet agony as the turbulence of his passion swirled around her. She was a glowing image of fire, passion—and love. Then she soared to awesome, shuddering ecstasy. "Kit!"

Diablo did not stop, but continued his loving torment until he reignited the dying flame of her passion into blazing splendor. Never had he felt so strong, so virile, wishing it never had to end. But eventually his body took over and he poured himself into her.

"Are you awake, sweetheart?"

"Aye. Must you leave already?"

"Not yet, there's still time for us to love again, but first there's something I need to say."

Devon tensed. Did she really want to hear Diablo's words? Intuitively she sensed what he wanted to say and thought it better left unsaid. She wanted their parting accomplished without tender sentiments, without either of them revealing personal feelings that could never become reality. "Kit, won't it keep? This is hardly the time for—"

"There's no better time, sweetheart. I love you, Devon. I never thought I'd say that to any woman, but you're different from any woman I've ever known. I want to spend the rest of my life with you. I want children from your body. I want— God's bones, sweetheart, I want us to be together forever. No matter what it takes, I'll find a way."

"Kit, nay, you don't know what you're saying." Diablo's words thrilled Devon whether he meant them or not. Her own heart was filled with so much love for him she had to bite her tongue to keep from crying out her feelings.

"I know exactly what I'm saying. You don't know how much I love the sound of my name on your lips. My real name. I'd almost forgotten I had a name other than Diablo."

"Kit, listen to me!" Devon pleaded. "I must leave. This attraction between us is doomed. There's more than love involved here, there are other people to consider. There's my father and—and my fiancé. You and I are from different worlds. It would never work. How could I stay with you, knowing that one day word would come telling me you'd been caught and hanged?"

"What I feel for you goes beyond mere attraction," Diablo confided. "If we were from the same culture, contemporaries, so to speak, would it make a difference?"

"Possibly," Devon admitted slowly. "But what good is conjecture when we both know what you are and how your life will end?"

"When I return, sweetheart, there's a story I want to tell you. One that will shock you, but one I think will make a difference in what you feel for me."

"I seriously doubt there's anything you could say that will change things."

"I've bared my soul to you, Devon. Me, Diablo, a man notorious for his secrets and proud of his female conquests. Who would have thought I'd be brought to my knees by a woman half my size, one who makes love like an angel? God's bones, Devon, why can't you love me as much as I love you?"

Devon flushed, biting her tongue to cry out her own love but knowing it would only cause them more grief. "If it helps, I do care for you, Kit. More than I care to admit. But it's senseless to talk about something that was doomed from the beginning."

"I agree," Diablo grinned wolfishly. "Especially when I want desperately to make love to you again. Just think about what I've said while I'm gone. When I return, perhaps my explanation will persuade you otherwise."

"Devil you might be, but when you make love to me you take me to heaven," Devon sighed, melting into the warmth of his body. "Take me to heaven, Kit."

"Gladly, sweetheart, if you take me along with you."

Diablo was gone. She'd never see his captivating smile again. Tears of remorse watered Devon's eyes as she recalled their passionate parting just before dawn colored the sky. She knew that Diablo hadn't the slightest inkling she'd be gone before he returned. His parting words reaffirming the love he bore her were nearly her undoing. Choking on a sob, Devon could only wish him God's speed, too distraught to speak. If she so much as opened her mouth she'd blurt out that she loved him, that she'd never forget him, and that Winston would never take his place in her heart. But she remained mute. How could she stay with Diablo knowing that one day they'd be torn apart and she'd likely be forced to watch him hang from the gallows? Better to part now before children came along to complicate their lives. How would she tell their offspring their father was a notorious pirate responsible for countless deaths?

Though Devon's appetite was virtually nonexistent, she appeared in the dining room for breakfast, not wishing to arouse undue suspicion. Tara was extremely perceptive and might take it upon herself to alert Kyle should Devon act other than normal.

Devon had just spooned the last mouthful of food in her mouth when Kyle joined her, looking decidedly unhappy. Devon knew immediately what bothered him and understood his disappointment. Being left behind to guard over a woman certainly was no task for a man accustomed to adventure on the high seas.

"I'm sorry to be so much trouble, Kyle," she said sincerely. "I know how much you want to be with Diablo. If it were up to me you'd be aboard the *Devil Dancer*."

"Aye," Kyle agreed glumly. "But Diablo wouldn't have left me here with you if he didn't care for you."

Devon flushed, unable to meet Kyle's eyes. What would he say if he knew she meant to leave Diablo before the day was out? Then suddenly a disturbing thought entered her mind. What would Le Vautour do when he found Kyle attending her? Surely the pirate wouldn't hurt Kyle, would he?

Excusing herself, Devon went upstairs to pack clothes necessary for her journey. Kyle watched her slow progress up the stairs, puzzled by her odd behavior. He had hoped she'd remain for some stimulating conversation, but it was not to be. Unaccustomed to the vagaries of women, Kyle shrugged and left the house to see to the onerous duties concerning the plantation that Diablo had dumped in his lap.

Hidden in a shallow cove on a neighboring island, Le Vautour watched with unconcealed glee as both the *Red Witch* and *Devil Dancer* cleared the shoals and sailed away from Paradise. Scarlett had played her role admirably in leading Diablo from his roost. Le Vautour waited until the ships were out of sight before navigating the reef and finding his way to Diablo's hidden cove. When the *Victory* was anchored in the bay, Le Vautour's men swarmed ashore, finding little difficulty subduing the women and children left behind. With no one to stop him, Le Vautour walked boldly up to the devil's lair.

When he reached the house he became more cautious, deciding to conceal himself until he scouted the lay of the land and learned if Diablo had left someone behind to guard his prize. His caution proved prudent, for he had just scuttled for cover when Kyle walked out the door.

Hiding behind a dense thicket of bougainvillea beside the house, Le Vautour watched as Kyle walked toward the rear of the house. Le Vautour assumed he was going to the cane fields, and waited until he was out of sight before exposing himself. Making certain no one was in sight, Le Vautour sidled through the front door.

Luckily Tara was working in the kitchen connected to the house by a dogwalk, and the other servants were engaged in duties elsewhere. Having been told by Scarlett which room belonged to Devon, Le Vautour climbed the stairs and entered her room unannounced.

Devon had just placed the last of her belongings in a bag when she whirled to find Le Vautour standing at her elbow. "You could have knocked," she bit out, more angry than frightened.

"I didn't want to alert the servants. Are you ready?"

"Diablo left Kyle behind."

"I know," Le Vautour replied anxiously. "He just left the house, so we must hurry. My men are prepared to raise anchor the moment we're safely aboard." He grasped her arm to hurry her along.

"Wait! My bag. I've packed a few necessities."

Le Vautour spied the bag, scooped it up, and urged her down the stairs. Devon had intended to leave Diablo the locket she wore around her neck as a small memento, but at the last minute decided she couldn't part with it for it bore the likeness of her mother. He would just have to make do with his memory of their time together.

Le Vautour's hand was on the doorknob when Kyle walked unexpectedly into the hall from the back of the house. So great was his shock he had no time to react or even to defend himself as Le Vautour dropped Devon's bag and drew his cutlass. Though the Frenchman aimed for Kyle's heart, the big Irishman had the presence of mind to turn aside at the last minute so that the blade sliced through his arm and into his side.

Devon screamed as Kyle started a slow spiral to the floor. "You've killed him! You heartless brute, you've killed Kyle."

"Non, *ma chère*," Le Vautour denied, nettled by Devon's

outburst and anxious to be away. "He'll survive. I strongly advise you stop that screeching before you alert the whole island. I thought you wanted to leave."

"I—do, but I didn't want anyone hurt. Are you certain he'll be all right?"

"What's this all about, lass?" Kyle found the voice to ask. "Are you leaving Diablo? How did Le Vautour find Paradise?"

"Forgive me, Kyle," Devon sobbed, heartbroken over how things were turning out. "I didn't mean for this to happen. I wanted to leave here quietly with no one the wiser. Le Vautour is taking me back to England where I belong."

"You can't trust him, lass," Kyle warned, growing weak from loss of blood. "Mark my words, Diablo won't let you go so easily. And you, Le Vautour, make the most of your time for your days are numbered."

Le Vautour laughed nastily. "I fear neither man nor devil." Then he picked up Devon's bag, gripped her arm, and dragged her out the door.

"Devon, don't go, you don't know what you're doing," Kyle pleaded, depleting the last of his strength.

"I can't leave him like this," Devon balked, straining back toward Kyle.

But Le Vautour was not to be denied. He wanted Devon nearly as much as he wanted the reward for returning her to her father. He pulled, prodded, and pushed her all the way to the village, her meager strength no match for him.

The *Victory* was the only ship riding at anchor in the protected bay, and Devon could see men scurrying about the deck in preparation for sailing. When they reached the beach, the helpless villagers stood by as Le Vautour wrestled the devil's lady into a waiting longboat. Within minutes they were rowed to the ship and Devon was unceremoniously dumped aboard. Soon the *Victory* slipped its moorings and Le Vautour was negotiating the narrow river and gliding through the treacherous reef protecting the island.

Once they were in open water, Le Vautour turned the wheel over to his lieutenant and rejoined Devon where she stood at the rail watching forlornly as Paradise disappeared over the horizon. For a short space of time the island had truly become her paradise.

"Don't fret, *ma chère*," he soothed. "In two or three weeks, depending on the winds, you'll be with your family and I'll be all the richer for it. 'Twill be my pleasure to make your journey a pleasant one. Come along, I'll see you to your cabin."

Le Vautour's leering grin set Devon's teeth on edge, but she was determined to ignore his sly innuendos. In the two weeks or so it would take to reach England she vowed never to be alone with the devious pirate or to place herself in a compromising position.

To her chagrin, Devon felt reasonably certain the cabin to which she was assigned was the captain's domain. It was richly decorated and completely masculine, and none but Le Vautour would possess so many fine things. When he returned to the bridge to set the course and issue orders pertaining to their journey, Devon carefully examined her surroundings.

Innocently naive, she believed that Le Vautour intended to occupy other quarters, that collecting ransom for her safe return was uppermost in his mind, and she would be safe from his lust for that reason. So far he had done nothing to disabuse her of that notion, and she clung desperately to that hope.

Devon retired early after supping alone, and finding no lock on the door was determined to ask to have one installed the next day. Before she fell asleep, she uttered a prayer for Kyle's swift recovery and thought wistfully of Diablo, the man she loved more than her own life but could never have.

Le Vautour stood before Devon's door for a long interval, his loins throbbing with the need to possess the beautiful blonde goddess occupying his bed. Considering himself too wise to be ruled by his lust, he finally turned away. Time was on his side. First he'd attempt to seduce Devon, and failing that, resort to more forceful methods. After watching her and Diablo couple on the ground like two animals, Le Vautour was determined to have her as hot and eager for him as she obviously was for her devil lover.

The following days passed pleasantly enough despite the despondency Devon suffered. The knowledge that she would never see Diablo again had sent her spirits plummeting. Lately she had come to think of him as Kit, not Diablo, for the name suited him better. He was hardly the devil people made him out to be. Once Kyle had confided that Kit had never deliberately killed anyone. He attacked mostly merchantmen, frightening them into submission by putting a shot across their bows and waiting patiently for surrender. Often a ship was captured without striking a blow. Only when the *Devil Dancer* was challenged by navy vessels did a fight ensue and men were injured or killed. Moreover, Kit's prisoners were never treated harshly. Some were ransomed, but usually passengers were left on the ships to make their way back minus their cargos.

The name "Kit" gave Devon little clue as to Diablo's origins. She had originally thought him Spanish, but detected no sign of an accent. He spoke flawless English—not the low street dialect but with perfect diction. The man was not only a mystery but a contradiction. Kind, tender, gentle, loving. Arrogant, overbearing; a pirate notorious for unscrupulous deeds, most of them embellished lavishly as they passed from mouth to mouth and country to country. Who was he really? She was destined never to know, for their paths would never again cross.

The fourth day out Devon awoke to overcast skies and brisk winds. "Looks like a storm brewing," she remarked when Le Vautour joined her on the deck.

"I doubt it," he said, sniffing the air. "A bit of a blow, mayhap, but nothing serious. "'Twill be naught but a brief summer storm."

Le Vautour truly believed the coming tempest would be of short duration, and he chose tonight to seduce Devon. Each passing day sorely tested his patience, until he had to have her or explode. He thought himself amazingly forebearing given his Gallic temperament, and could wait no longer to enjoy the wench.

Devon remained skeptical despite Le Vautour's assurance that a major storm wasn't in the offing. "I'll take your word, Le Vautour," she said doubtfully. "About the lock on the door, it still hasn't been installed." So far the Frenchman had ignored her frequent requests for a lock, promising vaguely to have it done as soon as time permitted.

"*Ma chère*," Le Vautour replied, feigning concern, "have you been disturbed since setting foot on my ship? Have any of my men accosted you?"

Grudgingly Devon admitted that Le Vautour ruled his ship and men with an iron fist. She knew he dealt swift and cruel punishment, for many times in the past days she heard the whistle of the whip followed by grunts, moans, and screams of agony. So far she had managed to hold her tongue about Le Vautour's handling of his men.

"Nay, I've not been molested."

"And you won't be," he stated arrogantly. "My crew knows I demand strict obedience. But enough of that, I've ordered cook to prepare a special feast for us tonight. A small offering to celebrate our alliance."

"Hardly an alliance," contradicted Devon.

"What else would you call it, *ma chère*? I would say it is mutually beneficial. You get your freedom and I get—what I want," Le Vautour said cryptically. "So, about supper . . ."

She could hardly refuse, Devon considered thoughtfully. Angering Le Vautour was the last thing she wanted. She had willingly placed herself in a vulnerable position and already regretted it. She had never meant for anyone to be hurt and fervently prayed Kyle was recovering from his wound. Of Diablo, she tried not to think. When she did the pain was unbearable.

"Of course I'll sup with you," Devon allowed with grudging acceptance. "I'm grateful to you even though I deeply regret your rash actions concerning Kyle. It was a senseless act and could have resulted in his death."

"But a necessary one if we were to leave without interference. I assure you the man will live. So, *ma chère*, until tonight." With a gallant gesture totally at odds with his calling, Le Vautour brought Devon's hand to his lips. Then he spun on his heel and strode off with a jaunty bounce.

Distraught, Devon paced the confines of the cabin, fully aware of the grave mistake she had committed by placing herself at Le Vautour's disposal. Though he'd not touched her, his black eyes all but devoured her each time they met, and she despised the way his probing gaze rested far too often on her bosom. Kyle was right, the man did not inspire trust. At least she knew what to expect, she reasoned, and was prepared to deal with it.

A short time later Le Vautour arrived accompanied by two crewmen bearing assorted dishes from which the tempting aroma of food wafted. The pirate had dressed himself like a dandy, sporting a blue velvet frockcoat and a white shirt dripping with yards of lace. Prancing about the cabin, he saw to the placement of food and drink and then dismissed the men with a lazy wave of his hand.

"You look ravishing, *ma chère*," he purred once they were alone.

Actually, Devon had done nothing to enhance her natural beauty, merely wearing one of the dresses she brought along with her.

"Shall we eat?" she suggested. "The food smells delicious and I'm famished."

"Excellent idea," Le Vautour agreed. His hawk-like features sharpened and he ogled Devon as if he'd prefer to taste *her* rather than the food. Though he was not unhandsome, his sly regard of her set her nerves on edge.

While they supped, pelting rain lashed at the windows and the howling wind made eating difficult. Their meal was interrupted when several dishes slid from the table to the deck.

"It's all right," Devon assured a disgruntled Le Vautour. "I was finished anyway."

"This is not how I planned the evening, *ma chère*," he apologized, rising. Bracing his feet on the swaying deck, he helped Devon to her feet and over to the bunk. "You'll be safer here until the storm abates." But instead of leaving as Devon expected, he settled down beside her.

"Aren't you needed on deck?" she asked, her voice strangled with rising panic.

"Peck is quite capable at navigating through the tempest. As I said before, the storm will be of short duration. Perhaps we can create a storm of our own inside this cabin," he hinted slyly.

"I prefer that you leave," Devon insisted indignantly. "I wouldn't want to keep you from your duties."

"You're no innocent, *ma chère*, you know what I want." Le Vautour's narrow face assumed a predatory gleam as he reached for her. "You knew what to expect when you sailed with me." Grasping her waist, he dragged her into his arms.

"You promised!" Devon cried, pounding her fists against his chest. "You said you'd deliver me to my father unharmed.

"Harming you is furthest from my mind," Le Vautour said smoothly. "I know Diablo has enjoyed you and I merely wish the same privilege."

"Let me go! You're nothing like Diablo. What happened between us has nothing to do with you. Besides, one word from me and my father will send you packing without a cent."

"Your father will pay—and pay well," Le Vautour laughed. "As long as I hold you hostage I can name my price. Besides, you'll not see your father until the reward is in my hand. By then I'll be long gone and it will be too late to cry foul. I want you, *ma chère*—now."

Driven beyond restraint, Le Vautour seized Devon's lips in a kiss so forceful it pressed the breath from her lungs. Suddenly his hands were everywhere, on her thighs, her breasts, her hips, squeezing her buttocks until she cried out in pain. Drawing renewed strength from somewhere within her slender body, Devon fought back furiously, the turbulence of the storm matching the turbulence of her struggles. Forced down into the surface of the bunk, she felt the weight of Le Vautour's considerable bulk smothering her.

"You brute!" she gasped as he fought to subdue her.

"I didn't want it to be like this, *ma chère*," he wheezed breathlessly. "I had hoped you'd submit willingly, but if not I'm prepared to use force. Which will it be?"

"Damn you, Le Vautour! Now I know why neither Diablo nor Kyle trusts you. You're crazy if you think I'll submit to a bastard like you."

"I'm a better lover than Diablo. Scarlett can vouch for that."

Hearing Diablo and Scarlett linked together in that manner served only to reinforce Devon's rage and she renewed her struggles. But she soon became aware that her efforts were futile in the face of Le Vautour's lust for her. She felt the pull and heard the sound of cloth being torn as her bodice split and slid away from her body. Le Vautour's black eyes gleamed with salacious intent as he stared at Devon's pale breasts laid bare by his heavy hand.

"*Mon Dieu!* You're magnificent, *ma chère.* Once I put my brand on you you'll want no other man."

"You arrogant, conceited pig!"

Le Vautour's face hardened and he began tearing at Devon's clothes, her careless words stripping away the veneer to reveal the cruel streak in his flawed character. "You little bitch," he sneered menacingly. "Am I not good enough for you? What does Diablo have that I lack?"

"A heart!" spat Devon, condemnation ripe on her tongue. "Leave now and I'll say nothing to my father."

Le Vautour was far too aroused to worry about the earl hundreds of miles away in England. Shifting, he began tearing at his own constrictive garments.

When Devon realized how close she was to being ravished, she opened her mouth to scream, but the sound was lost to the wailing wind. Instead of subsiding, if anything the violence of the storm had intensified, but Le Vautour was aware of nothing but his overwhelming lust. Then suddenly fate intervened to save Devon from his vile intentions.

The ship keeled sickeningly, balanced precariously for what seemed like hours, then righted itself . . . only to lurch in the opposite direction before once again leaping upright. The two struggling bodies rolled to the edge of the bunk, then slid off to land with a thud on the deck.

"*Mon Dieu!*" exclaimed Le Vautour, scrambling to his feet. He had his hand on the door when a loud crash signaled more danger. He turned to shout at Devon over the din of the raging elements, "I'm not finished with you!" Then he was gone, prying the door open against the onslaught of lashing rain and whipping wind.

A small sob left Devon's throat as she crawled onto the bunk and slipped beneath the covers, hanging on to the sides to keep from being thrown off. God had heard her plea and granted her a reprieve, but what would happen when Le

Vautour returned? she asked herself despondently. Would she have to go through this again?

The storm continued to unleash its fury and Devon began to wonder if she'd survive the terrible tempest. The sea was a cruel mistress who destroyed indiscriminately and jealously kept what she claimed. Devon was convinced she would die an ignoble death, never to be heard or seen again. Would she be missed? She wondered glumly. By her father, surely, and perhaps Winston, and maybe Diablo, for a short time. Until he found someone to take her place.

Diablo—Kit—What would he think when he returned and found her gone and Kyle wounded because of her? Would he hate her? Perhaps it was best if he did. Whatever it was that had lured him away from Paradise could have only been some trick cooked up by Scarlett and Le Vautour, Devon reasoned, and Diablo was bound to be furious when he discovered the hoax. Did he care enough to come after her? For his own good she certainly hoped not. Returning to England would be tantamount to writing his own death warrant.

A terrible crash brought Devon's thoughts skidding to a halt. The sound of shouts and cries rising above the roaring wind cleared her mind of all but the necessity for haste as she leaped from the bunk and threw a cloak over the tattered remnants of her clothing, certain the ship was in danger of sinking and determined to leave the confines of the cabin.

Her hand was on the door latch when the panel burst open, forcing her backwards. Several men, soaking wet and looking half-drowned, pushed into the cabin bearing the body of a man. Devon recognized Le Vautour immediately. She made way as they carried him to the bunk. Only then did she notice the piece of jagged wood about a foot long protruding from his thigh and the peculiar angle of his right arm.

"What happened?"

"The mainmast snapped and the cap'n couldn't get out of the way fast enough," growled Peck, Le Vautour's lieutenant.

"Will he live?"

"Who's to say?"

"Where's the doctor?"

"Dead. Crushed by the mast. He wasn't as fast as Le Vautour."

The man's callous reply shocked Devon. "Who's to treat him if the doctor's dead?"

Suddenly another crash rent the air and Peck said hurriedly, "Do what you can. I'll leave one man to help, but the rest are needed on deck." Then he was gone, followed by all but a small, grizzled pirate obviously too old to be of any use on deck.

Devon stared at Le Vautour with something akin to horror. That he was badly wounded was obvious. For what he intended to do to her she felt she had every right to let him die. But she couldn't. He was a human being, albeit a miserable one, and she was humanitarian enough to help. Not that she was all that versed in the art of healing. Far from it.

"What ye gonna do, lady?" the ancient pirate asked, staring uncertainly at his bleeding captain.

"What's your name?"

"They call me Gabby 'cause I like to spin yarns."

"Well, Gabby, what do you suggest? I'm willing to do what I can, but I've not done this sort of thing before."

"I've helped the doc some, lady, but I ain't particularly knowledgeable. I'd say that splinter gotta come out," Gabby advised, "and the bleedin' stopped. Then we can set that right arm."

Gritting her teeth against a sudden rise of nausea, Devon helped Gabby remove the large splinter from Le Vautour's leg. Then they cleansed the gaping wound by dousing it copiously with rum, and managed to stop the bleeding to a trickle while the captain remained blissfully unconscious. Luckily no bones were broken in the thigh. After binding the wound with clean cloths, they set to work on the broken arm.

Devon sent Gabby in search of a board to serve as a splint. While he was gone, Devon determined the break was in the lower arm between elbow and wrist. When Gabby returned, they pulled the bone into place and taped the arm to the board. Then they administered a liberal dose of laudanum found in the doctor's bag retrieved by Gabby.

Afterwards, Devon collapsed in a chair and closed her eyes while the grizzled pirate cleaned up Le Vautour and put him into a nightshirt. Only then did she realize that the storm had abated and the ship had somehow ridden out the tempest. She was amazed to find she was still alive and unharmed, though the damage to the *Victory* had to be heavy.

During the following days the pirate crew was much too busy to bother with Devon as they worked tirelessly to repair their ship. Not wanting to appear conspicuous, she remained safely inside the cabin. Too hurt to be moved, Le Vautour remained in the cabin, forcing Devon to sleep on a pallet. Gabby came in and out freely, bearing meals and performing more personal duties for his wounded captain. Peck appeared daily to check on Le Vautour's progress, as well as to receive orders once the captain had regained his senses. It spoke well for Le Vautour's leadership that his men were willing to continue under his rule rather than elect a new captain.

By some miracle, or perhaps the generous rum bath, Le Vautour's wound did not fester and was healing slowly but surely. A week later he was able to hobble to another cabin, supported between two burly pirates. He was vain enough not to want Devon to see him in diminished health. It was obvious; though, that his right arm would never regain its previous dexterity. Still, he had much to be grateful for. But being the kind of man he was, he was more bitter than grateful. On the verge of possessing Devon, fate had conspired against him and deprived him of the very thing he had spent considerable time planning and plotting for. Now, due to his injuries, it looked as if he'd have to forego the pleasure of her body and settle for the earl's reward, for he was in no condition to pursue his former objective and unlikely to be so for some time to come.

No one was more thankful for Le Vautour's disability than Devon. Unable to continue with his plan of seduction, but still desirous of receiving full payment from her father, he kept his crew from molesting her. When he was finally able to hobble around under his own steam, he visited Devon in her cabin.

"So, *ma chère*, the trip didn't go exactly as I had planned," he began breezily. "I'd hoped by now we'd know one another intimately."

"I'd not wish you unnecessary pain, but I'm not sorry. You'd have raped me if you hadn't been injured," Devon maintained.

Le Vautour's lips thinned sourly. "Rape is a harsh word. You had only to cooperate."

"What do you want, Le Vautour?" Devon asked, adroitly changing the subject.

"If I were able I'd show you what I want. But as things stand we'll reach England before I'm strong enough to do you justice," he complained bitterly. "Four or five days should bring us to the mouth of the Thames."

Home, Devon thought with a rush of emotion. Would she be able to move effortlessly into her former life after knowing and loving Diablo? Facing Winston after willingly sharing Diablo's bed would be no easy task. More difficult still, she thought glumly, would be marrying her fiancé—if he still wanted her. Seeing her father again promised to be the one bright spot in her bleak future. She'd just have to learn to live without the handsome pirate she had come to love. Suddenly a disturbing thought entered her head.

"How can you just sail into London harbor? Aren't you taking a big risk? Won't you be arrested?"

"The British flag will fly from our mast," Le Vautour grinned slyly. "It should work if we do nothing to incur suspicion. I plan to be in and out of London before the authorities realize I've even been there. Where will I find your father?"

"Probably at our London townhouse," Devon replied thoughtfully. "Father doesn't much care for the country since mother died."

"Excellent, *ma chère*," Le Vautour gloated.

The *Victory* encountered no difficulty sailing up the Thames into London harbor. To her chagrin, Devon learned she was not to go ashore immediately but must wait until Le Vautour contacted her father and collected his reward. She could do no more than pace the cabin while the pirate made his way ashore. Before he left he posted a guard at her door to prevent an ill-advised escape.

The one thing Devon regretted was having to part with the locket she always wore around her neck bearing her mother's photograph. But she knew her father would never believe Le Vautour without proof. When he had asked her for something her father would readily recognize, it was the only thing she had to offer.

Chapter Ten

"Are you telling me my daughter is aboard your ship, safe and unharmed?" demanded the Earl of Milford?

"*Mais oui*," Le Vautour replied smoothly. "Lady Devon will tell you herself how I risked life and limb to rescue her from the devil's lair."

"God's blood, man, where is she? Why isn't she with you? Or is this all a hoax?" His face grew beet red and a fierce scowl distorted his features. "I've suffered untold anguish over my daughter's abduction. Who are you?"

"Lady Devon is aboard my ship, monsieur, unharmed and in good health." Le Vautour was unperturbed by Lord Harvey's rage. "I am called Le Vautour."

"Le Vautour!" spat Lord Harvey, recognizing the name instantly. "A bloody pirate! No doubt you and Diablo are in cohoots to bilk me out of my money. It won't work, Le Vautour. Get out of here before I summon the authorities. There's a price on your head."

"Tsk, tsk, *mon ami*, you misjudge me."

"I am not your friend, Le Vautour. I think you're lying through your teeth. Devon's fiancé and I have not been idle these past weeks; not even the Royal Navy could find a trace of that scoundrel, Diablo, and we despaired of ever seeing her again. That blackguard's promise to return my daughter was nothing but empty words."

"Do you recognize this?" Le Vautour dangled the locket belonging to Devon by its slender gold chain before Lord Harvey's nose.

"Where did you get that?"

Snatching the locket from Le Vautour's hand, Lord Harvey

examined it thoroughly before releasing the catch. The moment he saw the picture of his dead wife he knew the pirate spoke the truth. Devon would never willingly part with her treasured keepsake except under unusual circumstances.

"Now do you believe me?" Le Vautour taunted. "I have caused your daughter no harm and intend to deliver her safely into your hands."

"How much, Le Vautour?" Lord Harvey was prepared to pay and pay dearly for his beloved daughter.

"You are astute as well as wise," Le Vautour replied. "I will not haggle with you, monsieur. I want three thousand pounds. In gold. I went through great hardship to bring your daughter to you and incurred much expense." He was thinking of Scarlett who demanded a full third, as well as his crew who would also share in the windfall.

The earl's mouth flew open. "My God, man, that's robbery! I don't keep that much cash on hand."

"But you can get it with little difficulty," Le Vautour advised smoothly. "I will allow you sufficient time to procure the necessary funds. Give me half now and the rest when your daughter is delivered to you. If you value her life you will tell no one about me or alert the authorities of my presence in England until I am well away from these hostile shores."

A man of power and the brains to go with it, the earl was not a man prone toward rash judgments. Yet his daughter was dearer to him than his own life. His answer came swiftly, the only one available to him under the circumstances.

"You'll have your money, Le Vautour. Half now and half when Devon is released. Furthermore, you have my solemn word the authorities will know nothing of this until you are safely gone."

Le Vautour was no fool. He recognized the earl's caution and applauded it. "Agreed," he said.

He looked on greedily while the earl opened his safe and

counted out fifteen hundred pounds, noting that the man had spoken the truth. That sum had nearly depleted the amount kept in the safe. "There's one condition, Le Vautour," the earl said, holding the sack of gold coins well out of the pirate's reach.

Shifting his gaze from the bag of gold, the Frenchman narrowed his eyes suspiciously. "No tricks, monsieur," he warned ominously, "or your daughter will suffer."

"I'm in no position to offer tricks," Lord Harvey snapped. "I value my daughter's life too much. I'm only requesting that you tell me where to find Diablo. I aim to see him brought to justice and hanged for what he did to my daughter. The spies I dispatched to Nassau returned with very little information. All they learned was that Diablo had his own hideaway somewhere in the Bahamas. But either no one knew its location or they feared Diablo too much to talk. Yet it is common knowledge that Devon was in Nassau for a short time."

"It's true Diablo inspires fear in many, and few would betray him," Le Vautour muttered sourly. "Diablo's island is well protected and virtually impregnable unless one knows the secret." The Frenchman was ever resentful of the awe and respect shown Diablo by his peers. His name ranked in importance with Blackbeard, Calico Jack, and Stede Bonnet.

"But you know how and where to find him, don't you, Le Vautour?" the earl said shrewdly. "Will you share your knowledge? For a price?"

The pirate needed little prodding. Betraying Diablo was exactly what he had planned from the beginning. "Add another five hundred pounds and the information is yours," he said slyly. "I've just come from Diablo's Paradise and know the route. But even after you find the island, getting to Diablo is difficult. He's only on Paradise for short periods of time, and the island is surrounded by a barrier reef that protects it from intruders. None but shallow draft ships may enter, and then only if one knows exactly where the break in the reef is located and how to find the secret entrance to the lagoon."

"Will you help me, Le Vautour? I want to see Diablo captured and punished. I want that devil hanged for his crimes."

Le Vautour had nothing to lose by divulging Diablo's secret, and much to gain. Disposing of Diablo would fulfill a promise of long standing, one he had made when Diablo brought about the death of Black Bart and stole his friend's ship. The debt of honor had been outstanding far too long, and it was time Diablo was made to pay for leading the mutiny that took the life of Black Bart. But in the unlikely event that Lord Harvey's plan failed, Le Vautour wanted no one to know who had betrayed Diablo. If it got back to that devil, his retribution would likely be swift and lethal.

At length, Le Vautour said, "Diablo is no friend of mine. I will tell you his secret only if you promise not to divulge a word of this conversation to anyone, including your daughter, who saved my life when I was injured during a storm at sea. I certainly wouldn't want her to think badly of me."

Lord Harvey couldn't imagine Devon coming to the aid of a thoroughly despicable man like Le Vautour, until he recalled his daughter's gentle and caring compassion for all human life. "You have my word, I will not tell Devon. But I make no such promise concerning her fiancé, who wants Diablo brought to justice as badly as I do."

Le Vautour considered the earl's words for the space of a moment. "You are a man of honor, and therefore I agree with your terms. Listen closely while I tell you how to reach Paradise. Or better yet, bring pen and paper and I'll draw a map.

A quarter of an hour later Le Vautour left to return to his ship while Lord Harvey hurried to his bank to withdraw the outstanding amount due the pirate. Arrangements had been made to meet at the wharf in London harbor where the *Victory* was moored.

As she stood at the rail of the *Victory*, Devon's heart beat with trepidation as a closed carriage bearing the Chatham coat of arms drew to a shuddering halt beside the quay. The door opened and her father's beloved face searched the deck until he found her. Eagerly she ran to the gangplank but was stopped by Peck, who looked to Le Vautour for orders.

"Not yet, *ma chère*," Le Vautour cautioned. "Your father and I have business to conduct before you are free to join him."

The pirate had returned just an hour ago and informed Devon she was to leave shortly, as soon as her father arrived and the ransom was delivered. Devon assumed that an agreement had been reached and she couldn't wait to leave this vile ship. She was ecstatic when Le Vautour allowed her on deck where she could be readily seen by the earl. Now, seeing his dear face, which had aged dramatically these past weeks, she knew her decision to leave Diablo had been the right one, though it had left her heart permanently damaged. She watched warily as Le Vautour limped down the gangplank, favoring his injured leg. His right arm was still in a sling, but all his injuries were healing well.

Lord Harvey stepped from the carriage before his footman could aid him, his anxious eyes riveted on Devon's slim form.

"You have the gold?" Le Vautour asked when he faced the rotund earl.

"Aye, all of it. Release Devon."

Nodding, the pirate turned and signaled Peck, who sent Devon on her way down the gangplank. She took off at a run, throwing herself into her father's protective arms. Only then did the earl place the bag of gold into Le Vautour's hands. Moving with utmost haste, he lifted Devon into the carriage where she collapsed in a sea of tears against his ample chest. Abruptly the carriage jerked forward, leaving Le Vautour standing on the quay, happily counting his money.

"There, there, sweetheart," the earl soothed clumsily. "It's all over. You're safe now."

Lord Harvey had no way of knowing that his endearment succeeded only in bringing on a fresh torrent of tears, for it brought to mind all those times Diablo had called her sweetheart. Sometimes teasingly, sometimes coaxingly—but always with love.

"Was it so terrible, m'dear?" the earl asked when Devon's tears showed no signs of abating.

"Nay, Father, not really. I'm sorry if—if I gave you that impression. Diablo didn't harm me. He was quite gentle, in fact, though he had ample cause to treat me harshly. I—I shot him the day he brought me aboard his ship. It wasn't a dangerous wound, merely disabling him for a time."

Lord Harvey's florid face went blank with shock. "Good God, girl! You shot Diablo and lived to tell of it? The man is a cold-blooded killer, it's a miracle he didn't order your immediate death."

"Diablo—he's not what people think," Devon said lamely, trying to explain the man she had come to love.

Lord Harvey regarded Devon through narrowed eyes. "Has the scoundrel bewitched you, daughter? He's taken dozens of lives, stolen thousands of pounds worth of goods, and sunk countless ships. Only the devil knows how many women he's ravished. The man is devoid of all honor. He promised to set you free, but proved by his failure to do so that his code of honor consists solely of lies and deceit."

"Diablo *was* going to set me free, Father, but a storm blew us off course. He was also quite ill from his wound at the time and unable to order my release. He—"

"Cease, Devon, I've heard enough of that man's virtues! I

didn't want to dredge up painful memories, but under the circumstances I feel I must. Did Diablo do anything to— harm you while he held you captive?"

Devon's eyes became shuttered. She knew exactly what her father referred to. It was no more than any parent would ask, yet a simple answer was impossible. In the end she spoke the truth—or as near the truth as she could come without hurting either Diablo or her father.

"If you're asking if Diablo raped me, the answer is no. I told you I wasn't harmed." Her flushed cheeks revealed more than her cautious words.

What Devon failed to reveal was that what had begun as her seduction had ended with their mutual pleasure . . . that in a shockingly short time she had gone to Diablo willingly, welcomed his intimacies, craved his love, responded to him with wanton abandon. She could tell none of these things to her father.

Devon's words did little to ease Lord Harvey's suffering. He found it difficult to believe she had escaped Diablo's clutches unscathed. It was widespread knowledge that the devil devoured beautiful young girls like Devon. But for his own sanity as well as hers, he chose to accept her words.

"Thank God. I was so afraid he—ahem—well, never mind, m'dear. All is well now, and you'll never have to think about your ordeal again. I promise that blackhearted devil will soon hang for his crimes."

Horrified by the thought, Devon fell silent, content for the moment to bask in her father's love. She was astute enough to realize that her welfare came first with him and he would go to any lengths to protect her from harm. Their silence continued until the carriage ground to a halt before Chatham House. Lord Harvey alit first and helped Devon descend, then he guided her to the door, his arm curled solicitously around her slim shoulders. But before they reached the entrance, another carriage came careening around the

corner, skidding to an abrupt halt behind the Chatham rig.
Both Devon and her father turned to watch as a slim man of
medium height with brownish hair and a thin mustache
bounded out.

"Devon, thank God you're safe!"

"Winnie, how did you—"

"I sent a message, m'dear," Lord Harvey explained hurriedly. "'Tis no more than right, Winston is your intended
husband. Your abduction has been hard on both of us. The
poor boy's been distraught."

"It's all right, Father," Devon allowed, though all she truly
wanted was to go to her room and collapse on her bed.

"Come inside, Winston," invited the earl. "The street is
no place to air family discussions."

Seated in the familiar comfort of her father's study, Devon studied Winston from beneath lowered lids while the
earl told him of Le Vautour's visit and Devon's safe return.
Had she ever really looked at the foppishly dressed man
she had agreed to marry? she asked herself distractedly. He
was handsome enough in a classic, effeminate way, she allowed, but compared to Diablo's virile face and form, he
appeared soft and weak. His muddy brown hair hung lank
on his forehead and his eyes were a pale shade of blue. His
skin lacked the dark, healthy glow of a man accustomed to
long periods of time in the open. He was adorned like a
dandy in peacock-hued satin that did little for his pasty
complexion.

Yet something must have attracted her to Winston, Devon realized. Perhaps it was his devotion to her. Or his
pretty manners, which had once seemed an admirable trait
but now struck her as being sissified. It certainly wasn't his
ardor for her that drew her, for Winston was totally lacking
in that department. She might once have thought such reti-
cence desirable in a man, but after experiencing Diablo's

exuberant loving it had lost all appeal. Suddenly she became aware that the men had stopped talking and were staring at her curiously.

"Is something amiss, m'dear?" Lord Harvey asked anxiously. He had noticed Devon's distraction and worried about her state of mind. He knew of few women who could survive what she had just gone through and took great pride in Devon's courage and fortitude.

"'Tis nothing, Father," Devon assured him sweetly. "I suppose the shock of being home when I never expected to see you again has left me quite fatigued. I'd like to be excused."

"Can you spare another moment, dear?" Winston asked solicitously.

"Of course, Winston," Devon agreed, thinking she owed him that much for betraying his trust.

"I want us to be married immediately, and your father agrees."

"Immediately? Why such a rush?"

"He's right, m'dear," concurred the earl. "Neither of us want you hurt by gossip mongers. They'll have a field day once they learn you're back."

"That's correct, Devon," Winston added. "The only way to save your reputation is by marrying immediately."

"Hang my reputation!" Devon snapped. "I've done nothing wrong. I didn't ask to be abducted."

"We know, dear," explained Winston patiently, "but the first thing everyone will think is that your virtue has been compromised."

"What if it has been? Would it matter to you?" Devon questioned bluntly.

"Well, ahem, of course not, dear. Nothing matters as long as you're restored to us safe and sound."

Devon was appalled by the thought that society would

condemn her even if she hadn't been a willing participant in her abduction. It was to Winston's credit that he was still willing and eager to marry her. But an immediate marriage held no appeal for her. Besides, so much had happened in the past weeks that she needed time to sort through her feelings and consider her future.

"I hardly think a hasty marriage will solve anything, Winnie. I need time to think. I've just gotten home, let me recover before rushing into anything."

Winston's smooth brow wrinkled into a frown, his displeasure obvious. "Our marriage is scheduled to take place in a few weeks. What I'm suggesting is not unreasonable."

What neither Devon nor her father knew was that Winston was close to financial ruin and in desperate need of Devon's generous dowry to satisfy his creditors. He would have married Devon no matter what Diablo had done to her. He strongly suspected she was no longer a virgin, but that was the least of his worries. It merely saved him the distasteful task of deflowering her himself.

Recognizing Devon's obstinacy, Lord Harvey came to the rescue. "My daughter has been through a harrowing experience and is exhausted. Let the subject rest for tonight. Perhaps Devon will change her mind once she's had time to think about this."

"Of course. How callous of me to force the issue when Devon is obviously distraught and needs rest. Good night, dear," Winston said, bending to place a chaste kiss on her forehead. His lips were cool and dry, and Devon gave an involuntary shudder.

She nodded in reply, glad to see him leave. When had her feelings changed so drastically? she wondered dully. At one time she considered Winston everything she wanted in a man. Before Diablo cast his spell on her.

"I'll see you out, Winston," Lord Harvey offered.

"I'll be in my room, Father," Devon called as she rose to

follow them out of the room. Both men watched as she disappeared up the stairs.

"I won't have Devon badgered," the earl warned Winston when they were alone. "I'm sure she'll come to see the advantage of wedding without delay once she's had time to consider the consequences. Right now there's something of more importance to discuss. I know how and where Diablo can be found."

"Devon told you where that bastard is hiding?"

"Nay, but the pirate Le Vautour did. He seemed none too reluctant to part with the information, for a price. The man is totally lacking in scruples. He even drew a map to aid us."

"Let me go after him," Winston said, his eyes bright with dreams of glory. "Think what destroying that menace to society will do for my reputation. Even the king will have to sit up and take notice. I'll have no difficulty obtaining three men-of-war from the navy to join my own *Larkspur*."

"No warships, m'boy. Le Vautour told me Diablo's stronghold is guarded by a coral reef preventing all but shallow draft vessels from entering the sheltered harbor through the narrow passage. The map shows where the break in the reef occurs and pinpoints the entrance."

"Shallow draft vessels. Hmmm," mused Winston thoughtfully. "A little more difficult to obtain, but not impossible."

"How long will it take to find and prepare such ships? I want the bastard brought to justice."

"I shall be knocking at Diablo's door within a month; six weeks and I'll be back in London," boasted Winston.

"Splendid, splendid," beamed the earl. "We'll plan a wedding six weeks from today."

"What if Devon isn't willing?"

"She will be," promised the earl.

Diablo paced the bridge as the *Devil Dancer* plowed smoothly through the blue-green water. He was bored, restless, and angry. The *Devil Dancer* and the *Red Witch* had crisscrossed the Atlantic for weeks looking for the elusive Spanish galleons. He strongly suspected there never was a Spanish fleet laden with riches. But what did Scarlett have to gain by lying? He intended to find out tonight. He'd signaled the *Red Witch* earlier inviting Scarlett to sup with him aboard the *Devil Dancer*. Both ships would seek shelter that night in a secluded inlet on the coast of Puerto Rico.

The moon reflected thousands of tiny diamonds on the sparkling water when Scarlett stepped aboard the *Devil Dancer* and was shown directly to Diablo's cabin. She looked fetching in tight breeches, flowing white shirt, and high boots that molded the long length of her legs. But Diablo, dressed in unrelieved black, saw neither her beauty nor the seductive pose she struck for his benefit. Unaccustomed to being ignored, Scarlett stomped over to the chair Diablo held out for her and sat down with an angry thud.

"Our meal will arrive shortly. Would you care for a drink while we're waiting?"

"Brandy, if you have it."

"Of course."

Scarlett regarded Diablo with riveting attention as he busied himself with their drinks. She loved the way his muscles rippled beneath his shirt, the movement of his taut buttocks when he walked, the bold display of his manhood inside the tight confines of his trousers. But to Scarlett's dismay, all her efforts of seduction had failed since Devon had come into his life. She longed to tell him the witch was gone but wisely decided it was in her own best interests to let him discover that for himself.

Scarlett sipped her brandy with obvious relish while their supper was being served. "I'm afraid the fare is poor tonight," Diablo said. "That's one of the reasons I asked you here tonight. Our stores are severely depleted, and I assume yours are too."

"I thought you asked me because you like my company," Scarlett said coyly.

Diablo frowned. "I'm tired of this wild goose chase. We've tracked back and forth across the ocean with nothing to show for it but an empty hold and men grown edgy from lack of action. Not even a merchantman has crossed our path. Scarlett, I'm beginning to think you invented those Spanish galleons."

"Why would I do that?" Scarlett asked with feigned innocence.

"Aye, why?" Diablo repeated. "What will you gain from lying?"

"Nothing, I wasn't lying. Finish your meal, Diablo, 'tis a good supper considering supplies are short."

For several minutes Diablo devoted himself to his food, then shoved his plate aside and stood. "I'm setting our course for the Bahamas tomorrow. Do what you want, but don't count on me for help."

Scarlett pushed her own plate back and rose to her feet. Swaying seductively, she walked to within inches of him, the tips of her unfettered breasts brushing the incredible breadth of his chest.

"You're going back to *her*," she accused, her voice a sultry whisper. "You know I can give you everything she can, and more. What does a lady like Devon Chatham know about pleasing a man?" Her hands played teasingly over his chest, her fingers skillfully unbuttoning the buttons of his shirt. "I can offer you more, so much more. We're alike in so many ways."

Boldly Scarlett's hand dropped to the bulge straining against Diablo's tight trousers, and she chortled gleefully when his manhood jumped in response. "You want me, admit it!"

"I'm a man, Scarlett," Diablo ground out, grasping her wrists in a viselike grip. "My body may respond to manipulation, but my mind and heart reject you utterly. This may come as a surprise, but I love Devon. She moves me as no other."

"Love, bah! You're not capable of love. Forget about that witch and be my lover again."

"Nay, Scarlett, there's but one woman I want to make love to, and I'm going back to her tomorrow."

"You poor besotted fool! Wake up! The lady doesn't want you."

Diablo's silver eyes narrowed dangerously. "What do you mean?"

Sensing her danger, Scarlett immediately sought to placate him. "Nothing, I meant nothing. I'm only trying to convince you that women like Lady Devon have no place in your life."

"Get the hell out of here, Scarlett! I refuse to listen to anything you have to say about Devon."

Recognizing Diablo's rage and the tight control he was exerting to maintain his temper, Scarlett turned and fled the cabin, happy to escape unscathed. She had seen the results of Diablo's fury before and had no wish to experience it herself.

Diablo navigated the barrier reef with practiced ease, yet he couldn't shake the sense of foreboding that had plagued him since his conversation with Scarlett. As the *Devil Dancer* sailed into the snug little harbor, people gathered on the beach to welcome their returning men. By the time the ship docked beside the single pier and Diablo walked briskly down the gangplank, Kyle was there to greet him. The glum look on Kyle's face did nothing to ease Diablo's worry, nor did the sling holding Kyle's arm in place against his chest.

"The *Devil Dancer* is riding too high in the water for her hold to be filled with riches," Kyle said in sober greeting. "Did the Spanish fleet elude you?"

"Either that or there never were any galleons out there to

begin with," Diablo grumbled crossly. "I'm beginning to believe the whole thing was a figment of Scarlett's imagination, though I've no idea what she hoped to gain from it. But enough of the elusive galleons, how is Devon? Why didn't she accompany you to the beach? I hope the little hellcat has missed me."

There was so much love in Diablo's eyes that Kyle cursed Devon and Le Vautour a thousand times over. "Sweet Jesus, Kit, I'm sorry. I—it happened so damn fast, there was nothing I could do." Kyle's disjointed reply sent fear lancing through Diablo's heart.

A string of oaths left his bloodless lips. "You're not making sense, Kyle. What happened? Has something happened to Devon?" Though Diablo felt it necessary to ask the question, his keen intuition had already supplied the answer.

"There's no easy way to tell you, Kit," Kyle explained contritely. "Devon is gone. I've failed you." Never had Kyle felt so woefully inadequate.

"Somehow I already knew it," Diablo replied grimly. "What happened? How did she get off the island? Was she taken by force? By God, I'll kill the bastard who took her!"

"No force was necessary," Kyle said regretfully. "She went with Le Vautour willingly enough."

"Le Vautour!" spat Diablo with fury. Suddenly his eyes fell to the sling cradling Kyle's arm. "Is that his handiwork?"

"Aye. I tried to stop him, but it happened so quickly he skewered me before I could draw my weapon. I swear, Kit, I'll never be caught unaware again."

"I can't believe Devon would stand idly by and watch Le Vautour wound you without interfering. He could have killed you. Doesn't she know the kind of man she's dealing with? Why in God's name would she go with Le Vautour when she could scarcely stand the man?"

"Don't misjudge her, Kit. She did not condone what Le Vautour did to me. If not for her he would have killed me. Le

Vautour offered to take the lass home to England, and she struck a deal with him." His voice held a note of accusation as he added, "You should have returned her to her father as you promised."

"Don't lecture me, Kyle," Diablo warned, his eyes holding all the warmth of cold steel. "And don't make excuses for Devon. She planned this behind my back, scheming and plotting with a man who's totally lacking in scruples."

"I tried to tell her, Kit, but the lass has a mind of her own."

"So I've noticed," Diablo concurred dryly. "Are you well enough to assume your duties?"

"Aye, what are your orders?"

"How soon can you have the *Devil Dancer* replenished for a long voyage?"

"Surely you're not going after Devon?" Kyle asked, stunned.

"How soon, Kyle?"

"Barring misfortune, the lass is already in England. She's been gone over a month."

"How soon, Kyle?"

"Twenty-four hours."

"See to it. Consult with Akbar about repairs and replacement of crewmen."

"Why, Kit? Why are you so adamant about chasing after Devon when she obviously doesn't want you?"

"Have you forgotten that I'm responsible for scores of lives on Paradise?" Diablo asked tightly. "Devon knows too much about Paradise and its secrets."

"Surely you don't think . . ."

"I've not lived this long by placing my trust in chance. I'd like to think Devon won't tell her father or fiancé how or where to find us, but I'm far too realistic to take her silence for granted. I'm going up to the house to speak with Tara. Please see that my orders are carried out without delay."

Dismissing Kyle with a curt nod, Diablo whirled and walked briskly past the cluster of women and children who were joyously greeting their men.

Hiding behind his stoic expression and empty eyes, Diablo concealed the terrible hurt over the ease with which Devon had abandoned him. The world must never know how a fragile girl had nearly destroyed him. How she must have laughed when he bared his soul to her, declaring his feelings like a lovestruck adolescent. No wonder Devon had not shared her own feelings with him, for her heart had remained untouched while his own beat hot and strong with a passion born of perfect love.

Chapter Eleven

"Sail ho!"

Diablo came instantly alert. "Where away?"

"Astern to starboard."

Diablo swung to the starboard, his spyglass sweeping the horizon. "She flies no flag. Does she look familiar to you, Akbar?" He handed the glass to the huge Turk.

"She's still too distant to tell."

"May I look?" Kyle asked, reaching for the glass. "Hmm, her lines are familiar but I'm not certain. Do you suppose it's Le Vautour's *Victory*?"

"By God, I hope so," swore Diablo fervently.

"And if it is?" Akbar challenged. "What if the lady is still aboard?"

"'Tis my guess Devon is in London by now," Diablo returned, "unless she remained aboard the *Victory* to serve as Le Vautour's mistress."

"Oh come now, Diablo," Kyle scoffed. "The lass would never—"

"By the Prophet's beard, it *is* Le Vautour!" Akbar sang out gleefully. "I'd recognize the *Victory* anywhere." Kyle had returned the spyglass to the Turk, who avidly followed the course of the approaching ship. He passed the glass back to Diablo, who confirmed Akbar's suspicion.

"I think you're right, my friend." Diablo smiled with grim satisfaction. "Send the men to battle stations."

There was a wild scurry as men from every part of the ship, armed with cutlasses, daggers, pistols, and boarding axes, hurried to their stations at Akbar's command. When all was in readiness, Diablo stepped forward, his voice booming loud and clear above the din and excitement.

"Have you the stomach for a fight, lads?"

A resounding collective "Aye" was everything that Diablo hoped for.

"I'll tell you now 'tis one of our own and she's unlikely to be carrying booty," Diablo said.

"'Tis Le Vautour, I recognize her rigging," shouted Dancy.

"Aye, lads," Diablo concurred. "He's stolen my lady and launched a vicious attack upon my lieutenant. I've sworn vengeance. Are you with me, lads?"

"We're with ya!" shouted Rooks, naming himself spokesman.

"You'll not be sorry. I'll personally reward every man loyal to me out of my own pocket to make up for lack of booty. Good fortune, lads."

"Do we sink her?" Akbar asked, aware that Devon could very well be aboard the *Victory*.

"Nay, Akbar, not until I'm certain Devon isn't aboard. When we're close enough, put a shot across her bow and see what happens. Mayhap Le Vautour will surrender without a fight."

Le Vautour recognized the *Devil Dancer* immediately, and a string of oaths spewed from his lips. He should have known the devil would come searching for him. He had hoped the British navy would finish Diablo off, but he'd not back down from a confrontation now, nay, he welcomed it with eager anticipation. Already his men were occupying their battle stations, prepared to defend their ship. The sky was cloudless, the sun bright and warm, and Le Vautour decided it was a good day to avenge the death of Black Bart.

"Fire!" Akbar shouted, and the starboard guns belched a

stream of gray smoke. The shot cleared the bow of the *Victory* according to Diablo's instructions. Immediately the *Devil Dancer* tacked sharply while its starboard guns were being reloaded. An answering volley from the *Victory* fell short of its mark.

"Le Vautour wants to fight," Akbar chortled gleefully. The two ships were evenly matched, but he knew the Frenchman could not match Diablo in skill and cunning.

"Aim the cannon into the rigging," Diablo ordered curtly. "I want to bring the bastard to his knees without harming Devon if she's aboard."

"I always said the woman would bring you trouble," Akbar grumbled beneath his breath. "She chose to go with Le Vautour, so I see no need to worry about her fate."

"You have your orders, Akbar, see to it." Diablo's tone demanded instant obedience, and Akbar called for another round, this to be aimed high in the rigging.

His efforts were amply rewarded when the shot sheared off the top of one of the *Victory*'s masts. Le Vautour's gunners had not yet found their mark as their answering shot soared over the *Devil Dancer*'s prow to fall harmlessly into the sea. Or perhaps it was Kyle's superb handling of the wheel. Whatever the reason, Diablo's gunners managed to disable a second mast. Then the *Devil Dancer* took a direct hit, but luckily the shot did no more damage than put a hole in the hull above the waterline. Fortunately it missed the cache of ammunition stored on deck, and the fire it started was quickly doused.

Diablo smiled with grim satisfaction as he noted the several small fires burning aboard the *Victory*. None looked serious enough to sink her, but so many men were involved in putting them out that most of their guns fell silent. Diablo used the lull to his advantage, maneuvering the *Devil Dancer* to within boarding distance of the floundering *Victory*.

"Run out the boarding planks!" he shouted above the din

of battle and wild cheers of his crew. "Le Vautour is mine," he cried as everyone surged over the side.

Within minutes the crew were swarming aboard the *Victory*, dodging burning rubble and engaging in hand-to-hand combat. It had been far too long since they'd enjoyed a rousing fight, and each man was eager for blood.

Diablo spied Le Vautour standing on the quarterdeck, cutlass in hand, his mouth curved into a snarl. "Come ahead, you devil's spawn," the Frenchman challenged. "I've been waiting a long time for this. Ever since you killed Black Bart and stole his ship."

A puzzled frown furrowed Diablo's dark brow. "Black Bart brought about his own demise." Slowly he advanced up the ladder to the quarterdeck. "If not me, someone else would have led the mutiny. Bart was a cruel, perverted man, and the world is a better place without him. Why should it matter to you?"

"Black Bart was like a father to me. I've waited years to avenge his death." He aimed a vicious slash of the cutlass to Diablo's middle, forcing him to suck in his breath as the blade whizzed by with a fraction of an inch to spare.

"Where is Devon?" Diablo asked, easily deflecting Le Vautour's second thrust with the flat of his cutlass. "Is she aboard the *Victory*? Woe be to you if you've done her any harm."

Le Vautour laughed crazily, slicing again at Diablo's vulnerable midsection. "Your whore came with me willingly enough."

Filled with incredible fury, Diablo clenched his jaws as he danced sideways, parrying Le Vautour's thrust. "You bastard, is Devon aboard your ship or not?"

"You're too late, Diablo, the lady is in England. She's a delectable piece, I understand fully your reluctance to part with her. We became quite—intimate—during her stay aboard the *Victory*. It was part of the bargain we struck," he boasted, embellishing the lie with a sly grin.

"You lying, blackhearted braggart! Devon would never let you touch her."

Then all talk ceased as each man concentrated on killing the other, the larger battle raging around them with increasing vigor. Both crews were evenly matched, equally cunning and brave, but Diablo's men, driven by fierce loyalty, slowly began turning the tide in their favor. By now Diablo had received several minor cuts, but so had Le Vautour. Suddenly two of Le Vautour's men leaped up the ladder to the quarterdeck, brandishing cutlasses, followed closely by two crewmen from the *Devil Dancer*.

Inadvertently one of Diablo's men jostled him, and he fought for balance, dropping to one knee. Chortling gleefully, Le Vautour saw victory at hand, and lunged viciously at his fallen enemy. But Diablo, who had outfoxed many a wily foe in his numerous ventures, was too quick-witted for the sly pirate. He deliberately let down his guard when he stumbled, inviting Le Vautour's thrust to his vulnerable chest. Grinning evilly, the Frenchman plowed forward, and was stunned to find that Diablo had nimbly rolled aside and now raised his own cutlass up and under Le Vautour's guard, driving the blade into his gut. Le Vautour's eyes widened, then went blank as he fell, dead before he hit the deck.

The battle ended swiftly with Le Vautour's death. A thorough search of the ship turned up a cache of gold hidden in Le Vautour's cabin as well as other money and a rich store of valuable objects. Though the hold was indeed empty as Diablo suspected, the *Victory* yielded a surprising amount of booty for the crew of the *Devil Dancer*.

When offered a choice, Le Vautour's surviving men eagerly joined the ranks of Diablo's crew. Once all the wounded were transferred aboard the *Devil Dancer*, the *Victory* was torched. His face an inscrutable mask, Diablo watched stoically as the *Victory* upended and slid beneath the sea. He thought it a just end for the man who had brought him nothing but grief. With Devon now in England she was all but lost to him. Suddenly Diablo's life, once filled with excitement and adventure, held little meaning.

"What are your orders, Diablo?" Kyle asked, sensing his friend's dark mood. "Do we go to England after the lass?"

"Nay, Kyle, 'tis too late for that. Devon has made her choice." His eyes were bleak, his face as if carved from stone. "Let's go home."

"I wouldn't worry about Devon betraying the secret of Paradise," Kyle offered lamely. "She knows what would happen to the people living there."

Kyle wouldn't have spoken so confidently had he known what was taking place a few hundred miles south on the small island called Paradise.

Diablo sailed the *Devil Dancer* through the coral reef with an ease born of practice. But as the ship neared the sheltered harbor it became apparent that disaster had struck the tiny settlement. The buildings lining the beach had been reduced to splintered rubble, and the huts beyond were leveled to the ground. A pitiful few survivors stumbled from hastily erected shelters to greet Diablo as he sprinted down the gangplank. A slim woman rose from where she knelt offering comfort to the wounded and waited for Diablo, her back hunched wearily. By now Kyle and Akbar had caught up with their captain, all three too stunned to do more than gape at the wanton destruction and careless loss of life.

"It happened a few days ago," Tara said, her voice a dull parody of itself.

"God's bones, Tara, who did this?"

"The English. Three ships led by the *Larkspur* sailed into the cove and began shelling without warning. They gave no quarter, offered no mercy. It made little difference to them that only women, children, and old men occupied the island. They could see for themselves that no ships were anchored in the cove." She raised sad brown eyes imploringly to Diablo. "Why, Diablo? Why would they do such a thing? How did they find their way to Paradise?"

Diablo had no answers. In his anguish his face was terrible to behold, his sensual mouth a thin line, his silver eyes as cold and murky as death. Suddenly the answer came to him, driving the breath from his lungs with the force of a sledgehammer. "I'll kill the treacherous little slut!"

"Diablo, surely you don't think that Devon . . ." Kyle began.

"Have you some other explanation, Kyle?" Diablo ground out remorselessly. Kyle flushed, unwilling to admit that Devon had betrayed them but unable to draw any other conclusion. "I thought not." Diablo turned his attention to Tara. "Are these the only survivors?"

By now the crew had clamored down the gangplank and were frantically searching among the survivors for their loved ones.

"There are a few more people up at the house," Tara revealed. "And most of the Arawaks working the cane fields were spared."

"The house still stands?"

"It can't be seen from the beach, so that's probably why it wasn't destroyed. The English must have been angry to find you gone when they arrived, for they set about destroying everything in sight. Then they left. We've buried the dead, and most of the wounded have been treated."

"You've done well, Tara, I'm grateful. I hold myself entirely responsible for this—this senseless massacre. If I hadn't foolishly brought Devon here, none of this would have happened."

Akbar muttered his wholehearted agreement, intense hatred burning from the depths of his black eyes.

Though Kyle prayed it wasn't so, he had to acknowledge

the overwhelming evidence pointing directly to Devon. Who else could have betrayed them?

"We'll start rebuilding immediately," Diablo said.

"Why?" Kyle shrugged. "The English know the secret entrance and can find their way in here any time they please."

"This time we'll build across the cay on the opposite shore."

"What about the reef? It circles the entire island. How will we get in and out?"

"I've prepared for just such an eventuality," Diablo revealed. "If you recall, I've thoroughly explored the entire cay on those occasions when the *Devil Dancer* was being repaired and my presence was not needed. There's another navigable passage that I've told no one about. I've never attempted it, but I'm sure the *Devil Dancer* can slip through the gap. See that the survivors are loaded aboard the ship, Kyle. We'll leave immediately and begin rebuilding. We're fortunate to have Le Vautour's men to help."

"What about your house?" Tara asked.

"'Tis nearly the same distance from either shore and it suits me well enough. I'll continue to use it while on Paradise. Meanwhile, I've plans to make."

"Plans?" Kyle asked, fearful that Diablo was thinking of doing something rash. "Surely you're not—"

"Aye, Kyle," Diablo nodded soberly. "When I'm finished with Lady Devon Chatham, the deceitful bitch will rue the day she was born."

"Where have you been, Winston?" Devon asked listlessly. "You've been gone ever so long."

"Did you miss me, dear?" Winston smiled feebly. He had assumed that Devon wouldn't even notice his absence while he was off on his expedition. "How are the plans progressing for our wedding?"

"Didn't Father tell you?"

"I haven't seen him yet." Remembering that he hadn't greeted Devon properly, he kissed her lightly on the forehead. "Is there some problem?"

Problem? Devon nearly laughed aloud at Winston's innocent question. What problem could there be besides loving a man totally wrong for her, a man wanted for committing vile crimes against mankind? No other man, Winston included, could take Diablo's place in her heart. Yet Devon knew exactly what kind of future awaited her if she chose to remain a spinster. She'd have the protection of her father's name while he lived, but if there were no male heirs the title and bulk of his estate would go to a distant relative. That's why the earl was anxious for Devon to marry and have a child. Not that he'd force her to marry someone she detested. But if she remained single she'd be dependent on a distant cousin for her livelihood.

"You haven't answered my question, Devon," Winston persisted.

"Well—er—there is somewhat of a problem," Devon stuttered. "We can't be married until October."

"But that's weeks away!" protested Winston. Would his creditors wait that long? he wondered.

"Only four weeks, Winnie. What's four weeks compared to a lifetime?" That terrifying thought brought a shudder to her slender frame.

"Four weeks *is* a lifetime," declared Winston gallantly. "Why the delay?"

"The dressmaker needs more time to complete my gown and those of my bridesmaids. A girl only marries once, you know."

Devon had only decided to marry Winston a week ago. Until then she had remained adamantly opposed to the match. An incident that had recurred with alarming frequency for several mornings had changed her mind. There was no longer a doubt in Devon's mind that she was carrying Diablo's child. She had yet to miss her second cycle, but every instinct told her she'd bear Diablo's baby. She had to marry Winston, for she'd not shame her father by bearing an illegitimate child.

Winston sighed, distressed by the delay. "October first, dear, no later," he stressed. "I've waited a long time to make you my bride."

"October first," Devon concurred. Abruptly she changed the subject. "Where have you been these past weeks? Father said you took the *Larkspur* on a mission. I thought you'd resigned your commission."

"'Twas a routine mission, dear," Winston lied smoothly. "But fear not, I plan on resigning once we're married and devote all my time to you."

"How is your father? You haven't mentioned him recently."

"Same as usual. He knows little of what's going on around him but defies us all by living." His callous words shocked Devon.

"I'm sorry," she muttered.

Just then Lord Harvey entered the room, his face lighting up when he spied Winston. "Welcome back, m'boy," he blustered. "When did you arrive?"

"Just hours ago."

"Devon, m'dear, there's a matter I would discuss with your fiancé. Will you excuse us?"

"Certainly, Father, I need to visit the dressmaker anyway." She paused at the door. "I'm glad you're back, Winston."

Her words so lacked enthusiasm that Lord Harvey frowned, wondering if he was doing the right thing by urging Devon to marry Winston. But at the moment more pressing matters occupied his mind.

"Well, m'boy, tell me quickly, was your mission successful?"

"Only partly," Winston returned sourly. "Diablo wasn't on

his island, but we made damn certain he'd return to a pile of rubble."

"You shelled his settlement? Was that wise? I want Diablo, not the lives of innocent people."

The thought that lives had been lost made Lord Harvey decidedly uncomfortable. It also hinted at a serious flaw in the young man's character, one never before revealed.

"How can you call people who live in Diablo's stronghold, under his protection, innocent?" defended Winston. "They are all pirates and outlaws."

He deliberately failed to mention that no one but women, children, and old men had been seen in the village before the shelling. Some of his men had been appalled by the carnage left in their wake, especially since Diablo was not in residence, but Winston cared little about the lost lives.

"Perhaps, but I like it little," the earl said with a frown. "Have you and Devon settled on a wedding date? I must admit she waited until the last minute before agreeing to the marriage."

"October first."

Lord Harvey nodded. "I think marriage is just what Devon needs. This incident has changed her, and frankly I'm worried. She's no longer the same girl I knew before that devil carried her off."

"I hate to broach so delicate a subject, Your Grace, but do you think Diablo raped her? I know she denied it, but perhaps she is reluctant to talk about her ordeal."

"Devon wouldn't lie to me," the earl said huffily. "Are you having second thoughts about the wedding?"

"Of course not," Winston objected. "I'd marry Devon tomorrow if she'd agree. I feel fortunate she chose me from a long list of suitors." What he didn't say was that he needed money so badly he would have married Devon even if every pirate in the Caribbean had raped her.

"All right, m'boy, October first it is. I'm sure you'll make her happy."

Actually, Lord Harvey was beginning to harbor strong doubts about Winston's character. He loved Devon too much to give her to a man unworthy of her love and respect. The last few times he'd visited his club he heard bits of distressing gossip about Winston's unusual sexual preferences, but they were so outrageous he dismissed them out of hand. Hearing about the indiscriminate shelling of innocent people today only added to the earl's uncertainty. But Lord Harvey considered himself a fair judge of character and he rarely listened to gossip. As long as Devon seemed happy with her choice, he would not interfere.

The rambling mansion on London's fashionable Grosvenor Square appeared in need of refurbishing, but was nonetheless impressive. The man poised at the front entrance was richly dressed in an elegant dove gray satin waistcoat and matching pants, fine hose of the purest silk, lemon satin brocade vest, and leather shoes sporting fashionably high heels and large silver buckles. He wore a fancy powdered wig and carried a sword of the finest Toledo steel strapped around his slim waist. Yards of Brussels lace dripped from his cuffs and shirt front. He would have cut a handsome figure even if his muscular body had not been a perfect example of masculine beauty.

Raising his large calloused hand, he lifted the brass knocker and rapped sharply. He wasn't exactly certain what had brought him to Linley Hall, but something deep inside him had guided his steps to the place still committed in his memory though it had been many years since he'd called it home. He fidgeted nervously while waiting for someone to answer his summons. He identified immediately the aged butler who answered the door, but the staid old man appeared not to recognize the elegantly dressed stranger.

"May I help you, sir?"

"I would like to speak to—the Duke of Grenville."

"I'm sorry, sir, but the duke lies near death in his home in the country and does not receive visitors. Perhaps the viscount could help you."

"The viscount?" He was startled to hear of the duke's illness, but his expression remained carefully blank.

"Aye, sir, the duke's son. Fortunately you've found him at home."

"By all means, then, let me speak with the duke's son."

"Whom shall I say is calling?"

"Just tell Winston that a—relative wishes to speak with him."

Reluctantly the butler stepped aside, allowing the man to enter. Peters had been with the Linleys for many years and knew of no living relatives. "Please wait here."

The visitor took interest in every facet of the entrance hall, lavishing attention on several portraits adorning the wall. Peters found him engrossed in the portrait of a former duchess when he returned a few minutes later. "Sir, the viscount will receive you in the study, but only briefly. He has another appointment within the hour."

Before Peters could point out the direction, the elegant visitor nodded, making his way directly to the study, which the old man thought rather odd.

Peering over a stack of unpaid bills, Winston regarded the imposing man standing before him with a certain misgiving. "Peters said you were a relative," he remarked without introduction. His blunt greeting was utterly lacking in social grace. "If you're looking for a handout you've come to the wrong place." Winston did not really think the steely-eyed stranger needed money, or anything else, but he saw no reason to mince words.

"I don't need your money, Winston. I could probably buy all you possess and still leave the bulk of my fortune intact. I'm sorry to hear about your father." He didn't sound sorry at all.

"A stroke," explained Winston. "He can't speak, walk, or communicate in any way. I don't know what keeps the old fool alive. If your business is with him you're too late. Who are you? I have no relatives that I know of."

"Look closely, Winston, and think back fifteen years. Are you certain you don't recognize me?"

Squinting myopically at the tall, lithe man whose rugged, sun-bronzed face bore no familiarity, Winston was about to order him from the house when something in those silver-gray eyes nudged his memory. Winston's brow furrowed in deep concentration, stripping the years from the fuzzy layers of his brain. Suddenly his face turned as white as death and he could not control the shaking of his hands.

"Nay! By God, it can't be! You're dead! They swore they killed you." Great heaving sobs conveyed Winston's shock, and his terrible fright was clear.

"So you finally recognize me."

Words began spilling from Winston's mouth. Damning words, words that laid bare secrets long buried in lies and deceit.

"I knew nothing about it, Kit, I swear it. It was all my father's doing. He's the one who hired the men. After your father died there was nothing standing between him and the Linley fortune but one small boy. He was greedy. He wanted it all, wealth, title—your entire inheritance."

"So he hired men to kill me and dump my body in the Thames," Kit accused coolly.

"I knew nothing about it until years later. I thought—everyone thought—that you'd met with an accident, or were the victim of foul play."

"I was. Treachery is the worst kind of foul play. Your

father—my uncle—has had control of my money all these years."

"After seven years you were declared dead and the title and fortune passed down to Father. What happened? Why didn't you come back when you were able?"

"If you're implying that I should be dead, you're right. Fortunately, greed saved my life. The men your father hired to kill me saw a way to earn extra money. They sold me to a press gang, and for years I slaved aboard a ship under a harsh master and conditions I'd not wish on a dog. A twelve-year-old grows up fast when each day of his life consists of the worst kind of depravity and cruelty imaginable."

"My God, Kit, I had no idea. You've got to believe me. But—how did you become—er—wealthy? Surely you haven't been at sea all these years. Why haven't you contacted us sooner? Do you care nothing for your title or inheritance?"

"At one time I cared a great deal," Kit revealed bitterly. "I spent years planning my revenge. Then suddenly it no longer mattered. The only family I cared about was gone. I had new friends, and my life took an entirely different direction. Besides, from the looks of things," he added, staring pointedly at the stack of bills, "it appears there's little left to claim but an empty title."

Winston flushed guiltily. "Father made some unwise investments, with disastrous results. Then there was his gambling. He always was a terrible businessman. But if you saw him now you'd know he's paying dearly for what he did to you. He's an empty shell, more dead than alive."

"'Tis no more than he deserves," Kit observed remorselessly.

"I'm doing my part to restore the family fortune," Winston added quickly. "I'm marrying an heiress on the morrow. Her father has arranged to finance a complete restoration of Linley Hall and our country estate."

A burst of raucous laughter erupted from Kit's throat.

"You? Marry? Surely you jest. Does your bride to be know that you're—?"

"Kit, please! Few know my secret."

"Don't you think your bride deserves to know?"

"I'm perfectly capable of doing my duty where she's concerned, and begetting an heir should prove no hardship," Winston declared somewhat uncertainly. Actually he had no idea if he could pull it off but was willing to have a go at it.

"Funny," Kit mused, "I thought I was the only one able to provide a Linley heir."

"You're dead! I mean," Winston corrected, "everyone thinks you're dead. Why did you come back? Do you expect to right a wrong committed fifteen years ago? Is that why you're here? You're too late, Kit, Father is dying a slow, painful death."

"Curiosity brought me back," answered Kit truthfully. "I've thought about this house so often through the years I had to return. I was a twelve-year-old boy uprooted in the cruelest fashion. Ten of the past fifteen years have been pure hell."

"I swear I knew nothing about it," repeated Winston, sweating profusely. This man he barely recognized looked powerful enough to tear him limb from limb if he so desired. "What do you intend to do? I'm going to be married, Kit, you can't deprive me of all I've come to expect in life. Have pity!"

"Pity, bah. Don't grovel, Winston, it ill becomes you. Did anyone show me pity? I don't know if you're guilty of conspiring with your father or not, and evidently he's in no condition to tell, but I've not come to rob you of your ill-gotten gains. As I said, curiosity brought me here. But you needn't worry, I'll be leaving England soon enough."

Kit knew it was dangerous to remain in London, for there were some who could identify him. He had come to London for a purpose, and it wasn't to reclaim his lost title and possessions. Still, the urge to confront his uncle had been too great to resist. But all thought of revenge fled when he learned the man responsible for his terrible ordeal lay near death. And since Winston had been a lad of eighteen at the time, Kit couldn't be certain his cousin had had anything to do with the crime.

"Thank you, Kit," Winston breathed shakily.

Kit had no way of knowing that Winston was not nearly as innocent as he pretended. He had indeed known of his father's plan to do away with the heir to the Linley fortune, having overheard his father talking with the men hired to do the job. He could have warned Kit in plenty of time to foil the devious plot, but chose not to, for one day it would all pass down to him.

"Don't thank me, Winnie," Kit said tersely. "If you're guilty, your day of reckoning will come. In the meantime, I wish you joy of your—your—bride." Kit's statement was accompanied by a scarcely suppressed snicker. "And God pity the poor unsuspecting wretch. Don't bother to show me out, I know the way."

Pausing outside the mansion, Kit wondered what perverse desire had brought him to Linley Hall. Everything it stood for had been cruelly denied him fifteen years ago, and there was no turning back. Stepping smartly into his hired rig, he signaled to the driver and forced himself to relax, anticipating with great relish the mission that had brought him to London.

Tomorrow, Devon thought dully as she prepared for bed. Tomorrow she'd be climbing in bed with Winston, allowing him to use her body in the same way Diablo had. How could she bear it? How could she stand to have another man touch her when it was only Diablo she desired, only Diablo she loved? Yet Devon realized that her child's future depended on her wedding Winston. There'd be talk enough when her child came early, and sooner or later Winston would have to be told.

Sighing despondently, Devon still wasn't certain she could actually marry Winston. Perhaps she'd confess everything to her father in the morning and accept his condemnation.

Facing away from the partially open window, Devon found that her hopes of finding sleep were not to be realized. It was long past midnight and a chilling breeze blew through the narrow opening past the fluttering curtains, bringing a shiver to Devon's slight form. She did not see the figure dressed in unrelieved black who had just stepped through the opening and stood very still, blending into the shadows. A sudden chill swept through her, and Devon arose and walked toward the window, certain that the draft was preventing her from sleep.

Just enough moonlight danced in the room to illuminate Devon's face. Diablo's silver eyes narrowed with hatred as he greedily devoured her entrancing face and form. Though he could barely stand the sight of the traitorous bitch, it didn't stop him from appreciating her beauty. His hands clenched tightly at his sides as he struggled to control his raging temper. He wanted Devon to know exactly why he was going to kill her. He was determined that she hear all the gruesome details of the unprovoked attack on innocent people before she died. Diablo wanted her to realize fully what terrible havoc she had wrought by betraying the secret of Paradise.

Devon reached the window and lowered it. But something had distracted her. She sensed she was not alone, and every nerve in her body screamed with awareness. How many times had she inhaled that spicy, musky odor while held so tenderly in those strong arms? She would recognize his scent anywhere, know the moment he walked into the room even if she were blindfolded.

"Diablo . . ." The name whispered across her lips like a summer breeze, soft and yearning—and oh so gentle.

Diablo stepped from the shadows, the light from the window falling across the stark planes of his face. Devon gasped, the hatred blazing from his silver eyes so fierce that she retreated in alarm. Like a stalking panther Diablo followed, grasping her shoulder and spinning her around to face him. Devon winced, his cruel grip confusing her. Never had he touched her with anything but tenderness. Had he changed so completely because she had left him? Or was it because she had left with Le Vautour?

"Diablo, please! You're hurting me."

"You traitorous bitch! The reason I didn't kill you immediately is because I wanted you to know what you're dying for." His face was hard, cruel, unforgiving, his voice remorseless.

Horrified, Devon did not recognize this cruel man. He was an avenging stranger, one bent on murder. "What have I done?"

Diablo's huge hands left Devon's quaking shoulders, rising to grasp the slim column of her neck. "It would be so easy," he drawled menacingly, "to snap that pretty, deceitful neck. A little pressure here," he applied just enough pressure to make her head spin dizzily and gasp for air, "and all the needless deaths you caused would be avenged." Abruptly the pressure eased, and a shuddering breath filled her aching lungs.

"Tell me, Diablo," Devon rasped painfully, "what did I do? If I must die at your hands I want to know the reason."

"I hope you're pleased with your handiwork. Because of you, dozens of innocent women and children lost their lives. But you knew that when you directed the British to Paradise," he accused. "You knew I'd be gone, leaving no one to protect the defenseless people in the village. Before I kill you I want to hear from your own lips why you did it. Did you hate me so much?"

Diablo's face was carved in stone, and Devon marveled at the fleeting memory of his gentle kisses, for surely this angry, ruthless stranger could never display such tenderness. But it was his words and false accusations that stunned her. She'd told no one, not even her father, how to penetrate Diablo's stronghold. In fact, she'd thought it strange that she was not questioned more thoroughly about the time she'd spent in the pirate's strong-hold. Though her aching throat was dry and hoarse, she had to try to make Diablo understand she was guiltless. Not only her life but the life of her unborn child—Diablo's child—depended on it.

The pink tip of Devon's tongue flicked out to moisten her dry lips. "I didn't do it, Diablo. No matter what you believe, I told no one about Paradise. I'd never do that."

"You let Le Vautour skewer Kyle. How do I know how far you'd go to repay me for keeping you on Paradise against your will? God's bones, Devon, I loved you! How you must have laughed at my trite words. Why did you have to hurt innocent people to punish me?"

"I swear I had nothing to do with it!" protested Devon. "Couldn't the British have found the way on their own?"

"Impossible!" Diablo roared. "The island is impenetrable unless one knows the secret passage."

"Maybe one of your friends—" Devon suggested lamely.

"Believe it or not, pirates live by a code of honor. Only a selected few know my secret, and none would dare betray me. Nay, my lady," he sneered sarcastically, "'tis you who told and you who'll pay the price."

The pressure on her neck increased, and Devon closed her eyes, words no longer possible as Diablo's face twisted into a grimace.

Devon had no way of knowing that the terrible grimace on Diablo's face was caused by the excruciating pain in his heart. His hands shook with the effort to maintain his hold on the slim column of Devon's neck, and the anguish visible on the pale oval of her face made his quest for revenge all but impossible.

He had loved her so dearly, trusted her so implicitly, that her fervent denials gave him pause. There was a possibility, albeit a remote one, that Devon hadn't betrayed him. She was so breathtakingly beautiful, so exquisitely formed, and felt so right in his arms that Diablo feared he could never destroy so perfect a creature, no matter what her crime. Though his love for her had died the moment he saw the destruction wrought by English guns, he had never before killed a woman. The remote possibility that Devon was innocent, combined with a force far stronger than his thirst for revenge, caused him to falter. Devon felt the pressure on her neck ease. Though the unholy light in Diablo's eyes continued to blaze with mistrust and doubt, the will to live flamed in Devon's heart. Instinctively she knew that the next moments would be crucial in determining whether she lived or died. It was that thought that compelled her to reveal her secret. She was responsible for a life other than her own, and it was time Diablo knew of it.

"Kill me, Diablo," she croaked hoarsely, "and your child dies with me."

Stunned disbelief met Devon's words. "What lies are you spouting now?"

"'Tis no lie, Diablo, I'm expecting your child. Go ahead and end my life if you care nothing for your child."

He swore, an outrageous stream of vile oaths. "If I find you're lying I'll derive great pleasure from your death."

Drawing herself up to her full five feet five, Devon taunted calmly, "Do it now if you don't believe me."

A long silence ensued while Diablo stared pointedly at Devon's middle, his eyes hooded. "'Tis far too early to show," she said, sensing his unasked question.

Suddenly a horrible thought occurred to Diablo. "I'll not be duped into claiming Le Vautour's child."

Devon drew her breath in sharply, too stunned to do more than sputter angrily as she drew her hand back and slapped Diablo's face with resounding force. "You despicable cur! I'd never let that slimy creature touch me!"

Somehow Diablo believed her. But that hardly solved his dilemma. Though he might hate Devon, that hate did not extend to the child she carried—his child—if she did indeed carry a child. What in the hell was he going to do about it?

Ever astute, Devon perceived his problem and offered her own solution. "I'm going to be married tomorrow, Diablo. You need not worry about your child. I'll love it, of course, and Winston need never know it's not his."

Diablo froze as bells went off in his head. "Winston? Winston Linley? Your fiancé is Winston Linley?"

"Have I never mentioned his name? I'll become Winston's bride tomorrow. He's only a viscount now, but upon his father's death will become the Duke of Grenville."

"God's bones!" If Lord Harvey hadn't been hard of hearing he would certainly have been roused from his deep slumber by now. "Are you daft, Devon? Do you know what you're letting yourself in for? What must your father be thinking to allow you to marry a man like Winston?"

"You don't know what you're talking about. Winston is sweet and sensitive, and he loves me. He'll provide a good home for your—my child. If it's a boy, he'll become the future Duke of Grenville."

A fierce smile stretched Diablo's lips into a grimace. "Aye, he will, won't he. Too bad Winston will never get the opportunity to claim my child." The moment Devon uttered Winston's name Diablo knew exactly what he must do. "Get dressed," he commanded, "you're coming with me."

"I'm going nowhere with you," Devon resisted stubbornly. "You should be grateful to Winston. You don't need the responsibility of a child."

"Let me be the judge of what I need or don't need," Diablo retaliated sternly. "If you don't get dressed immediately I'll carry you out in your bedgown."

"I'll scream, and Father will come to investigate."

"If you value his life you'll remain quiet and do exactly as I say."

The cold, implacable expression on his harsh features told Devon he was perfectly capable of carrying out his threat, and she moved stiffly to the wardrobe, pulling out the first dress she touched. While she quickly dressed, Diablo lit a candle and began stuffing articles of clothing from drawers and wardrobe into a large pillowcase. He worked efficiently and quickly, knowing which things Devon would need until he could provide her with others. When he finished he pulled a warm cloak from a hook and threw it over her shoulders.

"Surely you don't expect me to go out the window!"

"And risk harming my child? If there is a child," he added skeptically. "Nay, sweetheart, we'll leave by the front door."

"Someone will hear us," she said hopefully.

"Not if we're very quiet. I'm certain you love your father and wish him no harm." His threat was perfectly understood. "Let's go."

"Wait! Let me write a note to Father. He's no longer a young man, the shock of losing me again could kill him. Please, Diablo, if you ever held any feelings for me, allow me this small favor."

Perhaps it was the huge tears rolling down her pale cheeks, or the pleading in her blue eyes. Whatever the reason, a small crack appeared on the hardened surface of Diablo's heart and he nodded reluctant agreement. "Make it brief."

Diablo had to turn away from Devon's blinding smile as she sat down at her desk and scrawled a hasty note. Suddenly he ripped the paper from her hand, wadded it up, and replaced it with another.

"Tell him you're leaving with me of your own accord and he's not to come after you," Diablo directed. "Also leave a message for Winston saying you had no intention of marrying him. You might suggest to your father that he investigate Winston's background more thoroughly."

"What!" Devon asked, pausing in midstroke.

"Just do as I say. One day you'll thank me for saving you from this marriage—if you live long enough," he added ominously.

Still numb with shock and consumed by grief over Diablo's unjust accusations and his threat to kill her, Devon finished the note and handed it to Diablo to read. He gave the contents a quick perusal, nodded his satisfaction, and set it where it was sure to be found. Then he blew out the candle, grasped Devon's hand, and led her out of the house into the blackness of the night. With a stab of regret, Devon realized it might be the last time she set foot in her beloved home.

Chapter Twelve

"By Allah's beard, Diablo, what are you thinking of?" hissed Akbar when he saw his captain leave the house by the front door dragging Devon behind him. "If you couldn't do the job yourself, why didn't you allow me the privilege of killing the woman? I'd not turn squeamish like you obviously did."

"Enough, Akbar. Let's get out of here before the whole town comes clamoring after our heads," Diablo grumbled. Deep in his heart he must have known he couldn't bring himself to hurt Devon.

Ignoring her protests, he lifted her into the hired coach and leaped in beside her. Closing the door with a bang, Akbar, muttering dire predictions, climbed into the driver's box and whipped the team through the darkened city.

"You'll not get away with this," Devon warned, glaring at Diablo angrily. "The authorities will catch you before you clear London harbor."

Diablo smiled with deceptive charm. "Do you think I'm stupid enough to sail into London harbor? I suggest you try to rest, Devon, for we've a long journey ahead of us."

Devon eyed the door, but Diablo was one step ahead of her. "You'll not do anything to harm my child, so forget about leaping from the coach. After my son or daughter is safely delivered, you can do whatever you want with your life."

"Surely you wouldn't be cruel enough to take my baby from me!" Devon gasped. "You loved me once."

"Aye, once I *did* love you," Diablo admitted softly. "That was before you dealt with Le Vautour behind my back and betrayed me. While I was falling in love, you were plotting revenge. Was I too far beneath your social standing to take seriously? An earl's daughter and a pirate, how you must have laughed at my simple love."

"I never laughed, Diablo, truly," whispered Devon with sadness. "Why can't you understand? I had to leave. A love between us was doomed from the start. The horrible thought of having to watch you hang from the gallows one day prevented me from following my heart."

"Lies, all lies!" Diablo responded with a disgusted sneer. "But you needn't worry, I'll not kill the mother of my child. If you really are pregnant, you'll be cared for until my child is born, then you'll be free to go—alone."

Shocked by his cruel words, Devon fell silent, the thought of abandoning a child of her flesh heart-breaking. Diablo retreated into a brooding silence, vivid memories tugging at his mind. Nothing had been sweeter than Devon's warm, willing body responding to him, eagerly accepting his caresses, returning them with ardor, taking him deep into the secret passages of her flesh, joyfully and without restraint. What a consummate actress she was to make him believe she was beginning to care for him.

Diablo's musings were interrupted when he felt a weight resting against his shoulder. Glancing down at Devon's sleeping form, he was startled to see her blonde head nestled trustingly against him. His hands clenched into tight fists in an effort to keep them at his sides instead of placing his arms around her slender shoulders and snuggling her against the curve of his body. Ultimately he did exactly what he fought against, holding her as one would a delicate flower. Until their child was born, her comfort and care lay solely with him. He had taken her from the safety of her comfortable home and was glaringly aware of his responsibility to see that nothing harmed her or their baby. With that thought in mind, Diablo tightened his arms around her supple form, the soothing motions of the coach lulling his troubled mind and body into restless slumber.

* * *

Three days later the coach entered a small town on the rugged Cornish coast. Thoroughly exhausted, Devon had begun to think the long journey would never end. Every bone in her body ached from the constant jostling on the rutted roads. Though they had made brief stops along the way to eat and refresh themselves, Devon was never allowed far from Diablo's sight, much to her embarrassment. Nor did they spend a night in one of those inviting inns. Instead, Diablo and Akbar took turns driving, pulling off to the side of the road only during the darkest hours of night to rest the horses, relying on lanterns during the twilight and early morning hours.

Very little conversation had been made between Devon and the two men. Akbar's dark, condemning looks were enough to render her mute, while Diablo retreated beneath a facade of cool disdain, making silence far preferable to his verbal abuse. The coach rattled through the town of Penzance, heading toward the sea. If she hadn't been so upset and exhausted, she would have thoroughly enjoyed the wild, bleak moors and unrivaled scenery passing before her eyes.

High on a windswept cliff overlooking a snug cove sat an ancient weathered castle whose crumbling walls attested to its antiquity, and somehow Devon wasn't surprised when the coach turned up the road leading to the imposing edifice. A lone man waited on the stone steps as Diablo leaped nimbly down from the coach to greet him and be welcomed in return.

"So, my friend, you're back. I trust your mission was successful."

The man spoke in a booming voice that commanded attention from friend and foe alike. He stood nearly as tall and broad as Akbar, sporting a full head of curly black hair and a generous ebony beard reaching nearly to his barrel chest. He appeared somewhat past thirty with intelligent blue eyes beneath shaggy brows and a wide mouth all but hidden by his beard. The bulging muscles in his thighs and arms spoke eloquently of the active life he led and the hard physical work he did.

"My mission was—enlightening, if not successful," Diablo said cryptically. "Be prepared for a surprise, Cormac." He turned back to the coach and literally dragged Devon through the open door. "Meet Lady Devon Chatham."

"You brought the wench here!" Cormac blasted, aghast. "Are you daft, man? I thought you intended to get rid of the girl, not bring her with you."

Devon clung to Diablo's arm, cringing beneath Cormac's obvious disapproval and ferocious countenance. Hardly aware of his protective gesture, Diablo placed a supportive arm around Devon's quaking shoulders.

"There's an explanation for this, Cormac," he informed the man. "You'll hear it later. But first things first. Is there a place Devon can rest? She's exhausted."

"Aye," Cormac replied, eying Devon with the practiced eye of a connoisseur of women and liking what he saw. "There's plenty of empty rooms in this pile of rocks."

Following Cormac inside, Diablo propelled Devon forward, Akbar following close behind with the bundle of clothes. The room assigned to Devon was on the second floor.

"I'll arrange for a bath and see you're brought a meal," Diablo said curtly. "Then I suggest you rest. I'll not have you endangering my child." Turning abruptly, he left the room. His mouth hanging open, Cormac followed close on his heels.

Now that she was alone at last, rage conquered Devon's exhaustion. How dare Diablo abduct her again and dictate her life, she fumed impotently. The man wanted to kill her, for God's sake! And still might, once her child was born. Escape, that's it, she thought, rushing to the door. Only to find it locked from the outside. The windows were out of the question, for the room looked over the sea with only jagged rocks below to break her fall.

Diablo himself unlocked the door later to admit a blank-faced maid and two rather disreputable-looking men with the tub and hot water for Devon's bath. Much to her relief, Diablo did not linger. Afterwards, a tray of food was brought by the same dour maid while Diablo stood nearby waiting to relock the door once the woman left. Though the food looked appealing enough, Devon had little appetite, and she wandered over to test the bed. Climbing between the musty sheets, she soon fell into a deep, troubled sleep.

"'Tis amazing how your life has become hopelessly complicated in so short a time," Cormac remarked, his lips twitching suspiciously. Truth to tell, this new development greatly amused him and he was sorry he would have to miss out on the fireworks that were sure to follow. "I don't envy you, Diablo. What are your plans concerning the wench?"

"I can't harm a woman carrying my child." Diablo frowned, his distress evidenced by his black scowl.

"The wench might be lying to save her hide," Cormac suggested slyly.

"My thoughts exactly," Akbar concurred sourly. "Diablo is far too trusting. It proved fatal once, and I thought he had learned his lesson. My advice is to—"

"I don't need your advice," Diablo interjected, "nor did I ask for it. I thought you said dinner was ready, Cormac, I'm starved."

Seated at the table and eating the hardy fare provided by their host, a friend of long standing who often fenced loot for Diablo, and a smuggler to boot, Diablo asked a question that took everyone by surprise. "Is there a minister in Penzance?"

His simple request brought a roar of protest from Akbar.

* * *

A night of uninterrupted sleep was just what Devon needed. These past days, so hectic and fraught with upheaval, had left her drained. In her heart she knew she had come close to death. Having nearly met her end at the hands of the man she loved had jolted her badly, leaving her shaken and unsure of her future.

Diablo quietly entered Devon's room and saw that she was still sleeping soundly despite the bright sunlight pouring through the arched windows. He intended to awaken her but instead paused beside the bed regarding her with a mixture of loathing tempered with the great love he once bore her. He tried desperately to maintain the impenetrable wall he had erected around his heart. She looked so sweetly innocent. He quickly discarded that notion when he considered the loss of lives she had been responsible for. Recalling the reason that had brought him to Devon's bedside, Diablo softly spoke her name.

Devon's eyes opened slowly, fear clouding her vision. "What is it?" The strange gleam in Diablo's silver eyes nudged her from sleep into the cold reality of his hate. Had he changed his mind about sparing her life?

"You must get up now," he said coolly. "The *Devil Dancer* will return for us today and there's still much to be done. Come downstairs when you're ready." Abruptly he turned and stalked from the room, as if he could barely stand the sight of her.

Daring to breathe again, Devon scrambled from bed, quickly washing and donning a clean dress from her bundle, which had been placed in her room the night before. The door had been left unlocked and she descended the stairs to where Diablo paced below, impatiently waiting for her.

"Come along, your breakfast is waiting."

"I'm not hungry," Devon replied sullenly.

"Your tray was untouched last night. You'll eat today if

I have to force-feed you." He grasped her arm and propelled her into the dining room. Only one place was set. "We've already eaten," came his terse explanation.

The oatmeal stuck in her throat, but hot tea helped wash it down. When she had choked down enough to satisfy Diablo they left the crumbling mansion. The coach, with Akbar handling the horses from the driver's box, awaited them at the front entrance. With nary a word of explanation, Diablo boosted Devon inside, settling down beside her. She was surprised to see her bundle of clothes neatly tied and placed on the floor. Then Cormac joined them in the coach, looking fierce and frightening dressed in the rough clothing of a border lord, but nevertheless imposing. The door was barely closed before the coach jolted forward.

"Where are we going?" Devon asked sharply.

Cormac's shaggy brows flew upward. "Haven't you told the lass?"

"She'll do as I say," Diablo responded curtly, then fell silent.

"I'll do nothing of the sort," Devon balked. "I have a right to know where you're taking me."

More silence. Cormac merely shrugged and directed his attention out the window. Soon the coach entered the village at the foot of the cliff, continuing its furious pace until it clattered to a halt before a small weathered building at the far edge of town.

"What is this place?" Devon asked, a frisson of fear shivering down her spine.

"The town is called Penzance and this building serves as our church," Cormac saw fit to explain. Diablo said nothing, maintaining his brooding silence, while in the driver's box Akbar could be heard muttering Turkish obscenities.

"Church? I don't understand." Devon was truly puzzled and looked helplessly at Diablo for an explanation.

Realizing the time had come to reveal his plans, Diablo broke his long silence. "We're here to be married."

"Married! But I thought you hated me? Nay, I won't do it," she protested vigorously. "I had always hoped the man I married would love me."

"Like Winston?" Diablo mocked cruelly.

"Well, aye, like Winston," Devon freely admitted. "Why are you doing this?"

"It should be obvious even to you. I won't have my babe come into this world a bastard. Believe it or not, Winston isn't the paragon of virtue you think him."

"What makes you so certain?" Devon challenged. "You don't even know Winston."

Diablo's tightly clamped jaw told her he would say no more on the subject. Instead, he dragged her toward the small church. Cormac opened the door, and she soon found herself being forcefully led down the long aisle where a somberly dressed man awaited them.

"Ah, there you are," he said and smiled warmly. "I was beginning to think you changed your mind. What a beautiful bride," he complimented, beaming at Devon. "Shall we proceed?"

"Aye, pastor, begin," Diablo nodded curtly. "We sail within the hour and are anxious to be wed."

The pastor asked no questions, knowing Cormac as he did and aware of the other man's profession. Were it not for smuggling and piracy, half the families in Penzance would be starving and the other half destitute. His own little church couldn't survive without help from men like Cormac. Opening his prayer book and facing the young couple, Pastor Clement began reading the brief ceremony that joined Devon and Diablo in marriage.

Stunned, Devon opened her mouth to protest but was silenced by Diablo's harsh whisper. "Don't give me reason to carry out my original plan. I could still kill you."

Her world spinning crazily on its axis, Devon did not hear Pastor Clement address Diablo as Christopher, or Diablo's answer to the time-honored question. She wasn't even aware that it was time to speak her own vows until Diablo nudged her in the ribs. Inhaling deeply, Devon muttered, "I will," in a voice so soft the pastor asked her to repeat it.

Then it was over and Diablo was sliding a heavy gold band on the appropriate finger. She was married! Lord help her, she had just become the devil's bride! Diablo's kiss was cool and perfunctory and quickly over, but Cormac bussed her soundly on the cheek. From Akbar she received naught but a dark scowl.

In a self-induced trance, Devon signed the marriage paper, taking no notice when Diablo added his signature. If she had noticed, she would have been astounded to see the name Christopher Douglas Linley, Duke of Grenville, inscribed therein. Then she was outside the church, being hustled into the coach. And so began her first day of married life.

The coach left the town immediately, traveling along a high, spectacularly beautiful and lonely road closely following the sea. Several miles later they ground to a halt on a bleak windswept stretch overlooking a small, deep cove where the *Devil Dancer* rode at anchor.

During the bumpy ride from Penzance, it had appeared that Devon was all but forgotten as Diablo and Cormac discussed ships and cargos and schedules. Had she dreamed her marriage to Diablo? Was this all a terrible nightmare from which she'd wake up safe in her own bed? Nay, the heavy gold band on her finger was too real, its weight more like a tight noose than a token of love. Could she ever hope to win back Diablo's love? she wondered bleakly. Did she even want to?

Suddenly the conversation between Cormac and Diablo came to a halt and Diablo stepped out of the coach, lifting his hand to help Devon. "We must go the rest of the way on foot," he informed her. Cormac scrambled into the driver's box newly vacated by Akbar.

"Fair winds and the devil's own luck to you," grinned the huge smuggler. "Come again when your hold is bursting with French wine or Spanish spices and oil and I'll guarantee the best prices. Luck to you also, my lady," he said to Devon, certain she'd need luck if she expected to live harmoniously with her volatile husband.

"Farewell, my friend," said Diablo, "and thank you for your hospitality as well as the loan of your coach." After Akbar retrieved Devon's bundle of clothes as well as those of Diablo and himself, the vehicle clattered off down the deserted road.

"Come along, Devon." Grasping her upper arm, Diablo propelled her toward the edge of the cliff.

At first Devon thought he intended to toss her into the sea, until she saw Akbar disappear down a well-trodden path leading to a narrow crescent of beach below. Though the path was steep it was not particularly arduous, and Devon negotiated it easily with Diablo's help. For the sake of his child and for no other reason, Devon suspected he would let nothing happen to her. Thank God it wasn't the vindictive Akbar who had been entrusted with her safety, else she doubted she would have reached the beach alive.

"Are you all right?" Diablo asked anxiously when they reached the bottom. Breathless, Devon nodded. "Here comes the longboat."

Within minutes the longboat sent from the *Devil Dancer* bumped into the shore. Two men leaped out to hold it in place in the rolling surf. Sweeping Devon into his arms, Diablo carried her through the knee-deep turquoise water and dumped her unceremoniously into the boat. She noted the look of stunned disapproval on the men's faces when they recognized her. Did Diablo's entire crew hate her for committing an act she knew nothing about?

Devon learned how much she was despised the moment her feet touched the deck of the *Devil Dancer*. An angry clamor raced from one end of the ship to the other until Diablo saw fit to put an end to it.

"What's that bitch doin' aboard, cap'n?" called out Dancy. "Did ye bring her so's we all can watch her hang from the yardarm?" Dancy had lost a woman and child in the shelling of Paradise Island.

"Give her to us!" shouted another. Only once before in her life had Devon felt such overwhelming fear, and that when Diablo had had his fingers curled around her neck.

"Cease, lads!" Diablo commanded, thrusting his hand into the air to gain attention. Most complied, though many continued to grumble. "Lady Devon became my wife this day. We were legally married in Penzance by Pastor Clement not an hour ago."

A collective roar of protest and violent disapproval greeted his words.

"Traitor!" shouted one of the pirates.

"Why did you do it?" called out another.

"If the man who called me a traitor will step forward, I'll be happy to disabuse him of that notion." His dark scowl and forbidding features produced no challengers. "Lady Devon is my wife, and I'll allow no one to treat her with disrespect. Now, lads, we've a ship to sail." Grumbling among themselves, the men hopped to obey as Akbar barked orders that put the ship into motion. They were still in English waters and all too aware of their danger.

"Why didn't you tell them I wasn't guilty?" Devon demanded to know.

"How could I tell them something I don't know myself?" Diablo answered, glowering with fierce resentment.

Suddenly Kyle appeared at Diablo's elbow, and Devon smiled in genuine welcome, certain she had at least one friend aboard the *Devil Dancer*. But Kyle's condemning frown and cool words left Devon little doubt that she could no longer count Kyle among her friends.

"I'm happy Diablo didn't kill you, lass," he remarked dryly, "but if I thought him capable of wringing your neck I'd never have let him return to England in the first place. What puzzles me is his reason for marrying you and bringing you here where you're hardly welcome. Whatever possessed you, Diablo?"

"Kyle, please believe me, I had nothing to do with the attack on Paradise," Devon pleaded.

Kyle seemed not to hear. "What did you hope to gain by talking Diablo into marrying you? Are you prepared to live with his hate?"

"I didn't talk him into it, he—"

Her explanation was lost to the wind when Diablo crudely announced, "Devon is carrying my child."

"Holy mother of God! Is that true, lass?"

Devon's face turned bright red. She had hoped to hide her shame for a while longer. "I—I believe it to be so," she admitted in a strained whisper.

Instantly Kyle's fierce scowl melted into a look of pity. He didn't envy Devon living with a man whose love had been turned into hate and mistrust by her deplorable act. Uneasily he wondered what Diablo's plans for his wife would be after their babe was born. Kyle knew that Diablo could be utterly ruthless at times and feared that his implacable resentment would force him into something he might later regret. He found no words in his heart to encourage Devon, using his silence to convey his feeling of inadequacy. If Devon had been guilty of divulging the secret of their cove, then she richly deserved whatever punishment Diablo provided. Kyle's response to Diablo's astounding news was to repeat, "Holy mother of God."

Devon did not step outside Diablo's cabin for three days, not that she had any wish to. The profound animosity of the pirate crew drove from her mind all desire to walk among them. Her daily exercise consisted of pacing the narrow confines of the cabin and basking in fresh air and sunshine obtained by standing at the open windows over-looking the ship's stem.

She had not seen Diablo since he'd left her standing in the center of his cabin while he collected his personal items, which Devon assumed he had moved to wherever he was sleeping. She had more than sufficient time to dwell on the months and years to come, if she was allowed to live that long. After her babe was born would she be discarded like an old shoe, never to see her child again? Nay! she shook her head in vigorous denial, she'd not allow that to happen. Who would care for her child? Tara? Scarlett? The thought was more frightening than that of her own death.

As Devon paced the cabin, a nagging pain tugged at her gut. For two days the pain, sometimes sharp and unrelenting, other times vague and diffused, had made Devon all too aware of her vulnerability. Her very life depended on Diablo's good will. When the old pirate, Pegleg, who supplied her meals and saw to her comforts, carried in her supper, she refused it with a polite shake of her head, which was duly reported to Diablo.

That night Devon retired at her normal time, aware that something strange was happening inside her body, something she could not prevent. It was a long time before sleep claimed her, and nearly dawn when she awoke in excruciating pain. She knew immediately the cause of her agony. The sudden rush of blood told her that her monthly courses had resumed with a vengeance and she hadn't been pregnant after all! She strongly suspected that the upsets in her life these past months had stopped her monthlies. Wracked by pain, Devon crawled out of bed, cleaned herself up, and removed the soiled sheets from the bunk. Summoning the last of her depleted strength, she rolled up in a blanket and lay down on the bare mattress.

Then the tears came one after another, deep, soul-destroying sobs that spoke of her despair. She felt as if her insides were on fire, and the thought that she'd not have Diablo's babe to love only added to her pain. She normally experienced pain at the onset of menses but nothing like the crippling cramps that were tearing her apart now. Curled into a ball, Devon fell into a light sleep, her cheeks streaked with tears.

Pegleg cautiously entered the cabin after receiving no answer to his discreet knock. With pounding heart he stared at Devon's blanket-shrouded form curled up on the bunk. What little he could see of her face appeared white and drawn. Then his eyes fell on the bloody sheets wadded up and tossed in a corner. Abruptly he turned and fled as swiftly as his peg leg would allow.

Minutes later Diablo burst into the cabin, pulling Devon from the depths of a druglike sleep. She moaned groggily as he grasped her shoulders. "Devon, are you ill?" Her pale face and wide blue eyes blank with pain frightened him badly.

Finally Devon realized what he was asking. "Go ahead and kill me, Diablo," she stunned him by saying. "But I wasn't lying, I truly believed I was pregnant."

"Have you lost my child?" Devon had assumed that his harsh voice and stony features conveyed rage while in truth he was feeling a far different emotion.

"Perhaps there never was a child," Devon admitted dully. Then a severe cramp spasmed her gut and her face screwed up into a grimace.

"Are you in pain?" Diablo's solicitous words contrasted oddly with his furious scowl. Devon merely nodded, unable to speak with her insides twisted in agony.

Diablo whirled and left the cabin, returning almost immediately with Kyle. Kyle knelt before Devon, smoothing the tangled hair from her damp brow. "Have you lost the babe, lass?" he asked anxiously. What little doctoring he performed hardly included treating female problems. Then his eyes fell on the soiled sheets. "When did it happen?"

"During the night," Devon said weakly, "but I'm not certain now there ever was a child. My life has been in a turmoil of late and . . ."

"Shh, no need to explain," Kyle soothed. "Has there been much pain?"

"Aye," Devon acknowledged, "but 'twill pass. It always does."

"Are you still bleeding?"

"A little, the worst is past."

Kyle said nothing, assuming that Devon knew her own body far better than anyone else. When she appeared to be dozing, he rose to face Diablo, who hovered anxiously at his elbow.

"Well, what do you make of it?" Diablo asked.

Kyle directed his gaze to the blood-stained sheets, then back to Devon's pale face. "She's lost a fair amount of blood," he opined with careful thought. "It's entirely possible Devon's monthly time resumed after an interruption due to stress. But," he pointed out, "it's more likely she miscarried. You've been far from gentle with her, and the shock and upheaval she's suffered is enough to make her lose the babe."

"What can we do?"

"Nothing. As long as she's not hemorrhaging, her young body will heal itself in time."

"Is there no way to tell if Devon was truly pregnant or merely lying to save her skin?"

"I'm no doctor," Kyle reminded him. "I know little about female ailments or cures. Setting broken bones and sewing wounds is as far as my knowledge stretches. But I do think a dose of laudanum would do more good than harm."

Diablo agreed.

"You won't hurt Devon now that she's no longer carrying

your child, will you, Kit? I know what she did, or what *we think* she did, but killing her will solve nothing."

"You think I'd kill my own wife?" Diablo asked, glowering darkly.

"I happen to know why you married Devon. So do most of the crew. They're still angry at you for bringing her aboard the *Devil Dancer*."

"My plans for Devon's future are no one's concern," Diablo bit out. "And I'm perfectly capable of protecting what is mine. Sooner or later I'll find out if she betrayed us. Until then she'll not be harmed. See to your duties, Kyle, I'll see to my—Devon's—care."

During the following day and night Devon awoke frequently, always to find Diablo sitting beside her, offering water or food and wiping her brow. Though she refused the food with a shake of her head, she never failed to drink deeply. When she finally awoke to the light of day, her mind was clear, her pain greatly diminished, and Diablo gone. She was amazed to find herself lying on clean sheets, dressed in a fresh bedgown and her hair neatly brushed. When had Diablo turned ladies maid? she wondered, the thought bringing a wan smile to her lips. Somehow she couldn't picture him performing that duty. But if not Diablo, then who?

Feeling much better, Devon decided to get up and dress for the day. She was just sliding her long legs off the side of the bunk when Diablo entered the cabin bearing a tray. He stared at her legs, bared from the thighs down, with more interest than he'd shown her since he'd taken her from her home. She blushed profusely and made a futile attempt to tug down the hem of her bedgown.

"Pegleg was busy so I brought your breakfast," he said, raising his eyes reluctantly. "Are you feeling better?"

Eying him uncertainly, Devon nodded. "Aye, and hungry, too." His moods were so unpredictable she never knew how to proceed where he was concerned. Mostly he glowered at her with hate-filled eyes, his expression wavering between downright hostility and bare civility.

Devon noted that Diablo was letting his beard grow again, reminding her of the first time she had seen him, standing defiant and proud with a noose around his neck. Even then his virile masculinity had beckoned to her, and his charm eventually won her love. She wasn't certain when she first realized she loved the handsome rogue. Perhaps it was the very first moment she laid eyes on him. Diablo might be a pirate, but Devon intuitively knew that he was nothing like the crude men who sailed the seas in search of blood and booty. Something in his background suggested gentle breeding, for whenever he let his guard down he displayed the fine manners of a gentleman.

"Kyle thinks you should remain in bed another day or two," Diablo said, interrupting Devon's thoughts.

"I feel fine," Devon insisted.

"Nevertheless, it's best you follow orders." He set the tray on her lap, then perched gingerly on the edge of the bunk. "I want the truth, Devon, no more lies." Given his words, his voice was oddly gentle. "Did you tell me you were pregnant in order to save your skin?"

Devon shook her head, sending her tangled mass of blonde tresses flying. "You might as well kill me now if you think that, Diablo. I wouldn't lie about something as important as that. The only reason I agreed to marry Winnie was to give your child a name."

"Winnie," Diablo mocked. "An apt nickname. Has he given you no inkling about his—sexual preferences?"

"I—don't know what you mean." Devon was truly puzzled. She knew that Winston had none of the passion and fire she'd come to expect from Diablo, but she assumed he kept his under tight rein in deference to her innocence.

"I can excuse *you* for not recognizing the truth, but not

your father. Your marriage to the man would have been a sham. Winston has no use for women. Now do you understand?"

Devon's delicate brows arched nearly to her hairline as she became vaguely aware of Diablo's meaning. In certain areas her education was woefully lacking.

Her puzzled expression brought a snort of disgust from Diablo's lips. "To put it bluntly, Winston is the type of man who prefers men in his bed."

Devon's face turned a brilliant red, then green, before settling into a ghostly white. "You mean—Oh, surely you're mistaken. Why would he wish to marry if he was—that kind of a man?"

"Surely you're smart enough to figure that out for yourself."

"I don't believe it. How would you know such a thing? Father would never agree to that kind of marriage."

Rather than mention things he wasn't ready to divulge, Diablo said, "Eat your breakfast, Devon, I've a ship to run. If you're feeling well enough tomorrow, you can get out of bed. Meanwhile, rest and regain your strength."

"Diablo, wait! Where are you taking me?"

He grinned, but the smile never reached his eyes. "To Paradise."

"Go to the devil!"

"I'm afraid he's already claimed me."

Then he was gone.

Chapter Thirteen

The sound of belching cannon brought Devon leaping to her feet. Three days had elapsed since her illness and she now felt well enough to dress each day. Her appetite had returned and her paleness was replaced by a rosy glow. Just as Kyle predicted, Devon's youthful exuberance quickly reasserted itself, returning her to good health. She was young, healthy, and Diablo's wife. No matter what he had threatened, she was still alive and suddenly eager to face her future. Diablo had loved her once and there was no reason he wouldn't do so again.

The guns boomed with deafening redundancy, and Devon flew to the door. She was far too curious to remain inside while her husband faced danger, or even death.

Diablo stood on the quarterdeck, feet spread apart, hands on slim hips, directing fire at the Portuguese merchantman doing its best to evade the *Devil Dancer*. "Fire another round across her bow, lads," he shouted above the deafening roar. "She's lightly armed and no match for us. She'll surrender without a fight."

The cannon boomed again, and just as Diablo predicted, a white flag replaced the Portuguese banner flying from the mast. As often happened, Diablo had subdued the captain and crew without striking a blow. In a short time the *Devil Dancer* had maneuvered alongside the merchantman, and men were using grappling hooks to secure the two ships together. When the Portuguese captain spotted Diablo pacing the bridge, he shouted across the distance, "Who are you and from where do you hail?"

"From the sea!" returned Diablo, giving the traditional

pirate reply. Then he leaped to the deck below, grasped a line, and swung nimbly across the narrow strip of sea separating the two ships. He landed neatly at the captain's side. Throwing caution to the wind, Devon rushed to the rail, hoping to hear something of what was being said.

The Portuguese captain trembled before Diablo, who towered nearly a foot above him. He had heard of this devil disguised as a man but had never had the misfortune of encountering him. He wondered if the pirate was truly a Spaniard as rumored and addressed him in Spanish. "I am Diego Figuero, captain of the *Louisa Esperez.*"

In perfect Spanish, one of the three languages he spoke, Diablo replied, "I am called Diablo. What cargo do you carry?"

Captain Figuero licked his dry lips, looking decidedly uncomfortable. "We are carrying nothing but passengers this trip." He deliberately neglected to mention that he had been sent to England to return the ship owner's beautiful daughter to Portugal in time for her wedding.

Diablo snorted in disgust. He had hoped to rid the *Louisa Esperez* of much riches. "Assemble the passengers on deck."

Devon silently observed the proceedings as a group of frightened men, women, and children spilled from the passageway onto the deck, prodded by Akbar. Last to appear were two women, both young and beautiful. But judging from their manner of dress—one richly garbed and adorned with jewels, the other more plainly attired—they appeared to be mistress and maid.

Diablo looked over the poor selection of hostages, fuming over the lack of booty and silently considering which, if any, were worth holding for ransom. Not that he took the captain's word that the *Louisa Esperez* carried no cargo. His crew were turning the ship upside down in search of booty, and if nothing of value was found he'd have to look to the passengers for a source of income in order to placate his men.

Diablo's narrowed gaze stopped abruptly before a stunning, richly dressed and bejeweled woman—no more than a girl, really—and regarded her with interest. She was a fiery wench, loudly protesting her rough handling, and a satisfied smile teased the corners of his lips. He was willing to bet the volatile senorita was the pampered daughter of a rich don, one willing to part with a fortune in ransom.

"What is the meaning of this?" the senorita spouted angrily as Akbar nudged her forward. "Do you know who my father is?"

"This one is more trouble than she's worth," the huge Turk grumbled crossly.

"Why no, senorita, who is your father?" Diablo asked, assuming a placating tone.

The girl's dark eyes grew large and luminous at the sight of Diablo's imposing figure and handsome features. She thought him the most dashingly attractive man she'd ever seen. Her huge orbs devoured him greedily and her sensuous lips curved in a smile meant to entice and beguile as she posed artfully before him, pushing her rounded breasts forward to full advantage.

"My father is Miguel Esperez, owner of this ship and many others like her. I am Carlotta Esperez and this is my maid, Marlena. We have been visiting relatives in London." She offered far more than Diablo had asked. "Who are you?"

"They call me Diablo. Your father must be a wealthy man, Senorita Carlotta," Diablo probed.

"Extremely wealthy," Carlotta concurred guilelessly. "And not without influence. If I am harmed, Father will be relentless in his pursuit of you."

"I do not harm beautiful women," Diablo denied, "but neither am I stupid enough to let you go without relieving your father of part of his fortune. If your father is as rich as you say, he'll agree to whatever ransom I demand."

"My father loves me and will pay anything," Carlotta replied confidently.

Privately she thought it would be a great adventure to spend time with the handsome pirate. He didn't appear at all cruel or threatening. Besides, once she returned to Portugal her strict parents would put an end to her wild ways and she would marry a man she despised. In London she had taken several lovers and seriously doubted she could settle down to any one man. Despite her young age, she had been introduced to sex early by a handsome footman in her father's service. Her marriage had been arranged years ago to an elderly friend of the family, and she dreaded the thought of returning to Portugal and the dull life of a married woman when she was still so young and vital. She viewed Diablo as a way to delay her return as well as experience an adventure of a lifetime, the handsome pirate a bonus thrown in.

"Senorita Carlotta, you must not give this devil so much information," Captain Figuero cautioned, dismayed by his charge's lack of propriety. "Your father entrusted me with your safety, and I fear I have let him down." He turned to Diablo. "The lady is gently born and reared. Her reputation will be severely damaged if you insist on holding her for ransom. Have mercy."

"Senorita Carlotta will not be harmed," Diablo contended, smiling beguilingly at the haughty girl. His roguish grin filled her with an excitement she found difficult to contain. "I will do nothing to compromise her virtue."

Then Diablo called his lieutenant and quartermaster, ordering the *Louisa Esperez* thoroughly searched and anything of value removed before returning with the crew to the *Devil Dancer*.

"Your crew and passengers are free to continue on your way, captain," Diablo informed Figuero. "I ask only that you relay a message to Senor Esperez concerning his daughter.

Tell him neither Carlotta nor her maid will be harmed unless he fails to deliver the ransom in Nassau in two months' time. I will be there to receive it exactly sixty days from today. Once the ransom is in my hands the women will be released."

"What ransom do you demand?" Figuero asked.

"Five thousand pieces of eight."

"What! That's preposterous."

"Surely I am worth that much," Carlotta sniffed with a toss of her glossy black head.

"I wholeheartedly concur, the lady is worth at least that much," Diablo agreed, swallowing a chuckle. "You have my word the women will not be harmed."

"The word of a pirate? Bah!"

"Nevertheless, you have it. And now, senorita, allow me to escort you to my ship."

Carlotta trilled excitedly when Diablo swept her into his arms. "Hang on, senorita, I won't let you fall. My lieutenant will see to your maid."

Carlotta's slim arms circled Diablo's neck, the corded muscles rippling enticingly beneath her touch. "I'm not afraid," she replied, her heart beating in vigorous tumult. "You're so strong, I know you'd not let anything happen to me."

Easily supporting her slim form, Diablo grasped a dangling rope and swung gracefully across the chasm to the *Devil Dancer*, his wild flight not hindered in the least by Carlotta's meager weight.

A frown marring her smooth brow, Devon observed the proceedings aboard the *Louisa Esperez* with annoyed interest, caring little for the brazen way one of the women strutted before Diablo. Even from a distance she could tell the woman was young and radiantly beautiful in a dark, exotic way. When Diablo swept the woman into his arms, Devon nearly exploded with jealousy and rage. Did he intend to keep the lissome beauty for his own pleasure? Considering his voracious appetite, it was entirely possible, for it appeared he had little desire for his own wife. No matter what had persuaded him into marriage, Devon reflected, she was now his wife and shouldn't have to put up with his infidelity.

Diablo dropped lightly to his feet scant inches from where Devon stood, Carlotta still clinging to his neck. Amused and flattered by Carlotta's not so subtle attempts at seduction, he took his time untangling her arms and setting her on her feet. He noted Devon's fierce scowl and looped an arm around Carlotta's tiny waist, gaining perverse pleasure from provoking Devon's anger.

"What are you doing out here?" Diablo scolded, finally acknowledging Devon's presence.

Devon had no intention of admitting she had left the cabin because she feared for Diablo's safety. "I wanted to see what was happening."

"Now that you're here you may as well meet Senorita Carlotta Esperez. Senorita Carlotta, this is Lady Devon." The moment Carlotta saw Devon her smile turned sour. She viewed the lovely blonde as a serious contender for Diablo's affections.

Devon fumed with silent rage. She should have known Diablo wouldn't acknowledge her as his wife when he obviously expected to share Carlotta's bed.

"Who is this woman?" Carlotta asked in heavily accented English, surprising Diablo. He should have known the woman spoke the language, having just spent time in London. "Another hostage like myself or your—*puta?*"

Red dots of rage exploded behind Devon's eyes. She wanted to fly at the sly senorita and tear her eyes out. Realizing her intent, Diablo's placed a restraining hand on her arm.

"My relationship with Lady Devon is none of your concern, Carlotta." His censuring tone was like a dash of cold water in Carlotta's face.

Diablo's words did little to relieve Devon's hurt over his

deliberate slight. She felt strongly that he should have introduced her as his wife. Then Kyle arrived with Marlena, Carlotta's maid. Though the girl looked frightened out of her wits, her beauty could not be denied. Smaller than her mistress, her shiny black tresses had come loose from her demure chignon and curled around her face in charming disarray. Devon thought the girl to be about her own age. From the way Kyle was devouring her voluptuous form and lovely features, it was obvious he thought her more than attractive.

"Are you all right, Carlotta?" Marlena asked, more concerned for her mistress than herself. Having served the haughty young woman since the age of twelve, Marlena felt familiar enough with Carlotta to address her informally.

"Of course, you goose, Diablo would not allow anything to happen to me." Carlotta directed a glowing smile at Diablo. "When we are in the company of others, Marlena, we will speak English. You understand and speak the language as well as I do."

"Si, Carlotta," Marlena agreed. "What will happen to us now? I'm frightened."

"No need for fright," Diablo assured the tiny brunette. "No one will harm you. When Senor Esperez sends ransom you will both be freed."

"Truly?" she ventured, unable to believe his words after hearing of the despicable deeds visited on defenseless women by pirates.

"Truly," Diablo returned, thinking the girl quite fetching. Then he turned to Devon. "Pack your things, Devon. Carlotta and Marlena will occupy your quarters. 'Tis large and can easily accommodate both of them."

"Why, thank you, Diablo," simpered Carlotta coyly. "That's very thoughtful of you."

"Where will I sleep?" Devon demanded to know. It took all her considerable willpower to control her temper.

"You may have my cabin, Devon," Kyle offered generously. "'Tis no more than a cubbyhole but far better than sleeping on deck." He bent Diablo a censuring glare, unaware that he had spoken up before Diablo could suggest just such an arrangement himself.

"Come along, ladies, I'll show you to your quarters," Diablo said, returning Kyle's scowl. "Your trunks will be delivered shortly."

Flinging Devon a condescending look, Carlotta took Diablo's arm as he led her to the cabin that was to be her home for the next several days. Marlena followed meekly behind.

Though Kyle's small cabin offered none of the amenities she took for granted in Diablo's comfortable quarters, Devon was nonetheless grateful for a place to sleep. Did her husband hate her so much that he expected her to sleep on deck among men who despised her? she wondered, exasperated by the inconsiderate lout's neglect. It gave her a smidgeon of satisfaction that Diablo didn't plan on sharing Carlotta's bed, for if he did he'd hardly assign Marlena to the same cabin.

Kyle's cabin sported only one porthole, a far cry from Diablo's airy quarters with two full-length windows overlooking the ship's stern. Nothing was said about confining her to her cabin, and since Devon had recovered completely, she spent most of the following days sitting in solitude on a pile of ropes on the ship's bow. When time permitted, Kyle stopped to speak with her, and so did Marlena, but the little maid was kept far too busy by her demanding mistress to allow for lengthy conversation.

Though Diablo mostly ignored her, he did ask after her health from time to time. What truly rankled was the way Carlotta seemed to dominate Diablo's free time, often joining him on the bridge or coaxing him into strolling the deck with her. It hurt Devon to think that Diablo paid the fiery

Spanish beauty attentive court while all but ignoring his own wife. Yet more than once Devon caught Diablo regarding her through hooded eyes, his silver gaze fixed on her slim form with an unreadable expression that puzzled her. When she was brave enough to meet his stare, she'd find herself the object of his intense scrutiny. And today was no exception.

Their eyes collided across the expanse of rolling deck, reaching out toward one another yet unwilling or unable to breach the gap separating them. The silent message conveyed by the intensity of Diablo's gaze brought a flood of color to Devon's cheeks. Then the spell was broken when Carlotta deliberately strutted into Diablo's line of vision, smiling archly and batting her long dark lashes. Reluctantly Devon turned away, too proud to admit to her jealousy as Carlotta looped her arm through Diablo's and purposely led him in Devon's direction, pausing often to admire the view.

When they drifted past the spot where Devon sat, the wind flung bits of their animated conversation back to her. The dark Spanish beauty leaned intimately against Diablo, her words, those that Devon heard, sounding suspiciously like an outrageous invitation.

"Marlena will do exactly as I say. If you come to me tonight she will remain discretely on deck and not interfere."

Diablo's reply was lost to her, but Devon read eagerness in his laughter and approval in his eyes. She had no way of knowing that Diablo's laughter was due entirely to amusement. Not only did Carlotta's audacity and daring amuse him, but amazed him as well. Originally he thought her an innocent virgin, but as the days passed he seriously doubted he'd find her virginal should he accept her blatant invitation to share her bed. As for his smile, it was directed at himself for thinking her merely a young flirt testing her wings when her actions clearly labeled her a woman who had partaken freely of love's bounty with numerous lovers. And now Carlotta wanted to add him to her list.

Diablo thoroughly appreciated Carlotta's exotic beauty, but was aware that her shiny ebony locks were not the vivid gold of Devon's. Though her complexion had the look of creamy ivory, pale and glowing, he much preferred Devon's more vibrant coloring, reminding him of fine apricot brandy with a sprinkling of cinnamon freckles scattered across the bridge of her nose. And Devon's blue eyes were as stormy as the sea he loved so much, while Carlotta's flashing black orbs revealed nothing but her own feelings of self-worth. How different things could be between them if Devon hadn't betrayed him.

The thought of becoming a father thrilled Diablo. Especially with Devon as the child's mother. He knew of no other woman he'd want to bear his babe. If she'd had a miscarriage as Kyle suggested, he could not fault her, for he had put her through hell and treated her atrociously before bringing her aboard the *Devil Dancer*. But if she'd deliberately lied about being pregnant, he'd never be able to forgive her. Unfortunately, he'd never know for certain.

"Diablo, did you hear me?" Carlotta prodded, pouting prettily. "I've just invited you to share—the evening with me."

"Perhaps another time," Diablo hedged, wondering why in the hell he didn't jump at the invitation. Then he saw Devon staring at him as if he'd just plunged a dagger in her heart, and knew exactly why the thought of pleasuring himself with Carlotta gave him little joy.

"What exactly is Devon to you?" Carlotta asked, following the direction of Diablo's gaze. There was anger in her voice as well as jealousy. Accustomed to being doted upon by all her acquaintances, she did not enjoy Diablo's straying attention.

"Ask Devon," Diablo said cryptically. "Please excuse me, Carlotta, I've duties to perform." Shrugging off Carlotta's clinging arms, he turned and made his way back to the bridge.

From the corner of his eye he noted that Devon had joined Marlena and Kyle as they strolled by. When Carlotta approached them, Devon politely excused herself and left. With rapt attention Diablo observed the seductive sway of Devon's skirts, convinced he'd never seen a woman move with such sensual grace. He'd thought of nothing but making love to her since he brought her aboard the *Devil Dancer*. At first he was too damn angry to trust himself anywhere near her, then her illness had prevented him from consummating their marriage. Nothing stopped him now but his own stubborn pride. He didn't need a wife, wasn't certain he still wanted Devon, but he had to have her or go out of his mind.

The supper Pegleg brought lay untouched on the narrow table. Devon pushed it aside, having no stomach for food when Diablo was in another cabin making glorious love with Carlotta. Devon was haunted by the grim specter of the man he had been before he thought she betrayed him. Humorous, loving, passionate, tender, not this cold, brutal stranger who delighted in taunting and humiliating her. Stripping off her clothes, Devon lay down in her thin shift, deciding the night was too warm for the constricting bedgown. Since they had entered southern waters the weather had changed dramatically, making the small cabin hot and stifling. Devon knew they couldn't be far from the Bahama islands and wondered what fate awaited her in Diablo's home. Would he still pay assiduous court to Carlotta once they were on Paradise? Sprawled atop the narrow bunk, Devon fell into a fitful sleep. And then the dream began. The same dream that had plagued her constantly since she had left Diablo weeks ago.

In her dream Diablo was making love to her. Sweet, tender love in the gentle way she'd grown accustomed to. With a flick of the wrist he removed her gown, peeling off his own clothes and joining her in bed. Then he was pressing her down against the unyielding surface. Suddenly the usual course of the dream altered as Diablo became a sneering stranger, taking her with passionate violence instead of gentleness. Devon's eyes flew open, as she became aware that no dream could feel so real. And she was right. The flesh-and-blood Diablo crouched above her, nude to the waist and grinning like the devil he was named after.

"Diablo! What are you doing here?"

"You're my wife, Devon," Diablo reminded her.

"I'm sorry to hear you admit it," came Devon's scathing reply. "I'd so hoped it was all a bad dream. What about Carlotta?"

"Carlotta? What about her?"

"Have you finished with her already? I mean—I assumed you'd spend the night with her."

"I don't want Carlotta, though her offer quite dazzled me."

"I don't believe you."

"Then we're even, for I don't believe you. You're the only one who could have betrayed me. But that doesn't stop me from wanting you. Lord knows I've tried, but I have no pride where you're concerned. You're my wife and it's your duty to satisfy my needs."

Devon exploded in furious anger. "Duty! I owe you nothing. I became your enemy and bride at the same time. Twice you've abducted me, once on the eve of my wedding. And don't for a minute think I believe that drivel about Winston. I'd prefer your cruelty to our loveless coupling."

"Cruelty!" Diablo sneered. "You know nothing of cruelty. I could tell you, but I'd rather demonstrate."

His mouth slanted over hers brutally, hurting her, making her gasp out a protest. He paid no heed to her obvious distress, his arms encircling her like steel bands, holding her so tightly she could scarcely breath. The fury of his kiss forced her mouth open. Immediately his tongue penetrated deep inside with none of the tenderness she knew him capable of. He took her mouth and used it ruthlessly, forced it to his will, conquered it without mercy. The sudden unleashed violence badly frightened Devon and she feared she might faint.

His hand closed over her right breast, burning through the thin material of her shift to her skin. Against her will her nipple puckered against his palm, sending a shaft of pure fire straight to her loins. His kiss deepened savagely while his hand plundered the tender mound, caressing, kneading, searing her skin like a brand. His fingers thrust inside the shift and the fine muslin gave with a soft ripping sound. She lay trembling, helpless beneath his ravening desire. Then her shift left her body with a controlled savagery that made her heart shiver in her breast. Even if she wanted to protest, she could not have. Her blood surged hot and fierce in her veins, her legs trembled, and a fierce need erupted within her to equal the devouring hunger revealed in his face.

The silvery moonlight behind Diablo cast his head in dark silhouette, making it difficult for Devon to read his expression. His initial savagery startled her, but strangely she no longer felt threatened as he stared at her without moving for a long, breathless moment. She felt her breast beneath his fingers swell and tighten, bringing a jolt of both pain and pleasure. Instinctively she arched, offering him more of her tempting curves. A harsh, ragged growl left his throat. Then, in a movement so swift it startled her, he came down on top of her, his weight crushing her into the hard surface of the bunk.

"God's bones, sweetheart, I don't know who's suffering more, you or me. How can I hurt you when all I want is to love you? Your sweet body was fashioned expressly for mine. I touch you and you respond instantly. I want to be inside you so badly I hurt."

His arms wrapped around her slender body, crushing her to him, all thought of brutality long forgotten. His mouth closed over hers, and he kissed her with a fierceness that made her head spin. The wiry mat of hair on his chest was abrasive against her breasts, and she shivered in response to the stimulus. He must have felt her arousal, and it fired his own, stifling the impulse to take her swiftly to ease his terrible need. It had been so long—too damn long—and he'd had no other woman since Devon. As his lips moved to suckle the tender tips of her breasts, his fingertips slid down between her thighs, parting them as he sought to arouse her fully.

"God's bones, you're so hot and wet and oh so sweet I want to slowly savor every inch of you."

He lowered his head then, spreading light kisses over the triangle of golden curls nestled between her thighs before sending his tongue sliding along the tender cleft. He heard her call his name but ignored her breathless gasp to delve ever deeper into the warm moist cave welcoming his loving invasion with a rush of secret fluid. His tongue continued to caress her gently as he savored the sweet essence of her body. Devon was too pleased by the marvelous sensations he created within her to be shocked by the way he made love to her. Then the wonderful quickening inside her exploded, splintering into a whirlwind of light and colors and shapes.

Before Devon fully regained her senses, Diablo had discarded his trousers and thrust inside her, so deep she thought his hugeness would split her in two. She gasped, grinding her hips against his urgent, instinctive response as her passion began to slowly renew itself.

"Kit, oh God! When you're loving me like this I don't even know my own name."

Suddenly Diablo cried out, thrusting again and again, and then one final time to hurry Devon to her own reward. Her cry echoed his, quivering as Diablo wrapped his arms tightly around her, holding himself deep inside her until she was still.

For several long suspenseful minutes they lay motionless, entwined together, collecting their thoughts as well as their breath. Diablo's face was completely shadowed so that Devon could not decipher his expression. He shifted his weight to lay beside her, and Devon lifted one slender hand to touch and then slide down his hip. Her light caress set off a reaction in him that Devon hardly expected as he swore, the words harsh and shocking.

"You're a damn witch and I'm a bloody idiot." The words were no sooner out of his mouth than he was jerking her hard against him, his mouth assaulting hers with hot hungry kisses.

It rankled to know that no matter what Devon had done he continued to desire her. He was finally ready to admit to himself that he had married her to keep anyone else from having her. With Devon he had known the joy of love, the bitter anguish of betrayal, and an erotic pleasure he could not adequately describe in words. He despised his vulnerability where Devon was concerned, deplored his reaction to her pleading blue eyes and lying lips. Suddenly the thought of all the suffering and destruction that Devon had visited on Paradise brought Diablo's wild caresses to an abrupt halt. Expelling a snort of self-loathing, he leaped to his feet.

"Damn your bloody hide! You're like a drug in my blood. Your sweet kisses and siren's body have the ability to move a statue, and I'm not made of stone. Do you expect me to forget and forgive so easily?"

"You've nothing to forget, Kit, for I've done nothing that needs forgiving." The name slipped easily from Devon's lips, and since Diablo did not protest she repeated it. "Kit, please, why don't you trust me?"

"Trust a woman who ran off with a man like Le Vautour? Surely you jest."

"I'm certain Father can clear up this misunderstanding," Devon suggested. "The longer I think on it, the more convinced I am that Le Vautour betrayed your secret."

"Are you suggesting that your father is responsible for shelling a defenseless village and taking innocent lives?"

Pulling on his pants in angry motions, Diablo whirled, his hard features all but obscured by the darkness. Though she couldn't see them, she knew his eyes were as cold and colorless as ice, and a shudder passed through her body.

"No, oh no, Father would never do that." Suddenly a thought came to her. Perhaps it was wild speculation but it had enough merit to mention. "Do you know the names of the ships that attacked Paradise?"

Devon held her breath, waiting for his answer. She recalled that shortly after she returned to London Winston had left aboard the *Larkspur* on a mission lasting a month or more. Afterwards he resigned from the navy to prepare for their wedding. He had been very secretive about where he had been, and now all the pieces began falling into place. Le Vautour, hoping for a more generous reward and driven by his hatred for Diablo, must have told her father about Paradise Island. And of course Father had passed on the information to Winston. Her abduction by Diablo must have affected Winston greatly, prompting him to attack a village inhabited by defenseless women and children.

"Tara did mention the *Larkspur*," Diablo reflected. "Why, does the name mean anything to you?"

Devon sucked her breath in sharply. *Larkspur*! Winston's ship. Without her knowing it she was indirectly responsible for the shelling of Paradise. If not for her Le Vautour would not have ventured to England in the first place. "The—the *Larkspur*," she stuttered, "'tis—'tis Winston's ship. But I swear . . ."

"You bitch!"

". . . that I said nothing to him," Devon finished lamely.

"It had to be Le Vautour. He hated you though he tried to hide his feelings. He waited a long time to avenge the death of Black Bart."

" 'Tis logical," Diablo allowed grudgingly, "but can you deny you brought Le Vautour to England? Akbar was right, you've caused me nothing but trouble. I was too besotted to listen to him. God's bones, Devon, I fancied myself in love with you!"

"And now?" Devon prompted, sitting up and pulling the sheet to her chin.

"What I feel for you now is pure and simple lust," Diablo said, his voice laced with self-disgust.

"Then turn around and take me back to England. Since I'm not carrying your child, you owe me nothing. Forget I ever existed."

The mattress sagged under Diablo's weight as he perched on the edge of the bunk and lit a lamp so he could look at Devon. "Forget you? I wish to God I could. Have you forgotten we're man and wife? What's mine I keep. Besides, after tonight you just might be carrying my child."

"How long will you keep me, Kit?" Devon challenged. "One day you'll be caught and hanged, or killed in a sea battle. What will become of me then?"

Seeing Diablo's stricken look, Devon pressed on. "Perhaps I'll be passed on to your men? Or do you propose the other pirate captains draw lots for me? What if there's a child? How will we survive?"

To his profound regret, Diablo could answer none of those poignant questions.

Chapter Fourteen

Sleep eluded Diablo after Devon posed her evocative questions. It rankled to know that everything she said was true. Should he meet an untimely end, Devon would be left completely at the mercy of unscrupulous men. He'd wish that fate on no woman. No matter how difficult it was to admit, he still cared too much for Devon to abandon her to pirates and scoundrels.

So exactly what were his options? he asked himself grimly. Until Devon challenged him he had thought himself invincible and piracy the only way of life. Every day was a rousing adventure filled with an excitement found in no other profession. He thrived on danger, welcomed the hazards involved in every venture. And the rewards were well worth the risks. Piracy had made him rich enough to provide for future heirs for generations to come. It was the thought of those potential heirs that gave Diablo pause.

Did he want his sons and daughters living on the edge of society, shunned and reviled the world over? The answer was a resounding no.

Perhaps, Diablo reasoned, it was time to change the course of his life and mend his wild ways. He could become a planter on Paradise, or settle in America. England and most of Europe were out of the question, for the possibility would always exist that he'd be recognized as the scourge of the sea.

Leaving the brotherhood was something Diablo had never before considered, but then he'd never had a wife, or the possibility of children. He meant what he said when he told Devon he kept what was his. The thought of returning her to England to marry a man like Winston was reprehensible. Giving up pirating was definitely something he should contemplate, Diablo decided as he rolled up in a blanket and tried to find a comfortable position on the hard deck. With three women aboard, there were no cabins to spare and he deliberately refrained from remaining with Devon in her bunk. He greatly feared the effect she had on him and needed a clear head to run his ship and control his crew.

Devon's hair flowed like thick honey down her back as she raised her face to the warm sunlight. In the distance the Bahamas sparkled like jewels tossed upon the shimmering surface of the water. The blue-green water sliced beneath *Devil Dancer*'s hull as wind filled her burgeoning sails. The swiftly approaching islands were an inspiring sight despite Devon's misgivings about her future on those sundrenched, verdant shores. It had been two days since Diablo had come to her cabin and made love to her. Evidently their passionate coupling had affected him as much as it had her, for since that night she often caught him staring at her in pensive contemplation. She knew that her provocative probing made him delve deeply into his conscience and wondered if he had reached a decision about what to do with her.

"Are those distant islands our destination?" Carlotta sidled up beside Devon, joining her at the rail where she stood enjoying the balmy breezes.

"Aye," Devon replied, none too happy to have her solitude interrupted by the fiery senorita.

"He's a handsome devil, isn't he?" Carlotta sighed, shifting her gaze to where Diablo stood on the bridge. "His eyes—they're like none other I've ever seen. When he looks at me I forget I am a lady. He has only to ask and I'd—"

"I'm sure you would," Devon interjected rudely, wishing the woman would leave her in peace. She didn't care how often Diablo bedded Carlotta. Or so she tried to tell herself.

Carlotta's dark eyes blazed in sudden defiance. "What is Diablo to you? I know you don't share his bed so you can't be his mistress. And Kyle is paying too much attention to Marlena for you to be his whore. Perhaps one of Diablo's crew claims you," she suggested.

Devon's temper flared, her eyes shooting blue flame at the smirking Carlotta. It was long past time for the Spaniard to be told the truth. "I am Diablo's wife."

"You lie!" Carlotta screeched, capturing the attention of everyone nearby. "You're nothing but a *puta*! You might be Diablo's whore, but never his wife."

"Ah, but Devon is indeed my wife, Carlotta," Diablo interjected with a smile. Caught completely off guard by Diablo's sudden appearance, Carlotta could only stare at him, her eyes huge as saucers. "Devon would not lie about something as important as our marriage."

"Why wasn't I told this before?" Carlotta demanded to know.

"Because it didn't concern you. I rarely reveal details of my personal life to people I hold hostage. Or have you forgotten your position aboard the *Devil Dancer*?"

Devon's mouth flopped open and she gaped at Diablo with stunned fascination. His contempt was obvious for the fiery brunette who had made a game of practicing her seductive wiles on him. How many men, Devon wondered, had Carlotta lured into her sensual web?

"Married, bah!" Carlotta spat derisively. "Isn't it customary for husband and wife to share a bed?"

"Why, Carlotta," Diablo wagged his finger playfully, "have you been spying on me? Do you keep track of my movements every minute of the day and night?" He looked pointedly at Devon and winked, evoking memories of the teasing, captivating pirate who had landed in her lap at his own hanging.

"I surely hope not, for I'm certain a chaste young woman like yourself would swoon with embarrassment if she spied on my activities."

"Oh!" Carlotta fumed, stomping her foot in frustration. "You're horrid! But what else might one expect from a pirate?" Wheeling, she flounced off, her skirts swirling in angry motion around her slim ankles.

Devon giggled delightedly. "I'm afraid you've made Carlotta angry."

"She's a spoiled young woman who cares for no one but herself. Besides, I already have a woman who more than satisfies my needs." A smirk appeared at the corners of his mouth, and when he looked at her there was a gleam in his eye, bringing a becoming blush to Devon's face. Diablo thought she looked adorable and found it exceedingly difficult to remember that Devon was a deceitful witch who had betrayed him.

From the corner of his eye Diablo caught a glimpse of Akbar's glowering features and knew that his Turkish friend was reminding him in his own way that women couldn't be trusted. Noting the direction of Diablo's gaze, Devon looked pointedly at the ferocious Turk.

"Akbar doesn't like me. He never has."

"Akbar has no use for women," Diablo revealed. "He was once a guard in the sultan's palace where he caught the eye of the sultan's favorite concubine. Normally Akbar wouldn't be allowed anywhere near the harem, but Tallah bribed the head eunuch and soon Akbar was visiting Tallah regularly. Another concubine, jealous of Tallah's position and popularity with the sultan, eventually betrayed them."

"How terrible," Devon murmured, seeing Akbar through new eyes. "No wonder he feels about women as he does. Did he love Tallah?"

"Who's to say? When Tallah was questioned she tried to save her skin by saying Akbar forced her. It didn't work. Tallah was placed in a sack and thrown in the sea. Because Akbar had distinguished himself in the sultan's service, he was spared death. Instead he was sold into slavery and ended up as a galley slave aboard a Spanish galleon. For many years he was chained to the oars, and his hatred of women became an obsession."

Devon shuddered. "How did he escape?"

"Black Bart attacked the galleon, and Akbar was freed. He joined the brotherhood and that's how and when I met him. Most of the galleon's slaves are still part of my crew. I saved Akbar's life once and he appointed himself my guardian. He's repaid me many times over by saving my skin more times than I can count. He feels strongly that women are a dangerous lot, good for only one purpose."

"I wish he'd realize I present no danger to either of you."

"That remains to be seen, doesn't it?"

Diablo insisted upon taking Devon to the old village first to view the destruction he believed her responsible for. Everything looked peaceful at first glimpse, but as they entered the cove through the hidden river, Devon saw the devastation of the once bustling little village.

She stared in horror at the pile of bleached, splintered wood littering the beach. "Fortunately the fields and house weren't torched, and the Arawak laborers fled into the woods to hide until the English marauders left."

"Your house is still standing?" Devon asked, amazed as well as pleased.

"Aye, the English didn't bother to come ashore, else I fear it would have been destroyed as well."

They didn't remain anchored long in the cove, and Diablo said little, still too upset over the sneak attack to discuss it without growing enraged. When he was certain that Devon had viewed every aspect of the senseless destruction, the *Devil Dancer* returned the way she had come.

"Must you blindfold me?" Devon asked crossly as Diablo tied a scarf over her eyes. He did the same with Carlotta and Marlena.

"I'm taking no chances. I trusted you once but no more."

"I'd never tell," purred Carlotta.

Diablo all but ignored her. "Kyle will keep you company while I take the ship through the reef," he told Devon.

Devon slumped against the rail. "He'll never trust me again, will he, Kyle?"

"Can you blame him? All those people killed in the shelling were his responsibility. Many of our crew lost women, and in some cases, children.

"I had nothing to do with it, Kyle, why won't you believe me?"

"I—perhaps you didn't," acknowledged Kyle reluctantly. "It could have been Le Vautour, just as you said. But for the present, Diablo is too angry to think sensibly. Give him time."

"What are you two talking about?" queried Carlotta curiously. The conversation told her nothing but the fact that Diablo was angry with Devon for some offense, and perhaps she could use it to her own advantage.

"It's none of your concern, Carlotta," Kyle scolded. He thought the young aristocrat spoiled and vain and disliked her callous treatment of her little maid.

"Humph!" huffed Carlotta, fingering her blindfold. "Can I remove this yet?"

"Aye," Kyle allowed, "we're inside the reef now and already sailing up the secret passage."

At first glance Devon thought it looked like the same place she had just left, until she noted the raw new wood of the huts lining the beach, so different from the weathered dwellings in the old village. There were even two new warehouses on the beach where a long pier jutted out into the deep water of the cove. To Devon's thinking, this side of

Paradise was equally as beautiful as the other. She learned just how narrow the cay was when they walked to Diablo's house.

Sensing Devon's question, Diablo explained, "The cay is several miles long but less than two miles wide. The barrier reef circles the entire cay, and my explorations discovered only two places where it could be breached. The secret canal we entered on the opposite shore flows through the interior of the island and exits here. This cove is deeper than the other but much more difficult to locate."

"What's to stop the same people who shelled the old village from entering at the same place and sailing around the cay to where we are now?" Devon asked.

Diablo grinned, his teeth a white slash in his tanned face. "Sandbars. Too many to count. A ship attempting to circumnavigate the cay inside the reef would run aground the moment they left the deep water of the cove. 'Tis virtually impossible."

Tara was on hand to greet them, as beautiful and poised as Devon remembered. "Welcome home, Diablo." A wide smile split her exotic features.

"You've done well, Tara," Diablo complimented.

"The field hands and Le Vautour's crew did most of the work. I did no more than supervise their efforts," she said proudly.

"Le Vautour's crew!" Devon exclaimed. "Is that scoundrel here?"

"Le Vautour is where he'll cause no more trouble," Diablo said tightly. He turned away, but Devon was not about to drop the subject.

"What do you mean?"

"I sank the *Victory*. Le Vautour went down with his ship."

Devon's breath left her lungs in a loud gasp. "You killed him! Now we'll never know if he was the one who betrayed you."

"Devon, there's no longer a need to pretend. You're my wife now, and I'll not harm you for your deception."

"Are we to spend the rest of our lives at odds over my supposed betrayal? I'll convince you of my innocence if it takes a lifetime."

Wisely Diablo chose not to reply and they entered the house. He took Devon directly to the large, sunny room on the second floor she had previously occupied, while Carlotta and Marlena were shown to another part of the rambling structure by Tara.

"This will be our room," Diablo said, daring Devon to defy him. "You're my wife and there's no reason I should deny myself. I never denied I wanted you, and your body's response to my loving tells me you desire me just as fiercely. Living as a eunuch was never my intention."

Devon bit back a peppery retort. But in the end she decided not to protest. After experiencing Diablo's loving again aboard the *Devil Dancer*, she knew it was impossible to resist him; it was glorious being in his arms again, the sweet magic of his loving claiming her mind and body. Since they were now man and wife, she had no reason to withhold herself from him or act the outraged virgin. It was far too late for that. She was determined to make Diablo love her again, to trust her and accept her as his wife in every way.

The good Lord only knows why he had married her, except for the undeniable fact that her body gave him great pleasure. Call it lust, if you will, Devon smiled inwardly, but she'd have his love one day. And his trust.

Carlotta did everything in her power to complicate life for Devon while she remained on Paradise. And to make matters worse, Tara blamed her for the death and destruction wrought by the English. While waiting for Carlotta's ransom, Diablo chose to remain close to his home base. He also occupied Devon's bed every one of those nights. At times

Devon thought him the same teasing rogue she had grown to love. Then suddenly she'd find him staring at her oddly, a scowl furrowing his brows, and he'd be instantly transformed into that steely-eyed, inscrutable stranger she no longer knew and often feared.

Somehow Devon sensed that her father could explain exactly how Diablo's secret had been discovered, but she also knew him to be incapable of ordering senseless killings. Too bad, she lamented, that Le Vautour had died before he could be questioned. If pressed, he might have cleared up this whole mess. How could she go through life with Diablo hating her? With everyone on the island hating her?

Devon thought often of her father and wondered how her going off with Diablo had affected him. Did he also hate her for deserting him? That unbearable thought brought tears to her eyes and a piercing pain in her heart. And what of Winston? Were Diablo's crude remarks about him true? More importantly, how did Diablo know such a thing? True or not, Devon realized now that she could never have married Winston while loving Diablo as she did.

From where he stood in the sheltered doorway, obscured by evening shadows, Diablo silently observed Devon. She looked sad sitting in a cane rocker on the veranda and staring forlornly into the distance, the gentle breeze ruffling her honey-colored tresses. She did not notice him, but it was still light enough for Diablo to see the sparkle of tears on her cheeks. They reminded him of tiny diamonds on pale satin. He realized that her life was far from happy here among people who despised her, and Carlotta's petty jealousy only added to her distress.

Thank God that haughty Spanish bitch would soon be gone, he thought sourly. With that prickly problem disposed of, he hoped his life with Devon would become less complicated. As long as he remained a hunted man it was unlikely they could live a normal life. Yet he could not bring himself to send her away. Though he hated to admit it, he loved her too much to part with her, even though their future promised no happiness for either of them.

He stepped out from the shadows. "Devon." The name was a caress on his lips.

"You startled me."

"You're crying."

"Crying? I'm not," she denied, a sniffle belying her words.

"Ah, sweetheart, let me dry those tears."

Dropping to one knee beside her, he curled his hand around her nape, drawing her face down to his. Then she felt the moist tip of his tongue gently flick the pearly drops from her cheeks, savoring the salty texture against his lips.

"Lord help me I've tried to hate you," Diablo whispered into the pink shell of her ear. "No matter what you've done, I still want you with a deep abiding longing. Come, sweetheart, I want to make love to you—now."

Mesmerized, Devon clasped his warm hand and allowed herself to be drawn deeply into the seductive web he wove around her senses.

"Disgusting!" Carlotta snapped acidly. "Look at them, they behave like animals. It's a wonder they don't couple right here on the ground."

She and Marlena had stepped out onto the veranda in time to observe an exceedingly intimate moment. Her cruel remark failed to produce the desired effect, for Diablo merely laughed, catching Devon up in his arms and bounding into the house and up the stairs with an urgency born of need.

"Animals!" Carlotta repeated, stomping her tiny foot in a jealous rage. It wasn't fair that Devon should have such a virile man as Diablo when she was destined to become an old don's bride.

"I think it's beautiful," sighed Marlena wistfully. "I wish—"

"Banish those thoughts from your mind," Carlotta snapped. "Your future does not include love and marriage. If you are fortunate, one day some man might bed you, but nothing will come of it. You'll soon bore him and find yourself discarded like an old shoe. Come along, a short walk before I retire might improve my humor."

Diablo set Devon on her feet, her lush body slowly sliding down his long length. When she lifted her head his eyes were turbulent with passion and she felt a surge of lazy heat spiral through her loins. His hands slid down the front of her body, over breasts and belly and the soft place between her legs. Slowly he began peeling away the layers of her clothes until she stood gloriously nude before him. Then he kissed her, his mouth warm and gentle and softly persuasive.

His hands cupped her bottom, his fingers lightly stroking the soft rounded flesh. "I thank God for your passion," he whispered, loving the spark of desire his touch had ignited. "I don't want to hurt you, only love you."

His words had the desired effect as Devon melted against him. She belonged to this special man, she always would, no matter what fate dealt them. Without breaking eye contact, Devon's nimble fingers worked furiously at the fastenings holding together Diablo's clothes. Laughing, he pushed her fingers aside and swiftly shed his offending garments. Standing proud and naked at last, he scooped Devon high in his arms and fell with her across the bed. He rolled with her so that she was sprawled on top of him.

Her eyes bright with passion, Devon gently stroked his furred belly, her fingers walking through the soft wedge of curly dark hair that stretched across his chest. The gulf between them was still enormous, but each time they loved a tiny portion of their differences melted away, and Devon sought to make the most of it. She wanted to put their troubles behind them, heal his mistrust, and make this moment a magical interlude out of reality.

Bending low to place small teasing kisses on Diablo's face,

Devon was stunned when he deftly eluded her, his hands clutching her shoulders and pushing her upright. Obediently she sat up, his hands sliding down the front of her body, moving intimately over her breasts and belly and bright thatch of hair between her legs. Then he shoved her thighs apart so she could straddle him. Her eyes widened but she made no objections.

"I want to see all of you when we make love. Your breasts are so beautiful . . ." He reached up to touch them, then scraped his thumbs teasingly across her nipples. Shafts of pure fire shot through her. "Do you like that?"

"Yes, oh yes."

Smiling with wicked delight, Diablo abandoned her breasts to guide his hands over her ribcage, tiny waist, the delicate curve of her hips, the tautness of her belly. Heat melted her bones and she begged him to quench the fire he ignited inside her.

Devon gasped as the warm strength of his hands caressed her knees and slid up the silken length of her inner thighs to rest lightly on her soft mound. She froze as exploring fingers parted the curling nest of hair, stroked over it gently, finally discovering the secret wellspring of passion nestled there. When his fingers worked magically against her, Devon jerked, cried out, her head falling forward and her eyes closing at the sudden intensity of her passion. Her hands braced against his chest kept her from collapsing.

Finding her nipples so close to his lips, Diablo took first one ripe bud then the other into his mouth, sucking vigorously, licking, rolling the tiny nubs between his teeth until Devon's body began vibrating with compelling need. When his fingers delved deeply into the moist heat of her, she shrieked with joy. Watching her face with intense longing, Diablo continued his loving caress until the last tremor left her body.

"Now I want you to love me." His voice was a husky whisper against her ear.

Devon's head lifted and her eyes struggled open as she tried to make sense out of his words. His meaning became clear when his hands moved to her hips, lifting her upward and lowering her carefully onto his steely length. She gasped as his fiery heat probed against her. Then he was inside her, his hands tugging her down—down, until his hugeness stretched and filled her.

"Love me, sweetheart," he repeated, the words thick on his tongue, his eyes glazed, his face flushed with passion.

The muscles in his neck corded, standing out in stark relief against his bronze skin as he fought to hold himself in control, wanting Devon to set the pace. Grasping her hips, he guided her in the motion he sought, then waited for her to learn the rhythm and take the lead. Sensing his intent, she quickly grasped his lesson and gave him what he desired, her hips moving against his in seductive invitation. Then he released her to find her breasts. She cried out as his hands cupped them.

Diablo groaned and pulled her down so that he could suckle the tender mounds. He nursed them with savage delight, his hands hot and demanding on the silken roundness of her bottom as he ground himself upwards into her. She gave herself up to the fierceness of his passion, responding with a passion of her own. Finally, a hoarse cry left his throat and he clutched her close, trembling beneath her. As he held himself inside her, Devon felt something deep within her break loose and she cried out, swept up in a firestorm of exploding ecstasy.

Afterwards they lay quietly in each other's arms, quivering with exhaustion and sated passion. "You're mine, Devon, I'll never let you go. If you leave me now I'd search the world to find you."

The weeks passed swiftly, and since Diablo and Devon had come to an understanding of sorts, life became more bearable.

Not even Carlotta's constant bickering succeeded in spoiling the time Devon spent with the man she loved. Diablo was her whole life now, and though she knew he still withheld his trust, he did seem to care for her. Maybe not love her as he once did, but it was a beginning. He certainly was possessive of her, and her own love was as unwavering as it had always been.

Devon greatly admired Diablo's stamina in withstanding Carlotta's attempts at seduction, and credited him with good sense as well as strength of character. Perhaps their marriage actually did mean something more to him than a piece of paper. If only she could convince him to give up piracy their prospects for a life together would be greatly enhanced. It was a wish she prayed for nightly.

Lord Harvey was a broken man. He wore his worry and concern etched in the deep lines on his face. It was inconceivable that Devon would leave on the eve of her wedding with a man wanted by every civilized nation in the world. Had Diablo bewitched her? There appeared to be no simple explanation for Devon's behavior. And why would the notorious pirate risk capture and death to come to London for Devon? Was there something Devon had failed to tell him, something about her relationship with the pirate that she was too ashamed to reveal?

The moment Lord Harvey learned of Devon's disappearance he sent immediately for Winston. When the jilted bridegroom bounded into the earl's study, the older man merely handed him Devon's hastily scrawled note.

"The bloody sod! How could this happen?" Winston exploded, showing more spirit than Lord Harvey had given him credit for.

Winston was livid with rage. Not only had his cousin come back from the dead to haunt him, but his bride-to-be had jilted him for the notorious pirate whom he, as well as half of London, believed had ravished her. If he wasn't in desperate straights and in need of Devon's fortune he'd say to hell with the whole mess. Kit's return had shaken Winston badly, for his cousin could do all kinds of damage to him and his father, should he so desire. The thought of facing the many creditors hounding him was just too much, and he flew into a frenzy.

"How could Devon do this to me? I offered her love and protection from the gossips who would make hash out of her reputation. Is this how she repays me?" Winston's face contorted into an ugly mask, shocking Lord Harvey. Few people had seen Winston's violent side. Most thought him a pleasant, even-tempered man somewhat lacking in spirit with mild manners and rather insipid charm.

"I refuse to believe this note is Devon's doing," the earl offered, leaping to his daughter's defense. "It may be her handwriting, but 'tis my theory Diablo forced her to it. 'Tis my belief she intended to go through with this marriage."

Somewhat mollified, Winston whined, "Devon changed after she returned to England. No one really knows the truth about what happened between her and that pirate. Devon spoke little of that time. How do we know Diablo didn't—"

"That's enough, Winston!" thundered Lord Harvey. "I don't care what happened between them. None of it matters, and I supposed you felt the same. If you didn't want to marry Devon, you had only to say so. The stress of being held captive affected her greatly, but Devon never let it destroy her. Lesser women would have buckled under the strain."

Winston had the grace to flush, realizing he must tread carefully if he hoped to remain in the earl's good graces. "No offense meant, Your Grace," he blustered. "I'd marry Devon today if she were here. Or anytime she reappears."

His words seemed to satisfy the earl, for he beamed gratefully. "And so you shall, m'boy. How soon can you leave?"

"Leave, your grace?"

"To get Devon, of course. I know you've already resigned your commission, but I'll buy or hire any ship you want."

"After the shelling of Diablo's hideaway I doubt he can still be found there. By now he's moved his base to another cay," Winston contended.

"Perhaps, but I want my daughter back. I'm prepared to risk all I possess to wrest her from the clutches of that blackguard. She's all I have left in this world. How soon can you find a ship?"

Winston's hesitation brought a curse to Lord Harvey's lips and a generous offer Winston could not afford to turn down. "If you leave within two weeks I'll settle twenty thousand pounds on you the day you marry Devon. That's in addition to her dowry."

"Your Grace, I don't know what to say." Winston was stunned. With so much money he'd be free from financial worry for the rest of his life and able to pursue his dreams. "Of course I'll go. I love Devon."

The words dripped from his lips like warm honey. Though he held a certain fondness for Devon, he wasn't capable of the kind of love expected of him. He was confident he could do his duty and father an heir for the earl's fortune, but it wasn't something he looked forward to.

"I'm aware that Diablo might have changed his base, and there's dozens of islands and cays where he could hide, but I expect you to search diligently. I want that bloody bastard and I want him bad. But most of all I want my daughter."

Two weeks later Winston sailed from London harbor. Lord Harvey's wealth made it possible to hire a shallow draft schooner carrying thirty cannon whose original destination had been China. The *Mary Jane*'s captain happily changed his plans when approached by Winston and offered a fortune for the use of his ship.

Chapter Fifteen

"What are you thinking, sweetheart?" Diablo asked, his voice a husky purr. They had just made love and Devon still lay warm and trembling in his arms. Only much too introspective for Diablo's liking.

"Nothing important, Kit." In their private moments Devon nearly always called him Kit. It didn't seem right to call one's husband "Devil."

Diablo refused to let the matter rest. "Are you so unhappy here on Paradise?"

"Oh, no, it's not that."

"Then what? I know Carlotta is a terrible burden, but she'll soon be gone."

"Carlotta's not the problem," Devon said with a hint of sadness. "You'll leave soon, your men are getting restless, and so many things could happen to you while you're gone."

"Do you care so much?"

"I—I've always cared. I realize you must sail soon to keep your men happy, but I can't help wondering what will happen to me should you fail to return."

Diablo frowned. He had given that nagging worry much thought of late. "Nothing is going to happen to me, sweetheart."

"You can't be certain, Kit. Will your men choose lots to see who gets me if, God forbid, you're killed or captured? What if there's a child?"

"Are you—"

"No, but it's bound to happen."

"Are you suggesting that I give up piracy?" In truth the

idea had been much on his mind of late. So were Devon's thought-provoking questions. Having a wife was so new to him that he hadn't yet become accustomed to considering someone else's feelings besides his own.

"If you truly cared for me you'd give up the dangerous life you lead. Aren't you rich enough?"

"Aye," Diablo admitted grudgingly. "I suppose I am. Enough to keep you and our children in comfort for life with a good bit left over."

"Then give it up, Kit. We can stay here and raise sugar cane, or settle anywhere you say. I know England is out of the question, but what about America?"

"Is preserving my life so important to you? I hardly know what to think, you guard your emotions so close."

Devon hesitated. Though Diablo freely admitted his love for her, she had yet to utter those words. Fear held her back. Fear that the vast differences in their lives and circumstances would one day tear them apart. Yet she loved him more than her own life.

"Your life is—is more precious to me than my own," Devon admitted slowly. The words did not come easily. She had withheld them so long it was like losing a part of herself. She wanted to say she loved him, but for the time being this must suffice. "I know you still don't trust me, but I can live with that as long as you don't hate me."

"Hate you! God's bones, woman, you're everything to me. I loved you even when I thought I hated you. Does it hurt so much to say the words? Why can't you express your feelings like a normal woman?"

"Fear," Devon whispered. "Stark fear. There are so many things conspiring against us, I don't want to tempt fate. You know as well as I that there can be no real future for us as long as you continue to ply the seas for plunder."

"You want me to give up my wicked ways?" Diablo teased, flashing the dimple Devon loved so much. Since returning to Paradise he had shaved his beard, exposing the devastating dimple in his cheek.

"Can you? Will you?" Devon was so serious that Diablo immediately sobered, maintaining a tense silence that made Devon fear she had angered him.

"Aye," he said finally. "I've given a great deal of thought lately to choosing another profession."

Devon was stunned; she hadn't expected Diablo to capitulate so easily.

"Oh, Kit, you don't know how happy that makes me!" she cried, throwing herself into his arms. "When? How? Where?" She had so many questions they came tumbling from her mouth one after another.

Diablo laughed. "Not so fast, sweetheart. When I return from Nassau I'll share my plans with you. But at the moment I expect you to be appropriately grateful."

"Kit, not again!" Devon squealed as Diablo lifted her and settled her astride his lean hips.

"Aye, sweetheart, and again and again, until I've had my fill. Though I seriously doubt, considering the way I feel now, 'tis likely to happen any time within the next hundred years."

Two days later the *Devil Dancer* sailed out of the cove. She carried a full complement of men in addition to Carlotta and Marlena. Their destination was Nassau where they would collect Carlotta's ransom. Unwilling to expose Devon again to the rough, rowdy men who congregated in Nassau, Diablo left her behind, this time certain she would be safe.

Winston whooped with joy, his grip tightening on the telescope clapped to his eye. "There she is, Block! I knew if we hid long enough in these blasted islands, that blackhearted bastard would show himself. Mark well her course, Block, for we're going in as soon as she's out of sight."

"What if the devil has the woman with him?" Block asked. Jonah Block was the proud owner and captain of the *Mary Jane*, the ship hired by Lord Harvey to rescue his daughter.

"You heard the gossip. Diablo is expected to arrive soon in Nassau to exchange a Spanish don's daughter for ransom. Seems the devil's been up to his old tricks. I'm willing to bet he's not taking Devon with him into that den of iniquity. We'll find out soon enough. Do you think you can find the way in?"

"If there's a way through the barrier reef, Jonah Block will find it," the captain bragged. "Fortunately we stopped in Nassau first and learned Diablo had moved his stronghold. It saved us from endless hours of searching."

"Aye," Winston concurred. "Lucky for us that sailor, Patch, held some kind of grudge against Diablo. He didn't mind at all repeating the rumor that Diablo had moved his stronghold to another spot on his island. Since I already knew the exact location of Paradise, the rest was easy, although we lost considerable time and nearly ran aground trying to reach the bloody village by sailing inside the reef."

"Aye, who would have thought there'd be so many bloody sandbars blocking our path?"

Once the *Devil Dancer* slipped into a passage between two cays and was out of sight, Winston ordered the *Mary Jane* out of the hidden inlet of a neighboring cay. When they neared the dangerous reef, Captain Block set a parallel course, guiding his ship with an expertise born of years of experience. When they located the place he'd been looking for, Block turned the wheel and sailed directly into the reef, apparently bound for total destruction. Winston gripped the rail and waited for the crunch and jolt of the hull being ripped apart by the jagged coral. But Block was a skilled seaman who had marked well Diablo's passage earlier. His only concern was that the *Mary Jane*'s six-foot draft might not be shallow enough to scrape clear of the reef. It was—just barely. And to Winston's amazement they were safely inside the reef.

The river was much more difficult to find, but Winston used his previous knowledge of the secrets of Paradise to good advantage. It took nearly the entire day to locate the entrance to the cove. Rather than wait till morning, they sailed in at twilight, anchoring a short distance from shore.

"Shall I order the guns out?" Block asked, eying the peaceful village with misgivings. It was obvious that none of the pirates had remained behind, and Block wasn't the type of man who enjoyed senseless killing.

"Nay," Winston decided. "There's nothing to be gained from it. I intend to go in after Devon and get out as quickly as possible." He recalled Lord Harvey's dismay over the previous shelling and had promised him he'd not take innocent lives unless necessary. "I'll take a landing party ashore immediately."

Devon stretched lazily, enjoying the spectacular sunset descending over the peaceful cay. The sight was so inspiring she hated to go inside. Besides, the house seemed so cold and empty since Diablo had left that morning for Nassau with Carlotta and Marlena. She had no idea when he'd return, certainly not until he had Carlotta's ransom in hand. How pleasant it would be without the disruptive and volatile woman around to whine and complain.

Devon looked forward to Diablo's return for more than one reason. He had promised to seriously consider giving up piracy during his absence and reveal his plans for their future. Had he finally come to realize they had no future together unless he gave up his wild ways and lived within the law?

They'd been so happy these past weeks, Devon thought wistfully. Diablo gave every indication he had come to trust her again. Hopefully they'd learn the truth about the sneak attack upon Paradise one day, and then nothing would interfere with their happiness.

Suddenly Tara came running from the direction of the village, out of breath and frantic with fright. "There's a strange ship in the cove!"

"Are you certain it's not the *Devil Dancer?*"

"Nay, I'd know the *Devil Dancer* anywhere. "'Tis an English ship."

"Navy?" Devon asked fearfully. "How . . ."

"Nay, 'tis no naval vessel. I can't imagine how they found their way here. They were preparing to come ashore when I left, and I ran all the way back. What shall we do?"

Devon bit deeply into her lower lip, her mind working furiously. "I'll go down to meet them. If there's only one ship, perhaps they mean us no harm."

Tara balked, remembering the last time ships had found their way inside the reef. "Nay, don't go. I fear they're up to some mischief. Come with me, I know a perfect hiding place. Diablo would want me to keep you safe."

"Do what you want," Devon shrugged. "I'll go alone if I must."

It hadn't occurred to Devon to hide. Why would the English wish her harm? She considered it a good omen that they hadn't shelled the village and felt it her duty to greet the visitors. Perhaps Diablo had sent them.

She arrived in the village out of breath and panting from her exertion just as two longboats filled with armed men scraped against the shore. Immediately spotting the assortment of weapons the landing crew carried, Devon panicked. What if Tara was right? she asked herself. What if these men meant her harm? As the men leaped from the boat and splashed ashore, Devon came to a sudden decision. Turning on her heel, she fled in the opposite direction, hoping to lose herself in the woods lining the beach.

"There she is! Don't let her get away!" Though the voice was vaguely familiar, Devon did not stop to investigate. Only when she heard someone call out her name did she hesitate. "Devon, don't run! 'Tis Winston."

She skidded to an abrupt halt. "Winston?" She turned slowly and waited for her ex-fiancé to catch up to her. "What are you doing here?"

"Your father sent me. He's worried sick about you."

"How did you find your way inside the reef?"

"That's not important. What does matter is that I found you and you're going home. We'll be married immediately."

"I won't go," Devon refused, backing away. "Didn't you get my note? I came with Diablo willingly. I'm his—his woman."

"Obviously the man has cast some kind of spell over you," Winston said disgustedly. "But don't fret, dear, I'll not hold it against you. Our wedding will take place just as planned. Come along."

"Nay, I won't go," she repeated stubbornly.

Winston's eyes narrowed. He was vividly aware that Diablo had been bedding Devon and probably had from the very first. But that bothered him less than the knowledge that he couldn't afford to lose Devon's fortune.

"I didn't risk my life to come away empty-handed," Winston pronounced with grim determination.

Before Devon realized what he intended, Winston grasped her about the waist and dragged her toward the beach. "Let me go!" she shrieked, aware that no one was likely to come to her aid.

"Stop struggling, Devon, 'twill do you no good."

"I can't leave like this. What will Diablo think?"

"Let him think what he will."

It was like a repetition of a bad dream. Only this time Devon was leaving the island against her will. But Diablo wouldn't know that, he'd think she'd left him, just like the last time. The fragile love that had grown between them these past weeks would wither and die if he was given no explanation. That thought brought a renewal to her struggles.

Winston cursed. "If you don't come quietly, I'll order Captain Block to shell the island. What will your lover think when he returns and finds nothing but rubble?"

Devon's struggles ceased instantly. "Nay, please, Winnie, there are innocent lives to consider. I'll go with you willingly if you promise not to destroy the village."

"Now you're being sensible, dear. I see no reason to attack women and children." He took her arm and propelled her toward the beach.

"You did once," Devon accused. "I know it was your *Larkspur* that attacked Paradise while Diablo was elsewhere, destroying the village and killing dozens of people."

"I don't know where you heard that," Winston denied, refusing to meet her glare. The less Devon knew about that fiasco, the better.

Devon would have delved more deeply into the matter, but they had reached the beach now and Winston lifted her into the longboat while two dozen armed men looked on. As soon as she was settled they all scrambled into the boats and shoved off, rowing at a furious pace to where the *Mary Jane* rode at anchor.

Seething with rage, Tara watched as Devon calmly accompanied the Englishmen to their ship. She had failed to see Devon's struggles earlier, and was aware only of her willingness to leave Paradise. It broke her heart to think this should happen when Devon had finally won Tara's trust. Tara pitied Diablo, for she knew he loved Devon with all his heart. How could Devon abandon Diablo so easily? Did she have no feelings? No conscience?

Hours later, her heart heavy, her cheeks wet with tears, Devon watched sadly as the *Mary Jane* carefully cleared the reef and set a course for England.

* * *

A few days later Diablo made a triumphant return to Paradise. Don Esperez had been so anxious to have his daughter back that her ransom arrived on time, delivered in person by Carlotta's elderly fiancé. When he saw the man, Diablo better understood the desperation that drove Carlotta. Don Fernando was probably older than Carlotta's father. His stern, dark visage and proud bearing left little doubt that he'd accept no foolishness from the youthful Carlotta. Still, Diablo thought the fiery senorita would prove more than a handful for her elderly husband.

Carlotta's plight was complicated by Marlena's adamant refusal to accompany her mistress home. When it came time to leave, Marlena clung to Kyle with desperate pleas that she be allowed to stay. Anguish twisted Kyle's handsome features, for he had come to care a great deal for the little maid. In the end he proposed marriage, and Diablo invited Marlena to accompany them back to Paradise. He knew that Devon would welcome another woman on the island, and it would certainly ease Kyle's mind to have Marlena safe on Paradise.

Carlotta was livid, flying into a rage and ordering Marlena to accompany her aboard the Spanish ship that would carry her home. But for once in her life Marlena obstinately refused to obey her mistress, saying she had nothing to look forward to in Spain but a life of servitude. She had chosen to remain with the man she loved, and nothing could change her mind.

Taking over the wheel, Diablo sailed the *Devil Dancer* into the cove, noting with satisfaction that all appeared serene in the little village. Several women could be seen engaged in various chores and children cavorted in the surf. With an expert hand he maneuvered the ship into its berth beside the pier and ordered the gangplank run out. He was the first to leap ashore, leaving Akbar and Kyle to tend to the docking. Anxious to see Devon and discuss his new plans for their future, Diablo raced all the way to the house. During the time he was gone he had decided to give up piracy and devote himself to legal pursuits.

Such was Diablo's preoccupation that he took little notice of the people gathered on the beach to welcome him, or their pitying expressions. Everyone on Paradise was aware of Diablo's obsession with Devon and what her leaving was likely to do to him. They watched in silent commiseration as he walked briskly toward his house.

Tara came out to meet him, her face grim, her generous mouth tightened into a thin line. Diablo scarcely noticed his housekeeper, looking past her for his first glimpse of Devon. When she failed to appear, he looked questioningly at Tara, her expression sending his heart plummeting.

"Nay, not again!" he cried, refusing to acknowledge what Tara's expressive features revealed. "Tell me it's not true!"

"I can only speak what I know," Tara replied with infinite compassion. She hated to be the one to disillusion Diablo, but there was no help for it. "Your wife is gone."

"How? Why? I know Devon wouldn't leave here willingly. Who carried her off? Were they corsairs?"

"Pirates? Nay, English. An English ship arrived the same day the *Devil Dancer* left the cove. I urged Devon to hide, but she refused. Instead, she walked to the beach to meet the intruders. I hid in the woods and watched Devon speak to one of the Englishmen. Then she left with him aboard his ship."

"You mean she was taken against her will, don't you?" Diablo asked hopefully.

A long, tense silence ensued as Tara carefully considered her reply. "I saw no struggle. Devon simply walked with the man to the beach, and he carried her out to the longboat."

Torn between disbelief and rage, Diablo cried out, "God's bones, she's played me for a fool once too often! Her lying lips drip with honeyed words that hold no meaning."

"What is it, Diablo?"

Diablo whirled to find Kyle and Marlena standing behind him, having walked up from the village at a slower pace.

"Devon's gone, Kyle. The little bitch left aboard an English ship."

"That's impossible," sputtered Kyle, stunned. "How in the hell could a strange ship find its way in here?"

"There's only one way," Diablo said grimly. "They were spying on us when we left the cay. Tara said they arrived the same day we left, so I assume they were hidden somewhere nearby, watching our comings and goings.

"I can't believe the lass would leave without a word," Kyle refuted. "She loves you." Marlena added her own agreement to Kyle's words.

"The woman is incapable of love," Diablo observed with a bitterness born of shattered pride. "Her words, her actions, were lies meant to beguile me until the time came for her to leave. Akbar has the right idea. Women are good for but one purpose, to be used for what God intended them and promptly discarded."

"Had you listened to me you would have been shed of the witch long ago," Akbar said with a scowl, arriving in time to hear nearly all the conversation. "No woman is worth the anguish you're suffering."

"Perhaps you haven't met the right woman, Akbar," Tara injected, her dark eyes hinting that she might be the woman to teach the Turk about love and trust.

The beautiful Indian woman had long admired Akbar, for his cunning, his courage, and his devotion to Diablo. But thus far she hadn't been able to crack the hard shell of mistrust guarding Akbar's heart. Though she had tried many times to prove herself worthy of his trust, Akbar had made it perfectly clear he had no use for her—or any woman. But Tara stubbornly refused to relent, hoping that one day Akbar would notice her many fine qualities and regard her with fondness.

Akbar slanted Tara a sharp glance, then promptly ignored her. Actually, he wasn't as immune to Tara as he let on. Little by little her gentle nature and loving regard were beginning to erode the wall around his heart, but he refused to acknowledge it. He had lived too long with his reputation to change now.

"Aye, you were right, Akbar," Diablo agreed bitterly. "I loved too deeply and unwisely."

"Are you going after the lass?" Kyle asked, ready to risk life and limb to reunite Diablo with his wife.

"Nay!" Diablo thundered, glowering fiercely. "Not this time. I know when I'm defeated. Round up the men, we sail with the tide in search of riches and adventure. The first ship sailing to England from Nassau will carry a letter to Devon telling her I never want to see her again. If she ever steps foot on Paradise or anywhere in this part of the world, she'll find herself in deep trouble for I'll not be charitable a second time."

Diablo sprawled drunkenly in a chair at the Wheel of Fortune Inn, resting his swimming head in his hands, the image of utter dejection. He'd kept the *Devil Dancer* at sea two months, attacking, pillaging, robbing, until his men had had their fill and insisted on putting in at Nassau to replenish their supplies and slake their lust with the many whores plying their trade in the rough port. First he set Kyle and those of his men with women ashore at Paradise, but Diablo did not tarry there himself. Already too many ghosts were haunting him without spending a night in the house where he and Devon had loved one another all those long, passion-filled nights.

He missed her, missed her with a deep abiding ache that often plunged him into a despair so profound he could not find his way out. More nights than he cared to count he drank himself into a stupor, hoping to lose himself in a drunken mist of forgetfulness. On most nights he succeeded, but when he failed, Devon appeared in his dreams to plague his darkest moments and plunge him into the depths of hell. If he weren't such a brilliant captain, drunk or sober, his crew would have replaced him long ago.

Now, blurry-eyed and disheveled, he paid little heed to the ruckus around him as he concentrated on filling his glass without spilling a drop. He failed miserably.

"What in the hell have you done to yourself?"

Diablo raised his heavy head, squinting as two wavering figures finally merged into one stunning redhead. He grinned crookedly. "God's bones, Scarlett, you're a sight for sore eyes. Sit down, both of you. Join me in a drink."

"Haven't you had enough?"

He flashed a roguish grin, reminiscent of the Diablo of old, his bold black beard enhancing the aura of mystery surrounding him. "Who's to say what's enough?"

"That highborn bitch has done this to you, hasn't she?" Her words were met with a black scowl. "Did you think I wouldn't hear how you're making a fool of yourself over a woman? Word spreads quickly in this part of the world."

"My problems are no one's business. I don't want to talk about D—her."

"First we'll get some food in you and then put you to bed," Scarlett said briskly. She turned to speak to a passing serving wench, then sat down to wait until the food arrived. After watching him eat a meal he scarcely tasted, she engaged a room and helped Diablo up the stairs and into bed. Then she flopped down beside him.

The next morning, Diablo awoke slowly. Dawn had arrived with subtle hints of mauve dusting the dingy room. His head was pounding; he couldn't remember when he'd last awakened without a fuzzy brain and thick tongue. As he stretched and tested his limbs, he became aware of a softness pressed against him, and the word slipped smoothly over his tongue. "Devon."

Scarlett stirred, snuggling closer. "Are you awake?"

"Ummm," Diablo answered dreamily, savoring the delicious softness he'd missed so desperately these past months. "God's bones, I've missed you, sweetheart." In his heart he knew it wasn't Devon teasing his flesh, but he couldn't bear another day of emptiness, so he pretended. The dream was too real, too vibrantly sensual to give up so soon. "Devon."

"You bastard! Your precious Devon is gone," Scarlett lashed out. "Wake up and realize I'm flesh and blood, not some elusive dream."

He was fully awake now, and enough light filtered into the room for Diablo to see a naked and enraged Scarlett bending over him. "What in the hell are you doing here?"

"I slept here last night, remember?"

Diablo frowned, the effort bringing a frustrated groan to his lips as he recalled Scarlett helping him up the stairs. Then he drew a blank, for he had no recollection of what transpired afterwards. He tried to rely on humor to placate Scarlett, but she merely snorted in disgust when he said, "I hope I pleased you."

"Please me! How could you please me when you fell asleep almost immediately?" Suddenly her expression softened and she ran her hand along the hard ridges of his chest. "But now that you're awake it wouldn't take long to put you in the right mood to please me. I know what you like, Diablo." Her hand slid beneath the sheet draped loosely around his middle, boldly brushing against his manhood.

Diablo jerked, but not from desire as Scarlett assumed. In the first place, she wasn't Devon. In the second place, he needed a drink. And lastly, as expert as he knew Scarlett to be, his body might cooperate but his mind rejected the idea of making love with anyone but Devon.

"I'm in no condition to make love, Scarlett," Diablo hedged. "Besides, I need a drink."

"Has the witch stolen your balls?" Scarlett said with a smirk, her disparaging remark not only vulgar but hitting a raw spot.

Had Devon hurt him so terribly that she had robbed him of his manhood? Diablo wondered bleakly. Since Devon had left him he'd bedded no other woman, wanting no one but his wife to lavish his love upon. Abandoning him as she did had turned him into a bitter lush who found solace in a bottle. Suddenly it all became quite clear, though he had rejected Kyle's dire predictions that he was on his way to self-destruction. Hearing Scarlett echo his friend's sentiments just now opened his eyes. He had become a man mired in self-pity, traveling the well-worn path to total ruin. Only Devon had the power to change him, and she had chosen to leave him, Diablo thought despondently.

"Leave me alone, Scarlett," he growled testily. "I didn't ask for your help and I certainly don't need your pity."

"Have you forgotten how Devon left with Le Vautour?" Scarlett baited. "The moment you turned your back she was gone. Is it any wonder she did it again?"

Diablo's eyes narrowed suspiciously. He never did find out how Le Vautour had learned the secret of Paradise Island. "What do you know about it? I never considered that you, one of the brotherhood, would betray me. Did you? Did you tell that bastard Le Vautour how to find Paradise?"

"We've been through too much together, Diablo," Scarlett lied smoothly, afraid of Diablo's reaction should he learn the truth. "I believe Le Vautour chanced upon the entrance by accident. Or he spied on you."

Had Diablo not been so hung over he would have debated the point, but feeling as rotten as he did and unwilling to pursue so painful a subject as Devon, he dropped the issue. "Just get out of here. But if I ever find out differently, you'll wish for an easy death."

Scarlett flounced out of bed, flaunting her voluptuous charms before him. "I don't know why I bother with you, I have lovers aplenty. Call me when you're in better humor."

She began throwing on her clothes, ignoring Diablo's sour look. Scarlett hadn't been in Diablo's bed since Devon came into his life and it drove her wild with jealousy. The little witch had ruined him for any other woman. Someday, she didn't know when or how, Scarlett vowed to get even with Lady Devon Chatham.

Chapter Sixteen

Woodes Rogers, a former privateer, had been given permission by King George of England to develop the Bahamas. It was April when his expedition reached New Providence Island. His arrival marked the beginning of the end of the golden era of piracy in the Caribbean. Rogers' first order of business was to wipe out the pirates who made Nassau their home base. He was received royally in the town amidst cheering men and much merrymaking. At the end of the feasting and drunken revelry, Rogers, speaking for the king, offered unconditional amnesty to men who willingly denounced piracy and embraced a new way of life.

Before the week was out, over six hundred pardons had been granted. Among the receivers were Diablo, Scarlett, Kyle, and after much soul-searching, Akbar. Hardened pirates like Blackbeard and Calico Jack departed for other bases. Eventually some of the men who accepted amnesty drifted back into the life, while the smart ones took their treasures and settled elsewhere. A good number went back to their homes to eventually die in poverty. Many ended up in England.

Diablo had debated long and hard before deciding to accept amnesty. He didn't like what he had become or where his life was leading. Kyle was all for changing his way of life, especially since he had Marlena to think about. Piracy was being eradicated the world over, so he was all for accepting amnesty and beginning anew. Akbar wasn't too certain about living a dull, conventional life, but if Diablo decided to live within the bounds of the law, he could do no less than give it a try.

Diablo, one of the wealthiest pirates, sailed boldly into London harbor several weeks later, flying the Union Jack from the *Devil Dancer*'s tallest mast. Despite the harsh words written in a letter to Devon, Diablo knew he was in England only because of the love he bore her—a love that refused to die though he had tried to pound it to death with alcohol and unnecessary danger. One day, when his good name was restored, he would find Devon and try to make her understand that the letter was a result of the terrible pain he was suffering.

Upon hearing that Diablo had accepted amnesty, Scarlett followed him to England a few weeks later, the hold of the *Red Witch* carrying enough wealth to last several lifetimes.

"Come now, m' dear, don't you think Winston deserves better than you've accorded him?"

"I told you before, Father, I can't marry Winston. I don't love him."

Lord Harvey sighed wearily, having gone over the subject time and again. "There's plenty of other swains around, take your pick." Devon chose not to reply. "I know you fancy yourself in love with Diablo, but a young and impressionable girl like you is easily duped into submitting to the base desires of a man with his experience. He obviously has worked some sort of magic on you. How else can you explain your fascination with him? What hold does he have over you?"

"There was no magic involved, Father," Devon replied, sick unto death of being badgered, no matter how kindly. "I love Diablo, and he loves me. Or he did before Winston carried me off. Now he hates me."

"How do you know that?"

Devon sighed dejectedly, unwilling to reveal the extent of Diablo's hatred and how she knew for certain how he felt. "I just know."

"Be reasonable, Devon," the earl cajoled. "There's no future for you with that—that pirate."

Devon deliberately withheld the knowledge that Diablo had made her his wife. What purpose would it serve other than upsetting her father more than he already was?

"I purposely refrained from delving too deeply into the relationship between you and Diablo," the earl said slowly, "and I won't do so now. You're my daughter, and I love you no matter what occurred. But it seems to me if Winston is still eager to marry you despite your—er—adventure, you should at least consider his proposal. You were willing enough once to have him as your husband."

"That was before . . ." Her words faltered and she fell silent, letting her father draw his own conclusion.

"Aye, before that devil got his hooks into you," the earl muttered, tossing his hands up in defeat. "If you want that scoundrel so badly, I'll see that you're taken back to him. That's the least I can do to make you happy."

Devon blanched, recalling the letter delivered to her one day when her father was away. It was a message from Diablo spewing hatred and vile accusations and telling her he never wanted to see her again. He promised swift retribution if she showed up on Paradise again.

"Nay, Father, I can't go back. Diablo doesn't want me. Don't speak of it again."

The poor earl was truly puzzled by Devon and was sorry he'd had her dragged back to England against her will, but if she wouldn't return to the man she professed to love, then why wouldn't she consider Winston? "What do you have against Winston?"

Suddenly Devon recalled the odd things Diablo had said about Winston. "Father, have you heard anything—er—any strange gossip involving Winston?"

"Everyone has his enemies, m'dear. You know I put no store in gossip. Winston risked his life to restore you to me. I personally find no fault with the man. His father died while you were gone, making him a duke."

Truth to tell, Lord Harvey had heard odd snippets of gossip about Winston, but could put no truth to it. Rather than add to Devon's distress he kept it to himself. As far as he was concerned, any misgivings he harbored about Winston's life-style had been laid to rest when he succeeded in wresting Devon from Diablo's lair.

"Viscount, duke, it makes little difference to me," Devon said. "I can't marry Winston."

"Will you at least see him, and give him a chance to court you again?"

"Father, I—"

"For me, Devon, please. It's not doing your reputation any good to remain a recluse. Everyone knows you disappeared on the eve of your wedding, and all our friends are wondering why you deserted Winston at the altar. Fortunately, most believed my explanation that you'd had second thoughts and needed time by yourself to think. I hinted that you went to the country in order to reach a decision. Now that you've returned, I think it wise for you and Winston to be seen in public together."

"All right, Father," Devon agreed reluctantly, worn down by the earl's badgering. "I'll see Winston socially, but nothing will come of it."

Lord Harvey watched his beloved daughter walk from the room, saddened by the change in her. And all because of that devil's spawn, Diablo. It was obvious the girl pined for him. He could kill the man for what he did to her. Not only had he taken her innocence, but he had ruined her for any other man. Devon didn't have to reveal what happened on that island, Lord Harvey was no fool. Devon was young, beautiful, and desirable, no man could resist her. He blamed his daughter for none of the terrible things that had befallen her. She had been taken forcefully and made to bend to Diablo's will. Love, bah! The man didn't know the meaning of the word, and now Devon was suffering for it. Why couldn't Diablo have been hanged that day as the good Lord intended?

Christopher Linley paced back and forth in short, jerky motions across the palace antechamber, waiting for his private audience with the king. He had waited over two weeks for the meeting, and now that the moment had arrived he wondered what the hell he was doing here. Did he really want to reclaim his title after all these years? The answer was simple. Before he could approach Devon, he had to establish himself in society.

He had thought a great deal about Devon these past weeks, and the reason behind her leaving. It was much easier to do with a clear head. Kyle had been right, he had been destroying himself with drink without taking time to sufficiently analyze the situation. What he discovered had shocked him. Deep in his heart he felt Devon loved him, and that her reasons for leaving could be explained if he gave her a chance. He should have given himself time to think before sending off that letter, but his pride had been wounded and his heart broken. At the time he truly felt he never wanted to see her again. He had no idea he would see her night after night in his dreams and spend every waking hour thinking about her.

But first things first. He'd not confront his wife until he was the Duke of Grenville and a social equal. If the king refused to grant his petition, he'd join Blackbeard and men of his ilk in new ventures, and try his damnedest to forget the woman he loved.

The door opened and the king's secretary motioned him inside. Squaring his broad shoulders, Diablo walked into the king's chamber, his steps sure, his composure steady. Kit had no fear over his appearance, for he was impeccably groomed in the latest fashion, clean-shaven, and wearing a huge powdered wig, which he hated. He intended to throw it away the moment he reached home. Christopher Linley bore no resemblance to the fierce pirate feared by mankind. And if the king favored his petition, he'd be free to assume his rightful place in society and claim his wife.

Two hours later Kit left the king's chambers, his step lighter, his tanned face wreathed in a smile that crinkled the corners of his eyes. Without interrupting once, King George had listened to his story, fascinated by the tale of conspiracy, murder, and piracy. He scowled deeply upon learning that Kit's uncle had paid to have him abducted and murdered, but somehow his plan had gone awry. At times the story sounded so improbable that if the king hadn't known Kit's father personally he wouldn't have believed it. But King George recognized the Linley gray eyes and strong chin immediately. Besides, Kit was able to provide intimate details of his family which no one but the true heir could possibly know. The ring with the family crest on it was further evidence of his identity. Diablo had hung on to it throughout the years with a tenacity he could never understand.

Confessing that he was the infamous Diablo had nearly been Kit's undoing, for that feared and hated name brought an immediate reaction from the monarch. If Kit hadn't been determined to begin a new life, he might not have felt compelled to reveal his secret. Thank God he had persuaded King George that the life he led had been the natural result of his uncle's deceit and grew out of those desperate years he had endured more than any young lad ought to.

King George was sympathetic, but what really convinced him to look favorably on Kit's petition to reclaim his estate and title was the fortune in precious gems Kit presented to the monarch. It was a magnificent offering, but one Kit could well afford. As the king pointed out, since amnesty had been offered and duly accepted, he could hardly deny a repentant subject and duke of the realm—a very rich duke—his request to give a present to the king.

When Kit left the palace he had in his possession a document stripping the title from Winston Linley and restoring everything to Christopher, the long-lost heir. Kit had suggested that his other identity not be made public for obvious reasons, and the king had readily agreed. Kit had decided on some vague story involving kidnapping and loss of memory to satisfy the inquisitive. The less said about Diablo, the better.

"My God, Kit, why now? After all these years! Why couldn't you remain dead? You said you didn't care about the title, why did you come back? You realize, of course, that there's little money left. Father went through the bulk of your inheritance before he died."

Eying his imposing cousin malevolently, Winston felt his world come tumbling down around him. His respectability, his prestige, such as it was, everything he took for granted in life was suddenly being wrested away by someone who should have died years ago.

"I don't need money," Kit claimed, thoroughly enjoying seeing his cousin squirm. It was all he could do to keep from tearing the man apart limb from limb for the devastation he had wrought on Paradise. Winston was also probably the one who had carried Devon away from him. But in order to protect his identity, Kit could not confront the coward with the foul deeds he had perpetrated. Kit felt no compassion for his cousin, no need to take care of his future. Though he had no proof, Kit strongly suspected that Winston had known of his father's plan to do away with him. Aye, he had every right in the world to hate Winston.

"I suppose you'll want me out of here," Winston said tightly.

"I believe that would be best." Kit fought the urge to tell Winston that he was Diablo and Devon was his wife. All in good time, he thought, all in good time. Once he was firmly established and acknowledged as the Duke of Grenville, he'd find a way to punish Winston for his misdeeds. First he needed to see Devon, tell her the letter had been a mistake, and persuade her father to think of him as a son-in-law. Linley Hall needed a duchess, and no one but Devon would do.

"How am I supposed to live?" whined Winston. "I'm deeply in debt, my creditors are hounding me, and I've lost my fiancée."

"Are you referring to the heiress you were engaged to?" Kit probed.

Winston scowled. "Something—happened and the wedding was postponed. She's yet to set a date, and I doubt she'll have me once she learns I'm not only penniless but stripped of my title."

"The title was never yours," Kit reminded quietly.

"So you're tossing me out to fend for myself," Winston observed bitingly.

"You've had use of my title and money all these years, be content I'm not demanding restitution. Get out of my home, Winston, before I change my mind. Let me know where to send your things."

"You're a bloody devil, Kit," Winston gritted from between clenched teeth, his choice of words bringing a smile to Kit's lips. "What I'd really like to know is where you've been hiding all these years and how you obtained your fortune. Why did you decide to come forth now after all these years? I'll wager that's a tale worth telling. You couldn't have come by your wealth honestly. For now, I've no recourse but to leave, seeing as how the king granted your petition. We may be kin, but one day you'll pay dearly for what you've done to me."

He slammed out of the house, aware that his future depended on his ability to convince Devon to marry him. If not, he'd end up in debtor's prison.

Devon primped before the mirror, unable to muster enthusiasm for tonight's ball. Winston would be here soon, and she fervently wished she hadn't indulged her father by agreeing to accompany Winston to the party. She had disappointed him so often lately that she hadn't been able to resist his pleading in Winston's behalf. She also felt pity for Winston after learning that his long-lost cousin had returned after all these years to claim the dukedom. Devon knew it was a blow to Winston's pride, especially after years of considering himself the sole heir to the Linley estate. Though she wasted no love on Winston, Devon felt sorry for him.

Devon wondered how it could be that a man considered dead for years should suddenly show up alive and possessing great wealth. She had suggested he might be an impostor, but Winston assured her the man was indeed Christopher Linley and had a ring with the family crest he'd held onto all these years to prove it. Idly Devon wondered if she would meet the new duke tonight, for she knew he had been invited to the Smythes' party. For some unexplained reason a tingle of excitement raced up her spine at the prospect.

Winston's predicament wasn't the only problem plaguing Devon. She had finally accepted the fact that she was carrying Diablo's child. She had suspected it for weeks but refused to believe it until she began vomiting each morning upon arising. Tender breasts and having missed two monthly cycles added to her conviction. Somehow she had to find the nerve to tell her father, but as yet hadn't found the right moment. Weeks ago she would have welcomed the pregnancy, but now she wasn't so certain. Not that she wouldn't love Diablo's child, for she would, with her whole heart and soul.

Unable to delay the inevitable, Devon heaved a fretful sigh and left the room to join Winston, where he awaited her at the bottom of the stairs. She was surprised that Winston had been invited to the prestigious affair since he had been demoted to his old title of viscount. Perhaps the fact that the golden-haired Freddie Smythe and Winston were close friends accounted for Winston's invitation. Devon knew it couldn't be easy for Winston to lose everything he held dear as well as face the new duke tonight in public, and she felt a stirring of pity despite the fact that she hadn't forgiven him for carrying her away from Diablo against her will.

Kit arrived at the Smythes' palacious home while the party was in full swing, a gorgeous redhead gracing his arm. They had arrived fashionably late just so Scarlett could make a grand entrance.

Poised in the doorway, Kit bent to whisper in his companion's ear, "Are you ready, Scarlett? You've been waiting a long time to be presented to society."

"Damn right," Scarlett hissed in reply. Dressed in a gown of vivid purple that should have clashed horribly with her red hair but was actually enhanced by it, Scarlett clung possessively to Kit's arm.

Immensely wealthy from her ill-gotten gains, Scarlett had followed Diablo to London, posing as a rich widow newly arrived from France. Unaware of Diablo's true identity as the Duke of Grenville, she was stunned the day she had encountered him at Lady Davenport's afternoon affair. Since her arrival in London Scarlett had carefully courted the denizens of society, hoping for a smooth entrance into a way of life she had been denied all her life. A quick study, Scarlett had easily mimicked the manners of London's upper crust until she felt quite at home with the rich and titled.

Lady Davenport's affair was the first social function that Kit had attended as Christopher Linley. He had gone primarily to test the waters and gauge his reception by his peers, which proved excellent. He was immensely pleased by what he had accomplished. So pleased, in fact, that he felt confident enough to confront his father-in-law and claim his wife. Encountering Scarlett that afternoon at Lady Davenport's hadn't exactly thrilled Kit.

With the exception of Kyle and Akbar, Kit hoped to avoid all former acquaintances who could identify him as Diablo. When he finally claimed his wife he wanted no stigma attached to her name. So meeting Scarlett had left Kit with an uncomfortable feeling in the pit of his stomach as well as a strange premonition. It didn't help that Scarlett immediately attached herself to him with a tenacity that dismayed him. He held vague misgivings that Scarlett aspired to the title of duchess and sought to stake her claim.

Kit found it difficult to escape Scarlett's persistent badgering and soon became her reluctant escort to the Smythe ball. He couldn't wait to be shed of Scarlett and hoped that one of the many swains vying for the attention of the beautiful, rich "widow" would succeed in luring her from his side.

Chapter Seventeen

It occurred to Kit that he might encounter Devon at one of the affairs he had attended recently, but so far he had met neither his wife nor Winston. During his rounds he heard snippets of gossip about Devon and Winston since they were still believed to be engaged. There seemed to be much speculation whether the twice postponed marriage would ever take place now that Winston had lost the coveted title of duke.

Kit surveyed the room with cool disdain. Though he was officially one of the nobility, he felt little kinship with his own kind, having consorted with pirates and scoundrels most of his adult life. Yet he could not deny his place among them and was prepared to spend the rest of his days living the lawful life he had previously scorned. And all because of the woman he loved more than his own life. When he had found Devon gone from Paradise he tried to despise her, but now all he wanted was to claim her for all time.

"Everyone of importance is here," Scarlett enthused as they approached the intrepid butler whose duty it was to announce the guests.

Her green eyes glowed like emeralds as they swept over the large room congested with opulently dressed women wearing enormous powdered hairdos and satin-clad men sporting wigs. Powdering her hair or wearing a wig was the one current fashion Scarlett decided to forego, preferring her own flaming tresses. Kit bowed to the trend, donning his hated wig as a means of escaping recognition as Diablo.

"Christopher Linley, Duke of Grenville, and Lady De-Foe," intoned the butler loudly, the staccato beat of the long cane against the floor commanding attention.

Dozens of necks craned to observe Kit's slow progress into the room. More than one man envied him his companion, the flamboyant redhead known only as Scarlett DeFoe, a wealthy widow newly arrived in London.

"Bloody hell, I was hoping he wouldn't be here," Winston complained testily.

Devon turned, hoping to catch a glimpse of Winston's mysterious cousin, but she was too late. He and his companion had been swallowed up in a sea of curious people anxious to meet the darkly handsome duke.

Devon had been speaking with an old acquaintance when the duke's name was announced and missed the introduction of his companion.

"Did you know your cousin would be here?" she asked Winston. From what Winston had said, the duke was hardly a paragon of virtue.

"I suspected he might be," Winston allowed sourly, "but hoped he wouldn't. It didn't take him long to find a woman. The redhead on his arm is stunning. Wonder who she is."

The odd premonition that had plagued Devon all evening once again arose on hearing the word "redhead." Then it struck her: Wasn't Kit a shortened version of Christopher?

"Winston, do you call your cousin Kit?" Devon asked, shaking. Her breath came in little puffs of air that left her panting.

"Why, yes, how did you know?"

"Oh God, no! It can't be."

Devon's knees turned to rubber and a shudder passed through her slim form. She clutched her belly as if to protect her child and turned to flee—running straight into Kit's arms. Neither of them could have been more surprised. Unless it was Scarlett. If she thought Diablo no longer cared for Devon, the look on his face instantly disabused her. In all these weeks he had made no effort to see Devon, and Scarlett had assumed he had finally had his fill of her. Scarlett had no idea they were husband and wife, for Diablo's men had been forbidden to speak of the marriage.

Devon's body responded to his immediately as Kit clutched her close. A thrill of remembered bliss shot through her at the brief contact, and she gazed up into a pair of shuttered silver eyes.

"Is this your fiancé, Winston?" Kit drawled with lazy humor. "You've done well for yourself, she's a raving beauty. Aren't you going to introduce us?"

Scarlett's eyebrows shot up in wonder at what kind of game Diablo—she still had trouble thinking of him as Kit—was playing. She decided to go along with it until she learned his purpose and what she might gain by it.

Reluctantly disentangling herself from Kit's arms, Devon stilled her wildly beating heart, waiting for the devil to make his move. Knowing Diablo as she did, she assumed he would claim her immediately as his wife and find perverse pleasure in making her miserable for the rest of her life.

Winston, decidedly uncomfortable, made hasty introductions. Unwilling to stay and exchange small talk with a man he heartily disliked, Winston turned away to lead Devon onto the dance floor, politely excusing himself.

"I was hoping to dance with Lady Devon," Kit said, staying Devon with a firm grip on her arm. "As the head of the family, I should like to become better acquainted with your bride-to-be." Without waiting for Winston's approval, Kit swept Devon onto the dance floor, leaving a fuming Scarlett behind.

Ignoring Scarlett, Winston stomped away, itching to wrest Devon from Kit's grasp but afraid of causing a scandal. From the corner of his eye he caught a glimpse of Freddie Smythe observing him with unfeigned interest. Nodding his blond head toward the stairs, Freddie waited only until Winston signaled that he understood the implied message before drifting off. Winston waited a discreet interval before following, hopeful of salvaging something from this disastrous evening.

As for Scarlett, she was soon surrounded by men anxious for her attention and had little time to waste on Kit and Devon.

"I've missed you," Kit whispered, his eyes drinking in Devon's features like a man long denied the sustenance essential for life.

"That's odd. Your letter swore eternal hatred. Why didn't you tell me who you were?" Devon hissed in reply. She was angry—damn angry. How could Kit keep his identity from her while knowing that Winston was her fiancé? How could he now say he missed her after writing such a hateful letter? "Are you mad coming here like this? What if someone recognizes you?"

"Forget the letter. I have. After you left I was so hurt and stunned I hardly knew what I was doing. But it no longer matters, sweetheart." Kit grinned roguishly. "Haven't you heard? The king granted unconditional amnesty to pirates of the Caribbean. In return we had to agree to leave the Bahamas and give up piracy."

"And you agreed to that?"

"Aye. Over six hundred men have left the brotherhood. I am no longer in danger of losing my life, and the king has heard my tale and seen fit to grant full restitution of my title and estate."

"What tale? This is the first I've heard of amnesty. I've paid little heed to politics of late."

Devon was just beginning to recover from the shock of seeing Kit and learning he was other than what she knew him to be. All these weeks she had assumed he never wanted to see her again and had wallowed in remorse and dejection. Her first reaction had been one of overwhelming joy, which soon gave way to anger. The thought that Kit had neglected to tell her something as important as his real identity rankled. Surely he could have trusted her to keep his secret, couldn't he?

"Why didn't you tell me you were a duke?"

"What purpose would it serve? That sort of life was denied me. I saw no reason to reveal facts that would only confuse you."

"I'm confused now. Winston told me the Linley heir had disappeared when he was a mere lad. How did it happen?"

Kit could see that Devon was becoming more agitated by the minute and that people were beginning to stare at them. By the time the music stopped he had carefully maneuvered them so they stood close to the open French doors. While they were lost in the crush of people streaming from the dance floor, Kit whisked Devon out the door. Their escape did not go unnoticed as Kit had hoped. Scarlett observed their hasty departure, her green eyes narrowed dangerously.

"What are you doing?" Devon cried. "Take me back inside. Winston will wonder where I disappeared to."

"The hell with Winston," Kit returned tersely. Grasping Devon's small hand, he literally dragged her out into the blackness of the night.

"Wait! Where are you taking me? I don't want to go with you. You hate me, remember?" she taunted.

"I don't hate you, I never did. Will you forget that damn letter, it was a mistake. We need to talk. Privately. We were so conspicuous on the dance floor the gossip mongers were having a ball speculating on our relationship."

Despite Devon's protests, Kit's superior strength easily won out as he propelled her down a path leading to an orchard. When nothing of the house was visible but the twinkling of thousands of lights from the windows, he paused beneath the widespread branches of a gnarled apple tree, releasing Devon's hand long enough to pull her into his arms. With a small cry of surrender she melted into his embrace.

"God's bones, sweetheart, I missed you," he murmured against her lips. "I nearly lost my mind when you left me."

"I didn't leave you, Kit, I was—"

The words died in Devon's throat as Kit's lips slanted over hers, his drugging kiss flooding her mind and body with memories of rapture they once shared. She loved this man, though she had never mouthed the words for fear of tempting fate. Given his profession, it was inevitable they'd be parted one day.

Without breaking the kiss, Kit shrugged off his coat, letting it fall to the ground. Then he sank to his knees, bringing Devon with him.

"Kit, no," Devon pleaded. "You said we needed to talk. I'm ready to listen. Tell me how and why you went from duke to pirate?"

"Later, sweetheart. Can't you see how starved I am for you? I've dreamed of this moment for months. You're the reason I accepted amnesty. You're my wife, Devon, I need you."

"I'm Diablo's wife," Devon denied hotly, "not the wife of Christopher Linley, Duke of Grenville." The hurt of having been deceived sparked her anger. "You're a charlatan, a pirate, a rogue—and worst of all, you lied to me."

"Had you cared to inspect our marriage papers you would have seen my legal name affixed to the document, my love, all legal and aboveboard. And now I'm aching to make love to my wife."

His tongue whispered across her parted lips, then slipped inside to sip the sweet nectar. His hunger for her was enormous, his desire a beast that ruled his body. Then his mouth bent to the high curve of her breast, his breath burning through the thin silk until Devon thought it would burst into flame. She scarcely felt his fingers working on the fastenings at the back of her gown until the cool night air caressed her heated flesh. Kit made no attempt to stifle a groan of frustration as he shoved the delicate material down to her waist. Her shift was the next to go. As if by magic the corset strings parted and moonlight bathed the perfect mounds of her pale alabaster breasts.

The virile scent of arousal teased Devon's highly aroused senses as Kit moved his hips against her, his member instantly erect. Suddenly the pulsing between her thighs became a roaring throb.

With great tenderness Kit pressed her to the ground, sliding his coat beneath her slender body. Then he gently tugged her gown and underthings over her hips until she lay like a gilded statue beneath dancing moonbeams. Kit sat back on his haunches, his silver eyes glowing with rapt appreciation.

"I dreamed of you so often like this. I thought I'd forgotten nothing of your beauty, but when I look at you now I find my memory a poor substitute for reality. You're exquisite, sweetheart, lovelier than I remembered. And I love you just as fiercely."

His erotic words turned her body to putty and her mind to mush as Devon reached out to caress his cheek, sliding down his neck to the buttons on his spotless white shirt. With a will of their own her fingers parted the material and pushed the garment over his broad shoulders. Pulling his arms free, Kit removed his trousers, stockings, and shoes while Devon's hands roamed restlessly over the wide expanse of his chest, his back, the lean curve of his hips. They played teasingly over flat male nipples, through dark, curling hair, wanting to explore further but suddenly turning shy. It had been so long since they'd been together like this.

But Kit was not so inhibited. Taking her hand he moved it to his fully distended member, letting her feel his great need for her. His breath exploded in his chest as her fingers curled around him. His groan echoed through the darkness of the night, eloquently conveying the exquisite torture filling every corner of his mind and body.

"God's bones, sweetheart, your touch sets me afire. Another minute of this torture and I'll leave you behind." Gasping hoarsely, he gently disengaged her hands. "Lie back and let me love you."

His head dipped down and Devon felt the wetness of his mouth on her breast as he licked then suckled first one then the other diamond-hard tip. Her nipples puckered deliciously beneath his tender caresses as he nipped, licked, and pulled them deeply into his mouth. Then abruptly the pleasure abated as Kit's mouth slid downward over her ribcage to sip lovingly at the tiny indent of her navel, and a new pleasure exploded in her loins. Moving restlessly beneath his tender assault, Devon invited deeper caresses by arching upward, and Kit gladly obliged by pushing her thighs apart to nuzzle the mound of tight golden curls he found there.

Cupping his hands beneath her, he pressed the searing heat of his mouth against her, spreading her legs wide. A delicious weakness set her to trembling as Kit's mouth came hungering, dipping into her and exploring her roughly, his tongue bolder and more urgent. She grew dizzy as the bright flame of desire swiftly ignited a blazing ecstasy that brought a low moan of surrender to Devon's lips, and she called out his name in blind and mindless rapture. The first penetration of his tongue brought a shriek to her lips, sending her senses spiraling out of control as tremors of ecstasy jolted through her.

She was half-sobbing when he rose above her at last, and she screamed with incredible pleasure when he plunged deep, deep within her. She screamed again as he stroked her to climax, the sensation so strong and volatile her insides contracted into a hard knot. While Devon writhed and spasmed with exquisite pleasure, Kit had yet to gain his own release, thrusting wildly into her, wanting to reclaim her in the most primitive way. He pierced her deeply, again and again, and then cried out his own rapture.

Embarrassed, she buried herself against the slick dampness

of his chest and tried not to think of all the wanton things she had done.

"Don't be embarrassed, sweetheart," Kit said, his soft breath fanning her cheek. "I love your passion. Don't ever change."

Scarlett didn't linger to see Kit and Devon consummate their love. The moment she saw them sink to the ground she hurried back to the house and began searching for Winston. It was much later when she saw him at the top of the stairs with his arm linked through Freddie Smythe's in a manner suggesting more than friendship. Wise in the ways of the world, Scarlett smiled slyly as she watched the couple part and descend the stairs in a more circumspect manner. She waited until Freddie headed off in a different direction before accosting Winston.

"I must talk to you," she whispered, startling Winston with the intensity of her words. "Alone."

"Of course, Lady DeFoe," he replied, his brows angling upward. He had no idea what his cousin's beautiful companion could want with him. "Let me see if I can find Devon first. I wouldn't want her to think I've deserted her."

"You won't find her, she's not in the house," Scarlett said. "Where can we be alone?"

"The library," Winston returned, recognizing her urgency as he led the way to another part of the house.

The library was deserted and he ushered Scarlett inside where a lamp glowed invitingly. Before Winston could mouth his question, Scarlett blurted out, "They're together, you know."

"What! To whom are you referring?"

"I'm speaking of your cousin and your fiancée."

"Impossible!" Winston denied hotly. "They just met. Has Kit been annoying Devon and creating gossip by dancing with her more often than good manners decree? Where are they now? I should have known Kit would try something like this. Isn't it enough that he took my title?"

"Sweet Jesus, you are dense, aren't you?" Winston had the sense to look affronted. "I saw them just minutes ago in the orchard, engaged in more than friendly banter. Had I chosen to remain I'm certain I would have seen them coupling on the ground like animals."

Winston blanched. "Your assumption is absurd! Devon wouldn't do such a thing. Besides, she and Kit just met."

"Winston, you're either very stupid or incredibly dense," Scarlett snorted. " 'Tis difficult to believe you know nothing about Kit when he's your own kin."

"Know what? For years I thought him dead until he showed up just recently to claim his title and estate. If you know something that I don't, you'd better tell me."

"You've heard of the pirate Diablo, haven't you?" Scarlett asked.

"Of course, who hasn't? But what's that got to do with—" Suddenly comprehension dawned. "Bloody hell!" Winston exploded. "I should have realized something like this when Kit returned rich beyond belief refusing to reveal the mysterious void he's existed in for the past fifteen years." He paused, his mind working furiously. The thought that suddenly occurred to him left his face drained of all color. "If Kit is Diablo, then he and Devon are—are—lovers! Dammit, I won't allow it! I'm bankrupt. I need her dowry to keep out of debtors' prison. If I was hounded by creditors before I lost my title, you can well imagine what it's like now."

"What are you going to do about it?" Scarlett goaded mercilessly. "Obviously Diablo and Devon have resumed their— illicit relationship."

"Why, I'll—I'll . . ." Winston stammered to a halt. Obviously he was no match for his cousin's superior strength and cunning and could do little to wrest Devon from his grasp if Diablo wanted her. Besides, where did Scarlett fit into all this? How had she become so knowledgeable about the pirate? "I sense your concern is more than mere interest. Why are you telling me this?"

Scarlett fixed Winston with a baleful glare. "I have my heart set on becoming Duchess of Grenville. I want Diablo, or Kit, or whatever you care to call him. I've always wanted him. We were lovers before Devon interfered. The only reason I accepted amnesty was so I could follow Diablo to London."

"You're a pirate?" Winston's mouth hung open in stunned disbelief.

"Aye, but that's all in the past. I'm a lady now, and rich enough to be accepted by society."

"What do you want from me?" Winston asked. "I understand Diablo is a ruthless killer who takes what he wants. And he's proven time and again he wants Devon. Only a fool would think himself capable of taking from Diablo something he considers his property."

"Coward!" hissed Scarlett.

"Unless . . ." mused Winston thoughtfully.

"Unless——?" prompted Scarlett.

"If I went to the king and told him about Kit he'd——"

"——do nothing. You are a fool," sneered Scarlett. "The king knows all about Diablo. Don't you understand? It no longer matters who he was. He's been granted amnesty and can no longer be punished for piracy."

"It might make a difference to some people," sniffed Winston, miffed at being considered a fool. "What would you have me do?"

"Take Devon away. Force her to marry you. Anything to keep Diablo from claiming her."

"You're the fool, Lady DeFoe," Winston retorted. "Devon has refused to marry me countless times during the past weeks. Being penniless hardly helps my cause."

"What about her father? Can't you enlist his help? If he

loves his daughter he won't want her involved with a pirate and scoundrel like Diablo, duke or no. He should be grateful to you for wanting to save Devon from Diablo's cluches."

"I can't do it! 'Tis a damn bloody mess! Find some other way to get Kit for yourself."

Scarlett's eyes narrowed into dangerous green slits and her mouth thinned into a stubborn line, which should have given Winston warning of the length she was prepared to go to gain her own end. "You'll do exactly as I say or find yourself ostracized by your peers. Think of Freddie's family. The shame will kill them."

A horrified expression crept over Winston's face. "Wha—what are you talking about?"

"How long have you and Freddie Smythe been lovers?"

Absolute silence reigned as Winston's face turned a sickly shade of green. "I—I—"

Scarlett grinned smugly, Winston's dismay serving to re-inforce her theory. "I wasn't born yesterday. Mayhap you can dupe your peers but you can't fool me, I've seen too much of the world. One has but to see you and Freddie together to know you're lovers."

"That's blackmail!" Winston sputtered lamely. He was astute enough to realize that Scarlett would not stop at vile methods to obtain her goal.

"Aye, I'd attempt anything to get Diablo. I may no longer be a pirate, but I've forgotten nothing of my former life."

"What do you want from me? I'm virtually powerless against my cousin."

"Take Devon someplace where Diablo can't find her. Wed and bed her. Better yet, get her with child. You *are* capable, aren't you?" Scarlett mocked.

"Of course," Winston said uncertainly. Though the idea sickened him, he thought he could perform if he had to. "But I told you before, Devon won't have me. I think she fancies herself in love with Diablo."

"Devil take you! Have you no guts? Use your head, man. If Devon isn't taken to where Diablo can't find her within forty-eight hours, your abnormal sexual preferences will become common knowledge. And Freddie Smythe will be exposed as your lover."

Winston blanched, his mind racing furiously. If Devon refused to marry him, Scarlett's disclosure would make it impossible to pursue another heiress, and he would surely have to flee England or go to prison. His only salvation lay in convincing Lord Harvey that Devon must marry him in order to save her from Diablo. With luck and the earl's cooperation, it could work. The old man loved his daughter and would go to any lengths to save her from a disastrous liaison.

"Well," Scarlett said, tapping her foot impatiently. "Have you come to a decision?"

"Do I have a choice?"

"None that I can see. Where will you take her?"

"If all goes well I'll take Devon to Cornwall. I'm sure Kit has all but forgotten the family hunting lodge near Penzance. We'll be safe enough there until I can arrange a marriage."

"If Devon returns before I'm wed to Diablo, I'll see you ruined," Scarlett warned ominously. "Or perhaps I'll revert to my old ways and slit your gullet. Even if you have to hold her against her will, keep Devon away from London until I send word that I'm Duchess of Grenville."

Winston swallowed the lump of fear rising in his throat. He didn't doubt Scarlett's ability to kill him should she so desire. But instinctively he knew it would take more than his efforts alone to keep Devon confined against her will. First he had to inform Lord Harvey of Kit's identity and impress upon the man the threat that Kit posed to Devon. Next he had to hire a couple of unsavory characters to help carry out his plans. But first there was the problem of money.

"I'll need cash to accomplish all this—hire a carriage,

hire someone to help, feed us while we're in hiding. I have no money. Kit stripped me of everything."

"I'll see to it." Scarlett nodded with smug satisfaction. "Come around in the morning and you'll be taken care of." She turned to leave. "Say nothing of this to anyone if you value your worthless hide."

"You're coming home with me, sweetheart," Kit said, his arms tightening possessively around Devon's slender form. "I'm afraid I'll lose you again if I let you out of my sight. You make a habit of disappearing the moment I turn my back." His voice held a hint of censure, and Devon turned in his arms to peer up at him.

"I didn't want to leave you. Winston threatened to shell the village if I didn't go with him. I couldn't allow that to happen again."

"Bloody bastard!" Kit spat venomously. "I was too easy on the coward. You have no idea the anguish I suffered because of him. The thought that you could leave me so easily nearly broke my spirit, and I became someone I scarcely recognized. I penned the letter to you in a moment of despair so profound it nearly destroyed me. You don't know how often I regretted acting so rashly."

"It didn't take long for you to find solace with another woman," Devon accused, bristling angrily. "How long have you and Scarlett been together?"

"We've never been 'together,'" Kit denied. "Not in the sense you mean. I brought her to the ball tonight for the sole purpose of introducing her to society. Scarlett accepted amnesty and is posing as a rich widow. I've not wanted another woman since the day I saw you. It's always been you—only you I love and want. I've had no other woman since you entered my life."

"Oh, Kit, I love you, too," Devon exclaimed, her mind searching for the words to tell him about the baby. "I was desolate when I thought I'd never see you again. I want to know how and why you disappeared years ago and never returned to claim what was rightfully yours."

"It's a long story, and not a very pretty one."

"Please, Kit, you owe me an explanation."

"My father died when I was a lad, and my uncle, Winston's father, became my guardian," Kit began slowly, all those years of hurt and pain spilling from his memory in a flood of bitterness. "I had no idea my uncle coveted the title and estate for himself and his own son, but, alas, I learned too late the extent of his hatred."

Kit licked his dry lips, recalling the betrayal and disillusionment he suffered as if it happened yesterday. "One day I was abducted from my home by two men hired by my uncle. They were under orders to kill me, but being greedy as well as lawless, they sold me to an unscrupulous sea captain to serve aboard his ship, obtaining his promise never to allow me to go ashore, fearing I'd escape and make my way back to England."

"My God!" Devon gasped, stunned. "Did—did Winston know of this?"

"He says not, but who's to prove or disprove it? His father is dead and there's no one else to question."

"Go on," Devon urged. "How did you become Diablo, and why didn't you return to England to the life you were born to?"

"I served aboard the ship under deplorable conditions nearly ten years before we were attacked by pirates. I chose to join Black Bart's crew rather than meet an untimely end. I was young and strong, and men looked to me as their leader. Fed up with Black Bart's depraved cruelty, the crew asked me to join them in a mutiny. I agreed. We took over the ship in a bloody battle and I was appointed captain. Black Bart was dead and I assumed the name Diablo, deciding to keep my identity a secret."

"You could have gone back to England," Devon suggested.

"By then the lure of excitement and adventure was too great to leave it. I'd been at sea over ten years. I was twenty-three years old and for the first time in full control of my life. Assuming my rightful place as Duke of Grenville held little appeal to me. If my uncle wanted the title so badly, I decided to let him keep it.

"From that day forward I embarked on a career that made it impossible to return to polite society anywhere in the civilized world. I've been Diablo for five years and not regretted one minute of it. And then I met the woman I came to love more than my own life, more than adventure, riches, and freedom to rule the seas. I fell in love, sweetheart, and my life was never the same afterward.

"There's so much sadness in my heart for that young boy," Devon said wistfully. "But life will be different now. I swear I'll make you happy, my love."

"You already have, sweetheart," Diablo vowed earnestly.

Now, Devon decided, was the time to tell Kit about the baby. "There's something—"

"God's bones, sweetheart, we can talk later, at home. I know we still have much to discuss, but I can't wait to have you all to myself in the privacy of our own home. Get dressed."

Kit's words brought back a sense of reality, making Devon aware that this was neither the time nor the place to bring up the subject of their child. She also realized that she couldn't accompany him back to Linley Hall. "Kit, I can't go home with you, not yet," she said, sighing regretfully. "We both owe Father the courtesy of an explanation. I've disappointed him enough already without disappearing again without a word."

"But you're not disappearing, sweetheart, you'll be with me." He couldn't bear the thought of another separation, no matter how short.

"Please, Kit, try to understand," Devon pleaded as she turned to receive Kit's help with the fastenings at the back of her gown. "Father is not a young man. He tries to hide it from me, but he isn't well. Let me prepare him first. Tomorrow we'll tell him together. Come for lunch."

"Dammit, Devon, you're my wife! I want you with me."

"I know, my love, I haven't forgotten. Please humor me in this. I want to be with you more than anything in the world, but what can one more day hurt?"

Reluctantly, Kit agreed, but not just to please Devon. He'd caused Lord Harvey enough heartache in the past without currying his disfavor yet one more time. Fully dressed now, he pulled Devon into his arms, reluctant to part with her, fearing that something was bound to happen the moment she was out of his sight, as it always did. All kinds of strange premonitions played havoc with his mind. Now that he and Devon were happily reunited, why did he sense danger? What could go wrong? he scoffed. Burying his fear beneath an outpouring of emotion, he slanted his mouth across hers, a driving desperation turning his doubt into fierce possession. His kiss softened when he heard a small whimper of protest float past her lips.

"I'm sorry, sweetheart, 'tis just that the thought of losing you again tears me apart. I didn't mean to hurt you."

"Kit, nothing can separate us now," Devon pledged solemnly.

"All right," Kit sighed, finally convinced but still reluctant. "I'll take you home."

"What about Winston and Scarlett?"

Kit frowned. "What about them?"

"Do you think we should let them know we're leaving?"

"The devil take them. I'm taking no chances now that our lives are on the right track. I don't give a damn what they think, we owe them nothing. Come along, sweetheart, my coach is waiting."

Arm in arm they strolled beneath the lovers' moon toward the line of vehicles parked along the circular drive outside the house. Stopping before the handsome carriage bearing the Linley crest, Kit opened the door and boosted Devon into the dark interior. Her gasp of dismay brought him instantly alert.

"What is it, sweetheart?"

"I suspected you'd try something like this." Scarlett's bright red tresses gleamed darkly in the moonlight as she leaned out the door.

"God's bones, Scarlett, why aren't you inside having a good time?"

"I saw you leave the ball with Devon. I'll not be dumped like so much unwanted baggage. We came together and we'll leave together." So saying she settled herself against the squabs, spreading her skirts about her with regal disdain.

Muttering an oath, Kit hauled himself inside, plopping down beside Devon. He'd be damned if he'd allow Scarlett to spoil a perfect evening. He signaled the driver, and the coach took off with a lurch. Then he relaxed, slanting Devon a secret smile that spoke volumes about his love, and his determination that no one would interfere with their lives.

But Scarlett succeeded in thwarting Kit's intentions, refusing to budge from the coach until Devon was taken home. Roaring mad but unwilling to resort to violence, Kit acquiesced with bad grace. He was forced to make do with the goodnight kiss he and Devon shared in the dark shadows of the doorway. Knowing that Scarlett sat fuming in the coach while he bid Devon goodnight added zest to his passion.

At the touch of his lips, Devon melted into Kit's embrace, molding her body into the contour of his hard-muscled form. Her mouth parted beneath the gentle probing of his tongue and Kit ached to partake again of her sweet warmth. Once would never be enough with his fiery love. He had to forcibly stop himself from stripping the silk material from her perfect breasts and savoring the taste and feel of those hard-tipped mounds.

"God's bones, sweetheart, if I don't stop I'll take you right here on your front steps," Kit breathed raggedly. "I'm stupid for not taking you home with me where you belong."

Blushing, Devon reluctantly pulled away, her own breath dangerously shallow. "Nay, Kit, I've already told you, we owe it to Father to explain how things are between us. Tomorrow, my love. Then I don't care if all of London knows we are husband and wife."

"I'm sorry about Scarlett. I should have kicked her out of the coach on her backside."

"Nay, I no longer fear Scarlett. Nor do I doubt your love. Tomorrow will be the beginning of forever."

Their parting kiss left Devon so unnerved she entirely forgot to tell Kit about the baby.

Tomorrow would be soon enough, she thought, smiling dreamily. Tomorrow they would begin their life with the knowledge that they would soon be a family. Tomorrow.

Chapter Eighteen

Reeling groggily, Lord Harvey staggered to answer the insistent racket at the front door. It was long past midnight and the servants had retired to their quarters on the third floor. Shuffling along in slippers and robe and holding a candle aloft, he mumbled a string of oaths. He knew it couldn't be Devon for he had heard her come in earlier. Hastening his steps, he prayed Devon wouldn't be awakened by his late-night caller, whoever he might be.

"I'm coming, I'm coming," he grumbled crossly as the pounding continued. He flung the door open, surprised to see Winston in the doorway beneath the candle's mellow glow. "What! What!" the stunned earl sputtered. "What the devil are you doing here at this hour?"

"Is Devon home?"

"Devon? Are you mad? She hasn't left since you brought her home."

"I didn't bring her home."

"She came home alone?" Lord Harvey asked, frowning with disapproval. "Did you quarrel?"

"N—nay, not exactly," Winston stammered, chosing his words carefully. "She left with my cousin."

"The Duke of Grenville? I wasn't aware that Devon knew the man."

"There are many things you're not aware of," Winston said cryptically.

"Can't it wait till morning?" the earl asked, yawning hugely. "I don't know what possessed you to stop by so late."

"Nay, Your Grace, it can't wait," Winston persisted, shoving his way past the older man. "This needs to be said now."

Seeing no way out of it, Lord Harvey sighed in weary resignation and led the way to his study. "Come along then, m'boy, just keep it brief."

Lord Harvey barely made it to the comfortable chair behind his desk before Winston blurted out, "That devil's got her again! He's put some kind of spell on Devon."

"What in bloody hell are you ranting about?" the earl asked, puzzling over Winston's words, "I thought you said your cousin brought Devon home."

"That's what I've been trying to tell you! My cousin and Diablo are one and the same. The Duke of Grenville *is* Diablo."

"Diablo? The pirate Diablo? He's in London? By God, that man has nerve!" Lord Harvey thundered. "But you're wrong about Devon, she's upstairs in bed. And what does your cousin have to do with that blackhearted scoundrel?" Still not fully awake, only half of what Winston said registered on the older man's mind.

"Have you heard nothing of what I've said, Your Grace? The mysterious earl is really the pirate Diablo. He was granted amnesty and came back to claim his estate. More than likely 'tis Devon he's after. Evidently she recognized him immediately tonight, for they disappeared shortly after they met and no one saw them after that. I feared he's carried her off again. Lord only knows what went on while they were alone," Winston hinted slyly.

"That bloody bastard! I won't have it!" The earl was painfully aware that Diablo had seduced Devon long ago and she hadn't been the same since. "Are you certain? You could be mistaken. I told you Devon came home hours ago."

"I was never more certain of anything in my life," Winston said with smug assurance. "I've been suspicious of him ever since he showed up after being thought dead all these years. He was kidnapped as a young lad and nothing was heard of him until a few weeks ago when he turned up with enough wealth to convince the king to strip me of all my possessions. It seems utterly beyond belief that a notorious pirate accustomed to adventure should choose to accept amnesty and return to resume the dull, rather colorless life of an English lord and all the restrictions placed on him by society."

"You—you think he came back for Devon?" Suddenly Lord Harvey clutched at his heart as a sharp pain squeezed the breath from him. He couldn't lose Devon again. Not to a man with no morals and a heart as black as his reputation.

"I'm certain of it. The same person who revealed Kit's identity to me intimated that Diablo intended to use Devon to satisfy the animal lust he developed for her. Nothing can save her from ruination once he gets his hands on her."

"She's virtually powerless against him," Winston continued relentlessly. "Diablo's proved time and again he has total control over her senses. Do you want your daughter corrupted by the likes of a man who attained his wealth by preying on others? What will happen to Devon when he tires of her? One day he'll look for a young and innocent wife, and I can assure you it won't be Devon."

Having done what damage he could to Kit's reputation, Winston waited for Lord Harvey's reaction.

The earl's normally ruddy complexion turned white, then went slack with terror. He loved Devon far too much to see her corrupted and humiliated by a pirate who would use and discard her at his convenience. He'd see Diablo dead first.

"Nay," he denied vehemently. "I'll not let that happen. I'll do whatever necessary to keep Devon away from that vile man."

"Let me help you," Winston pleaded eagerly. "I have a plan, but it won't succeed without your cooperation."

The pain in his chest was terrible, but not great enough to interfere with Lord Harvey's keen mind. "Tell me your plan. I'll not lose Devon again."

Casting a wary eye toward the closed door, Winston sidled closer to the earl. "Assist me in taking Devon away where Diablo can't find her. Once we're alone, I'm convinced she'll come to her senses. Why, when we return," he boasted, "she may even be carrying your first grandchild." At Lord Harvey's incredulous look, he hastily added, "Naturally we'll wed first."

"You'd hold Devon against her will?" the earl quizzed sharply. "It won't be easy."

"I can do it with your help. Once Devon is in the coach with me there'd be no turning back. I won't return till we've been properly wed and bedded. I know I could convince Devon to be my wife once she's away from my cousin's influence."

"It didn't work before," came Lord Harvey's skeptical reply.

"Would you hand your daughter over to Diablo without a fight?" Winston goaded. His devious words were meant to strike terror in Lord Harvey's heart in order to force his cooperation. He must not fail. Winston feared Scarlett's retribution almost as much as he feared Kit. If Lord Harvey agreed to help him in his efforts to take Devon to a secret place, it would give Scarlett time to capture Kit's heart. If anyone could do it, Scarlett could.

"By God, that devil won't have her!" the earl reiterated, pounding the desk to reinforce his words. "What must I do?"

Their voices lowered in conspiracy, Winston instructed Lord Harvey to arrange for Devon to be delivered to his coach, which would be waiting outside the front door early the next morning—just a few hours hence. Then he would take her with all haste to the little-used Linley hunting lodge near Penzance in remote Cornwall. Before he left he slipped the earl a vial of brownish liquid given to him once by a doctor for pain when he had broken his leg. There was still a goodly amount of laudanum left in the bottle.

Lord Harvey slumped dejectedly in his chair, burying his gray head in his trembling hands. Must he stoop to betraying his own flesh and blood to keep Devon safe? Was he doing the right thing? Surely Winston, weak though he was, was a better choice for his beloved daughter than a ruthless pirate like Diablo. Once she was married to Winston, not even Diablo—or the Duke of Grenville—would dare pursue her.

A terrible pain tore upward through his body and Lord Harvey stiffened, his pale face shiny with sweat. Then slowly his breathing eased and the pain subsided enough to allow the tortured earl to seek his bed for what remained of this eventful night.

Despite having retired late, Devon awoke early the next morning, lighthearted and happily expectant. In a few hours Kit would arrive and set things right with her father, and they could settle down to a life she'd always dreamed of with the man she loved. A dreamy look turned her beautiful features soft and wistful as she bathed, dressed, and went downstairs to breakfast.

"Father, you're up early," Devon trilled happily. "I'm glad, there's—" Suddenly she noticed his waxen complexion, his pinched features, and alarm seized her. "Father, you're ill! What is it?"

"Nay, daughter, I'm fine," the earl denied, managing a weak smile. "But I'm glad you're down early. I have an errand to attend to and I'd like you to accompany me."

"Of course, Father," Devon readily agreed, "as long as we return in time for lunch. I've invited a guest and—and I have something to tell you. But it can wait until later."

The earl knew exactly who to expect and was determined that Devon wouldn't be here when Diablo arrived. Refusing to look into Devon's trusting eyes, he nodded. "We'll be back in plenty of time." It was a deliberate lie but one he felt necessary under the circumstances. "Help yourself to break-fast, m'dear, the food is quite tasty."

Ravenous, Devon went to the sideboard and heaped her plate with the tempting array of food prepared by the cook. When she returned to the table, the earl had already poured her tea. Devon smiled her thanks and concentrated on her plate, unaware of her father's warring conscience and plagu-ing doubts over the terrible thing he must do in order to save his only child from corruption and ruin. When she finished, she sat back, replete, draining the last drop of tea from her cup.

"I'm ready, Father, whenever you are."

"Fetch your cloak, m'dear, and I'll see if the coach is out front. I've ordered it brought round early." Lord Harvey made a half-hearted effort to rise, then sank back quickly in his chair, as if the effort were beyond him.

"Perhaps we should delay this errand for another time," Devon suggested, gravely concerned over her father's obvi-ous weakness.

"Nay, I'm fine, truly. Run along now, I'll be waiting by the door."

Planting a kiss on his forehead, Devon hurried off, deter-mined to summon the doctor the moment they returned.

Rising somewhat unsteadily, Lord Harvey walked to the door, peeked out the side window, and saw Winston's hired coach waiting by the curb. Immediately a stab of guilt pierced his heart and he very nearly couldn't go through with it. But the thought of Devon being used and corrupted by Diablo firmed his resolve. Heaving a troubled sigh, he waited for Devon to reappear.

A frown furrowed Devon's smooth brow as she removed her cloak from the wardrobe and drew it over her shoulders. A strange lassitude turned her legs to rubber as she mounted the stairs, and her weakness increased with each passing minute. Pausing at the top of the stairs, she started down, clinging tightly to the handrail as she tried to think above the buzzing in her head.

Immediately Devon's hand went to her stomach. Was it the baby? The conspicuous absence of pain told her all was well with the child. Perhaps both she and her father were coming down with something. By the time she reached the front door where Lord Harvey waited, her vision was blurred and her knees trembled from the effort it took to remain upright. With keen perception the earl noted Devon's distress, and he took her arm, leading her to the door, his face a study of grave concern. Did he really want to do this?

"Father," Devon demurred, "perhaps I should stay home. All of a sudden I feel—strange."

"Nonsense," the earl blustered. "I'm sure it will pass once you're out in the air."

Thinking perhaps her lethargy was but another manifestation of her pregnancy, Devon reluctantly agreed, leaning against her father as he carefully helped her down the steps to the waiting coach. Suddenly Devon experienced a disturbing premonition that something was amiss. "This isn't your coach, Father. Where is the coat of arms?"

"This is a rented coach, Devon, mine is being repaired," the earl was quick to reply. "In you go, m'dear."

Even as he handed her inside, guilt rode him mercilessly. Was he doing the right thing by his beloved daughter? Would she thank him for protecting her from a liaison that would be disastrous for her reputation and ultimately break her heart? Or would she despise him for interfering in her life? Just when he would have snatched her back to the safety of his arms, the coach shot forward and Devon fell backwards into Winston's viselike embrace.

"Father! Help!"

"Please forgive me, daughter, I love you!"

Then darkness descended and she fell into a void as black as death.

* * *

A bubbling well of happiness burst inside Kit as he approached the front door of Chatham House. At long last he could let the world know that Devon was his wife. Last night was the longest night he had ever endured. He had rehearsed his speech to Devon's father over and over until he had it perfect, well aware that the man had little reason to like him. Hopefully he could convince the earl he had shed the identity of feared and hated pirate and was now a respected member of society. Setting the knocker into motion, Kit vowed that Milford's opinion of him would make little difference, for Devon was his and he meant to claim her with or without her father's approval.

Stating his request to speak with Lady Devon, Kit was stunned to learn from the dour butler that she wasn't at home. A strange prickling commenced at the back of his neck and intuition told him something terrible was wrong. He quickly asked for the earl and was shown into the library by the servant, who batted not an eyelash when given Kit's name and title.

"So, 'tis true, you are Diablo. You're a despicable scoundrel, sir, and a seducer of young virgins. If you are looking for my daughter, she's not here. With luck she's where your corruptive influence can't touch her."

Kit whirled to find the short, ruddy-faced earl staring at him with undisguised loathing. He leaned heavily against the door frame, his face a grimace of agony.

"I'm sorry you feel that way, Your Grace," Kit replied evenly. "You have every right to hate me, but I hope to change your mind."

"Never!" the earl denied vehemently. "What you did and continue to do to my daughter is unforgivable."

"Might I speak with Devon? I'm certain she'll—"

"I wasn't lying when I said she wasn't here," Lord Harvey repeated.

"I'll wait," Kit replied with staunch resolve.

"She may be gone for months."

"What! Impossible! Devon asked me here today with good reason. We hoped to explain our situation to you and gain your approval. I've been granted amnesty and fully intend to live within the bounds of society. We hoped you'd be as forgiving as our king, who restored to me all I once possessed but lost due to an act of treachery."

"You ask too much. How can I forgive what you did to my daughter?" thundered the earl. "What about all the innocent lives you've taken, the helpless women you've ravished, the shipping disrupted by you and those under your command?"

"No women were raped by me, and I've deliberately refrained from taking lives during my years of command," Kit defended stoutly. "I'll not deny I'm guilty of seizing cargoes and disrupting shipping, but in the beginning piracy was not my choice. It was thrust upon me. While my peers wallowed in luxury I slaved aboard a ship as a common seaman, driven by a cruel master. I grew to manhood hardened by years of servitude and abusive treatment. Devon was the only good thing to happen to me after I was kidnapped from my home by henchmen hired to kill me by my uncle. He was a greedy man who coveted my inheritance for himself and his own son."

Appalled, Lord Harvey sank into a chair, his face a mask of disbelief. "Kidnapped? By Winston's father? Do you expect me to believe that drivel?"

"'Tis true. The king believed me, and Winston admitted knowledge of the deed, though he denied knowing about it until years later. 'Tis also true I love Devon with all my heart and soul."

"If what you say is true, then I've done both you and Devon a grave injustice," the earl said slowly, his breath coming in short, painful gasps. "If Devon's actions these past weeks are any indication, I'd be safe in saying she returns your love."

Kit smiled, a shudder of relief passing through his body. "Devon is my life," Kit admitted. "Without her I'd have no reason to return to a society that rejected me."

"What are your intentions toward Devon?" the earl asked, still not completely convinced. Yet he had a niggling suspicion that he'd been thoroughly duped by Winston. Had he foolishly delivered his beloved daughter into the hands of a man who wanted her only for personal gain? A man capable of assisting in the murder of his younger cousin?

"My intentions," Kit responded with alacrity, "are for Devon to assume her rightful place as my duchess and my wife."

"Your wife! But—" The earl started to rise but fell back, stunned.

"We have been wed for many months. The ceremony was legally performed by a minister in Cornwall and duly recorded. For Devon's sake I have freely renounced my former life and accepted amnesty. Now, Your Grace, if you'd be so good as to tell me where I might find my wife."

Lord Harvey opened his mouth to speak, and though his jaw worked furiously, nothing but choking sounds issued forth. "Your Grace, what is it? Are you ill?" Alarmed, Kit knelt before the older man trying to make sense of his mumblings.

"Winston." It was the only word Kit could understand, but one that brought a chill of foreboding racing down his spine.

"Is Devon with Winston?" A slow nod from the afflicted man brought Kit his answer. "Where? Where has he taken her?"

Suddenly speech was beyond Lord Harvey as he clutched at his heart and slumped over in Kit's arms. Acting instinctively, Kit picked up the older man and darted into the hall and up the stairs in search of a bed. As he dashed past a startled servant, he called over his shoulder, "Summon a doctor, quickly! The earl's life depends on how fast you can run."

* * *

"Will he live, doctor?" Kit asked when the doctor joined him in the library hours later. "What ails the earl?"

Never having met Kit before, the doctor was reluctant to confide in him. But Kit seemed so genuinely concerned he decided to trust him.

"The earl suffered a heart seizure," came the doctor's solemn reply. "I warned him this might happen after his last examination when he complained of pain and shortness of breath. I told him the least little excitement—" He shrugged, looking at Kit helplessly, as if it were now up to a higher authority.

"Will he recover?" Kit asked anxiously.

"I've done all I can, 'tis up to God now. Time will tell." Then he looked at Kit curiously. "Who are you, sir?"

"I am the earl's son-in-law," Kit replied without hesitation. "Christopher Linley, Duke of Grenville."

"You're married to Devon?" the doctor gasped. "But I thought she and Winston—"

"We've been wed some months. We met shortly after she left London on—er—holiday."

"Of course—I didn't realize—I'm sorry, Your Lordship." Once the doctor realized he was dealing with nobility he immediately changed his tone.

"When might I speak with the earl?" Kit asked apprehensively. He despaired of saving Devon from Winston's machinations unless Lord Harvey recovered sufficiently to tell him where she had been taken.

The doctor shook his head sadly. "'Tis doubtful his grace will gain consciousness anytime soon. So severe was his pain I was forced to sedate him and will continue to do so until he is out of danger. It could be weeks."

"Weeks!" Kit blew up. "I can't wait that long! It's imperative I speak with him the moment he opens his eyes."

"I'm afraid it will gain you naught. I suspect the earl will be incoherent and confused long after he awakens. Where is your wife, my lord, she should be with her father at a time like this."

"Devon is—visiting out of the city," Kit improvised. "I'll see that the earl is properly cared for and your orders strictly adhered to. Someone will remain with him night and day."

"Excellent," nodded the doctor. "I've left medicine and instructions with Mrs. Givens, the housekeeper. I'll stop by twice a day, more often if needed."

After he left, Kit was in a state of panic. How would he find Devon if the earl was incapable of speech? What if the earl died and he never learned where Winston had taken her? God's bones! He couldn't bear it. He'd nurse Lord Harvey back to health himself, Kit vowed, if it would help.

Once he composed himself, Kit gathered the staff, introduced himself as Devon's husband, and issued orders for the sick man's care in a crisp, no-nonsense voice that demanded instant obedience. His commanding air of authority left no question in the minds of the servants that the Duke of Grenville was anything other than what he claimed and as such must be obeyed. But when Kit questioned them about Devon's destination that morning, he was met with blank stares. So after looking in on Lord Harvey one last time, Kit returned home to ponder his dilemma. If need be he'd search London from end to end to find the woman he loved. In the meantime, he'd hover over the earl day and night until the man regained his wits. Nothing mattered but finding Devon and keeping her safe for the rest of their days. A love like theirs happened only once in a lifetime and he'd be damned if he'd allow anything or anyone to keep them apart.

Chapter Nineteen

Devon was aware of nothing but the bouncing of the coach over rutted roads and being forced to swallow a loathsome liquid from time to time. Just when her head began to clear, the bitter brew forced between her lips sent her plunging back into a dark void. Once she roused herself long enough to recall being carried into an inn and put to bed by a sympathetic maid who worried over the "poor woman's" illness. After another dose of her "medicine," Devon soon drifted back into a bottomless abyss, too confused to ask for help.

Two more nights slipped past in the same manner before Devon fully awoke to find herself in an unfamiliar bed in a strange room. Devon's hands flew to her stomach, relieved when her fingertips brushed the slight swelling where her child rested. Gingerly she pushed herself to a sitting position, gulping back the rise of bile in her throat and struggling against the dizziness that threatened to plunge her back into darkness.

Surging to her feet, Devon stood with difficulty, but managed to remain upright until her head cleared and her vision returned to normal. The china water pitcher across the room drew her like a magnet to its thirst-quenching promise. Empty! Another urgent need was appeased when she found a chamber pot beneath the bed. Then determination stiffened her wobbly legs and carried her to the door. It opened before her hand found the door-knob.

"You're awake! Good."

"You've done it this time, Winston," Devon flounced with angry indignation. "Why have you drugged me and brought me to this place? Father will have your hide for this!"

"This may come as a surprise, but I have your father's blessing," came Winston's smug reply. "He agrees with me wholeheartedly. We had to get you away from my cousin's corrupt influence. You know Lord Harvey hates Diablo and all he stands for."

"Father knows about Diablo?" gasped Devon with alarm. "How did he find out? I wanted to be the one to tell him about Kit."

"I told him," Winston revealed slyly. "I had your best interests at heart. I know you fancy yourself in love with Diablo, or Kit as he's now called, but the man is a notorious pirate, a defiler of women, and a murderer. I thought your father should know the truth."

"But how did *you* know?" Devon persisted. Then abruptly the answer came to her. "Scarlett! I should have known. The woman hates me. She's always wanted Kit."

"It doesn't matter who told me, only that I learned the truth in time to save you from being ruined beyond redemption. Your father made it possible to take you away where Kit can't find you. He expects us to return as husband and wife."

"Father drugged me?" Devon gasped, disbelief coloring her words. "I—nay—he wouldn't do such a terrible thing. He loves me."

"That's why he did it. He loves you too much to see you corrupted by an evil man like Diablo. My cousin may be a duke, but his past will never allow him to live a respectable life or fit into society. He'll only use you, then discard you when he tires of you."

"Nay! You're wrong about him! Kit loves me and I love him. He was to call on Father and explain about us, but now you've ruined everything. Why, Winston? Why are you doing this?"

"To save you, of course," Winston lied smoothly. "You're going to marry me, Devon, do you understand? Your father expects us to wed before we return. Until you agree to become my wife you'll remain here. I don't care how long it takes. You'll learn to love me once you banish my cousin from your mind and heart. I'm not such a bad fellow. You were prepared to marry me once."

"I can't marry you, Winston, I told you that weeks ago."

"It doesn't matter that you've bedded Kit, my dear," Winston allowed magnaminously. "All that's in the past. After we're wed we'll travel abroad for a year or two and soon you'll forget that pirate ever existed. Your father would be thrilled should you return with a child in tow."

"Marriage is out of the question for us," Devon tried to explain. "Truth to tell, I can't marry anyone. I'm already—"

"Bloody hell, Devon, I've tried to be patient with you, but you are being exceedingly difficult. We'll see if your disposition improves after a period of isolation. Perhaps if you're allowed sufficient time to ponder your wicked ways you'll come to realize I'm offering a way to save your badly bruised reputation. I've always fancied you, my dear."

"You've always fancied my dowry," Devon corrected contemptuously. "Few men are generous enough or willing to overlook a woman's indiscretions unless money is involved. I know you're penniless, and no heiress would have you now that you've not even a title to offer. Besides, I can't believe Father would agree to this unless you deliberately lied to him."

"Have it your way." Winston shrugged, turning to leave. "Let me know when you change your mind."

"Wait! Don't leave me like this! I'm thirsty and hungry and—and filthy. I want a bath and food."

"I have no intention of starving or mistreating you, my dear," Winston said coolly. "I've hired a woman from the village to see to your needs. She's a deaf mute and has been told in sign language that you are slightly demented following the loss of a child. You'll be adequately cared for but not

allowed to leave this room until you agree to our marriage."
Then he was gone.

"Where am I, Winston? At least tell me that much!"

Her plea fell on deaf ears as the door was slammed in her
face and securely locked from the other side.

"Damn you, Winston!" Devon sobbed, pounding on the
door to relieve her frustration. "I'm already married!" The
sound of absolute silence told her it was too late for confes-
sions, Winston had removed himself to another part of the
house.

A short time later the woman hired by Winston unlocked
the door and sidled inside carrying a pitcher of fresh water
and towels. She was middle-aged, tall and stout with the
sturdy build of one accustomed to a lifetime of hard work.
Her graying hair, pulled back in a severe bun, provided a
perfect frame for her stern features. Yet Devon saw nothing
in her dark eyes to indicate cruelty in her character. The
woman eyed Devon warily but went efficiently about her
work. Though Winston had said the servant was mute, Devon felt she had to try to communicate in some way.

"Please help me," she begged as the woman turned to
leave. "Winston lied to you, he's holding me against my will."

Nothing registered in the servant's expression but a brief
flash of compassion that swiftly faded when she recalled her
instructions. She was being well paid to care for the poor
demented soul. She left quickly to prepare a meal for her
charge.

The next two weeks passed in a blur of suffocating bore-
dom and intense anger on Devon's part. Her attempts to
communicate with the mute servant failed miserably, as did
her efforts to speak with Winston. She was confident that
once he learned she was already married he'd lose all interest in her and release her.

As the days slid by Devon knew in her heart that Kit was
turning London upside down looking for her. She wondered

what had happened between Kit and her father when Kit appeared at her door and found her missing. It seemed inconceivable that her father hadn't told Kit where to find her once Kit explained everything to his satisfaction. Perhaps her father didn't know where to find her, Devon reasoned, searching for a plausible excuse for her father's failure to reveal her hiding place. She knew her father to be a stubborn man but not when his daughter's welfare was concerned. Just what had Winston told him?

Throughout her ordeal Devon's primary concern was her baby and keeping it from harm. Though Winston had never resorted to violence with her, she guarded the child in her womb jealously, fearing Winston might turn abusive once he learned her secret. She recalled how he had shelled Paradise at the cost of innocent lives without a smidgeon of remorse.

To Devon's chagrin, Winston ignored her for another week. All her efforts to escape were handily foiled by the stout servant who watched her like a hawk. When Winston finally did show himself, Devon was appalled at his appearance. Signs of dissipation clearly visible on his handsome features led her to believe he had been spending his lonely hours drinking far more than was his custom. His face was puffy, his eyes bloodshot.

"I hope you've come to your senses," he said sourly. "By now you must be thoroughly sick of your own company. Once you agree to become my bride you'll please not only me but your father. And you'll find your circumstances greatly improved. After we're wed we'll go on a grand tour; you can buy a new wardrobe and dine on the finest food the continent has to offer. What say you, my dear?"

Devon's answer astounded Winston as well as brought his world crashing down around his ears. "You simply must listen to me, Winston," she began with deceptive calm despite the wild tattoo of her heart. "I tried to tell you before why marriage is out of the question for us. I'm already married. Kit and I were legally wed months ago."

A blaze of anger turned Winston's features into an ugly mask. Blindly he struck out, catching Devon in the shoulder when she ducked, sending her sprawling across the bed.

"You wanton whore! You opened your legs for my cousin like a bitch in heat, caring little that he was a pirate and you were my intended bride. You women are all alike. You sicken me with your rounded thighs and jutting breasts, your sweating bodies and clinging ways. The thought of having to bed you makes me want to vomit, but I would have swallowed my revulsion and done my duty to get you with child and remain in your father's good graces. I'd have done anything for your inheritance, even though it made me physically ill."

Horrified, Devon watched helplessly as Winston continued to rant and rave. She hardly recognized him as the same man whose gentle wooing and flowery words had charmed her into an engagement months ago. And the terrible things he was saying! He sounded as if he hated women. She knew now that Kit had been right about Winston all along but she had been too stupid to see it. How had he managed to hide his true nature from her and most of their peers all these years?

Winston's angry tirade came to an end as abruptly as it began, leaving him sullen and withdrawn. Normally not a violent man, he turned away from Devon in obvious disgust. Her bombshell had left him more shaken than he cared to admit. His first thought was to wonder how Scarlett would react when she learned that Kit and Devon were already man and wife. Throw a fit, he reckoned, and was grateful he'd be nowhere around when she was told the news. She must be notified immediately. Locking the door behind him, he hastened to find one of his hirelings to send posthaste to London with a message for Scarlett and await further instructions.

* * *

"Scarlett, what in the deuce are you doing here?" Kit asked as he greeted the ex-pirate in his drawing room where she'd been cooling her heels.

"Where have you been keeping yourself, Diablo?" Scarlett asked archly. "I've seen little of you these past weeks. Have you no time for old friends?"

"I was under the assumption you were swamped with admirers these days." Kit's mouth slanted in a mocking smile. "You no longer have need of me, Scarlett."

"I'll always need you, Diablo," Scarlett said, her voice a husky whisper. "No other man can compare with you. Call yourself Kit, Diablo, or anything you want, I'll always find you fascinating. These dull creatures fawning over me and my money are poor excuses for men with their fancy duds and pompous airs. Give me a lusty buccaneer any day. This amnesty isn't all it's cracked up to be."

Scarlett put her arms around his neck and pressed her lush body to his. How many nights had she imagined stroking his hard-muscled shoulders, savoring the texture of his smooth, golden body, so lean and virile in comparison with her own softness? How many nights had she yearned to experience the sweet stimulation of his magic touch? Too many—far too many.

"You still want me, Diablo, I see it in your eyes," Scarlett murmured, her voice made ragged with desire. "And I want you. Touch me! Oh, please touch me, darling." In his anguished state he was vulnerable, as Scarlett shrewdly guessed. Her offer of a moment's oblivion her body could provide him was a temptation most men couldn't resist.

Taking his hand that rested at his side, she deliberately placed it on her breast, holding it there while she struggled to control the lust racing through her body. "Feel my heart, Diablo? It flutters like the wings of a hummingbird. All for you—only for you." She lifted her face. Her breath came thick and shallow as the tip of her tongue danced out to moisten her dry lips in eager anticipation of his kiss.

Her lips were red, inviting, slightly parted, her breath sweet. Had Kit not had a woman like Devon in his life he would have accepted Scarlett's generous offer instantly and responded with all the vigor his young, virile body afforded. Now it was out of the question. What he and Devon had together far surpassed the mere satisfaction of lust that Scarlett offered. Never would he defile the hallowed love that he and Devon shared by falling into Scarlett's silken web. No longer was he the notorious Diablo who loved and fought indiscriminately. He was Christopher Linley, Duke of Grenville, and Devon, wherever she might be, was his beloved duchess.

"If you're trying to seduce me, Scarlett, you've failed miserably," Kit said with cool disdain, his hand falling away from the soft mound of her breast. "I want no other woman but Devon. From the moment we met I knew she was the only woman I could ever love."

"Love! Bah!" blazed Scarlett contemptuously. "People like us don't need love to complicate our lives. Men are ruled by what's between their legs. Use your head for once in your life. If Devon loved you she'd be with you now instead of off somewhere with Winston. They're still engaged, aren't they?" she hinted slyly.

Kit's eyes narrowed dangerously. "Who told you Devon was with Winston?" Outwardly he was calm but inside he boiled like a witch's cauldron. Did Scarlett know something he didn't?

Unmindful of the anger bubbling below the surface of Kit's cool words, Scarlett continued blithely, "Why, Freddie Smythe told me he heard Devon and Winston had eloped and gone off on an extended honeymoon."

"The devil you say!" roared Kit. "Devon wouldn't do such a thing. She'd never marry Winston when—" Abruptly his words slid to a halt, aware that he was about to divulge information that did not concern Scarlett.

Scarlett watched Kit's face with avid delight. It had been part of her plan for Winston to casually mention to a few of his friends that he and Devon were eloping. And of course Freddie had been the first to hear it. The young man had been angry enough at losing his lover to spread the gossip throughout London. Eventually Kit had heard the rumor but knew better than to believe such rot. Kyle and Akbar, who helped him in his fruitless quest, had also reported hearing gossip to that effect, but in light of what Lord Harvey had revealed before suffering a stroke, Kit knew that Devon had been an unwilling participant in the supposed elopement.

"If Devon isn't with Winston, then where is she?" Scarlett asked sweetly. "Have you hidden her away somewhere?"

"Get the hell out of here, Scarlett, I've had all I can take of you," Kit gritted from between clenched teeth. "You've got nothing I want. If your heart is set on becoming a duchess you'll have to look elsewhere. Please excuse me, I have an appointment. You know the way out." Turning on his heel, he stomped from the room, leaving Scarlett shaking in impotent rage.

"Bastard!"

"Is the earl improving, doctor?" Kit asked as he paced anxiously outside Lord Harvey's sickroom. Every day for the past three weeks he'd kept a vigil outside the earl's door, hoping for improvement in the man's condition. His brief visits to the sickroom only added to his frustration, for the stricken earl had yet to utter a lucid word.

"'Tis my belief a full recovery is entirely possible." The doctor beamed. "Lord Harvey is a strong man, and he seems determined to recover. I'd like to credit my medicine, but in truth 'tis the earl's strong will that's keeping him alive."

"How long before he can communicate?"

"I have every reason to be optimistic, but I can't predict a time. 'Tis in God's hands."

"May I attempt to speak with my father-in-law?" Kit asked.

"Of course, just see that you don't tire him," the doctor advised. "I'll be back tomorrow."

Kit entered the sickroom and nodded to the housekeeper, who quietly left the room at Kit's signal.

"Lord Harvey," Kit prodded with an urgency that belied his calm exterior. "Can you hear me?"

At first the earl remained absolutely motionless, then slowly, oh so slowly, one eye cranked open, then the other.

"Can you hear me, Your Grace?" Kit repeated with an excitement he hadn't felt in weeks.

An awareness that had been absent since the earl's seizure flickered in the watery depths of his eyes, and Kit's spirits soared. The old man's pale lips opened, but try as he might, nothing but garbled words issued forth. Words without meaning or clarity. Then the light faded, replaced by a familiar blankness that pierced Kit's heart. Please God, he prayed fervently, let him find his love before Winston forced her into something beyond her control.

"Rest, Your Grace," he said kindly. "I'll return tomorrow. Perhaps by then you'll feel more like talking."

"You have a visitor, m'lady," the dignified butler announced when Scarlett returned to the sumptuously appointed house she'd purchased with her ill-gotten gains. "A rather—er—disreputable-looking fellow who says he has an urgent message that requires an immediate answer. He's waiting in the drawing room, which I'm certain the house-keeper will want to fumigate after he leaves."

"Thank you, Jeevers," Scarlett said, smothering a smile. She'd dealt too many times with unsavory characters during her adventurous life to be offended by one more of their ilk.

She wondered if the proper butler would look down his long nose at her if he knew he was employed by a notorious pirate captain. "I'll take care of it."

His disapproval evident, Jeevers replied, "As you will, m'lady. I'll be nearby if you have need of me."

Nodding her dismissal, Scarlett entered the drawing room to find a tall, gaunt man carefully examining a priceless sculpture that was part of her pirate's loot. His filthy, ill-fitting clothes gave him the appearance of a scarecrow. His obsequious smile revealed sparse yellowed teeth, and his offensive odor hinted at an aversion to bathing.

"Be careful with that, my man, 'tis worth a fortune," Scarlett snapped. Her commanding tone brought the man sharply to attention, and he released his hold on the sculpture immediately.

"The name is Tibbs, m'lady," the man said, pulling off his cap and bobbing his head.

"I understand you have a message for me, Tibbs." Scarlett wasted no time on formalities.

"Aye, m'lady, traveled night and day, I did, to bring it 'ere."

"Well," Scarlett said impatiently, "where is it?"

Hastily Tibbs extracted a much creased and begrimed slip of paper from a pocket and handed it to Scarlett. Wasting no time, Scarlett devoured the words, her frown deepening as she reached the end of the brief message. Then she flung the offending paper to the floor and flew into a rage.

"The bleedin' bastard married the slut!" she cried out viciously. "Why didn't he tell me?" Cursing and pacing, Scarlett had nearly forgotten Tibbs until she saw him cowering before her. "Have you read this?"

"N—nay, I 'aven't 'ad much schoolin'."

Satisfied, Scarlett said, "You'll have the answer before you leave. Go around to the kitchen, cook will fix you something to eat. You can sleep in the stable and start out at first light tomorrow. A servant will bring my message to you along with your breakfast. Be off with you, man!"

"Aye, m'lady," Tibbs obeyed, anxious to have a hot meal under his belt. Because his employer had stressed speed he'd wasted little time on amenities, camping out most of the time and eating cold food that had been packed for him.

Scarlett spent most of the evening forming her reply to Winston's startling revelation. If the perverted coward thought the news would alter her plans, he was badly mistaken. Scarlett was still determined to have Kit no matter what drastic measures it took. As a pirate she had made life-and-death decisions every day, so what did one more matter? Her message to Winston was concise. "Kill Devon."

Three days later Winston read Scarlett's terse note, blanching with horror at the words. A bolt of terror coursed through him at Scarlett's order. What would that vicious pirate do to him if he failed to follow instructions? he wondered bleakly. Kill him? Probably. Spread vicious gossip about him and Freddie, leaving their reputations in shambles? That too was a distinct possibility. But could he kill Devon? Nay. If Scarlett wanted Kit badly enough to kill, she'd have to do it herself. A second message was prepared and sent posthaste, once again carried by a disgruntled Tibbs. Winston's words were, "If you want Devon dead, do it yourself."

Tibbs cringed beneath a barrage of curses as Scarlett flung Winston's note in his face. "That lily-livered coward! How dare he defy me. I'll see him rot in hell for betraying my trust. He took my money in good faith, yet refuses to do my bidding. I can see this is something I have to do myself if I want it done right. Remain in London until I'm ready to leave for Cornwall, you can drive the coach for me. But there are things I must do first. You can sleep in the stable and eat in the kitchen."

Somehow Tibbs found the courage to protest. "Nay, m'lady, I've 'ad all of the country I can take. I don't like bein' away from me digs so long. Me mates will be wonderin' what 'appened to me. I'll not be returnin' to Cornwall. Ye can drive yer bleedin' coach yerself, I ain't goin'. This situation is gettin' too deep fer me."

So saying he turned and fled, leaving Scarlett staring open-mouthed at his departing back. Nothing had gone right since she'd left the rolling deck of the *Red Witch* and men she understood and who understood her, she reflected with an angry toss of her flaming tresses. Obviously she could depend on no one but herself in this world of fools and fancy-dressed idiots.

Her eyes narrowed into catlike slits, Scarlett set about planning revenge on Winston Linley. First things first, she thought, and smiled deviously. Before she departed for Cornwall she'd make damn certain all of London was rocked to its core by the news of the perverted love life shared by Winston and Freddie Smythe. Neither of them would be able to show their face in town again without being openly ridiculed.

Within hours Scarlett had planted the seeds of malicious gossip throughout the city. But if things went her way, Winston wouldn't be alive to hear any of it. Three days after receiving Winston's note, Scarlett left London, well pleased with her scurrilous deeds. With that out of the way, she could concentrate on ridding herself of Diablo's wife. Once Devon's death was reported, she'd give Diablo sufficient time to recover, then press her suit while he was still suffering and vulnerable. Aye, Scarlett reflected gleefully, she knew men and was confident of her ability to lure Diablo to the altar once Devon was disposed of.

Chapter Twenty

Devon languished in her bedroom prison while a vindictive Scarlett was planning her short future. Since Winston learned of her marriage Devon had seen nothing of him. She was adequately provided for and her needs attended to by the dour servant whose name she had yet to learn. She was allowed to bathe regularly, given a change of clothes, and fed nourishing but plain fare. And consequently her child thrived, evidenced by her increasing waistline, which was disguised by the ill fit of the clothing provided her.

For exercise Devon paced the room, back and forth, back and forth, until the mute servant took pity on her and accompanied her outside for brief strolls twice a day. During those outings Devon surreptitiously studied her surroundings, but they told her nothing about where she was being imprisoned. And the hawk-eyed servant remained staunchly by her side the entire time. Devon felt in her bones that something was amiss, the very atmosphere crackled with tension. Call it intuition, but Devon existed in a high state of expectancy, waiting with bated breath for something to happen.

It seemed inconceivable that her father hadn't relented and told Kit where she was being held. Assuming he knew, of course. And of late she began to wonder about many things, including exactly what Winston had told her father about Kit, and whether he was aware of Winston's sexual preferences. Devon couldn't imagine her father falling in with Winston's plans if he knew the kind of man he was dealing with.

* * *

The dilemma facing Winston was nearly more than he could cope with. If he remained at the hunting lodge he could expect Scarlett to show up and demand her pound of flesh. Winston never bargained for murder when he agreed to Scarlett's harebrained scheme. Marrying Devon was one thing, murdering her was another. Except for her bullhead-edness in refusing to marry him, Winston didn't hate Devon. Yet he realized that if he defied Scarlett he'd end up as dead as Devon was likely to be. Of course he could release Devon to find her way to London and safety, then quietly disappear himself and hope Scarlett wouldn't stalk him. It would be difficult without money, but there seemed to be little alternative. Those were his options, none of them attractive, when he decided to hie himself to the nearest tavern and drown his problems in a bottle using the last of the coins given him by Scarlett.

Leaving the mute servant in charge, Winston rode his hired mount to the village where the Hound and Hare stood at the end of a busy street. He had visited it on several occasions these past weeks and was greeted with familiarity by the innkeeper.

The tavern was crowded, it being the time of day when workers gathered for companionship and revelry. He found an empty table and ordered a bottle from the slovenly waitress, settling himself for a lengthy stay. He was well into the bottle when a voice he'd never expected to hear again interrupted his solitude.

"By God, Winnie, I never thought to find you so easily!"

"Freddie!" Winston exclaimed, ogling his handsome lover with astonishment. "How in bloody hell did you find me?"

"Pure luck, old son, pure luck."

"Sit down, Freddie, and tell me what brings you out here to this wilderness."

"You've had no word from London? Heard no gossip?" Freddie quizzed sharply.

"Nothing of importance," Winston shrugged, discounting Scarlett's brief missives. "Why, has something happened?"

"You may as well know," Freddie sighed bleakly, "seeing as how you're involved. It seems, old son, that our secret is out. Our—er—past intimacies are being bandied about London and spreading like wildfire. My parents are livid. They've kicked me out of the house and disinherited me. I've made them the laughing stock of London Town and they'll never forgive me."

"My God, Freddie, I'm sorry! I never thought the bitch would actually do it. I know what it means to lose one's birthright."

"The money is no problem, Winnie, I've a private fortune of my own, left to me by my doting grandmother. But what did you mean? You spoke as if you knew who blew the whistle on us. Was it Devon?"

"Nay, not Devon," Winston said bitterly. "Scarlett De-Foe."

"Lady DeFoe? But why would she . . ."

"It's a long story, Freddie. Join me in a drink and I'll explain."

When Winston had finished his story, Freddie shook his head in wonder.

"You can't imagine, old son, how hurt I was when it leaked out that you and Devon had eloped. I knew you two were engaged and your marriage inevitable, but after all those postponements I had hopes that you'd finally come to your senses. Grenville had his men out scouring London for Devon. That wild Turk was especially fierce. I assumed that Milford knew where you and Devon had disappeared to but withheld the information for reasons unknown to anyone but himself. And then I heard the old boy had a seizure and was hanging onto life by a thread."

"I'm sorry to hear about the earl, Freddie," Winston said. "I hope he makes it."

"Did Devon finally consent to marry you? The way Grenville has been acting of late, you'd think Devon was his fiancé instead of yours. It's all so confusing. I can't believe Lady DeFoe threatened to take your life if you didn't fall in with her plans. What are you going to do?"

"As it turns out, Devon isn't free to marry me. She's already married to my cousin."

"Grenville? But how? I didn't even know they were acquainted until just recently." Suddenly he snapped his fingers, comprehension dawning. "By jove, I remember now. Wasn't she kidnapped by Diablo the day he escaped from the gallows? I recall that escapade set London on its ears. Didn't she return and disappear again on the eve of your wedding? Seems like the earl said something about her going to the country to make up her mind."

"You've got the right of it, Freddie. One day I'll tell you the whole story, if I live so long. Including what drove Kit to take up piracy. But at the present time I'm enmeshed in a devious plot I've no stomach for. But before I get into it, tell me how you found me."

"After being booted from my happy home," Freddie began earnestly, "I made the rounds of all my friends. They treated me like an outcast, refusing to receive me or acknowledge my presence. Then I began hanging around the waterfront dives, hoping to book passage to France and start life anew. I've enough money to do as I please with my life. While drowning my sorrows one night, feeling particularly bereft after hearing that you and Devon had eloped, I met a disreputable character by the name of Tibbs."

"Tibbs! He was my hireling who failed to return on his last trip to London at my behest."

"The same," Freddie concurred. "He was well into his cups and began spouting off about being stuck in Cornwall

these past weeks, hired by a man to abduct a beautiful
woman who refused to marry him. According to Tibbs, he
got tired of being messenger boy and just stayed in London
during his last trip carrying messages back and forth to a
madwoman. After listening to your tale, I assume the madwoman is Lady DeFoe.

"I asked Tibbs to describe the lady being held in Cornwall
against her will and he gladly obliged. The description
matched Devon perfectly. Then I put two and two together
but still couldn't come up with four. Abduction didn't sound
like you no matter how desperate you might be. So I decided
to hie myself to Cornwall to see for myself. There was nothing to keep me in London. Discrete questioning provided
me with the directions to Penzance, but by then Tibbs was
too drunk to be of further use. I left immediately and stopped
at the first inn I came to in Penzance, intending to seek
knowledge of you. Imagine my astonishment when I saw you
sitting here."

"I'm glad you've come, Freddie, but it still doesn't solve my
problem."

"What problem? Devon is already married. What choice
do you have but to release her and allow her to return to her
husband?"

"Scarlett wants Devon dead."

Freddie blanched. He hadn't a violent bone in his body,
and what Winston told him shocked him badly. "Jesus, Winnie, you're no bloody killer."

"I know, that's why I told Scarlett I couldn't do it. She's a
devil, Freddie, disguised as a beautiful woman. She's proved
herself capable of evil by spreading gossip about our relationship and ruining our reputation. She's promised to kill
me if I failed her, and she's vindictive enough to do it. She
also wants Kit badly enough to do away with Devon. Hell,
Freddie, I don't know what to do!" Winston's anguished plea
tore at Freddie's soft heart.

"Calm down," Freddie advised, his mind working furiously. "First of all, killing Devon is out of the question, we both agree to that. Second, you've got to get back to wherever you're keeping Devon and release her immediately. And last, the sooner you place yourself out of Scarlett's reach, the better. The same goes for Grenville. Though I scarcely know him, he doesn't strike me as a man who forgives easily. Kidnapping his wife was a despicable deed."

"The first two can be accomplished easily enough, but the third is more difficult. It takes money to travel abroad."

"I've got plenty of money, Winnie. Come to France with me. I hear the French are more tolerant of our kind than the English. There are bound to be several ships in Penzance or Land's End bound for France. I'll inquire and book passage for the two of us. Later we can travel to Italy, or wherever you want."

Suddenly Winston's prospects didn't appear so bleak anymore. Freddie's providential arrival had been a godsend. His cool head and clear thinking—not to mention his money— had painted an entirely different outcome to his agonizing dilemma.

"You'd do that for me?"

"Of course, Winnie, all we've got left is each other. I've alienated my family, they never want to see me again. And my friends shun me like poison."

"Then we'd best leave now. Scarlett could show up at any time."

His shoulders slumped in dejection, Kit slowly opened the door to Lord Harvey's bedroom, fully prepared to encounter the same suffocating disappointment he'd experienced each time he visited the earl's sickroom. It seemed as if fate were conspiring against him and he'd never find Devon. She seemed to have disappeared from the face of the earth. Though he'd hired a veritable army, no one had turned up a single clue about Devon's whereabouts. That bastard Winston had chosen his hiding place well.

Shortly after Winston and Devon disappeared, gossip mongers had themselves a field day hinting at their probable elopement. Jealousy nearly killed Kit, but the knowledge that Devon harbored no feelings for Winston and was being held against her will saved him. Recalling how, when he was a young lad, he had surprised the eighteen-year-old Winston in a disgusting act with an older man, Kit felt confident Winston had little use for Devon as a woman. It shocked him that Winston had tried this crazy stunt, for his cousin was neither very imaginative nor excessively brave.

Yet Kit knew of no one else who would aid Winston in a scheme that could hardly succeed. Surely Devon had told Winston that she was a married woman, Kit reflected, more puzzled than ever by his cousin's devious thinking. Why hadn't Devon been released once Winston found marriage to her out of the question? Why hadn't Kyle or Akbar turned up a clue to Winston's destination? Someone in this city had to know. If Winston harmed Devon in any way, he'd make the man wish he'd never been born.

Then, just yesterday Kit had been privy to a rumor that Winston and Freddie Smythe had been carrying on a homosexual relationship. The rumor spread like wildfire, and Freddie's parents had banished their son from their home and disinherited him. Thinking, hoping, that Freddie might offer a clue to where Winston had taken Devon, Kit attempted to locate the young man, once more meeting with disappointment. Hounded by ridicule, Freddie had apparently hied himself from the scene of his embarrassment. Another dead end.

The first thing Kit noticed as he entered Lord Harvey's room was that the windows had been thrown open and the drapes drawn to allow fresh air and sunshine to circulate. Previously the room had remained darkened and suffocatingly close. Then he saw the earl sitting up in bed, clear-eyed but obviously highly agitated.

"Thank—God—you've come," Lord Harvey gasped, finding difficulty in forming the words. "I—asked the doctor to send for you—hours ago."

"I haven't been home, Your Grace," Kit confided, elated to find the earl awake and lucid. "This past month has been pure hell for me. I've prayed day and night for your full recovery, while searching relentlessly for my wife."

"Your wife," repeated the earl slowly. "So I didn't dream it. You and Devon are wed. Does she love you?"

"I have every reason to believe she does." The earl nodded, satisfied. "And I love her more than my own life," Kit revealed. "Please, sir, if you know where Winston has taken Devon, I beg you to tell me."

"Aye, Grenville, I'll tell you, but first tell me all that's transpired since I've been disabled."

"Not much, Your Grace, and please call me Kit. I'm worried that Winston hasn't released Devon once he learned we were married. It leads me to believe that something terrible has happened to her. It's been four weeks and I've turned London upside down to find her."

"Four weeks! Good Lord, that long? Winston's a bloody fool. He's taken her to Cornwall. Where exactly, I don't know."

"Cornwall! God's bones, why didn't I think of it before? I'd completely forgotten about the family hunting lodge near Penzance. 'Tis remote enough to provide strict privacy yet easily accessible. I'll leave immediately."

"Grenville—Kit, wait!" Kit turned, chafing impatiently to be off. "I want you to know that for my daughter's sake I'm willing to forget all that's transpired in the past. Devon must have seen some redeeming qualities in you or she wouldn't have chosen you. Bring her back, Kit, and as long as you make her happy I'll not interfere in your lives."

"My finding Devon doesn't depend on your forgiveness, Your Grace. I'd do it regardless. Devon is everything to me. Even when she betrayed the secret of my stronghold I loved her. I was angry enough to slay her but too consumed by love to wish her harm."

"What?" the earl gasped, stunned. "You blamed Devon for that? Nay, lad, 'twas Le Vautour who betrayed your secret. Devon refused to speak a word against you. I deliberately kept the knowledge of Winston's raid from her, fearing she'd hate us both for so cowardly an act. Though I take full responsibility for sending Winston to Paradise, I didn't order or condone his taking of innocent lives."

It was as if a great load had been taken off Kit's broad shoulders. "I believe you, Your Grace," Kit allowed, "and thank you for telling me." Then, seeing how quickly the man was tiring, he added, "Rest and get well. Fear not, I'll bring your daughter home safely. And if Winston has harmed her, you'll have his head on a platter."

The sound of voices somewhere in the house brought Devon instantly alert. At least two male voices drifted to her beyond the door. One belonged to Winston and the other sounded vaguely familiar. She hadn't seen the mute servant since early in the day, and that seemed strange also, for no one had brought her dinner. Suddenly the doorknob turned and Devon rushed forward, ready to assault Winston with harsh recriminations. How dare he keep her prisoner? If he didn't fear Kit's retribution he was a bigger fool than she thought. Kit would find her soon, she adamantly believed, stifling a smidgeon of doubt.

It worried Devon that Winston hadn't already released her. It was almost as if he feared letting her go. Was there someone or something he feared more than Kit?

Her pregnancy was another reason for Devon to fret. The past month had wrought a great change in her appearance.

Previously her pregnancy had remained largely undetected. Now into her fourth month, she seemed to have blossomed in more ways than one. Her breasts sorely tested the fabric of her bodice and her stomach curved outward into a small, hard bulge.

The door opened, and Winston stepped somewhat hesitantly into the room.

"You look well, Devon," he said. His words, meant to appease, only spurred her anger.

"No thanks to you!" Devon returned. Her eyes blazed with angry fire and a reddish tint crept up her neck. "Have you finally come to your senses and decided to let me go?"

Winston cleared his throat nervously. "Ahem, why—er—aye, you're free to leave. I've already dismissed your servant."

Stunned, Devon stared uncomprehendingly at the man she might have married had she not been tempted by the devil and learned to love him. "You—you mean it? My God, Winston, why did you wait so long? Why didn't you let me go immediately when I told you I was already married? You've earned nothing for your despicable act except Kit's hatred."

"Winston acted on my orders," a feminine voice from behind Winston said. "He kept you away from Diablo. And I'm here to see that the separation is made permanent."

A loud groan escaped Winston's lips. He had hoped to be gone long before Scarlett arrived to complicate matters. But Scarlett's untimely appearance answered many of the questions that had plagued Devon since Winston had spirited her from her home. Though Winston had proven himself capable of dastardly deeds, she had been mystified by his refusal to release her. It did not surprise Devon to learn that Scarlett was behind her ordeal. Somehow she didn't feel her life threatened by Winston, though she had to admit he acted with incredible stupidity. But Scarlett was another matter entirely, for Devon suspected Scarlett fully capable of committing murder.

"It seems I arrived not a moment too soon," Scarlett said coolly, her green eyes glittering maliciously. "I knew Winston was a spineless pervert but didn't think him witless as well. What did you think to gain by letting Devon go?"

Winston swallowed the lump of fear choking him. "I'm through with your crazy scheme, Scarlett. Murder isn't my way. I would have married Devon, but that's impossible now."

"Murder!" gasped Devon, looking from Winston to Scarlett. Apparently Scarlett wanted her out of Kit's life badly enough to kill her. "This isn't the Caribbean where piracy and murder flourish, Scarlett. You accepted amnesty in good faith and promised to live within the law. You'll be punished, you know."

"I'll take my chances," Scarlett replied, shoving Winston aside as she took a menacing step toward Devon.

"Don't let her do this, Winston!" Devon cried, flinging out her hand in mute appeal.

The tip of Winston's tongue flicked out to moisten his dry lips. Where was Freddie? he wondered anxiously. He'd left the house to ready their horses for a hasty departure and by now would be wondering what was keeping him. If there was some way he could stall Scarlett . . .

Realizing she couldn't depend on Winston, Devon turned to confront Scarlett, fear for her child making her desperate. "Kit is lost to you, Scarlett. Do you seriously think he'd turn in love to the woman who killed his wife?"

"Wife! Bah! *I* was meant to be Kit's duchess, not you. Who will tell him? There will be no witnesses left to tell the tale."

Winston's loud gasp brought a wicked smile to Scarlett's beautiful features. "You can't involve me in murder, Scarlett. I'm leaving," he blustered with false bravado.

"You're not going anywhere, Linley," Scarlett warned,

whipping forth a cutlass she had concealed beneath her voluminous cloak. Only then did Devon realize that Scarlett was garbed as she'd first seen her, in tight trousers, white silk shirt, and high black boots. Not only was there a sword in her hand but a small arsenal strapped around her slim waist. "Stand here where I can see you." She motioned to a place beside Devon.

Sidling around Scarlett, Winston stood hesitantly beside Devon, facing the notorious pirate while Scarlett stood with her back to the open door. She brandished the cutlass in their faces, enjoying their terror. It was just like old times when people quailed before her and the power of life and death lay as near as her cutlass. She savored the heady feeling to the fullest.

"Once you two are disposed of, no one need know what happened. Your murders will remain a mystery. I came to Penzance by ship, my own *Red Witch*, and rented a horse in town. My face was muffled and I spoke not a dozen words. I could have been anyone."

"Penzance!" exclaimed Devon. "I'm in Cornwall! Damn you, Winston, for bringing me here. If Scarlett doesn't kill you, I will."

"Enough!" Scarlett snarled, possessed by the need for vengeance and consumed by jealousy. Devon stood between her and all she desired. "You first, Linley. I'm going to enjoy this. Society will thank me for ridding it of a man of your perverted tastes."

The cutlass in Scarlett's hand pressed ominously into the soft flesh of Winston's neck. He whimpered in terror as a drop of blood trickled down his throat.

Devon stared in horror, powerless to stop Scarlett. Once Winston lay dead she knew it would only be a matter of seconds before she joined him. And her baby would die with her.

Just then the figure of a man loomed in the doorway

behind Scarlett, his hand raised menacingly. Before Devon
had time to blink, the heavy candlestick held in their rescuer's hand came crashing down upon Scarlett's head. The
cutlass clattered from Scarlett's hand, and she began a slow
spiral to the floor. Devon's gaze shifted from the pirate's
prone from to the man bending over Winston, cooing and
fussing with grave concern.

"Did the witch hurt you, Winnie?" Freddie asked, dabbing
his handkerchief at the thin line of blood oozing from the
tiny puncture in Winston's neck. "When you failed to meet
me outside I came to see what was keeping you. And lucky I
did. Scarlett must have entered through the rear entrance,
for I swear I didn't see her."

"I'm so grateful, Freddie," Winston croaked. His face was
white, his voice quivering with fright. Never had he been so
close to death.

"Freddie Smythe, what are you doing here?" Devon challenged. "Are you involved in all this?"

"Nay, Devon, Freddie is innocent," Winston quickly defended. "'Tis a long story and one I have no time to divulge.
Suffice it to say that Scarlett's vicious tongue made it impossible for Freddie to remain in London so he came looking for
me."

"Vicious tongue? I don't—" Then suddenly comprehension dawned. Everything Kit had said about Winston was
true. Obviously Winston could never have been a husband
to her, as she had begun to realize weeks ago. It rankled to
think that he only wanted her for her money. From the very
beginning it had been her money, not herself—never herself.

"You're—you're vile, Winston Linley!" she cried, shocked
by what she'd discovered. "And you, too, Freddie. I'd never
dreamed you two could be—that you—" Her tirade trailed
off as she was unable to understand the perverted acts the
two men engaged in.

"We've got to get out of here," Freddie urged, ignoring Devon as he cast a wary eye on Scarlett. She hadn't moved a muscle since being clubbed, and he wanted to keep it that way. "No telling when that bitch will stir."

"Is—is she alive?" Devon asked.

Dropping to one knee, Freddie felt for Scarlett's pulse. "Aye, she's alive. Too bloody tough to die. Let's go, Winnie, before she regains her senses. I don't fancy being skewered at the end of her sword." He turned to leave, Winston hard on his heels.

"Wait! What about me?" Devon was incensed to think they could leave without a thought for her safety.

Freddie frowned, as if suddenly remembering her. "You'd best leave too, Devon," he urged "From what little I heard, Scarlett wants your life. Winston and I are off to Land's End. I heard a ship is sailing for France on the morning's tide. If we're fortunate our past won't follow us there. You're welcome to accompany us if you want."

"Nay," Devon demurred. "I must get back to London. To Father—and Kit."

"Then you'll have to find your own way," Winston said impatiently. "I value my skin too much to remain in England. If Scarlett doesn't do me in, Kit will. Please believe that I never intended to hurt you. Aye, I needed your money, but once I learned you were married to my cousin I was willing to go on to greener pastures. But Scarlett made it all but impossible. She learned about me and Freddie and threatened us with exposure if I didn't comply with her wishes. I couldn't let her ruin Freddie, so I gave in. But I never would have killed you."

"Here," Freddie said, handing Devon several gold coins. "You'll probably find Scarlett's mount tethered at the rear of the house. Take it and make your way to London. Good luck."

Good riddance, Devon thought as the sound of pounding

hooves faded into the distance. Depositing the coins in her pocket, she grabbed her cloak, stepped gingerly around the unconscious Scarlett, and made her way to the back door with a haste born of fear.

At least she now knew she was in Cornwall and could make her way home easily enough. Devon didn't relish riding horseback the long distance to London in her delicate condition and thought it best to go first to Penzance and hire a coach and driver.

She found Scarlett's mount tethered to a tree, contentedly munching grass. Leading him to a rock, she hoisted herself on his broad back, and with the last rays of the sun to guide her, headed in the direction she assumed Penzance to be. Actually, it was a wild guess, for she had no idea where the hunting lodge was situated. Darkness descended on the wild moors not thirty minutes later, and she became hopelessly lost.

Riding was out of the question in the darkness, for Devon couldn't risk falling and harming her child. Sliding from the saddle, she gripped the reins in her hand and led the frisky animal over the rough terrain, tripping over roots and stones until she called a halt for safety's sake. Not a glimmer of moonlight lit her way. Nor were there stars to lend her comfort. To add to her misery, a cold drizzle pelted her, and she pulled her cloak tightly about her to ward off the penetrating chill.

A loud clap of thunder rumbled across the heavens and a streak of lightning hurtled to earth, frightening the horse so badly it reared high on its haunches, pulling the reins from Devon's nerveless fingers. With its ears plastered to its head it bolted off into the darkness.

"Damnation!" Devon spewed helplessly as she watched the frightened animal crash through the night. What was she to do now?

Chapter Twenty-one

Inky darkness flirted with the empty corners of the room as Scarlett struggled through the suffocating layers of unconsciousness. Her head was splitting and her hand came away with blood when she touched the swelling that throbbed so painfully. Intuitively Scarlett knew she was alone in the house, and a stream of unladylike curses spewed from her mouth. What had hit her? Who had hit her? God, her head hurt. When she found Winston and Devon, they'd pay dearly for the pain she was suffering.

Struggling to her feet, Scarlett slowly made her way from room to room, lighting a candle to guide her way. Nothing but gloom and darkness lingered in the lodge, and her first instinct was to leave immediately. But the roar of thunder and rush of rain changed her mind. Aware that rain would hamper her efforts to track her prey, she settled in a comfortable chair to await the coming of dawn. No one could travel far on a night like this, she reasoned as she drifted off to sleep.

Kit approached the lodge on silent feet. Chilled, hungry, and drenched to the skin, he had ridden till he was ready to fall out of the saddle, and he prayed it wasn't too late. Devon had been missing so long, all kinds of terrible things could have happened to her by now. If Winston had harmed her he wouldn't live long enough to regret it.

The house was dark save for one feeble light flickering from the front window. Circling around to the rear, Kit found the door open and entered, moving with the grace and stealth of a stalking cat. The winking candle drew him like a fluttering moth to the chair where Scarlett lay slumped in slumber. At first glimpse Kit assumed that the sleeping figure was Winston, but something about the long slender legs stretched out in repose soon disabused him of that notion.

As he sidled closer, Kit's keen eyes encountered the curving sweep of a feminine hip, the high arch of a breast. The fiery gleam of long red tresses caught and reflected the candle's dim glow. "Scarlett!" Kit hissed from between clenched teeth. He should have guessed she was mixed up in this, that Winston was neither bright enough nor brave enough to attempt something so foolhardy on his own.

Drawing his sword, Kit pricked Scarlett's shapely thigh, his gray eyes cold as cement as he watched her awake with a start. "Diablo! What—how did you get here?"

Kit was dressed in garb reminiscent of all those years he'd lived as Diablo the pirate. His flowing white shirt was tucked into black trousers that hugged his muscular thighs like second skin. A bright red kerchief covered his jet hair, and the the beginnings of a blue-black beard darkened his cheeks and chin. Shiny boots fashioned of the softest leather clung to his calves, widening at the knees. A gold loop swung from one ear. He looked every bit as dangerous as he had when balancing on the windswept deck of the *Devil Dancer*.

"By horseback, all the way from London," Kit snarled, answering her question. "Where is Devon?"

"Your *wife* is gone," Scarlett replied with bitter emphasis.

"Where? What have you and Winston done with her? If you've harmed one hair of her head . . ." His words trailed off, but his implied threat hung in the tense stillness.

"As far as I know, no harm has come to her. She left with Winston after I was attacked." Scarlett's pouting lips and narrowed green eyes warned Kit that Devon wouldn't have escaped so easily had she been left to Scarlett's tender mercies.

"Are you the brains behind Winston's rotten act?" Kit

asked disgustedly. "No one knows better than I just how capable you are of dastardly deeds, including murder. What did you hope to gain from Devon's disappearance? Would you actually have done away with her?"

"My original plan was for Winston to marry Devon, and if she refused, to keep her under lock and key until she complied. But it didn't work out that way. We learned too late that you and Devon were already man and wife. You cur! *I* deserve to be your duchess, not Devon," Scarlett spat. "Marriage was never important in the world we lived in, but amnesty brought many changes in my life. Now I want the respectability of marriage. I want to be your duchess, Diablo," she said with a sudden seductive smile. "You know me better than anyone."

"Aye, I know you," Kit concurred, a sneer hanging on the corner of his mouth. "I was a fool not to suspect you were involved. I realize now you were the one who told Le Vautour how to get to Paradise. I doubt that Winston has the guts to commit murder, but you do. Was jealousy your motive? Or is viciousness so ingrained in your soul you know no other way of life?"

"Damn you, Diablo! I've never loved any man but you! I accepted amnesty on your account, despite the fact I'd rather spend my days with my feet on a rolling deck and spindrift blowing in my face. I followed you to England hoping you'd return my love, but instead you ran into Devon's arms."

"I've given you no indication I cared for you," Kit said coolly, unmoved by Scarlett's passionate words. "And I've already wasted too much time listening to your nonsense. I want to know, and I want to know now, where Winston has taken Devon."

"I'm telling you I don't know! They were both here when I arrived several hours ago, but . . ."

"Go on." Kit's sword wavered menacingly before Scarlett's nose.

"When I was—er—talking to them, someone came up behind me and struck me on the head. When I came to hours later, the house was empty. Then it started to rain and I decided to wait till morning before—" Her mouth snapped shut, unwilling to divulge her true purpose in coming to Cornwall. But Kit knew exactly what Scarlett had intended to say.

"How did you find out Devon and I were married?" Silence. "Did Winston tell you?" More silence. "You might as well confess, for I'll find out soon enough." The point of his sword pricked the tender skin of her upper arm ever so gently.

"You bloody bastard! Aye, Winston told me and I ordered him to kill the little witch. But the cowardly pervert refused. So I came to do the job myself. But first I made damn certain Winston and his loverboy were exposed and their perversions made public knowledge."

Panting with repressed rage, Scarlett paused to catch her breath. "But your whore escaped me, and so did Winston. I'm only sorry I didn't find them before you arrived."

Kit's eyes were as cold as stone, his face implacable. "Devon is my wife; don't you dare call her names. Get up. You're coming with me."

"I hoped when I told Le Vautour how to reach Paradise that was the last I'd see of the witch," Scarlett complained bitterly.

"Hold your tongue and move," Diablo ordered tersely.

Glancing out the window, Scarlett noted that mauve streaks dusted the eastern sky and rays of early morning sun had chased nearly all the clouds away. Traces of moisture still clung to the branches and leaves and sparkled like giant teardrops amid damp blades of grass. Unwinding her long legs, she rose from the chair.

"Now what?" she asked.

"I'm taking you to a friend for safekeeping while I find Devon. Later, I'll decide what's to be done with you. Had you harmed Devon I'd have killed you without a qualm. And I still might. But I have no time for you now. Cormac is man enough to handle you until I return."

Prodding Scarlett with the point of his sword, Kit pushed her out the door to where his mount was tethered. After disarming her of the arsenal of weapons attached to her body, he hoisted her in the saddle, lashing her hands to the pummel. Then in one agile leap he sprang up behind her.

"Diablo, my devilish friend, what brings you to my remote castle?" Cormac's laughing blue eyes settled on Scarlett's shapely form and flaming head, and his shaggy brows rose to meet the bushy lock of ebony hair trailing down his forehead. "Who might the lady be?"

"I need your help, Cormac," Kit said, his expression grim as he pulled Scarlett from the saddle.

"You have it," boomed Cormac. "Join me for breakfast while you tell me what you want of me. The tale should prove quite interesting." While he spoke, his appreciative gaze lingered longingly on the exquisite redhead who appeared not the least bit cowed by Kit's rough handling. Never had he seen so magnificent a specimen of womanhood.

"Scarlett, meet Cormac, Duke of Pembroke and master of this crumbling castle and all the land as far as the eye can see. He's also the best damn smuggler in Cornwall. Cormac, this is Scarlett, pirate extraordinaire, and deceitful bitch who tried to rid me of my wife."

"Ah, the plot thickens." Cormac nodded sagely. His perceptive eyes roamed greedily over Scarlett's shapely form and lovely features. He liked everything about the glorious redhead, except what she'd tried to do to Devon. But women were made to be tamed, he reflected, and taming Scarlett was a task he would relish.

Over a plain but hardy breakfast Kit related all that had

transpired during the past months, including accepting amnesty, reclaiming his title, and Scarlett's attempt to get rid of Devon. Scarlett had been consigned to a cell-like room, enabling the men to speak openly without her interference or knowledge.

"What would you have me do, Diablo? I draw the line at killing women. Besides, Scarlett is too toothsome a creature to suffer an early death."

"I ask only that you keep Scarlett for me while I find Devon. What I do with her depends on Devon's condition when I find her. Presently I'm very close to strangling the red-haired bitch. Can I depend on you, my friend?"

"I won't let that gorgeous creature out of my sight," Cormac promised, his blue eyes glowing with wicked delight. "I'm just the man to make Scarlett repent her evil ways. She may be a handful but I'm up to the task."

Cormac's grin was infectious and Kit joined him in laughter despite his bone-weary fatigue and worry. "If you think to tame Scarlett, I wish you luck. But don't complain to me if her sting proves more potent than a scorpion's, for she'll not submit to taming without a fight. She's a taker, not a giver, and more deadly than a black widow spider."

"I'll take my chances," Cormac boomed, eagerly anticipating an encounter with the fiery pirate. "Never knew a woman I couldn't handle."

"You've never known a woman like Scarlett," Kit returned.

After he had eaten his fill Kit stuffed a sack with food, changed his tired mount for a fresh one from Cormac's stable, and left in search of his beloved.

A short time later Cormac carried a tray of food to his beautiful prisoner. A current of keen anticipation charged through his huge body at the thought of what awaited him on the other side of the door. He'd waited many years for a woman of fire and courage to come into his life, and from all indications Scarlett was just such a woman. According to Diablo she had a soul as black as his own, but he didn't hold that against her. Like a fractious mare, all she needed was a firm hand to guide her and a real man in the saddle.

"What in the hell do you want, you grinning toad?" Scarlett snarled when Cormac stepped into the room.

"Is that any way to greet a man offering food and friendship?"

"Friendship, my arse!" Scarlett flung back. Her vulgar language was meant to shock, but Cormac appeared unfazed as he carefully set the tray on the table.

"Now, lass, you'll find I don't shock easily. See what I've brought you? There's scones and jam and oatmeal and hot tea. Be a good girl and eat."

His cajoling tone served only to goad Scarlett into a towering rage. No one spoke to her in such a condescending manner and lived to tell of it. Didn't this bear of a man know she was the master of her own ship and feared by friend and foe alike? Casually she sauntered over to the table where Cormac had placed the tray, eying it with cool disdain. Then, before the huge man realized her intent, she grabbed it up and hurled it at his head. Fortunately he was alert enough to duck, receiving only splatters of food as the tray whizzed harmlessly by to crash against the wall behind him.

"That's what I think of your food and your friendship!" Scarlett sneered. "We both know what Diablo intends to do with me. If you really wanted to be my friend you'd let me go."

"Ah, lass, you know I can't do that. Then neither of our lives would be worth a damn. Right or wrong, I'll not cross Diablo."

"Then we have nothing more to discuss," Scarlett proclaimed, her chin raised at a stubborn angle. "Get out of here!"

From the corner of her eye Scarlett studied the powerful giant, thinking him every bit as imposing as Diablo. A bit more rough around the edges perhaps, but every solid ounce of his magnificent frame exuded male sexuality at its most powerful best. Not an ounce of flab resided on his thickly muscled and blatantly virile torso and legs. Not handsome in a conventional way, Cormac's features possessed a rough-hewn beauty that Scarlett found more sensual, more compellingly attractive than men with classical good looks. Of course she wasn't about to let him know how deeply he affected her.

Taking full measure of Scarlett's tall, lithe body, Cormac had no intention of allowing the lady pirate to outwit him. "You're a feisty wench, Scarlett, but you've finally met your match. I'm no puny coward afraid to challenge your authority. Clean up this mess," he ordered, pointing to the upended tray and spilled food dripping down the wall onto the floor.

"Go to hell!" Scarlett defied. "I'm no man's drudge. Clean it up yourself."

Her flaming hair flying in wild disarray around her head, Scarlett stood her ground as Cormac took a menacing step in her direction. She had never backed down before any man and she damned well wasn't about to do so now. "Come ahead, you hairy ape," she taunted boldly. "You'll find I'm no easy target."

A low rumble of laughter tumbled from Cormac's mouth. Scarlett excited him as no woman ever had before. His nostrils flared as he breathed in the musky scent of her, sending the blood pumping through his veins at a furious rate. He felt alive and vital, and he wanted Scarlett. Wanted her with a compelling need that transcended every other need that had ever plagued him.

Scarlett's green eyes narrowed dangerously. She recognized Cormac's lust and reacted to it as only a woman of her fiery nature could, preparing to do battle. Lord knows she was no innocent. She knew exactly the moment the smuggler wanted her the way a man wants a woman. She could smell his excitement, reach out and touch that vibrant part of him that yearned to possess her. They stood facing each other like combatants on a battlefield, legs spread, arms akimbo, challenging one another in the age-old battle of the sexes.

Suddenly the thin line separating lust and hate shattered. Like animals in heat they fell upon one another, tearing at each other's clothes, clutching, grasping, falling to the floor to continue the fight for sexual supremacy. They coupled energetically and swiftly with little tenderness, carried away by a heady lust that surpassed anything either of them had ever felt before. Rolling around on the floor like two healthy animals, each trying to impose their will upon the other, they speedily reached an explosive, noisy release that drained and bewildered them. Neither had the slightest inkling of the monster they had unleashed between them.

"My God," Scarlett gasped reverently, "I've traded one devil for another!"

Thoroughly drenched, her hair plastered to her head in wet strands, Devon trembled with cold as she pulled her sodden cloak tightly around her. She had stumbled along in the soaking rain for hours and hadn't encountered a solitary soul crazy enough to be out on a night like this. It seemed incredible that she hadn't passed a single cottage or crofter's hut or found the village. Since there were no stars to use as a guide, she had been literally stumbling around blindly for hours. Weary beyond belief, Devon could at least be grateful that Scarlett was unlikely to find her trail in such dismal weather. Since nothing remotely resembling shelter had presented itself, Devon forced herself to continue moving, sheer guts and determination keeping her on her feet.

The last of her stamina had nearly deserted her when a large shape loomed before her, rising ghostlike through the darkness and mist. A house! Thank God, she prayed fervently, help was at hand. Her flimsy shoes squishing with mud, Devon experienced a strange feeling as she approached the cottage. It appeared dark and deserted and far too familiar for her liking. Oh, Lord! A groan of despair passed through her chilled lips.

The hunting lodge! She'd been traveling in circles for hours. At the end of her endurance, she dropped wearily to her knees, tears coursing down her smooth cheeks, ready to admit defeat. Then suddenly something stirred in her and she clutched her stomach. The baby! For the first time the child she carried made its presence known. Kit's child. Spurred by a growing sense of responsibility and love for her unborn baby, Devon struggled to her feet and approached the lodge, determined to survive.

It suddenly occurred to Devon that Scarlett might be gone, or asleep if she had remained, and thus might be easily overpowered. The door opened noiselessly beneath her hand and she paused on the threshold until her eyes adjusted to the violet shadows inside. Outside, dawn was breaking through the lowering bank of dripping clouds.

Stepping into the room, Devon felt the emptiness surround her and shivered. Intuition told her the lodge hadn't been vacated long, and the candle burnt down to the wick proved her correct. It was just light enough to see her way as she moved stealthily from room to room. Empty. No sign of Scarlett remained except for the heavy candlestick on the floor where Devon had last seen her lying unconscious.

Returning to the room that had once been her prison, Devon laid a fire in the grate, eager to dispel the chill from her bones. Once the fire burst into flames she hastily shed her clothes and wrapped herself in a thick quilt. The thought that Scarlett might return gave her a moment's pause, but she quickly discarded that fear, certain this would be the last place Scarlett would expect to find her.

Padding to the kitchen, Devon found cheese, bread, apples, and a portion of cold rabbit still left in the larder. Preparing herself a veritable feast, she carried it into the warmth of her cozy room, sat before the fire, and devoured every morsel. By now every bone in her body ached from weariness and long hours of abuse pushing herself through mud and pouring rain; she felt as if she could sleep for a week. Curling up on the bed, she fell asleep just as watery rays of morning sun broke through the mauve and silver clouds. Evening descended long hours later, and Devon slept on.

Slumped in the saddle, feeling as if the whole world rode on his shoulders, Kit reined in before the hunting lodge. His search had taken him so close to the lodge, he decided to spend the night in one of the bedrooms instead of returning to Cormac's ancient castle and starting out again in the morning. Weariness had rendered him nearly incapable of coherent thought, but every instinct told him to stop at the place where Devon had been kept so many weeks. He hadn't had a decent night's sleep since he left London days ago, snatching only brief naps in the saddle. Deep lines etched furrows across his brow, and his mouth drew taut with anguish. Hours spent scouring the countryside had failed to yield any sign of Devon. He should have found her by now, he reasoned, unless Winston had managed somehow to spirit her out of England.

Suddenly Kit straightened in the saddle, a frisson of sensation prickling his spine. It was almost as if something within the silent house was beckoning to him with an invisible finger. Compelled by a force stronger than his bone-wrenching weariness, Kit slid from the saddle and stared at the lodge through the encroaching darkness.

Tethering his drooping horse where it could easily feed on tender blades of grass, Kit approached the lodge like a sleepwalker moving through a dream. The fact that the house appeared deserted barely registered on his numb brain as he strode unerringly toward one of the bedrooms, drawn by some mysterious voice inside him.

Warm embers glowed dimly in the grate, providing just enough light to see the slender figure slumbering peacefully on the bed. Stifling a cry of incredible joy, Kit stood above Devon, gazing at her like a man whose sight had just been restored. Unwilling to startle her from so deep a sleep, Kit turned and walked back through the house and out the door to where his horse was tethered. After unsaddling and rubbing down the poor animal, he carried his saddlebags inside and prepared a simple meal for himself and Devon from the remnants of food provided by Cormac's larder. By the time he bathed and shaved, the need for his wife was like a burning brand inside him. He crawled in naked beside her.

Devon stretched with catlike grace beneath the quilt, a delicious languor painting her cheeks a delicate pink. Still sleeping, she could almost feel Kit's tender regard, experience his gentle hands exploring the hidden secrets of her body. It had been so long—too damn long—since she'd tasted the magic of his loving, savored the unique essence of his being. God, she loved him. Would they never be reunited and free from Scarlett's machinations? she wondered even in her sleep.

Reaching out to grasp the elusive object of her dream before he evaporated into pure fantasy, Devon imagined she could actually feel Kit beside her in bed. "I want you—I want you so," she whispered throatily. Just as she had so many times in the past, she ran her tongue over his skin, recalling how he had done the same to her on countless occasions.

How salty he was to her taste! How rough and smooth his magnificent body felt to her lips! If only he were real. The texture of his skin alternated from the velvet of his shoulders to the pleasant hairiness of his chest and the smooth hardness of his belly, and then the toughness and power of his muscled thighs.

"I want you, too, sweetheart," Kit's voice answered, startling Devon from the last vestiges of sleep. "But if you keep that up I'll not be able to love you properly."

Devon's heart catapulted to her throat. "Kit! Am I dreaming or is it really you? Thank God," she sobbed. "What took you so long to find me?"

"Your father just told me where Winston had taken you. I've had men scouring the countryside for you all these weeks. I left London the moment I knew. I'm no fantasy, sweetheart, as your lips and hands discovered."

"It's been so long I despaired of ever seeing you again," Devon said, choking back the lump in her throat.

"I'd have found you even if I had to search the world over."

"Not if Scarlett had her way." Suddenly Devon froze. "Kit, Scarlett! She wants to kill me. What if she returns to the lodge?"

"Don't fret, Scarlett won't bother us. I found her here in the lodge when I arrived earlier and took her to Cormac for safekeeping. You've nothing to fear where Scarlett's concerned. She's confessed everything. She admitted it was her idea to abduct you and that she blackmailed Winston into doing her bidding. Where is that bloody coward? If I know Winston, he's probably hiding someplace hoping I won't find him."

"By now Freddie and Winston are on their way to France," Devon revealed.

"Good riddance," Kit said with bitter emphasis. "But how in the hell is Freddie Smythe involved in all this? I would never have expected it of him."

"He's not involved, really. At first he thought Winston and I had eloped. Then Scarlett spread gossip about Freddie and Winston. I should have believed you when you told me

Winston was—was—odd, but it seemed so far-fetched at the time. Somehow Freddie found Winston, and since he'd been turned out of his home he offered to take Winston along with him to France."

"It's beyond me how Freddie learned where Winston was when the men I paid to find him turned up no clues," said Kit. "If Winston sets foot in London again, I'll strangle him with my bare hands. Not only did he persuade your father to help him in this crazy stunt, but he caused me weeks of unbearable anguish."

"I don't understand why Father didn't tell you immediately where Winston had taken me. Didn't you tell him we were married? It's not like Father to hold a grudge. I know he doesn't like you, but he's not a vindictive man and I felt certain he'd capitulate once he learned we loved each other."

Kit scooped Devon into his arms, settling her comfortably against his chest as he searched for words to tell her about the earl. "He would have, sweetheart, but your father suffered a seizure the same day you left. I was with him at the time. I had just told him that we loved each other and were man and wife when he collapsed. He did manage to say that he would never have consented to Winston's wild scheme had he been told the truth about us."

"Oh Kit, no! Is—is Father—"

"Nay, love, your father was recovering when I left London. He temporarily lost the ability to speak, and it was touch and go for awhile, but he's a strong man and the doctor predicts a full recovery. The moment he was able to communicate he told me where to find you. He's sorry for what he did and hopes you'll forgive him."

"I don't blame Father. Winston has a glib tongue and probably convinced him you meant me harm. Evidently you changed Father's mind. The important thing is that we're together again."

"You talk too much, sweetheart," Kit rebuked teasingly.

"Didn't you just admit you wanted me? I can wait no longer to demonstrate how badly I want and need you."

Her reply was lost as his lips claimed hers, his hands cupping her face in a firm yet gentle grasp as he kissed her sweet mouth, her chin, her nose, while whispering her name over and over again in a delirious frenzy of wild longing. Then Devon cried out in blissful agony as his dark head lowered and his open mouth closed over the taut peak of her breast while his hands roamed the length of her spine, the small of her back, her firm buttocks, down the silky measure of her thighs.

"You've gained weight, sweetheart," Kit murmured, testing the weight of the soft mounds of her breasts in his hands. "But I don't mind," he assured her, leering wolfishly, "they fit my hands better."

As if to prove his point, he cupped those tender white doves, passing his thumbs back and forth over the sensitive buds till they puckered and stood erect. Then he captured them again with his lips, lashing them with the moist tip of his tongue before drawing them deeply into his mouth and suckling with gentle insistence.

A shudder of intense pleasure wracked Devon's body. Oh Lord, she wanted it, wanted him, wanted all he had to offer.

Raising his head, Kit sighed blissfully. "Ah, sweetheart, you'd tempt the devil, how do you expect a mere mortal to resist you?"

"Mere mortal? Nay, Kit. You're Diablo, the devil who wove a seductive web around my heart. I love you so."

His breathing was thickened and unsteady as his hands danced over her curves, sliding downward to cup the taut mounds of her buttocks. He stroked and caressed them, tugging her hard against his hips, letting her feel his eagerness, know how compelling was his need of her.

The intimacy was unbearable, destroying what little restraint Devon had left. Drawing a quick breath, she turned wanton in his arms, boldly touching and caressing and stroking his hard male body with her hands, mouth, and tongue, arousing him to a breathless need that bordered on madness. His tenuous grip on reality vanished when her tongue traced a hot, wet path across the flat muscles of his belly. Flipping her on her back, Kit nudged her legs apart with his knee and lodged his entire length in the tight, hot sheath of her body. A groan of pure ecstasy tore from his lips, spurring Devon's need to an aching throb. Then their bodies forged into one, hands searching, exploring, lips hungry and eager as Kit began to rock back and forth.

Although he had meant to be slow and sweet, the strength of his desire compelled him to strike a far more rapid pace as he plunged ever deeper into the soft sweet center of her being. He pushed harder, deeper, swifter into her, her murmurs spurring him to bring them both to tempestuous release as quickly as possible.

Locking her legs around his buttocks, Devon urged him deeply and snugly within her, turning him wilder, crazier. The explosion erupting within her turned her insides to liquid fire, but her legs remained firmly locked in place, unwilling to release him until he reached his own climax, until the last shudder left his body, the final sigh trembled from his lips.

"God's bones, sweetheart, I expected to find this kind of ecstasy only in heaven. Now I know what I suspected all along. You *are* my heaven."

In the aftermath of love he began caressing her, her breasts, her thighs, her stomach—where his hand froze on the undisguisable bulge just below her waistline. Devon drew in a ragged breath, realizing belatedly that Kit still knew nothing about their child. Now it seemed as if he had discovered it for himself.

"Kit . . ."

"God's bones, you're growing a babe! Why didn't you tell me I was going to be a father? Or had you decided to wait until you placed the babe in my arms? You should have told me at the Smythes' ball," he reproved, annoyed by her omission of something so important. "Had I known I would have been more gentle."

"You didn't harm me, my love," Devon replied, her blue eyes glowing with love, "or our child. He's fine. Here," she said, placing his hand against the hard little bulge, "feel him move within me. He's strong, just like his father."

A look of awe replaced the frown darkening Kit's brow when he felt the tiny thump against his hand. "Why didn't you tell me sooner?" he repeated. "How long have you known? My God, Winston could have harmed our child! If Scarlett had succeeded in her plan, I could have lost you both." A look of horror turned his features into a mask of repressed rage.

"I began to suspect about a month after I returned to England. I was going to tell you at the ball, but Scarlett interfered. Then the next day, Winston carried me off. In a little over five months you'll have a son, Kit. Are—are you happy?" Devon asked, her lips curved into a tentative smile.

"Ecstatic, sweetheart, but I thought a daughter would be nice first. A blue-eyed angel as beguiling as her mother."

"Nay, a son first, Kit, to carry on your name, then as many daughters as you wish."

"Not too many," Kit teased. "I've no wish to wear you out with constant childbearing, nor endanger your life each time I fill your belly."

"I want your children," Devon assured him. "I'm strong and healthy, nothing will happen to me."

"And you'll have them, sweetheart, but just enough to satisfy my male ego and feed your mother's instinct. I want you to always have time for me."

"There'll always be time for you, my love, beginning with right now. Love me again, Kit. Love me for all those lonely nights I've cried myself to sleep for need of you."

"I will, sweetheart, but first, the supper I fixed for us is waiting and I'm famished. I've been in the saddle for days and haven't eaten since I left Cormac this morning. If I'm to love you properly I need sustenance of another kind."

Blushing, Devon acquiesced, using the time Kit was in the kitchen preparing their tray to wash and freshen up. Then she wrapped up in the quilt and fed the fire, having a nice blaze going by the time he returned. Sitting side by side on the bed, they devoured every last bite of the cold repast. Licking her fingers, Devon lay back, replete.

"Ummm, good. I was hungrier than I thought. I slept for hours with little thought for food or drink."

"Are you still tired, sweetheart?" Kit asked, his silver gaze hungrily devouring her face before dropping to her full breasts, exposed where the quilt had slipped under her armpits.

"Sleep isn't what I crave right now," she hinted brazenly.

"Then 'tis more food you want." His teasing tone set her heart racing in her chest.

"Nay, not food." Her soft, throaty voice flowed over him like a caress, surrounding him in a warm cocoon of desire, and his weariness dropped away.

His kiss was unhurried, moving slow and sweetly over her mouth as his right hand gently stripped the quilt from her body. His fingers slid over the smooth swell of her breasts, circling the pale pink tips until they were firm peaks; then he slid his hand over her hip to draw her closer. His mood was so relaxed now that he felt no urgency, simply wanting to give her more pleasure than she had ever known. His hand slipped between her legs, parting tender flesh to slide a finger inside the warm crevice. His intimate caress yielded a moist response from her body that made Devon shift uncomfortably.

"This won't hurt you or the babe, will it?" Kit asked anxiously as his fingers explored with maddening effect.

"Nay," Devon gasped, rotating her hips in rhythm with his probing and spreading her thighs to allow him greater access.

Kit's thumb located the tiny hidden bud and stroked it to pebble hardness. He scooted downward between her legs, and the tip of his tongue replaced his thumb to send a jolt ripping through her body, arcing her upward.

"Kit! My God!"

"Relax, sweetheart. I want to love you in every way. Don't be afraid to show your joy. I want to give you as much pleasure as you bring me."

"Kit, please—don't—don't stop!"

"Never, my wonderful love, never."

Then abruptly her whole world shattered and she went spiraling out of control into a kaleidoscope of brilliant colors and shooting stars. Waiting until her body was completely still, Kit shifted upwards, impaling her with the swollen length of his manhood. Desire thundered through him, for he had teased and aroused himself by deliberately delaying his own pleasure while enjoying hers.

He moved within her, driven by a need more potent than the headiest wine, thrusting, withdrawing, rekindling the banked fires Devon thought had been thoroughly doused just moments ago.

"Aye, sweetheart, that's it. Come for me again. Let me feel those delicious tremors inside your sweet body. Hurry, love—ah, you're so tight, so warm—"

His highly erotic words had the desired effect as Devon caught fire and blazed out of control. This time they flew away together, reaching the highest level of pleasure God granted to a man and woman.

"Are you all right, sweetheart?"

"Ummm, wonderful," Devon sighed dreamily. "I never thought it possible to be so happy."

"Nor I," Kit concurred. "Had I chosen to remain a pirate I

could have been captured and hanged at any time, and lose you forever. I never dreamed I'd be a respectable citizen again with a beautiful wife and a child on the way. It frightens me to think that Winston and Scarlett nearly succeeded in taking you from me."

"What will happen to Scarlett?" Devon asked.

"I'd like to wring her beautiful neck," Kit muttered darkly. "But I've decided to turn her over to the authorities. She'll be charged with attempted murder and violating amnesty. She'll be punished for her crime according to the dictates of the law. I'm through taking the law into my own hands."

Feeling little sympathy for the woman who had resented her from the moment of their first meeting, Devon did not question Kit's judgment.

They lingered at the lodge three more days, resting, talking, and loving, sleeping late each morning and making love again in the bed still rumpled from the previous night's exertions. Sometimes they whiled away the afternoon making love yet another time, sharing a rapture that had long been denied them. Fortunately, enough food remained in the larder to keep them from starving, supplemented with small game that Kit caught. Devon proved a fair cook despite her woeful lack of experience, and Kit never tired of watching her at her domestic chores.

"We'll leave in the morning," Kit said as they prepared for bed one night. "Cormac will be sending out a search party if I don't return soon. Besides, Scarlett is probably driving him mad and he'll be anxious to get her off his hands."

"It's been so lovely here I almost hate to leave," Devon sighed wistfully.

"You'll be happy at Linley Hall, sweetheart," Kit promised. "And as soon as we're certain your father is recovering we'll sail to Paradise Island for a proper honeymoon. I left Tara in charge and need to make plans for the disposition of the island."

"I'd love to go to Paradise, Kit, providing we'll be back in time for the birth of our child." Devon recalled with pleasure the warm, sunny days and balmy, moon-drenched nights on the tropical isle. "Do you still have the *Devil Dancer?*"

"Aye. She's been engaged in commerce these past weeks. But I left orders before coming to Cornwall that she's to meet us in a cove close to Cormac's castle for the return trip to London. She's probably there waiting now. But enough talk, the night grows short and I want to love you."

"Will you always want to love me?" Devon teased. "What about when I'm old and gray and no longer beautiful?"

"In my eyes you'll never grow old, sweetheart. You'll always be as lovely and desirable as you are at this moment. Each time I make love to you, be it once or a thousand times, will be like the first. But if you keep asking silly questions we may never get around to that thousandth time."

Giggling happily, Devon held out her arms, inviting him into the warmth of her embrace, offering her lips and her body as a fitting sacrifice to their love.

Chapter Twenty-two

"Damn you, Cormac, you're not a man, you're a sorcerer," Scarlett accused, gasping for breath.

They had lain together each night since their explosive coming together three days ago, engaging in the most satisfying sex Scarlett had ever experienced. Cormac was a huge bear of a man, rough yet incredibly tender, completely lacking in finesse but compensating for it with erotic expertise. In the three short days she'd known him she'd not thought of Diablo once. Even more astounding was the fact that Cormac appeared as fascinated with her as she was with him.

It seemed to Scarlett as if she had waited all her life for a man strong enough to match her in strength of will and wits. She thought she'd found him in Diablo and would have been satisfied with her first choice if he hadn't fallen hopelessly in love with Devon.

"And you're a red-haired witch, Scarlett," Cormac laughed delightedly. "I've been looking forever for a woman like you. We're a matched pair, my long-legged wanton, and that's for sure. 'Tis doubtful which one of us will prevail, but I'm willing to bet we'll both enjoy the combat. Taming you might take a lifetime, but life would never be dull."

"Are you man enough to tame me?" Scarlett challenged. Her voice was a throaty purr, daring him to try.

"Aye. Are you woman enough to enjoy it?" Cormac growled in response, rolling to capture her tall frame beneath his huge body.

What followed next was a night of wild and unrestrained sex that lasted until pink streaks made bright patterns across the eastern sky. Exhausted, they fell asleep in each other's arms, neither stirring until the door to the bedroom crashed open to reveal the nude couple, limbs entwined, sleeping peacefully amid the rumpled disorder of the big bed they shared.

"What the hell!"

Kit and Devon had returned to Cormac's castle just moments before, finding no one about except stammering servants. Though the staff knew full well where their master had spent the last three nights, loyalty prevented them from speaking. Vexed, Kit made immediately for Scarlett's room, Devon close on his heels. Contrary to Kit's orders, the door was unlocked, and he flung it open. Empty! Turning abruptly, he raced to Cormac's chamber, thinking Scarlett had somehow managed to do away with the burly giant and escape. He would put nothing past the witch. Not bothering to knock, Kit propelled himself into the room, skidding to a halt just inside the door.

Cormac reared up, scrambling for the sheet wadded up at the foot of the bed. Sated after her night of sexual rapture, Scarlett was slower to react, stretching languidly before opening her eyes. When she saw Kit and Devon staring at her she made no attempt to cover herself, merely smiling like a well-satisfied kitten.

Kit's eyes rolled heavenward, highly amused but also much relieved to find that Scarlett hadn't flown the coop. "So, my friend, I'm pleased you found the onerous chore of keeping my captive to your liking. Scarlett can be a handful but quite entertaining when the mood strikes her. I trust you've enjoyed yourself?"

Cormac had the grace to blush, but wasn't inclined to explain or excuse his actions. Instead, he adroitly changed the subject. Now modestly covered by the sheet, he turned to Devon. "'Tis happy I am to see you, my lady, though I'd much prefer to greet you under—er—different circumstances. I'm hardly at my best dressed in a bedsheet. But I truly am glad Diablo found you unharmed."

Devon stifled a giggle. Never had she seen anything so hairy as Cormac's massive chest except on a four-footed creature. "Thank you, Cormac," she replied, swallowing the laughter bubbling in her throat. It did her heart good to see Scarlett looking so subdued lying beside her huge lover. "If you'll excuse me, I'll leave you to your privacy. I—we didn't mean to barge in." She turned to leave, and when Kit failed to follow, she tugged determinedly on his sleeve.

Reluctantly Kit gave in to Devon's prodding. "I'll wait for you downstairs, Cormac. I'm sure there's much we have to discuss," he threw over his shoulder.

"He's angry enough with me to slit my throat," Scarlett said when she and Cormac were alone.

"Nay, lass," Cormac denied. "No real harm has come to Devon, though I won't say you aren't deserving of his contempt. What you did was despicable." His stern visage sent Scarlett's heart plummeting. It sounded as if Cormac had no intention of allowing the past three nights of unequaled bliss to interfere with Kit's plans for her.

"I'd like a bath," she said testily, unwilling to grovel at Cormac's feet. She'd been caretaker of her own destiny far too long to relinquish her pride by begging for her life.

"Aye," Cormac agreed, his lips twitching suspiciously. "I'll see to it. Meanwhile I'll go down and face the devil. I strongly suspect he'll have some choice words about finding us like this."

"Did you seduce Scarlett or did she seduce you?" Kit asked.

"A little of both, I suspect," Cormac said with the barest hint of humor. "It just happened. I couldn't wait to get my hands on the witch, and she couldn't keep her hands off me.

I always thought men were masters of their own fate, but now I'm not so sure."

A look of stunned disbelief passed over Kit's face. "Are you saying you have feelings for Scarlett, knowing what she is and what she's done? She would have killed Devon without hesitation if given the opportunity. The woman is capable of murder. She's the one who betrayed me by giving Le Vautour directions to Paradise. Scarlett masterminded Devon's abduction. If she had harmed Devon or our child, I would have retaliated swiftly, with the same kind of mercy she showed my wife."

"Your child! Is Devon—"

"Aye, in five months she'll give birth to our babe."

"Thank God you found her," Cormac said sincerely. "What's to become of Scarlett?"

"I'm turning her over to the authorities, charging her with attempted murder and breaking the terms of amnesty. I doubt she'll escape the hangman, but if she does she'll rot in jail for the remainder of her days."

"Nay, I'll not allow it!"

"What? You want me to be lenient with a woman capable of murder and deceit? You want me to extend mercy to one who doesn't deserve it?"

"Aye, I want Scarlett," the huge smuggler admitted somewhat sheepishly. "At first I took Scarlett to prove my mastery over so vibrant a woman. I had no idea she would affect me so deeply. Now I find I want far more from her. I want to marry her and keep her with me forever. I promise as long as I live she'll not harm another soul."

"God's bones, you're mad!" Kit cried. "The treacherous witch will reward you with a knife in your ribs the first time you turn your back."

"I'm willing to take that chance," Cormac argued stubbornly.

Kit regarded Cormac with piercing scrutiny. He couldn't believe what he was hearing. Normally Cormac was a sensible man with good instincts. What had Scarlett done to him? The only explanation seemed to be that Scarlett had bewitched him. Yet Cormac seemed in full control of his senses. It also occurred to Kit that Cormac had never failed to come to his aid. Along with Kyle and Akbar, Cormac had been an integral part of his life.

But somehow Kit couldn't mouth the words that would free Scarlett and give her to his friend. Her underhanded dealings had fouled up his life too often in the past. He belatedly realized that Scarlett had been part of Le Vautour's scheme to lead him on a wild chase after Spanish galleons while Le Vautour took Devon from Paradise and wounded Kyle while making good their escape. Scarlett was a constant irritant, always trying to tempt and tease, though he told her long ago their affair was over.

Kit's mouth twisted in a wry smile as he was suddenly struck with a solution. "Since my wife is the one who's been affected the most by Scarlett's dirty dealings, I'll place her fate entirely in Devon's hands."

At first Cormac was stunned, but then he realized Kit's intentions. He also knew that Devon's heart was too soft and forgiving to condemn a woman to death. "Aye, 'tis no more than right," he agreed.

Minutes later Scarlett stood before Kit, her green eyes wary, body tense. Devon was also present, having been summoned by Kit.

"Kill me now," Scarlett said defiantly. "I'd prefer it to rotting in jail." She had expected Cormac to leap to her defense, but his features were deliberately blank.

"I've decided to place your fate in Devon's hands," Kit said evenly.

Devon started violently, gasping in horror. What in the world was Kit thinking?

"Since it's Devon's life and that of our unborn child you endangered, 'tis no more than right she should make the decision. I'll abide by her wishes."

"Child!" choked out Scarlett, aware that she was already as good as dead. In all her long illustrious days of pirating she'd never deliberately harmed a child or allowed her crew to do so. "I—I had no idea."

"Might I speak before you decide?" Cormac injected.

"Aye," Devon said with a nod. "Please do."

"I've told your husband of my desire to marry Scarlett. Once she's my wife I swear she'll not cause you further grief. I intend to make her a full partner in my smuggling operation. I believe she'll find sufficient excitement to keep her happy and content, so she'll have no need to return to London Town. I'd stake my life 'twill be enough adventure to satisfy any craving Scarlett might harbor in that exquisite body of hers."

Scarlett could do little more than stare at Cormac, flabbergasted by his suggestion. Would Kit allow it? Would Devon agree?

"You want Scarlett for your wife?" Devon repeated, as stunned as Scarlett.

"Aye."

"What does Kit think?"

"Ask him."

She cocked an inquiring eye in Kit's direction. "Well, my love?"

"The decision is yours, sweetheart. Keep in mind Scarlett is a conniving bitch who would have felt no remorse over murdering you."

"Is Scarlett willing?" Devon addressed the question to Cormac.

"I've good reason to think so. You have no idea how fantastic we are together, how we seem to explode the moment we come together. I want her, damn it! If Scarlett agrees, I'll marry her tomorrow. She'll become my duchess and full partner in a lucrative smuggling operation. But if she even thinks of returning to London I'll wring her neck—after I beat the daylights out of her."

Devon felt the weight of decision pressing down upon her narrow shoulders. Scarlett deserved everything she had coming to her for wanting to harm her, yet no human was without redemption. Perhaps all the woman needed was a forceful man like Cormac to take control of her life. Besides, Devon knew she could not order another person's death, and Scarlett would surely die confined in prison for any length of time.

Scarlett's hopes soared, despite the fact she'd never thought of herself married to anyone but Diablo. But Cormac was offering her a second chance at life in a most intriguing manner, one she couldn't refuse. Each time Cormac set his hands on her tingling flesh it was a unique and thoroughly rewarding experience. She knew if she lived as his wife she'd have neither the inclination nor the energy to return to London, not for any reason. The antics of the rich and titled were beginning to bore her anyway. Besides, if she married Cormac she could still be a duchess as she'd always dreamed.

"Do you agree to Cormac's terms?" Devon asked, finally turning to Scarlett.

A long, tense silence ensued before Scarlett spoke. "Aye. If Cormac wants me, I'm his, though he's getting no bargain." She turned to Cormac. "You'll find me difficult to tame, but I promise you exciting days and nights for your trouble. If you still want me, then you have my consent. I'll be your wife and partner."

"What say you, sweetheart?" Kit asked, awaiting Devon's final judgment.

"Let Cormac have her," Devon decreed, "and I wish him luck. He'll need it."

Whooping with joy, Cormac scooped Scarlett up in his arms and bore her out of the room and up the stairs where he began his domination by making wild, passionate love to her.

The next day Devon and Kit witnessed the couple's wedding, performed that evening by the same minister who had officiated at their own nuptials. On short notice the staff had prepared a magnificent feast, and when the bride and groom retired to their wedding bed, Devon and Kit sought their own privacy.

"Do you think we've done right by not turning Scarlett over to the authorities?" Devon asked as she undressed for bed. One small part of her hated to see Scarlett go unpunished for her evil ways.

Kit had already disrobed and slid beneath the covers. "I think we can trust Cormac to keep that hellcat out of our lives," Kit murmured, too enthralled by Devon emerging from her clothes to give Scarlett more than a passing thought. "Come to bed, sweetheart, I want to make love to you." Thrilled by his hungry impatience, Devon complied, slipping eagerly into his waiting arms.

The next hours were spent making tender, leisurely love, oblivious to everything but their obsessive need for one another. Devon's craving was so devastating that her entire body quivered uncontrollably as she was drawn toward an all-consuming flame. With lips and hands Kit brought her carefully to the brink of ecstasy, and when she could stand no more of his sweet torture, he invaded the last of her body's defenses, bringing them both to explosive climax.

In another room in the vast crumbling castle, Cormac and Scarlett created their own fireworks, his potent seed finding fertile ground in Scarlett's receptive body.

The following morning only Cormac was on hand as Kit and Devon prepared to leave, excusing his bride with a sly wink that said more than mere words. When they had gathered their meager belongings, Cormac drove them in the coach to the deserted stretch of beach where they were to meet the *Devil Dancer*. It was a comforting sight to see her riding at anchor in the secluded bay. A signal was sent out, and they waited on the beach while a longboat was dispatched to pick them up. Their last sight of Cormac was of the bearlike smuggler grinning from ear to ear and waving goodbye, obviously quite pleased with himself.

Four days later they reached London. A hired coach took them to Chatham House, where Devon was ecstatic to find her father sitting up in a chair engaged in a game of chess with the butler. When Devon and Kit burst into the room, the servant sent them a grateful smile and scooted from the room, happy to be relieved of the onerous task of entertaining the cantankerous earl.

"Devon, thank God!" the earl cried, opening his arms to welcome his beloved daughter.

"Oh, Father, I've been so worried about you! Kit told me what happened. How are you feeling?"

"Well enough, now that you're back," replied Lord Harvey in a voice made gruff with emotion. "More importantly, how are you? Has Winston been turned over to the authorities? I fully intend to press charges. The man is utterly devoid of scruples. He deliberately lied to me. Can you ever forgive me, daughter?"

"Winston hoodwinked you, Father," Devon soothed, concerned by the earl's significant weight loss and haggard appearance. "He fooled us both. Winston wasn't what he seemed, he was—"

"Devon," Kit cautioned, "don't tax your father with useless information. Suffice it to say Winston has fled England and no longer poses a threat to us."

Taking Kit's hint, Devon continued cautiously. "It's over

with, Father. I'm here with you and my—my husband, and we have something to tell you. Something wonderful."

Intrigued, Lord Harvey shifted his gaze from Devon to Kit, a man he'd been prepared to hate until Devon chose him for a husband. "Well, daughter, what is this wonderful news you're so anxious to convey?"

A foolish grin hung on one corner of Kit's mouth and his chest puffed out proudly. "Let me, sweetheart. Your Grace, your daughter will soon present me with an heir."

"Bloody hell! I just recently learned my daughter was wed, and now you're telling me she's to be a mother," Lord Harvey grumbled, feigning annoyance. "You've cheated me out of hundreds of pounds in trading goods over the years, but that wasn't enough, you had to steal my daughter. If I wasn't absolutely convinced Devon loved you I'd send you packing."

"'Tis too late, Your Grace," Kit argued happily. "I fully intend to raise my children and become the husband Devon deserves. I've been offered another opportunity to live my life as it was meant to be lived. Few men are allowed a second chance to make things right. So with or without your blessing, Devon will remain my duchess."

"Do you think I'd turn down the opportunity of knowing my grandchildren?" Lord Harvey asked incredulously. "I'll take my daughter's word that she's tamed the devil and Diablo no longer exists. I welcome the Duke of Grenville into our family and wish the two of you every happiness."

He extended his hand, a truce eagerly accepted by Kit.

"You'll not regret it, Your Grace. I'll make Devon so damn happy she'll find her heaven on earth."

"I think Father took it well," Devon giggled, resting her head on Kit's broad shoulder. They lay in bed gloriously naked, arms and legs entwined. They were home now, at Linley Hall, where Devon once expected to reside as Winston's bride. It was a house she knew well and had always loved. It seemed so right that she should be its mistress and Kit's wife.

"Well enough," agreed Kit, recalling the earl's eagerness to become a grandfather before he breathed his last.

A long, painful sigh escaped his lips. Once they reached London he promised himself he'd allow Devon several nights' rest without subjecting her to his lovemaking, but was having a difficult time keeping his word. After Devon's ordeal and their journey home, Kit decided that for his child's sake his wife deserved a period of uninterrupted rest.

"Did you mean what you told Father, my love?" Devon purred in a seductive whisper.

"That depends. I told him many things."

"You said you intended to make me so happy I'd think I was living in heaven."

"True enough," concurred Kit, perplexed.

"Then do it."

"Do what?"

"Make me happy."

"I thought you'd appreciate the rest tonight."

"The first night in my own home and you want me to rest?" argued Devon, jolting upright and glaring at Kit indignantly. Her action gave him an unrestricted view of her full breasts bouncing enticingly. "Perhaps you're the one who needs rest. I *have* been rather demanding lately."

"Are you questioning my virility, wife?" Kit roared in mock anger. "Have I given you reason to doubt my ability to perform?"

Grinning with wicked delight, Devon taunted cheekily, "Nay, but if you are tired I could make love to you for a change, so as not to tax your strength, of course. Why should men do all the work?"

"Devon, making love to you is no chore, but I don't think—"

"Then don't think, just relax and let me . . ." Her words trailed off as her lips slashed across his. With a groan of delight, he surrendered himself into her tender care.

Putting her mouth, hands, and tongue into good use, Devon taunted and teased unmercifully, filling her senses with the salty taste of him, his musky odor. Her moist lips hovered on each male nipple and her roaming hands sought out each sensitive point on his body, leaving a trail of white-hot flames. Unable to resist, Kit reached for her, wanting to crush her to him, but she glided out of his reach. When she began anew with her tender torture, Kit forced himself to lie back and endure the delicious agony of her loving.

Kit nearly flew off the bed when she brought her hand over his hip, resting it there for an eternity before attempting a caress of a far more intimate nature. Then her hand found him, tracking the incredible length of him with long, teasing strokes.

"God's bones, sweetheart, you're killing me!"

"Turnabout is fair play," Devon taunted, giggling delightedly. Then her lips replaced her hands and Kit howled as if in pain. Only then did she relent, straddling his hips and taking his massive staff into her body and sheathing it lovingly in her moist warmth.

"Oh no you don't, you little temptress!" Kit groaned, adroitly reversing their position. " 'Tis your turn now."

Though it cost him untold anguish, he withdrew from her, covering her body with tiny nipping kisses, deliberately ignoring the pouting tips of her breasts. He paid loving homage to the indentation of her navel, the soft mound of her stomach, the inside of satiny thighs, before finally returning to those ripe buds that begged for his attention. Drawing each nipple deeply into his mouth, he suckled them gently one at a time until Devon moaned and arched beneath him, a burning beginning in that place she yearned for him the most.

"Had enough?" Kit teased, a roguish grin bringing his dimple into play.

"Aye, please," Devon panted raggedly.

"Nay, I think not."

And then, before her shattered senses could anticipate his next move, he slid downward to the thickly thatched crest of her womanhood. When his lips invaded the tender, hidden slit, he thrilled to the liquid heat of her passion. Hungrily he parted her with his hard thrusting tongue, greedily exploring deep inside.

Crying out, Devon writhed beneath his tender probing, begging for mercy just as Kit had begged moments ago. Finally taking pity on her, he shifted upwards, lunging forward with a groan of pure ecstasy. Employing extreme patience, he moved carefully against her, ever thoughtful of their babe. His hand slid beneath her hips, lifting her to him, his need a throbbing ache now. Devon was suspended in a whirlwind of sensations that touched every nerve and sinew in her body. Now she was moving in gentle rhythm to his coaxing, consumed by such heat she could never again claim to being an identity unto herself. From now into eternity they would be forever one.

As Kit soared to lofty heights, he became Devon's possession, a living, breathing part of her never again to be separated.

Several weeks later the *Devil Dancer*, with Kit at the wheel, safely sailed through the jagged reef guarding Paradise Island. A surprising number of people, including reformed pirates and their families who had chosen to remain on the cay, came out to greet them. There was one other ship anchored in the snug bay; it belonged to members of Kit's old crew. Before he left, Kit had shown them how to navigate the reef so they might come and go as they wished. He was pleased to note that the village appeared to be thriving and that another pier had been built to accommodate increased traffic.

Kyle and Marlena had accompanied Kit and Devon aboard the *Devil Dancer*, as had Akbar, who seemed to have mellowed somewhat in his opinion of Devon after he learned she was carrying Kit's child. With infinite care Kit guided Devon down the gangplank. She was well into her pregnancy and absolutely blooming. By the time they all stood on the dock, Tara was running down the path from the house.

"Diablo! I knew you'd come back!" she squealed breathlessly, throwing herself into his arms.

Kyle received an equally joyous welcome, as did Marlena. Akbar was greeted last, but no less exuberantly. Devon was granted a sour smile but little else, for Tara still held Devon responsible for deserting Diablo as well as all the bad things that had happened on Paradise. Kit sensed Tara's animosity, and as they all walked to the house he carefully explained much of what had happened since leaving the Caribbean, including the news that Devon was expecting his child. Instantly Tara's disposition toward Devon changed and she offered a tentative smile, begging forgiveness. Devon freely gave it.

They spent a blissful month on Paradise before Kit decided it was time to take Devon home to England where expert care was available for the birth of their child. Besides, he'd promised Lord Harvey they would return in plenty of time for the big event. Kyle and Marlena, already an essential part of their lives, would also be returning to England. Kyle had money enough to go into business for himself and at Kit's urging decided to launch a shipping venture. His voice bursting with pride, Kyle informed everyone that Marlena was expecting a child.

That left only Akbar at loose ends. He had yet to indicate his intentions. It became increasingly evident that he missed piracy and was almost of a mind to return to the profession. London definitely had not been to his liking.

Several nights before they were to leave, Tara took matters into her own hands, seeking Akbar out in the small hut he occupied while on Paradise. "What are you doing here, Tara?" he growled, eying the lovely, dusky woman warily. In the moonlight her hair gleamed like thousands of black diamonds, and Akbar had a difficult time concentrating.

"Don't you know?" Tara asked softly. Beneath her sarong her heart beat a wild tattoo. Her pride suffered coming here like this, but if it won her her heart's desire it was well worth it.

"You're no whore!" he snorted. "You know I've little use for women except for an occasional lusty encounter. Do you want to share my bed on those terms? Is that why you've come?"

"Would you turn me away if I said yes?"

"By Allah's beard! Do you think me stupid? I've been desired by women before, and betrayed by one whose jealousy ate at her like a canker. Would you bed me knowing I despise all women, that I use them for only one purpose?"

"I think you've hidden behind your hate too long. 'Tis time to forget and forgive. Let me help you."

"Why?"

"I wish I knew. All I know is that when I look at you I tremble inside, and not from fear. Oh, you try hard to maintain that fierce exterior, but I sense a softness in you no one else has discovered."

"A softness!" Akbar roared, scowling furiously. "There is nothing soft about me." Roughly he pulled her inside. "Don't you know I devour women like you?" His lips slashed across hers with a violence that would have frightened lesser women. "Don't you fear me? You should."

"Nay, what I feel is not fear. What I do fear is never seeing you again."

Akbar could not believe his ears. Even when he paid women for their favors they still feared him. "Would it really bother you not to see me again?"

"It would make me very sad. You're—you're magnificent, Akbar."

Akbar regarded Tara from beneath shaggy brows, finding it difficult to believe that Tara found any redeeming qualities in his character. Didn't she know he distrusted all women? Only when Tara stepped up to him, slipped her slim arms around his huge neck, and lifted her lips did he respond to her gentleness. Suddenly all his years of enforced loneliness and bitter hatred, of distrust and unfounded discrimination, dropped away. Then his massive arms crushed her to him and his lips seized hers with a hunger he'd never known or allowed himself to dream about.

During all these years he'd told no one of his attraction for the luscious Tara, fearing to reveal too much of his soul. The knowledge that the ravishing creature in his arms returned those feelings melted the hard knot of denial he'd harbored in his heart since he'd caught the eye of the sultan's fickle favorite and earned her jealous friend's betrayal. Chained to an oar provides an adequate setting to nurture one's hate. Now Tara had set him free—free to express an emotion so foreign to him as to be nonexistent. Lifting Tara off her tiny feet, he bore her to his bed, closing the door to the outside world and opening his heart to love.

When the *Devil Dancer* sailed a few days later, Akbar remained behind with Tara. Kit never would have guessed that anything remotely resembling love existed in Akbar's huge body. Only Devon remained strangely complacent upon hearing the news. She knew that the power of love could work miracles, for hadn't she experienced it herself?

Actually, the arrangement was much to Kit's liking. Akbar agreed to act as overseer on Paradise and continue the production of sugar cane and rum. Kit arranged for the

Devil Dancer to return to transporting rum to markets around the world. It was also decided that Kit, Devon, and their children would return to Paradise whenever time allowed.

Standing at the rail, Devon watched the jewel-like islands disappear over the horizon. His arms wrapped around her ample waist, Kit hugged her close, thinking he held all his hopes and dreams of the future in his arms. As she snuggled into the curve of his body, the baby made its presence known in a most abrupt manner.

"Am I holding you too tightly, sweetheart? The babe's protesting." Kit laughed, his palm settling lovingly on the quivering mound of her belly.

"Nay, 'tis more like he's anxious to make his appearance."

"Not too soon, I hope," Kit said, eying her worriedly.

"You fret too much, my love. The babe is well and so am I. Join me in our cabin and I'll demonstrate just how wonderful I feel."

"Don't you think 'tis time you gave up that kind of strenuous activity?"

"Not for a few weeks yet, unless the sight of my inflated body disgusts you."

"Never! That's my child you carry inside you. You're as beautiful to me as the first time I saw you."

"I'll never forget the first time I laid eyes on you," Devon mused. "A ferocious black beard concealed much of your face and I thought you quite fierce, though not unhandsome."

"Did you now? I didn't notice you swooning in fear at Diablo's feet."

"Not even the devil is threatening standing on a gallows with a rope around his neck," Devon returned saucily.

"But he was dangerous enough to seize the woman of his dreams and take her to Paradise. And now you're suffering the consequences of his love."

"Consequences? Nay, my blackhearted rogue. You stole my heart and replaced it with your love."

"And the fruit of that love is precious to me. But as long as you insist it won't hurt him to love you, I'm more than willing to do my part."

Inside the cozy privacy of the moon-drenched cabin, time stood still while the star-crossed lovers rededicated themselves to love. For without the magic of love and the power of passion their story could not have been told. It would have ended where it all began—on the gallows.

INTERACT WITH DORCHESTER ONLINE!

Want to learn more about your favorite books and authors?
Want to talk with other readers that like to read the same books as you?
Want to see up-to-the-minute Dorchester news?

VISIT DORCHESTER AT:
DorchesterPub.com
Twitter.com/DorchesterPub
Facebook.com (Search Pages)

DISCUSS DORCHESTER'S NOVELS AT:
Dorchester Forums at DorchesterPub.com
GoodReads.com
LibraryThing.com
Myspace.com/books
Shelfari.com
WeRead.com

☐ **YES!**

Sign me up for the Historical Romance Book Club and
send my FREE BOOKS! If I choose to stay in the club, I
will pay only $8.50* each month, a savings of $6.48!

NAME: _____

ADDRESS: _____

TELEPHONE: _____

EMAIL: _____

      ☐ I want to pay by credit card.

☐ **VISA**   ☐ MasterCard.   ☐ DISCOVER

ACCOUNT #: _____

EXPIRATION DATE: _____

SIGNATURE: _____

Mail this page along with $2.00 shipping and handling to:
Historical Romance Book Club
PO Box 6640
Wayne, PA 19087
Or fax (must include credit card information) to:
610-995-9274

You can also sign up online at **www.dorchesterpub.com**.
*Plus $2.00 for shipping. Offer open to residents of the U.S. and Canada only.
Canadian residents please call 1-800-481-9191 for pricing information.
If under 18, a parent or guardian must sign. Terms, prices and conditions subject to
change. Subscription subject to acceptance. Dorchester Publishing reserves the right
to reject any order or cancel any subscription.